A Harvest of Aliens

By John Wilson Berry

Book 2 of the Harvest Trilogy

A Harvest of Aliens

Book 2 of the Harvester Trilogy

Contents

1 Lieutenant Nelino Pereira: Central Amazon Basin

Huge trees surrounded by a host of lesser vegetation crowded the banks of the small river. Massive branches covered with thick twisting vines stretched far out over the water. The mix of leaves made it hard to tell where one species ended and the next began. Plants in the Amazon fought for light the way animals fought for food. Green predators grew thick and high to slay the slow and weak with their deadly shade. The vines stole upward to strangle the life out of other plants like slow-moving snakes.

This never-ending fight for light resulted in dense vegetation along the river that made it difficult to see much from the water. Where the afternoon sun penetrated the foliage, everything became a multi-hued green explosion. Where it didn't, the shadows tended to be deep and dark. An army could hide in the brush a few feet from the bank and never be seen. All this was familiar to the crews on the two Brazilian patrol boats creeping up the river. But it made for bad territory to be scouting out dangerous alien monsters.

Chief Mercia Gasquey, the boat's pilot and second in command, turned her head in a slow arc as she surveyed the river. The sunlight caught the lower half of her face under her black cap, leaving her eyes in shadow. She kept one hand on the boat's wheel and the other on the throttle. Her jaw was clenched and her spine straight. The backrest of her tall stool hadn't seen any use in over an hour.

"I hate the way the jungle hums," she said in a low voice. "I miss the birds." She waved one hand toward the left bank. "The jungle creeps me out without them. It...it sounds sad."

Nelino glanced at her and nodded. A constant drone of life came from the surrounding rainforest. Changing local animal populations made the sound vary. But something always buzzed, grunted, or growled loud enough to carry over the soft rumble of the boats' muffled engines. But not a single bird song, chirp, nor cry could be heard from the thick foliage.

"Yeah, hard to believe so many died. I heard an estimate it was fifteen million or more," he said with a slow shake of his head. "But the jungle does sound creepy now. Too quiet, but not quiet. I don't like it either."

Her head continued to swivel as she scanned the water and riverbanks. It took a lot of concentration to steer the boat along the narrow river. She glanced over at him, her mouth a tight line above her strong jaw.

"I heard they died of fright," she said. "The night that thing came down. It made their hearts pop."

"Yeah, I heard that too. But I also read many of them died from flying into trees."

Gasquey shook her head. "So, they panicked and bashed their own brains out? Oh, that's so much better than having a heart attack. Thanks for the update, sir."

He cocked his head slightly. "Sorry, Chief, you brought it up."

Her focus stayed on the river as she gave a slight shrug. "Yeah. It just keeps bothering me." She cut her eyes over to him and said, "How confident are you in the army's reports? About the aliens not being this far north."

"Well, Chief, let's just say I have my doubts." He smiled at her. "We've never fought aliens before, and I think the army is too arrogant. They make assumptions and consider it fact. But hopefully we won't run into any trouble."

"This brush is as thick as I've ever seen." She nodded to the depth finder. "And the main channel is starting to narrow. We need to slow down a bit."

"Okay, signal Martell to ease it down. This is a good time to go quiet too."

She reached up and flashed the searchlight at the lead patrol boat. The lead boat's pilot, Sub-Officer Michel Martell, waved acknowledgement. Gasquey throttled back and the motor's throaty growl went to a soft watery murmur as the two boats slowed to the speed of a fast walk.

Once more, Nelino noticed himself chewing on his bottom lip and spit it out with an angry shake of his head. He just couldn't stop doing it. The habit his wife said, "Makes you look like a cute little rabbit," didn't belong on the face of a naval officer. Colonel Antinasio said it made him look nervous. In a stressful situation, it might make his crew think him scared or uncertain.

Well, right now, they'd be right. He felt very scared and uncertain. Who wouldn't be, when leading a patrol into hostile territory held by alien invaders — some of whom could fire deadly spikes out of their arms while others stood over twenty feet tall and destroyed whole villages. Most people called them demons. It was easy to see why.

Colonel Antinasio said it was normal to be nervous and wound up tight on patrol. But a good leader didn't show doubt or fear. So, Nelino resolved for the tenth time today to stop chewing on his lip.

Not that it mattered much. His team's confidence couldn't get much lower. And his lip nibbling had nothing to do with it. Distrust and anger filled the hearts of the boat crews. The reason for this, beyond pure fear of the aliens, stemmed from the passengers they carried. That their commander was displaying a high degree of tension went pretty much unnoticed. Hell, they all were. Even so, he tried to keep his teeth clenched together. It was a constant battle for him. His subconscious craved the small comfort the habit provided. On the most dangerous mission of his life, his lower lip kept sneaking between his teeth with a will all its own.

The boats entered another tunnel of interlocking branches so common along the back rivers of the Amazon. The light became a murky green as the tree limbs closed in and intertwined overhead. Mosquitos loved the perpetual twilight during these stretches and buzzed around them in a thick cloud. Marcus waved his hand back and forth in front of his face to keep them away from his eyes and mouth. It didn't really help much; he swallowed more than a few. They left an acidic, nasty taste in his mouth.

"Got a weird shadow, three o'clock, fifty feet up," came the call from Junior Petty Officer Sergio Lisboa on the starboard machine-gun.

Nelino tensed and looked in the indicated direction. Yes, an odd shape sat in the juncture of three large branches of a large kapok tree. A shadow within a shadow, something darker than the dark around it. Did the indistinct shape have spikes and too many legs?

"On it," called out Sailor First Class Natalia from the front of the boat. She swung around the dual fifty-caliber machine-guns mounted in the forward gun tub and elevated the barrels to point at the smudge.

"Hold your fire," Nelino said. No point in giving away their position unless whatever it was posed a threat. The bark of the twin fifties could be heard for miles. But what was it?

To keep the dark smudge in sight from the small bridge, he had to bend and do a slow pivot. The boat continued forward at a slow glide, forcing him to shift from window to window. He'd been on the river a long time. He knew its shadows and shapes.

Please God, let it be a monkey...or a sloth, or anything normal. Despite the boats' slow speed, the tree soon disappeared from sight. As the suspicious shadow faded from view, Nelino shook his head. *Have we been spotted by the demons?* For all he knew, they'd been watching the whole time. *There's just too much we don't know about them.* He began biting his lip again.

By now, he faced the open back of the bridge. After the tree disappeared, he looked down into the grizzled face of Sergeant Cyro Araujo. The sudden eye contact with the other man made Nelino conscious of his lip, and he spit it out with a soft, "phuut" sound.

"Your crew seems a bit jumpy," said the sergeant. "There are a lot of shadows in the forest."

You son of a bitch, Nelino thought. But he held his tongue. Their relationship was strained enough already. "Better too jumpy than dead," he said. That might have been pushing it a bit, but in his anger, he couldn't find it in himself to be civil.

To Nelino's surprise, Araujo gave him a crooked grin and nodded. "Perhaps," he said. Then he turned and gazed up at the shadow.

Beyond the sergeant, ten army special forces soldiers sat on benches located along both sides of the small compartment. They occupied seats previously filled by the marines of Patrol Boat Group

31. The marines' first encounter with the demons hadn't left them with enough men to conduct shore patrols.

This led high command to assign special forces troops to fill in. Rumor had it that the boats had almost been confiscated for the army as well. But the navy managed to keep that from happening. The soldiers below—these strangers—looked up at him with varying degrees of interest, suspicion, and in some cases, contempt.

They didn't stare long. The soldiers didn't respect him, but he was still an officer. A few gave noncommittal nods before turning away. Two of them shook their heads as if in disbelief at being on a boat commanded by such a loser. One actually rolled his eyes at him. The men resumed watching the tangles of vegetation along the riverbanks in search of potential threats, though they still cast distrustful glances at him or the crew from time to time.

Bad enough the fear of running into demons here at the edge of alien territory. But the distrust between the soldiers and the crew pushed the tension to a heart-hammering level. He fought off another urge to nibble his lip. His own people saw him doing it enough to overlook it on occasion. But what about the men in the troop compartment? No doubt they saw everything he did as a sign of weakness.

"Those special forces guys are making themselves hard to love," said Gasquey.

"Yeah, this whole thing is a mess," Nelino said.

She managed a faint smile and said, "I think you could win a prize for that statement, sir. You know, for being so insightful and all."

"Watch it, Gasquey, I'll tell my wife you've been abusing me."

"That's a low blow, sir," she said with a hurt tone. "No fair hiding behind Camila."

"Chief, I'll hide behind her if I damn well want," he said. "But you're right about those troops. We've never had issues with the special forces guys before."

Gasquey nodded. "Yeah, there's always some rivalry and one-upmanship, but nothing like this. The general's stupid little speech and all the rumors really screwed things up."

Nelino let out a soft sigh. It sounded loud in his ears. With luck, it went unheard in the murmur of the motors and sounds of wildlife from the surrounding forest. "Yeah. Well, we've got to rise above it. Stay sharp, Chief. I've got a bad feeling about this."

"Yes, sir. I know what you mean," she said, returning her focus to the river.

Rumors ran wild about PBG-31's marines battle with the aliens, none of them good. The crew got pissed off each time they discussed the latest rumor going around base. According to one, the boat crews abandoned the marines when the demons showed up. Then the marines lost over half their men in the ensuing fight.

What bullshit. The patrol boats had been dozens of miles away at the time and played no part in the battle. Another rumor implied the marines threw down their weapons and ran at the first sight of the demons. *More bullshit.*

It would be funny how stupid rumors could get if they didn't tarnish the remembrance of brave people. The stories about marines throwing away their weapons and running probably angered the crew the most. They'd lost a lot of good friends that day, and none of them had been cowards. When PBG-31 held its next cookout, there would be a lot of empty places at the long tables they always used. It promised to be a very quiet and somber affair.

There's nothing I can do about it right now. Nelino fought down his annoyance and dismissed the opinions of the special forces troops with a half-shrug. He turned and resumed scanning the river.

Ahead, the river flowed straight for about a hundred meters and then disappeared around a left-hand turn. The murky, silt-laden water hid a muddy bottom that challenged the limits of the shallow-draft boats. Nelino could have easily waded across the channel—the water would only come up to his knees at its deepest—though to do so would invite all sorts of nasty surprises from piranha, caiman, or electric eels.

Despite the main channel getting narrower, the waterway itself began to widen. It spanned fifty meters and more from one tree-lined bank to the other, although for the most part, the water would barely reach Nelino's ankles. Fewer trees reached out far enough to intertwine into tunnels along this stretch. Overhead, a bright streak of blue cut between the pressing green sky.

The odor of rotting flesh hung heavy over the river. The smell came from the carcasses of countless birds that died the day the aliens arrived. The whole ecology of the forest had been wrecked by it. Even though it had been a few weeks ago, the putrefaction of countless small bodies still clung to the trees and ground.

"Sir! Ten o'clock," said the chief softly, nodding toward the port side of the boat.

He looked in the direction she indicated and saw a stretch of stagnant water leading into a marsh, a common occurrence along the rivers. On one side of the murky pool, a vast carpet of feathers floated among a tangle of sodden roots. The brownish water stained the color out of the feathers. But their beauty shone through anyway. A very sad beauty. Nelino blinked away tears.

"Martell's about to go around the next bend," Gasquey said.

Nelino jerked his attention back to the lead boat. The long sleek vessel began to ease around the bend, and both he and Gasquey held their breaths. The wide yet shallow river allowed them keep it in in sight during the whole turn. Every gun pointed at one foliage-lined bank or the other.

After thirty seconds, they could see down the next stretch of open water. Another bend conquered. The chief let out a sigh and glanced at him with a nervous smile. Then she resumed scanning the jungle ahead and to the sides. The next bend started in about two hundred meters.

"I think that special forces CO is giving Martell a hard time," said Gasquey.

Nelino didn't need his binoculars to see what Gasquey referred to. The special forces commander, Captain Frontin, had refused to ride with Nelino. The man hadn't given a reason, but Nelino suspected it was a control issue. The captain looked angry and kept waving his hands in the air.

"I bet he wants him to speed up," Gasquey said.

"God, I hope not," said Nelino. "On this narrow river, that could lead to something bad."

She shrugged in reply, though from her expression he suspected she wanted to say more. Only her respect for the chain of command kept her silent.

Patrols like this tended to create a mixture of extreme tension and boredom. Maybe that's why the special forces captain felt frustrated. Not good on these back-country rivers.

Boredom could be the deadliest thing the boats faced. t It led to mistakes. Even he and Gasquey weren't immune to the hypnotic spell of constant sameness on the rivers. Mile after mile of never-ending trees and water. Endless numbers of exotic animals and beautiful flowers began to look the same after a while. But speeding up wasn't the answer.

Riverbends like the one they just passed always made him nervous. While Brazil hadn't fought a war in a very long time, he did have some combat experience. His boat came under fire on two occasions while on patrol. Both instances occurred a little less than three years ago. Drug dealers and revolutionaries liked to hide in the back country. Encountering them unexpectedly had proven costly.

Chief Gasquey was the only crew member still with him from those times. He knew she remembered the terrifying ordeals as well as he. As they approached each turn, she leaned forward over the wheel. Her fingers would begin tapping lightly on the throttle as she focused her attention on the river ahead. Good for her. If something bad happened, speed would be one of the jet boat's best defense. Nothing like getting shot at and surviving to hone one's survival instincts.

After the ambushes, he learned to operate in an in-between state between the bends. His eyes stayed alert while his mind drifted. As they glided slowly toward the next turn, his thoughts went back to the tension between the sailors and commandos.

The different branches always put each other down, mostly in a good-natured way. Once real work began, such silliness was forgotten. That didn't hold true for this mission, not since General von Jaeger gave his little speech to the special forces guys before they left.

The sailors often called him General Fancy Pants. That was probably the least inoffensive of his nicknames. Most of the others involved cleverly worded descriptions of pornographic acts. Usually with relatives or barn animals. Maybe even both at the same time.

Initially, Nelino refused to accept the bad reports about the general. About his stupidity and tendency to show favoritism. Also, how his political ties and rich family were the only reason he held such a high rank. The speech changed all that. Now Nelino firmly believed every bad thing he heard about the little general. One part of the speech especially sickened him.

He'd given the speech in clear hearing of Nelino and his crews. Surely the man knew what impact it would have on them. Near the end the general said, "The Naval Brasilia boats cannot be true fighting vessels. No true combat units have...*women* in them. So, obviously their marines weren't up to the challenge of fighting the aliens."

The way the man pronounced "women" made Nelino's skin crawl. The remarks about sailors like Jobim and Gasquey were unfair and unjust. Frustration and anger heated his chest each time he allowed himself to think about it.

Both women had proven themselves excellent crew members on multiple occasions, especially Gasquey. They were more levelheaded than most men in tense situations. Fancy Pants went on to deride their commander as well, saying Colonel Antinasio was the reason the sailors were incompetent cowards. Of course, he'd had nothing but praise for the honorable and brave special forces commandos.

Who the hell gives such a speech before sending the celebrated and maligned off together on a dangerous mission? In circumstances like this, the lives of the entire group depended on the actions of each individual. The lack of faith...of trust...could be fatal out in the bush, especially when facing a mysterious and dangerous enemy. The speech shattered any chance they'd had of building any such trust.

But here they were. Nine Brazilian sailors and twenty-two special forces commandos, spread between two boats probing into unknown hostile territory. Most of the time they searched for the enemy in the forest. But too often they glared at one another through suspicious eyes. It was a situation Nelino never would have imagined being in.

The river widened and the depth finder indicated it was also getting deeper. The shallows behind them acted a bit like a dam. This caused a small lake to form ahead, although Nelino doubted it could be very big. At least it gave them room to maneuver.

Sub-Officer Martell's boat started to pull ahead. This did not conform to standard operational procedures of the unit. Normally they would take the opportunity presented by this wider stretch of water to trade places. Rotating the boats helped maintain alertness. Being the lead boat tended to wear down a crew.

"Yup, I told you that Captain Frontin jerk would push the boy into speeding up," Gasquey said.

Nelino nodded but didn't say anything. It fit with the contempt the Army officer showed for PBG-31. No doubt Frontin thought the boat crews to be overly cautious.

Nelino shook his head in frustration. Turning, he met Gasquey's concerned gaze and gestured with his head toward the lead boat. Her mouth quirked down in disapproval as she increased their speed to maintain distance. This made the motors go from a bubbling murmur to a low growl that seemed very loud to Nelino. The forest sounds were masked by engine noise and the increased whisper of the wind—not a good situation when trying to sneak through enemy territory. The boats glided toward the next bend at a noticeably faster pace.

Martell's boat was about fifty meters ahead. Nelino lifted his binoculars and focused them on the bridge. The young sub-officer glanced back, uncertainty etched on his face. Nelino made a slashing motion across his throat. The uncertain look on the young man's face became strained, and he pointed at Frontin. The captain was now yelling and jabbing his finger upriver. *God, what a mess.*

"Slow down; don't listen to him," Nelino mumbled under his breath. "Maintain standard procedure."

Instead, Martell must have throttled up since his boat began to inch ahead again. This appeared to still be too slow for Frontin because he continued yelling. He started to wave his arms about like an oversized bird doing a mating dance. Martell stood with hunched shoulders and stared straight ahead, but his boat didn't pick up any more speed. The captain finally shook his head, threw up his hands in disgust, and glared back at Nelino.

"Stupid asshole," said Gasquey.

Nelino nodded, then reconsidered and gave her a stern look. It was not proper to express derision of an officer, no matter how much he may deserve it. She returned his gaze with one that said she knew this, but also made it plain she had no regrets. Nelino gave a half-smile. She knew him too well. Heck, he'd often spent more time with her during the last four years than Camila. Most of the members of PBG-31 were volunteers and tended to stay with the unit for a long time.

"Keep us within fifty meters or so, Chief," he said. The new navigation system indicated they should reach the drop-off point for the special forces troops in another twenty kilometers. Getting rid of Captain Frontin would be a big relief. *Good riddance.*

After they dropped off the soldiers, their next mission consisted of two parts. First, they needed to determine how far north the demons had reached. Supposedly they couldn't be as far as the boats were currently, but you never knew. The next part involved synchronizing the new navigation system to the actual terrain. The system had been developed by one of the American scientists, Paul somebody or another. The man had come up with a way to use the radio emissions coming from the White Mountains to take the place of the lost GPS satellites. It pleased Nelino to see the creatures' own jamming system used against them. A bit of poetic justice.

The software on the tablet took multiple readings, calculated their position, and displayed it on the screen. The displayed positions tended to be a bit off, but it was still a big improvement over a compass and dead reckoning. The screen currently showed the boat about two kilometers east. This would put them in the middle of the jungle. After they got back, the scientists should be able to better calibrate the system. Since the destruction of the satellites, navigation had become nearly impossible in the forest. The new system would be invaluable once they refined it a bit more.

The boats moved toward the bend at the speed of a fit jogger—much too fast for Nelino's taste. The river remained wider than usual and stayed deep as it rounded the bend. This was good. The farther they stayed from shore, the better. Plus, it meant there would be room for a quick turn if needed.

Gasquey leaned even further over the wheel with her right hand locked on the throttle as they neared the bend. She looked tense and more than a little pissed off. No doubt she felt the same way he did. These damn special forces assholes kept putting them at more risk than necessary. A stupid move in an already dangerous situation.

"Just a couple of more hours, Chief. Then we can unload them," he said.

The stern, hard-faced woman nodded, but didn't look away from the river. Her light brown eyes scanned back and forth, scrutinizing both foliage-lined banks. The generous, quick to smile mouth was pursed into a thin, tense line just above her strong jaw. If there had ever been Amazonian women warriors in these parts, then surely, they looked like her.

In the gun-tub at the front of the jet boat, Natalia glanced back at them. She didn't do this often. It signaled how nervous she felt about the situation. Nelino gave her a nod in reassurance and gestured for her to resume scanning ahead. She scowled and shook her head, then turned back around and began swinging the twin machine-guns slowly left and right.

On the port side, Sailor 2nd Class Ribeiro Pessoa manned a single gun. Nelino could tell from the set of his shoulders how nervous he must be. On the starboard side, Lisboa leaned back in his harness and looked more relaxed, though Nelino doubted this to be the case. He'd probably heard Sergeant Araujo's remark about the crew being high strung and wanted to appear nonchalant.

None of the three younger crew members had actual combat experience. But Nelino and Gasquey drilled them so often, they came pretty darn close. Their current speed led to a lot of bad things when they practiced ambushes during training. All of them kept this in mind as the boat rushed toward the next turn.

They'd all been present when their bloodied friends limped into Rio Estrada. The loss of two thirds of the marines struck them hard. They'd had a hard lesson in the demons' capabilities and murderous intent.

The lead boat slowed as it neared the turn and drifted a bit to port, per procedure, to let Nelino's boat pass. No doubt the poor sub-officer would be glad to let them lead. The army captain stood the side scowling at Martell with his hands on his hips. Well, with Nelino in the lead the jerk couldn't very well continue to harass the young man about going faster. Nelino's boat started to inch up on them.

The turn proved to be the beginning of a large, gradual horseshoe bend in the river. Such a feature showed up on the navigation system, but three kilometers north. It must be the same one. Not bad considering how new the software was. The bend would make a good landmark for their mapping.

The water began to get choppy, which was odd as the small lake was on the deep side. Also, there wasn't any wind to make waves, so something ahead must be causing them. As the two boats reached the center of the bend, they encountered a light mist. Another oddity. There had been fog this morning, but it was almost two o'clock and dry for the Amazon. All traces of the fog burned off hours ago.

The mist and the choppiness might indicate rapids ahead, or even a small waterfall. But nothing like that showed on their map. This was low country and the drops for such water features were rare. Of course, there hadn't been a nineteen-thousand-foot mountain range in the middle of Brazil three weeks ago either. The world had become a very different place with the arrival of the demons.

They neared the end of the turn, and it appeared the river straightened. But the mist grew thicker and obscured Nelino's view. According to the depth finder, the river ahead began to get shallower and narrower. The trees pressed in on both sides to form another shadowy tunnel. There was still room to pass, however, and Nelino pointed to starboard. Gasquey nodded and they continued to gain on the other boat, drawing nearly even with it.

Over the soft rumble of the motors, a hissing noise tickled Nelino's eardrums. *Is that moving water?* He poked his head around the side of the bridge and strained his ears. The hissing began to grow louder. *Yes, that definitely sounded like fast moving water.*

Gasquey cocked her head to the side and frowned. "Is that a waterfall?"

Nelino shrugged. The noise grew louder, but the mist made it hard to see more than a hundred meters ahead. As their boat closed on Martell's, Nelino saw Frontin waving his arms and pointing upriver again. But this time, Martell was yelling back and pointing at the other boat. The damn special forces captain continued to display remarkable stupidity. This was no time to distract the driver of the boat.

"Oh, sweet Jesus, save us." Gasquey said. The fear in her voice alarmed him more than the words.

Nelino followed her gaze. Shadows...big shadows moved in the mist not far ahead. For a few seconds, his mind couldn't grasp what his eyes saw. Almost entirely obscured by the vapor hanging over the water, large grayish shapes rippled and floated ten feet or so above the water. The mist parted a bit more, and he saw that the strange silhouettes went from the southern bank, into the water, and up the north bank. As the boat advanced, the mist thinned further. Moments later, the strange images snapped into recognition. Fear grabbed his stomach with cold, hard fingers.

2 David Morgan: In the Heart of the White Mountain

The conveyor belt forty feet above made an ungodly screech as it lurched into motion. The sound sent goosebumps along David

Morgan's chest and arms. He let out a soft sigh and scowled up at it. "I truly hate you, you son of a bitch," he said.

The thirty-foot wide belt ignored his comment and continued on with its grisly business. No surprise there. But it made him feel a little better to express his loathing for the thing.

Although he knew the damn belt was about to start, and had heard it dozens of times, the noise still made him jump. The conveyor always made that same screech when it switched on. And he cursed it every time. Something in the machinery sounded like a cross between a dentist drill cutting into your tooth and a rusty nail being dragged across a chalkboard — only it sounded ten times louder than either one. Josh said there must be a bad bearing or something.

Once the belt got up to speed, the screech faded to a constant, annoying squeak. Despite the terrible noise, the greenish-white conveyor ran with smooth efficiency. It never gave a lurch or a jerk as it carried the gatherers' plunder to the massive blender below.

Even after three weeks, he found the process gruesome and mesmerizing in both scope and horror. The belt and giant mixing pit represented the final stages of a mind-boggling engine of destruction. Trees, animals, plants, and sometimes even fish poured down the belt every hour of every day. Once organic material filled the two-hundred-foot-deep pit, a vile brownish fluid flooded into it from the bottom. Then, rotating blades two to three times David's height pureed the contents into a thick, reddish-brown soup. Afterwards, the concoction drained out through three ten-foot-wide openings in the bottom. David had little doubt this process represented an ecological disaster for the Amazon Basin, and most likely far beyond the confines of the forest.

The room's walls arched upward into a hundred-foot-tall dome. In the center of the dome and taking up most of the space was the two-hundred-foot-deep blender. A low barrier that came up to David's thighs bordered the pit, and a wide stone walkway encircled it. The walls of the dome were a dull white with dark streaks, the color of old, unkempt teeth. The surface texture felt like a cross between rough-hewn granite and sprayed concrete. David and the other survivors often debated what the material was made of, though in truth it hardly mattered. Various sized rods and pipes covered most of the dome. They protruded downward from the curved surface in a bizarre and random pattern. It reminded David of a giant pincushion turned inside-out. Most of the pipes looked like twisted and misshapen radio antennae.

In between the pipes, short straight rods cast glaring electric-blue light. This gave everything a strange tint and made for severe dark shadows. The strange illumination often made it difficult to see details in the pit below.

The air hung heavy under the dome. A sickly-sweet odor like chocolate chip cookies fresh from the oven mixed in with rotting flesh filled the cavern. This twisted, perverted cookie smells especially upset David. Although compared to the revolting activity around him, getting mad about the odor seemed kind of stupid.

Back when he'd been happy, before his mother died, she used to make the world's best cookies. The day before a tornado killed her, he and his sister helped with cooking a batch. The memory of that day always surfaced when he smelled fresh baked cookies—a wonderful, magical time despite a slight tummy-ache afterward. It was the last truly happy moment of his life. Now the aroma of baking cookies, which once made him feel warm and safe, would be forever tainted with images of terror, death, and blood.

A large, gray, leafy shape appeared in the shadows of the tunnel above and drifted down the belt. The darkness of the tunnel gave way to the harsh light of the chamber, and the shape transitioned into a jatoba tree, the same kind whose bark he'd used to save little Pedro's life. With a crackling roar of breaking limbs, the tall tree somersaulted off the conveyor and fell roots first. It struck the bottom of the pit far below with a loud, echoing boom. It made a mournful peal, like a massive bell struck by a giant. Echoes of the impact reverberated through the chamber and into the tunnels beyond.

A steady stream of Amazon plants and animals followed the tree down the conveyor. First came a bunch of smaller forms that must have been animals. Whitish webbing covered them to varying degrees, making it difficult to tell one animal from another. Next came numerous large bundles of broken branches and plants encased in the same material.

After these came a long string of trees. Trees tended to be the dominate item of the gatherer's plunder to come down the belt. Due to their size and since the alien mountain sat in the middle of the world's largest rainforest, this could only be expected. Trees were generally free of webbing, although many appeared to have been trimmed. Whoever or whatever did the trimming didn't do a very neat job. The ends of the branches were broken rather than sheared, leaving jagged stumps of wood protruding from the trunks.

After the gong-like peal from the impact of the first tree, the rest fell with crashes and crunches as wood hit wood. Or in the case of animals, sickening plops or splats, which occurred when the creatures hit the bottom of the pit or slammed into hard wooden boughs. One of the sadder things to see was when the animals still lived. Seeing their mummified forms struggling and squealing as they tumbled down sent unpleasant electric chills through David. Most of the time they disappeared into the foliage. But this didn't often silence them. Their muffled yet haunting cries would continue to drift up from the leafy mass below.

The monkeys were the worst though. They tended to be way too human for David's liking. Of all the animals, it seemed monkeys got caught by the gatherers the most. Or maybe when he fished the vat, he just noticed them more. Too often, they were conscious and screamed like frightened children as they fell. If they didn't die on impact, then they whimpered and cried. Although it only lasted until they drowned in the viscous fluid that filled the pit before each cycle, the sounds they made caused David to wince with sympathy. Yes. No doubt about it. The monkeys were definitely the worst.

Of course, people would be the absolute worst. But there hadn't been any humans on the conveyor since Josh rescued David and the others. He said he'd seen several hundred souls go into the vat that day. Several hundred people, and he managed to save four. A shudder coursed through David. Yeah, people would be worse. *Please God, don't let there be people today.*

He remembered enjoying fishing with his father off their boat in Alabama. It was nothing like fishing the pit for food. *Fishing the pit sucks. A lot.* While not hard, it tended to be stressful and depressing.

Watching the vat fill while tuning out the horror of the thing was a trick David had yet to master. Pulling up firewood with the grapple and winch was easy. But bringing in food took a lot of concentration and diligence. It required you to keep a close eye on the vat throughout the entire cycle since the time it took to fill often varied.

Once the pit was full, he only had a few minutes to pick a target, cast, and pull something out. Otherwise he would have to wait half an hour until the next cycle. Sitting here with nothing to do but watch the giant blender wore at one's soul. No... fishing the vat was not the least bit pleasant. But they had no other way to get food.

The huge blender tended to be well packed before the overhead belt stopped feeding it. At times, David wondered if something organized the trees and bundles to maximize the filling process. He had no way to know, of course, but this seemed likely.

Every so often, though, something went wrong with the process. On rare occasions, trees fell in such a way that their limbs or roots tangled together. When this happened with enough large trees, some of them could reach the low wall surrounding the pit. According to Josh, such a tangle allowed him to escape the vat. Then he rescued David and the others.

The small group now trapped in the mountain were an odd lot. Josh was an ex-special forces badass. Paula had been the well-traveled wife of the local lumber mill owner. Alessandra, an aspiring English translator, and young Pedro, a local Indian boy, both had lived in Rio Estrada their entire lives.

And finally, David—a fat, useless, video-game addict forced to come on a jungle expedition for what his sister had termed much needed self-improvement. *Is that what I am?* In all honesty, he had to admit that it was. He should tack on being a burden to his poor sister as well. Lord knows she worked hard enough at supporting him. And he never even appreciated it. Funny how being abducted, nearly killed, and then imprisoned by monstrous aliens made a person rethink their life. A slight smile quirked his lips. *Who knew?*

Now, the five of them lived off the leavings of the pit. Being trapped while waiting for alien monsters to come for them proved to be slow torture. They spent a lot of time brooding in silence. But occasionally they'd deliberate why the creatures left them alone and how long the situation might last. None of these conversations tended to be pleasant. Not that they could do much if the gatherers did come. The general consensus was the creatures didn't know they existed. So, they lived like mice in the walls, stealing food and fearful of the day the big bad cat noticed them.

David pulled his injured left arm out of the sling and moved it around a bit. The motion sent sharp pains lance through his shoulder, making him wince. He checked it at least five times a day. The injury was getting better, but it still had a way to go. At least nothing major seemed out of whack since Josh jerked the dislocation back into place. He'd have to continue one-arming it. This hampered him a bit, but he'd gotten used to it.

The vat had multiple blades like ten-foot-wide steel daisies set into the walls around it at different heights. The contents now covered the topmost blades, signaling it was time to get ready. He double-checked the rope. In fact, this made the fourth or fifth check. Nerves tended to breed repetition.

Alessandra made their ropes by braiding together webbing pulled from the vat. Making the grapples took a fair amount of effort. But nothing compared to the work she put into crafting each rope. They didn't want to cut the line every time they got hung up on something. To keep from having to do this, the rope fed through a hole drilled in the main shaft and back up. The other end was tied off to the winch frame with a bow knot. By tugging on it, the end of the rope could be freed and pulled back through the grapple. Sometimes.

He'd thrown an unsecured rope into the pit once in front of Josh and actually feared for his life. Josh screamed at him about his lack of awareness for several long, terror inducing minutes. David had been sure the hulking brute would toss him into the vat.

Screaming was how it seemed to David at the time. Thinking back, he couldn't really remember Josh raising his voice very much. It just felt that way. In fact, Josh's tirade about staying focused and being responsible sounded a lot like what Sally used to preach about. But with Josh, everything felt much more intense. The man was by far the scariest person he'd ever met. David now paid very close attention when tying off the rope. He wondered if Sally would have been proud of his newfound focus.

A small cascade of fifteen or twenty similar sized bundles fell off the conveyor. It appeared to be a whole troop of red-faced monkeys based on what he could see of them. Primates might be common, but these not so much. The red-faced monkeys moved fast as hell, and he wondered how the gatherers managed to catch them. Not that it mattered, he supposed.

Half of this small, forlorn group still lived. Those that did screamed in despair as they fell off the belt. He squirmed uncomfortably at their cries, like always. But he refrained from looking away, although he truly wanted to. One by one, they disappeared into the piles of leaves below with rustling splashes. Four of them hit on large branches and stayed in sight, but too far away. One landed on a thick tree trunk with a plop and rolled down close enough for David to have a chance at it.

He hefted one of the four-pronged wooden grapples—another useful tool built by Josh. He swung it about to loosen up and get ready. There were three more of the grapples beside the pile of rope at his feet. Each measured about a foot across, with thick sharpened sticks for the prongs. Good for snagging things. The downside was that it also snagged branches just as well.

Timing the cast could be tricky and a little dangerous. The rope by his feet was about seventy feet long. So, he needed to wait until things neared the top of the vat before making a throw. If David threw the rope too early, he risked having a tree land on it. If this happened, the winch might be jerked into the pit before he could untie it. Josh worked hard to build it, and David shuddered at the thought of getting the contraption smashed to pieces. Not to mention the chance of getting crushed as it went over the wall.

With a hiss, the thick brown fluid began creeping up the walls of the vat. It wouldn't be long before the start of the next cycle. David pulled some slack from the winch and hurried along the low wall for a dozen feet. He needed to get as close as possible to have a chance at a successful snag.

He stopped just above the monkey. The webbing entrapping the primate had hooked on a broken tree limb. The little creature struggled feebly just below him, but it didn't scream. Worse, it sobbed in a soft, sad, whimper. David's throat clutched, and he swallowed hard.

Damn, this one's still alive. David let out a sigh. He detested having to kill them. But food was food, and the group had been low on meat the last couple of days. He shouldn't complain. They'd been lucky where food was concerned, although he couldn't believe the weird stuff he ate these days. Anteaters, sloths, monkeys, and even snakes frequented their menu. A good thing being a picky eater wasn't among his many shortcomings. But still, he'd give a lot for a bag of Cheetos these days.

After twirling the grapple a few times, he cast it toward a spot on the far side of the monkey. It landed with a clunk on the wide trunk just a few feet beyond it. David moved a little to his right so that the rope lined up with the body. He pulled the slack out carefully to bring the grapple close. When it lay beside the monkey, he gave the rope a sharp tug. The monkey screamed as one of the tines pierced the webbing. David felt torn between yelling in jubilation and crying with shame. Again, he reminded himself they had to eat.

He scrambled back to the winch and began cranking it as fast as he could. Josh had hobbled the contraption together with branches and webbing. The spindle was made from a large log with notches cut in it. Four sticks protruded from the spindle for handles. The notches interlocked with another stick to keep it from turning the wrong way. Crude, but it worked well enough to make fishing a bit easier.

The latch went clicker-clack as he pulled the slack out of the rope. In a few seconds, the monkey began bouncing through the foliage with soft, pitiful cries. After a few more turns, it bumped into the side of the pit and started to rise. David winched it up and over the wall. Then he rushed over and cut its throat to stop the animal's suffering.

The giant blender emitted crunching and burbling sounds as the two-story-tall mixing blades started to turn. The entire mass inside gave a mighty lurch, hesitated, and then shuddered into motion. At first, it moved in sluggish twitches as though uncertain which way to go. But after a few seconds, the contents started going around and around, faster and faster.

Loud cracks and grinding noises filled the chamber. Splintered wood, leaves, and large drops of brownish fluid leaped into the air over the vat. The noise faded as the concoction took on the consistency of a thick soup with large chunks in it. After a few more minutes, the concoction began to look like a chocolate milkshake with occasional lumps floating on top. A small dimple appeared in the middle, very much like the blender back home. The thick fluid continued spinning until no more lumps rose from the depths. Then the contents of the vat started draining. Not long after, the level dropped enough to expose the cruel, dripping blades lining the sides.

David looked down at the monkey. Despite knowing they had to eat, he still felt bad. Knowing it had been doomed to die in pit helped. But the small limp body made his situation seem more real, and for reasons he couldn't explain, even more hopeless. No, fishing the pit wasn't fun, not fun at all.

With a grimace and a sad shake of his head, he wrapped the monkey in webbing and placed it to the side. While he did this, the vat finished draining. A few moments later, with another grating squall that made him jump, the conveyor lurched into motion.

David glared up at it and said, "You bastard." Then he sat down next to the winch. Time to watch the giant blender go through another grisly cycle. A small shudder ran across his shoulders. *Please don't let there be people.*

3 Nelino's Crew Runs the Gauntlet

"Back, back!" Nelino screamed. Even as the words left his mouth, Gasquey slammed the thrust-reverser handle over and hit the throttle.

Less than fifty meters ahead, the huge centaur-like forms of hundreds of harvesting demons churned across the water. Their passage roiled the river into a white and brown froth. Each creature stood twenty feet tall or more on four legs like oak trees. Their torsos alone were five to six feet tall and almost as wide. Muscles flexed under spiky. scaled skin along their chests and two powerful arms. Three-fingered hands were tipped with long sharp claws, and each could easily span the hood of a car.

To the left and right, both banks had been stripped of trees and foliage. Beyond the first horde, he saw more going in the opposite direction. These looked heavily laden. No doubt they were carrying the harvesters' plunder back to their mountain. Back and forth across the water, the things trudged, moving in twin lines like giant ants working to feed their nest.

The boat's twin engines roared as the thrust-reverser sent the waterjets full power blasting in the opposite direction, bringing the jet boat to a quick stop. They sat dead in the water, seemingly frozen for a momentary eternity. Even at seventy meters, the alien monsters loomed over them.

All of the harvesters stopped and turned in unison to face the boats. The alien army responding to a silent command. Hundreds of emotionless black eyes the size of softballs zeroed in on them. Nelino expected their foam-like webbing to spew from their gaping mouths at any moment.

Then with a surge, the jetboat leaped backward. Although Nelino knew what to expect, the sudden motion slammed him into the forward console. The force made him bite through his lip. But at least the pain cleared the fog enshrouding his mind. Thank God for Gasquey's alertness and reflexes. Although the sudden reverse caught everyone off guard, the gunners were strapped in for just such sudden motions. Not so for the special forces men. Loud thumps and cries of pain came from the troop compartment behind him. Nelino felt no sympathy. They'd pointedly ignored the briefing on the jetboats' proclivity for quick maneuvers.

They'd made many plans preparing for this patrol, but none of them included running into a mass river crossing by giant monsters. Nelino pushed himself away from the console and looked at the other boat. Sub-Officer Martell and Captain Frontin still faced each other, arms frozen in mid-gesture but with their heads turned toward the towering harvesters. They stood staring with mouths agape. If ever there was a textbook picture of men unprepared to confront a crisis, this would be it.

After an eternity that lasted four heartbeats, Martell shook off his paralysis and leaped for the controls. His hands moved in a blur as he slammed over the thrust- reverser lever and hit the throttle. The boat did the same sudden stop and backwards surge as theirs. But it was far too late. The delay caused by the pointless argument proved to be a disaster.

After the boats pulled apart to make room for Nelino to pass, they'd wound up closer to each bank. Towering trees limbs arched out over the water and small, multi-legged things moved along them. From the shadowy branches, a cascade of dark dinner plate-sized forms began to rain down. Nelino's boat accelerated backwards. The misshapen creatures fell right in front of the boat, missing the bow by mere inches. However, even as relief flooded through Nelino, panicked screams erupted from his left.

Spinning, he saw the other boat hadn't been so lucky. Stupidity tended to be painfully expensive, and the boat's occupants now paid for Captain Frontin's. A cascade of large spider-like shapes poured down on the hapless patrol boat. They landed amidships forward and flowed backward in a writhing mass toward the stern. Some of the aliens bounced off into the water, but nowhere near enough to help. At that close distance, Nelino could see the terror on Martell's face. The young officer desperately jerked the boat back and forth in a fruitless attempt to shake off the scrabbling spider-shapes. It didn't help in the least. In seconds, they began climbing up the sides of the bridge.

The special forces captain and his men managed to get their weapons into action, and a flurry of shots erupted. The small demons were armed with a razor-sharp, three-inch-long claw at the end of tentacle-like arm. The creatures scurried around and over the open-backed wheelhouse. In seconds, they flooded into it and then the troop compartment behind. Martell looked over at Nelino with a hopeless, incredibly sad look. This changed to agony as he fell while beating at something out of sight.

Martell's jet boat roared in reverse at full power at a good twenty knots. The young sub-officer disappeared from sight, and the boat made a sudden hard turn toward the bank. An instant later, it smashed into a large log sticking out of the shallow water. Six tons of boat and crew moving at high speed slammed to a halt with explosive power. The stern emitted a cracking thump and the impact lifted the front of the boat skyward. The hull twisted up and around and then down, flipping and spinning like a trained gymnast.

Parts of the boat, wood, bodies, and black wriggling shapes sprayed in every direction, each of them doing their own different crazy spin. The front half of the boat completed the backflip and slammed into the river. It landed upside down with a huge splash of brown and white water. As it hit, the screams and gunfire cut off with numbing abruptness.

Everyone on Nelino's boat, crew and passengers alike, stared at the wreck in shocked horror. If the chief had been a fraction of a second slower at the helm…Well, they would have been…like them. *Thank God, thank God.* Joy at life, guilt, and fear hit him all at once. His chest seemed to tighten around his heart. Breathing became something that required concentration. Shock, fear, and an almost gleeful happiness swirled in a mad dance through his gut.

The turmoil in his stomach made it heave, and he almost vomited. But a scream from the starboard gun squashed the reflex.

"Jesus! Sweet Jesus!" Petty Officer Pessoa screeched.

The yell jerked Nelino out of his emotional paralysis. He shook his head and turned as the roar of Pessoa's machine-gun filled the bridge. When he spotted what Pessoa was shooting at, he froze again. War demons!

Bear-sized monsters with six limbs and covered in scales and sharp spikes leapt out of the jungle. Powerful rear legs like those of a frog propelled them with incredible leaps. The middle limbs moved with a blur as the demons charged. The front arms with their deadly weapons stayed high and ready for action. Their first jump took them almost halfway to the boat on their port side. But the water depth seemed to surprise them for a second. For some reason, instead of jumping again, they splashed forward using quick crab-like motions. The water foamed around them as they plowed ahead in a dark surging wave.

"Oh God," he croaked and bit down on his already swollen lip so hard it brought more blood. *What to do? What can I do?* But Nelino could only watch as his crew fought the boat. They knew their jobs, at least under normal conditions. But dear Lord, he wished he had something to do. Drive, shoot, something. But any action he took in the heat of combat would probably cause more confusion than help. *Think, damn it. That's your job. Take in the situation and think.*

All the guns were firing in controlled bursts at the war demons. Good. That meant the gunners were sticking to their training. The special forces troops leaned out of the open top troop compartment and began shooting as well. Dozens of war demons fell, but more and more charged out of the jungle.

The closest came at them from the starboard side. However, instead of plowing through the water, they began to dive under it. The swum as fast as they leapt and moved toward the boat with the speed of eels. Living torpedoes closed on them with malicious intent.

Pessoa raked the water around the creatures with his gun. Bullets kicked up small geysers in stitches as he traversed it back and forth. But they didn't seem to have much effect on the nightmare creatures swimming toward them.

The demons began to gain on the boat as it charged backwards. *How can they move so fast?* Gasquey had the boat maxed out, going as fast as it could in reverse, which wasn't fast enough. She kept her head turned, looking over her shoulder while concentrating on driving the boat. This meant she couldn't see the creatures torpedoing toward them.

"Chief!" he yelled. She glanced at him, and he made a spinning gesture with his finger.

She nodded and tapped the horn once, this being so much a part of the routine she maintained the habit even now. A short, mournful hoot sounded. The crew braced themselves. But the men in the troop compartment looked around in confusion. Part of the price they paid for piss poor communications.

Gasquey's hands became a blur as she worked the controls. The boat went into an abrupt sliding turn that only a waterjet-driven vessel could make. The forty-foot patrol boat half-turned, half-pirouetted in an impossibly tight circle. Water shot out in an arc of white spray as it spun. Centrifugal force threw everyone forward and then sideways as the bow swung about in a near circle. The crew rode it out with practiced ease, still firing in all directions. But the sudden motions threw the men in the troop compartment about in tangled heaps.

Without a doubt, Gasquey pulled off the fastest, tightest turn of her career. But it still cost them speed and distance. The demons torpedoed forward seemingly faster than ever. At the same time, more of the aliens burst through the trees and launched a barrage of spikes at them. A window next to Nelino blew inward with a spray of hard, sharp plastic. Hot wind from something fast and deadly kissed his cheek, leaving a burning sensation in its wake.

Pessoa screamed and the starboard machine-gun went silent. Nelino grimaced and fought down another urge to vomit when he saw the top half of the gunner's head missing. *Damn!* Memories of their last barbeque where Nelino's kids had played football with Pessoa's flashed through his head. He set his jaw and shook his head to clear it. *No time for that now. Later. If there is a later.*

Rushing to the weapon-mount, he began tugging at the belts holding up the limp body. They needed this gun working, and right now! Another pair of hands lifted the body to take the weight off the buckles. He glanced over to see the strained face of Sergeant Araujo. Together they freed Pessoa and moved him out of the way. One of the other special forces men grabbed the gun grips. The man fumbled with the unfamiliar weapon for a moment. But it wasn't that unusual for him, and he quickly began firing at the demons.

The creatures swarmed toward the boat from every side. Loud cracks and thumps reverberated through the hull as they ran over several trying to cut them off. Nelino could feel the impacts through the bottom of his feet. Another volley of spikes hit the hull and two men in the troop compartment screamed, clutching at blooming blood spots on their arms and chests. Then another of the soldiers jerked and quietly folded in on himself as he collapsed straight down onto the deck.

The boat reached full speed, slicing through the water at forty-five knots. They pulled ahead of the creatures knifing through the water and left the initial attackers behind. But others burst from the foliage ahead. Thirty or more made those crazy long leaps into the water to intercept them. After the initial splash, they disappeared under the surface.

So, the demons had hidden and let them pass earlier. This was no chance encounter; the damn things had set an ambush. The boat reached the middle of this new group in seconds. A dozen or more of them lined up, forming a barrier in the water just ahead. The boat rushed toward the line, and Gasquey tooted the horn in warning again. Nelino grabbed the handrail and braced. Araujo had learned his lesson and did likewise. The boat gave a big lurch, along with a loud thump accompanied by a distinct crunch. The hull started to shudder violently as it cut through the water.

God, please hold her together, prayed Nelino in silence.

The alien warriors continued to rush them from every direction. Gasquey jerked the jet boat into a series of tight turns. There were some light thumps and then a hard one as they struck another demon square on. The boat lurched with a louder, even more worrisome crunch coming from below. A barrage of spikes hit them and then another, but no one got hit.

The jet boat began to move noticeably slower. But inch by inch, they managed to pull away from the war demons. The hull shuddered and shook around the large horseshoe bend. This put a strip of land between them and the demons.

They raced into the area where the river flowed wide but with a narrow channel. The boat continued to shake and shudder as it sliced through the water. Gasquey did something to the controls, and the front of the boat rose a bit. The shaking eased, although a distinct vibration still buzzed up through Nelino's feet. He realized his boat was dying. But they had left the alien bastards behind. For now.

He turned and found Sergeant Araujo kneeling beside Petty Officer Pessoa. The sailor was obviously dead. The sergeant looked up to meet Nelino's eyes and shook his head sadly. Deep lines in the man's face gave testament to his tension.

Nelino could feel tears flowing down his own face and blood dripping his chin from where he bit his lip. More blood dripped down his cheek from the hot kiss of the demon spike. He must have looked a mess. But the sergeant's expression showed no sign of contempt or judgment. At this point, Nelino wouldn't give a damn if it had. Between the two boats, five of his people died in front of him today, and by God, he'd cry if he wanted.

But...? Did Araujo's eyes have a look of respect? With lips pressed tight, the sergeant gave Nelino a slight nod as if to recognize their shared sorrow. Then he stood and turned to go check on his own men. Maybe the sergeant understood this. Maybe every soldier wasn't a complete asshole. Maybe.

With a final look at poor Pessoa, Nelino went to a side locker and pulled out a towel to clean his bleeding face. Turning to Gasquey, he yelled over the wind rushing through the broken bridge windows, "How bad is it?"

She shook her head. "Not good. I can keep her trimmed out for a little while, but the bilge pumps can't keep up with what's coming in. In this shallow water...?" She shrugged and said, "A few kilometers maybe. Then we'll ground out, if we don't hit something hard first. At this speed, the depth finder is pretty much useless."

Nelino nodded and started to say something stupid like, "Get us as far as you can." But the chief already knew that. Instead he just clasped her shoulder, nodded, and turned to go help wrap Pessoa's body in a poncho. He noticed the soldiers doing the same for three of their companions below. God, what a mess.

Nelino stepped down into the troop compartment to talk to Araujo. The commandos looked up from tending to their dead and wounded. He saw fear, sorrow, maybe uncertainty, but no contempt. At least not that he could tell. He tried to think of something to say about the dead. They'd lost even more friends today than the he had. Plus, their commanding officer. But no words came to mind. Silence seemed the best option. Nelino looked at the now shrouded forms and crossed himself. This must have sufficed as the men around him nodded in approval.

"Our captain," Araujo said in a voice that barely carried over the wind. "He should've listened to you."

Nelino felt a twinge of relief, but that seemed stupid and even disrespectful, considering what had happened. He shrugged and said, "We face an unknown enemy. I fear we'll have more tough lessons ahead of us."

Araujo snorted, "This is a very expensive school."

"Yeah. And I fear we have barely made a down payment. How bad is it back here?"

Araujo wasn't crying, but the strain around his eyes indicated that maybe he wasn't far from it. No one went through such an experience and walked away free of consequences. "Two dead, four wounded. One is very bad."

Nelino gestured toward the bow. "The boat is taking on water. We can only go a few more kilometers. Normally we'd beach her and call for help, but…" The sergeant didn't need him to say the radios didn't work. There would be no calling. "Well, I hate to abandon her, but we're way too close to the demons for my taste. We have two inflatable boats with small motors on them. We can take them downstream to the main river. From there, we should be able to contact another patrol. Worst case, the base wouldn't be that much farther."

Araujo nodded and Nelino turned to the starboard gunner. "Lisboa, I think we're clear for now. Start breaking out the inflatables." The man nodded and unstrapped himself from his gun mount. Nelino climbed back up to the bridge to help Gasquey. Not that he could do much besides watch out for logs.

A few minutes later, Lisboa poked his head around the bridge's bulkhead. He yelled into the wind, "No good on inflatable number one, sir. It took a bunch of spikes. It's too shot up to patch."

"Shit," said Nelino. "Okay, got it. Go ahead and prep number two."

The man nodded and worked his way along the narrow walkway beside the bridge toward the inflatable lockers. Chief Gasquey spared him a tense look, then resumed studying the river. Each inflatable boat could carry a maximum of six people. She could do the math as well as he. Some of them would have to hump it out.

Well, there was nothing for it. He stepped back down into the troop compartment and gave the news to Araujo. The sergeant looked even grimmer after hearing the situation.

Nelino said, "We can evacuate the wounded and two more in the inflatable."

Araujo looked back at his men and nodded. "My people are trained for the jungle. So, it makes sense we go. Which of your people will go with us?"

"I will," Nelino said without hesitation. He looked around at his three remaining crew members. "And Lisboa too, I suppose."

Araujo nodded. "So, we are in for a nice walk. Which way, do you think? The base is south, but we'd have to skirt their territory. Directly away from the White Mountain would put us into the middle of nowhere. I don't relish spending weeks wandering around in the jungle."

Nelino managed a strained smile. "I thought you special forces guys could eat rocks and tree bark?"

Araujo snorted. "Yeah, well maybe. But as for me, I prefer pasta and wine."

Nelino chuckled. Damn, he was starting to like this man. "Okay, south it is." He held up his tablet. "Following the river would take us out of the way. But we can cut across and intersect the Jauaperi River about here," he said, tapping the screen. "By then, the inflatable should have contacted base and alerted them to be on the lookout for us."

Araujo forced a grin. "Well, we have a plan, such as it is."

Nelino nodded and went back to the bridge and stood beside Gasquey. "When she starts to bottom out, try to get to the south bank. You take the wounded and Natalia down river in the inflatable. Make contact and get help. Lisboa and I will cut across land with the special forces guys."

She gave him a sharp look and shook her head. "With all due respect, sir, screw that. Lisboa smokes like a chimney. He wouldn't last a day. I'll go with you."

"But…"

"Don't even say it. I'm as much a soldier as any of the crew. Hell, better. And you know it. I'll go. Besides, Camila would skin me alive if I didn't go along to watch after you."

Nelino's mouth twitched up, but the smile wouldn't come. "Very well. I guess I can't deny you the pleasure of my company and a nice hike through the rainforest."

She grunted and raised her hand in acknowledgement without turning, keeping her attention on the river.

So now they walked. Not something to look forward to. Snakes, spiders, alien monsters, and God knew what else. Nelino thought of the men who died today and then of his wife and two children. Would he live to see them again? *God, please help me make it so.*

4 Sally Morgan in the Civilian Camp

"Son of a bitch," said Dr. Robert Allen. "This place just keeps getting crazier."

Dr. Allen had the classic grey hair and bushy beard one would imagine for a scientist researching the rainforest, but not the expected physique of a jungle explorer. He was a bit too short and round to look the part of a true adventurer. Looking over the area through his thick, silver-framed glasses, his grey eyes seemed as round as the rest of him. But Sally Morgan loved working for him. He'd been a great mentor to her and a sweet old bear at heart.

Sally nodded and gave a shrug. "The whole world is getting crazier. Why should here be any different?"

Sally squinted as she surveyed the scene below them. The yellow globe of the early morning sun sat low on the horizon. Being close to the equator gave its light a fierce intensity, at least when not masked by the frequent rain clouds.

The semi-marshy ground on the south side of the river was evolving into a fair-sized village, and a very bizarre one. The original refugees who escaped the carnage of Rio Estrada were in the minority now. Hundreds of people had flocked to the area, and more were arriving every day. Whether they came because of science, religion, or morbid curiosity, the mysteries surrounding the Earth's newest mountain range proved to be a strong enticement. Paul even met some people from a TV show specializing in extraterrestrial encounters. He said they seemed very smug about the arrival of the aliens.

It was indeed puzzling that even with the obvious dangers, people continued to come by the boatload—each for their own reasons and bringing along their own associated odd symbols or strange equipment. This no doubt fueled Dr. Allen's comment about the surrounding craziness.

The sound of chain saws echoed out of the jungle behind the camp as trees fell to the camp's expansion. Tents and huts of various shapes and sizes were springing up in every direction. Open fires sent columns of smoke into the air along with the smells of exotic foods cooking. Several restaurants, shops, and churches were in operation or under construction. It was a regular frontier boomtown.

The research camp sat on a choice bit of land on top of a small ridge. It overlooked a gentle slope down to a mud flat bordering the wide river beyond. Sally and Dr. Allen picked the location before the current influx of people.

The university camp was growing almost as fast as the surrounding village, especially with the aid of the Brazilian military. The Brazilians threw a lot of resources at the University of North Alabama team. They were desperate to gain as much information as possible about the alien threat facing them. However, the growth was little more than an empty shell of tents and supplies for now. Useful research equipment and people trained to use it were in short supply.

The harsh light made Sally's eyes water as the sunbeams lanced into the back of her brain. This did little to help comfort her headache. She rubbed her temples in a vain attempt to ease it. The pain had become a constant, unwelcome friend. She knew the cause. Tension and lack of sleep from working almost around the clock. Not that she got much sleep when she wasn't working.

Damn, but I'm tired, she thought. *How much longer can I keep this up?* She'd hoped the work would be exhausting enough to get some decent rest. Well, she achieved the exhausted part, but not the sleep. Nothing seemed to help her ward off the nightmares about the death of her brother and friends. Not to mention the other horrors she'd endured after the helicopter crashed into forest. Working hadn't helped, and pills and wine made her feel worse once they wore off. Funny how when she really wanted to sleep, she just couldn't.

Paul Sanders walked up carrying a backpack. At first glance, one would be quick to label the tall, reddish brown-haired man with thick glasses a nerd. To do so would be correct to some degree, but it was far from a complete description. The body of a world-class athlete lay beneath his always-wrinkled clothing. Paul held the South Eastern regional record for the triathlon. He and Sally had a thing a while back. But after a few hot months, the passion faded into a good friendship. They were both too engrossed in their studies for anything serious.

A strand of limp, dark brown hair fell across Sally's face, and she pushed it up with a frown. *Damn it, stay put already*. The humidity of the Amazon was not kind to her hair. The humidity turned it frizzy, and if she used enough hairspray to prevent that, it felt sticky and gross all day. Annoyance turned into a spark of humor, and the corners of her mouth twitched upward. If her hair were all she had to worry about, life would be much easier.

"Holy cow," Paul said with a grin. "Did you actually smile there for a moment?"

This brought another half-smile to her lips, if not her eyes. "Yeah, I almost collapsed in mirth." She nodded toward the pack and said, "I guess you got the data to save okay."

Paul held up the backpack. "Yeah, this military grade tablet is doing great. Thank God. This damn EMP level radio interference is a pain in the ass. It sucks having our units constantly burn out. We should be able to get better results from now on."

"That's good," said Dr. Allen. "I know the Brazilians will be disappointed we don't have more information today."

Sally gave a half-wave of her hand. "We have enough, a hell of a lot more than we did last time. So, are you gentlemen ready?"

The other two nodded and they set out down the ridge along a meandering trail. It led between tents, log structures in various stages of construction, and thatch huts. The path followed the edge of the large, nearly black mudflat bordering the river. During the wet months, the mudflat would be flooded. Now the surface had a crusty top layer that would give way when stepped on, leaving you knee-deep in stinky slime.

The distance from solid land to the edge of the river ranged from fifty yards to a couple of hundred. A dozen walkways made of rough wooden planks snaked across the mud. The makeshift pathways met at one of four wooden platforms spaced along the shore. A gangway floating on a combination of rusting steel drums and bright blue plastic barrels continued out into the river.

The gangways connected to four platforms floating in deeper water. These rough-hewn log docks sat on more multicolored barrels. A dozen boats, both big and small, were tied up to them. A steady stream of foot traffic flowed back and forth across the gangways and plank paths. Most people carried bags or boxes. But here and there small carts were being pushed along the rickety walkway. The makeshift docks saw more traffic than the old ones at Rio Estrada ever did.

Rio Estrada prospered on the forest frontier mainly because of the small, lazy river. There were no roads to speak of, and everything moved by water. It had looked over a wide stretch of the waterway that could almost be considered a lake and had been the final stop for travel into the deep forest.

The town might be gone, but the old docks themselves on the far side now saw more use than ever. But nearly all of it now was military. Brazilian soldiers unloaded equipment or trudged up a ramp to the top of the ridge in a steady stream. They marched in single file to leave room for numerous ATVs going both directions.

A small tugboat pushed a barge bristling with soldiers and more equipment cruised toward the right-hand dock. Two more barges carrying soldiers and equipment sat in the middle of the river waiting for the tug to return.

They neared the outskirts of the civilian camp, and the tents and other structures began to thin out. A line of trees separated the civilian camp from the main Brazilian military base on this side of the river.

Before they reached the trees, Sally noticed a line of planks leading to a small island. These hadn't been there the last time they went to the military camp. They seemed quite unusual because they led to the middle of a swampy area. The island was little more than a small hill in the shallow water surrounded by cattails and tree stumps. If not for the floating gangway, only a canoe could reach it. A lot of work went into building the walkway to access what had to be a pretty much useless piece of land.

Or maybe not. Someone was using it right now. On top of the hill stood a dozen or so people. All of them focused on a skinny, disheveled looking man in a brown robe. Brown now, anyway. Sally thought it might have been white at one time. Oddly enough for this part of the world, he was very pale with freckles, dark blond hair, and a long beard laced with grey.

With one hand, he grasped a long pole that had what appeared to be a crooked M on top. On occasion, he shook the staff at the crowd. With his other hand, he gestured in sweeping motions encompassing the river, the camp, and the White Mountains in the distance. He spoke with a lot of emotion and intensity. The people around him seemed mesmerized by the performance.

The theatrics of the man's gestures and passion in his voice led the three scientists to slow down and then stop. "What's he talking about?" Dr. Allen asked.

Sally paused and focused on the man's speech. The words were faint, but understandable even across the mudflat. "He says that the mountain is a sign from God. Now he's challenging them to explain how else such a monolith could appear from nothingness. He says we are in the presence of a miracle the likes of which the world has not seen in over two thousand years."

Dr. Allen rubbed his face. "Humph, really? Well, you know, he does have a point… sort of."

Sally shrugged. "In a way, yeah, I guess he does. The only bad part is he's telling them they need to go there on a pilgrimage. To meet God's angels."

"Oh, crap. That isn't good," said Dr. Allen with a frown. He stroked his beard while studying the group. "I guess it takes all kinds." Then he looked back at the growing civilian camp. "Never thought about this becoming a religious thing. I wonder how many of these people are here to worship."

"I saw a bunch of bald guys in red robes yesterday," Paul said. "I think they were Buddhist monks. And one of the Brazilian staff guys told me some Muslims were building a mosque out of logs. And there's already a Catholic church."

They watched the man a few moments longer. The energy of his voice and grand sweeping gestures were mesmerizing. But for some reason, he gave Sally the willies.

With a shrug, Dr. Allen said, "The guy's got pizzazz, you've got to give 'em that. Come on, we need to get to the briefing."

Paul didn't move, causing Dr. Allen to hesitate. The older man followed Paul's gaze across the river toward the towering mountains in the distance. "That preacher man isn't getting to you too, is he?"

"No," said Paul with a soft chuckle. "But the mountains… Every once in a while, they just seem to reach out and grab me. I mean...They're just so, so…impossible. It's hypnotic."

"And terrifying," said Sally. Both men nodded in agreement. "Little wonder religions are moving in," she said. "There's been nothing like this in human history."

The sight of the White Mountains still sent shivers up her back. She avoided looking at them as much as possible. But like Paul said, the towering white fangs thrusting above the horizon just pulled at your eyes. The next thing you realized, you found yourself staring at them.

Some called them the White Mountains. Others used the singular form and just said, "The White Mountain." *Montanha Branca* in Portuguese. However, singular or plural, English or Portuguese, it mattered little. Everyone knew exactly what you were talking about.

From where the three stood, the two tallest peaks dominated the horizon. The closest was the overriding one, both in size and distinction. A massive yellowish-white granite obelisk, it reached skyward for nineteen thousand feet, jutting up from a brown and gray rocky base. A bit beyond was another granite peak, though not as tall or impressive as the first. Smaller crags and spires dotted the rocky slopes below the two main crests. Some of these would be decent mountains in their own right. But they looked insignificant next to the two main summits.

Between the mountains and tree line on the other side of the river, the top of a sheer rock cliff face could be seen. Paul had determined that it stood over three thousand feet high. As far anyone knew, this rocky wall completely encircled the massifs. The alien stronghold was a giant mesa topped by the mountains. Surveys were going slow. But the best information available put it at nineteen miles long by nine or ten wide.

Thinking about how such a huge…thing…could magically appear made Sally's head spin. One night she went to sleep. Then a crazy storm threw her out of bed and bingo, a new mountain range literally appeared overnight.

"So, there's no doubt it came from space?" Sally asked in a soft voice.

Paul shook his head. "None. Turns out quite a few people actually spotted it coming in. Heck, the International Astronomical Union even gave it an asteroid designation, 2028 NS_3. But it came in very fast and then slowed down. That got people's attention in a hurry. As it approached, it ignored every law Sir Isaac Newton and Einstein ever thought of."

Paul bent down and picked up a river-polished pebble. He started to rub it with his thumb, as though seeking comfort in the smooth surface. "Got a letter yesterday…" He gave a little chuckle. "I can't believe I got an actual letter. And I've even written three of them myself. Can you believe it? I've never gotten a letter on actual paper in my life. It took over a week to get here. This whole thing is so… surreal."

He shrugged and then continued, "Anyway, the letter was from Dr. Compton in the physics department. He said the guys at LIGO went crazy when the asteroid got close."

"LIGO?" said Dr. Allen. "What's a LIGO?"

"Laser Interferometer Gravitational-Wave Observatory. There are four of them actually, but UNA has ties to the one in Louisiana. There've been less than a dozen gravitational waves detected in the last five years. But when the White Mountain landed, there were nine hundred and sixty-seven of them in the course of an hour and a half. Most of them measured several orders of magnitude greater than anything before."

Dr. Allen gave a low whistle. "So, that's what we felt? That was the weird storm that tore up the camp?"

"Well, not the gravitational waves themselves. The waves are warp fluctuations in space-time—actual ripples in reality, which is one of those quantum things that makes you crazy. Gravitational waves make us actually undulate like jellyfish in an ocean swell. We just don't feel or notice them. Normally we can't detect them unless they're crazy powerful, like two black holes colliding. Dr. Compton thinks these waves were offshoots of wormholes, actual tunnels through reality opening and closing every few seconds. Not as strong as black holes, but since they were so close, we could detect them. It makes my head hurt even thinking about it."

Paul gave his head a gentle shake as if to ward off an encroaching brain pain. "What rocked the camp and Rio Estrada were gravitational forces of extreme power, though muted somehow. That's what made it seem like everything kept tilting back and forth. Multiple appearances and disappearances of these extreme gravity wells overpowered Earth's gravity, and things fell toward them. But the formation of these wells distorted local space and created the gravity waves. They're related. So, in a way, yes."

Paul said, "The thing is, the forces should have been even stronger. Dr. Compton's deceleration calculations show the gravity sources involved should have ripped the Earth and Moon apart. The effects had to be muted or contained somehow. He has a theory the creatures create a wormhole to a powerful gravity source, like a sun or black hole. Then they open and close these focused gravitational wormholes like sailors adjusting sails to steer their ship, using them to control their speed to land. They must have enough control to balance them out and cancel some of the tidal stresses."

"No wonder people want to worship it," Sally said softly with a slight nod toward the man in the robe. "It's as close to magic as I ever want to come."

"Amen," said Dr. Allen.

One of the onlookers in the group below, a large dark-skinned woman in a dirty flowered dress, glanced their way. The woman stared for a moment and then gave a small flinch as though recognizing them. Even at this distance, Sally could see anger light her features. She hurried over to the man in the brownish robe and pointed in their direction.

He stopped speaking and quirked his mouth in annoyance. The annoyance turned to thoughtful consideration while he listened to the woman. As she spoke, the man turned his intense gaze toward them and his brow furrowed.

In thought or anger? Sally couldn't tell at this distance, but something about his manner made her suspect the latter.

"What's that about?" said Dr. Allen. "Do any of you know her? And is that guy giving us the stink eye?"

"Well...We were talking about them, weren't we?" said Paul. "Guess they can talk about us too. Maybe they think we're kings or something."

"Because we don't have shit all over us?" Sally replied. It was an automatic response they'd developed after watching an old movie they both really liked. It'd been some silly British comedy about King Arthur the student union used to play over and over. Later there was a play along the same line the school thespian club put on. Remembering it brought forth a soft chuckle. The feeling surprised her. *Wow, half smiles and chuckles, maybe there's hope for me yet.* The feeling of mirth faded quickly though, dampened both by her internal pain and the malevolent glare from the robed man on the small island.

The three scientists wore clean khaki pants and dark purple shirts with a lion's crest over the left breast, the symbol for the

University of North Alabama. Dr. Allen had wanted them to dress their best for the meeting with the Brazilian military. In contrast, everyone in the group on top of the hill looked disheveled and unkempt. The scientists definitely stood out.

Paul chuckled, then shook his head. "Maybe. But I don't think that's it. They look pissed."

"Well, everyone's got the right," said Dr. Allen. "Come on, we've wasted enough time." He placed his hands on their backs and gently pushed them into motion. "We've got to get moving."

As they walked, sweat trickled down Sally's back and made her shirt stick to her skin. She'd much rather be wearing shorts. But that wouldn't be professional enough for a presentation to a bunch of Brazilian officers. The others were sweating as well, although Dr. Allen seemed to sweat most of the time anyway. However, even Paul, Mr. Triathlon, had a sheen of perspiration on his face.

Paul would be good-looking if he'd stop wearing those thick-framed black glasses he preferred. He'd worn them as long as she could remember. Supposedly for their durability. But he'd look a lot better if he only put them on when he ran triathlons or extreme obstacle courses. Her brother called the glasses birth control goggles, an obvious reference to their effect on the opposite sex. She had no idea where David picked up the term, but it certainly fit. Of course, she and Paul were no longer dating, so it wasn't any of her business. But still…

Paul noticed her looking at him and gave an awkward smile, then looked away. Sally sighed. She knew he felt guilty about leaving David in Rio Estrada while he took an airboat to check on the camp. The boat hadn't been big enough for an extra passenger, so it was stupid to blame himself. Right after he left, the village had been destroyed and David…went missing. Sally kept telling herself her brother was only missing. Her friendship with Paul had been strained ever since. It didn't matter how often she told him not to blame himself. He still felt responsible. It seemed they both had a bit of healing to do.

Thinking of her brother brought on deeper pain. Sometimes she thought it might be better to know for sure he died in the attack. *Is that being a bad person? Maybe.* Wishing she knew for certain made her feel rotten inside. So much so, it made her stomach ache. But keeping hope alive could be a two-edged sword. On the one hand, when she imagined him being okay, it felt good. But in her heart, she knew it wasn't true and holding on dragged out the pain. Bit by bit, she was letting go. She had to. But she feared the guilt over forcing David to come to Brazil would haunt her for a long, long time.

After a short walk through the trees separating the two camps, Sally was surprised to see that the military camp had been growing even faster than the civilian one. A score of new log bunkers now surrounded the base. The long snouts of heavy machine guns poked out from them. An eight-foot-tall log wall ran between most of the bunkers. More logs were in place with teams of soldiers working to finish the enclosure. Several hundred, medium-sized olive-green tents sat inside, organized in neat rows. Larger tents of various dimensions sat in four separate clusters. A dozen camouflaged trailers occupied the center. Besides the men building the wall, more soldiers carried logs from the forest, stood guard, or worked on other tasks.

"Wow," said Dr. Allen. "Fort Amazon. All of this in just a couple of weeks."

A group of soldiers stood beside one of the nearby bunkers. An opening framed in wood in the log fence marked an obvious gateway. The three scientists headed in that direction.

The soldiers looked them over as they approached. Sally recognized one of the uniforms as belonging to an officer. She went up to him and said in Portuguese, "Greetings Lieutenant. Dr. Robert Allen, Paul Sanders, and Sally Morgan to see Colonel Antinasio. I believe he's expecting us."

The men around the gate tensed and stared at her, then stood a little straighter. Their expressions looked odd, almost as if they were amazed. Dr. Allen and Paul noticed the strange looks and glanced over at Sally. Several of the soldiers muttered, "*Matador de demônios.*"

The lieutenant snapped to attention and the soldiers did the same. The officer said, "Present arms!" The soldiers at the gate snapped a salute. Then the officer said, "Order arms. At ease." The men dropped their salutes and relaxed as he reached out a hand to Sally. "I'm Lieutenant Mauro Pinheiro. It is a great honor to meet you, Miss Morgan."

Sally stammered in surprise, "Uh, yes, certainly. The honor is mine."

With a smile and a nod, the lieutenant turned toward the bunker. He started to call out but stopped when a smallish soldier hustled out. The first true smile in a long while lifted the corners of her mouth when she recognized the diminutive form of Private Julio Arente.

"Sally!" the young soldier yelled as he ran up. He had a big smile too. It disappeared after he glanced at the lieutenant, and his face turned serious. He stopped in front of the officer and saluted. "I beg your pardon, sir. With your permission, may I escort our guests to Colonel Antinasio?"

The lieutenant returned the salute with a small grin of his own. "Of course. Please give the colonel my regards."

"Yes sir. Thank you, sir." Julio turned to Sally, the big smile once again lighting up his face. "Sall...Uh, Miss Morgan, so good to see you again."

Sally stepped forward and gave the young private a hug. "We are too good of friends for such formality, Julio. Please, call me Sally."

"Uh, yes ma'am. But, well, I really shouldn't. At least not in front of..." He glanced at the lieutenant.

Lieutenant Pinheiro's smile broadened and he said, "It's fine in front of me, Julio. But I'm sure the colonel...and especially the general...wouldn't approve. Okay?"

"Yes, sir," Julio said. His eyes swept over Sally's companions. "I'm sorry. I'm being rude."

"My fault," said Sally. "Julio, this is my boss, Dr. Robert Allen, and one of my colleagues, Paul Sanders. Gentlemen, I would like you to meet Private First-Class Julio Arente. Julio is the man who rescued me from the helicopter." The three exchanged smiles and handshakes.

The day after the White Mountains appeared, Sally and her best friend Myra Hamilton took off in a helicopter trying to reach the university's camp. Instead, they'd been shot down over the jungle. The helicopter crashed into the forest and got lodged in the branches of a giant tree. Everyone died but Sally, leaving her trapped and injured in the crumpled aircraft. She'd spent several days alone except for the rotting corpses of her friends.

Marines from Patrol Boat Group 31 found the helicopter three days later. Julio volunteered to climb up the tree and help her get down. The memory of her dead and mangled friends was one source of her nightmares. Oddly enough, the feeling of freedom after getting out of the tree became one of her happiest memories.

Sally noticed the lieutenant nod to one of the soldiers standing nearby, a young man who looked like a slightly bigger, older version of Julio. The young man walked over to her with a nervous expression on his face and said, "Pardon me, Miss Morgan. I'm Corporal Raoul Bastani. I want to thank you for saving the life of my little brother, Carlosa."

Joy filled Sally. "Carlosa made it? I'm so glad." This was the best news she'd heard in a while.

Julio nodded, though he looked sad. "He made it, but they had to take his leg. We just found out this morning."

"Oh," said Sally, the smile fleeing her face. "I'm so sorry."

Raoul smiled, his teeth looking bright white against his caramel skin. "No, don't be. Momma is very glad to have him home. She sends her thanks as well."

Sally nodded, tears moistening her eyes.

Julio cleared his throat and said, "Uh, we really need to be going. The meeting is supposed to start in a few minutes."

With a quick flurry of thanks and goodbyes, they headed into the base. As they walked, Dr. Allen asked, "What does madador...doo...demournus mean?"

Sally shook her head. "*Matador de demônios*. It's silly; it means demon slayer, or demon killer."

Dr. Allen and Paul exchanged puzzled glances.

Sally shrugged. "While we were out in the jungle, we got attacked by war demons and... well, I killed one of them."

Paul gave a start. "One of those things? Like the one we have in the lab?"

Sally nodded with a dismissive half-wave of her hand.

Dr. Allen said in an admiring tone, "But...why didn't you tell us?"

She frowned and shook her head. "It's not a pleasant memory. I…just got lucky." She squeezed her eyes shut for a moment, trying to clear away her internal turmoil. "Besides, I've had other things on my mind. I'll tell you about it later."

5 First Lieutenant Daniel Johnson: Bataan Task Force

Lieutenant Daniel Johnson opened the starboard hatch near the stern of the USS *Bataan* and stepped outside. He ducked as he eased through the hatch onto an observation walkway that ran under the flight deck. Then he stood up straight and arched his back. It felt good to stretch out his six-foot-four-inch frame. The close confines of the ship didn't suit someone his size. But then, this held true for most of the equipment in the Marine Corps.

Sometimes he wished the genetic combination of his Japanese mother and Norwegian father had been reversed. Instead of being an oversized Asian dude, life might be easier to be a small, light-skinned blond guy. Of course, he would like to keep his eyes. The girls really liked his bright green exotic eyes.

But being big did have some advantages. Even as a child, few people ever picked on him. His father stood a good two inches taller, and he did well in the Corps. Too well in Daniel's opinion. The Colonel, as his mother called him, spent a *lot* of time away from home. But overall, Daniel couldn't complain. Life treated him pretty well.

Warm humid air rushed past, making his uniform flap hard against his arms and legs. It carried the smell of wet wood, a faint fishy odor, and the sweet musk of a million different plants and flowers. A gust plucked at his hat, forcing him to snatch it off his head before it blew away. He took off the green camouflage cap and tucked it into his belt. The wind on his bare head felt wonderful as it caressed his scalp with invisible fingers through his short-cropped black hair.

The *Bataan* was a large ship that most civilians would mistake for an aircraft carrier. However, her proper designation was amphibious assault ship. The vessel did carry plenty of aircraft, though, both jets and helicopters but also landing boats, hovercraft, and amphibious armored vehicles. These could be launched directly into the water from the hold below via the five-story rear doors. With her sister ships in the strike group, the Marines could put a powerful force on shore in a hurry. Usually. But there was nothing usual about the situation they now sailed toward.

Daniel always knew the Bataan could travel faster than advertised. But the speed she put on display steaming up the Amazon blew away the official maximum of twenty-two-knots. At a guess, they had to be doing over thirty.

The four escort ships kept up easy enough. That made sense. No point in one ship being faster than the rest. The capability to get places quicker than expected could be a great advantage for any military force. Still, steaming up a river like this, even one as big as the Amazon, seemed a bit reckless. The Brazilians demanded the Marines get to Manaus as soon as possible. They also assured the Navy high command that river traffic would be alerted. From what Daniel could see, they hadn't done a very good job.

A lot of big ships made the thousand-mile journey between the Atlantic and Manaus. The city proudly boasted of being the only major port located so far inland. This meant locals were familiar with large, ocean-going vessels on the Amazon. But they never encountered ships this large going so fast. Certainly not five of them together. Huge waves churned in the wake of the ships, by far the biggest Daniel had ever seen on any river. Big enough to roil the surface of the mightiest river on Earth.

Despite the Amazon being over a mile wide in most places, the five-to six-foot waves wreaked havoc along the waterway. It didn't help that the five ships maintained a formation geared toward defense rather than minimizing traffic disruption. This meant they were spread out across the river rather than in single file. Waves coursed across the surface from bank to bank. They left smashed docks, flooded villages, and wrecked boats everywhere. Also, a lot of angry locals.

He imagined the Brazilians and high command would rethink their, "As fast as possible," order in the future—provided any other Marine Expeditionary Units were ordered in. Dear God, he hoped more would come. As powerful a force a s the 22nd MEU was, he feared they would be inadequate for what lay ahead.

The observation deck ran along the rear of the ship, wrapping around the stern. Someone stood at the curve just before the platform disappeared around the back of the ship. The man leaned against the rail, staring back along the ship's wake. He recognized the fit, medium height black man at once—Gunnery Sergeant Louis Stevens, Daniel's platoon sergeant. As he walked toward the older man, Stevens stood and began waving at someone behind the ship with exaggerated enthusiasm.

The wind dropped noticeably as Daniel stepped around the corner onto the stern. He leaned on the rail next to the sergeant and looked down. A short distance behind and to the side, yet still in the ship's wake, a local fisherman clung to an overturned boat. The boat looked small as it bobbed and rolled in the ship's wake. The fisherman screamed unintelligible curses at them and managed to let go of the gunnel on the bottom of the boat long enough to hold his hand up with his finger and thumb in a circle.

"What're you doing?" asked Daniel.

"Maintaining peaceful relations with the indigenous population," he said, his expression a mask of well-schooled innocence. "Just like the colonel asked us to."

Daniel shook his head. "I don't think that's helping."

"Look at him; he's giving me an OK sign."

"That's what Brazilians use to flip you the bird."

"Huh? Really?" Gunny shrugged. "Well, at least I tried." He stopped waving and gestured toward the jungle speeding by the ship. "Man, it sure feels weird going upriver in this thing. Especially this fast. It's like I'm on the world's largest ski boat."

"Humph? A fifty-thousand-ton ski boat?" Daniel looked beyond the river at the expanse of green moving quickly by and nodded. "But yeah, I get your point."

"When I was a kid, I saw a show where someone skied behind a cruise ship. I always thought that was so cool." Gunny shook his head and stared down at the rushing, burbling water behind the stern. "Actually, I think we're going too fast to ski."

Daniel chuckled. "I can see you trying to talk the captain into letting you try. And if he let you, when you fell, it would take a long time for the ship to come around and pick you up. This thing doesn't exactly turn on a dime."

Gunny shrugged. "That's okay. Maybe I'd just swim to shore. I'm not too wild about going on this mission anyway," he finished in a low voice.

"I know what you mean," Daniel replied with a frown. "No radios, no satellite communications, and no GPS."

Gunny nodded. "Yeah. But hey. No GPS. That's another thing. What the hell could blast every damn satellite up there out of the sky?" He fidgeted with his toe against one of the guard rail poles. "It feels like we're going back to the Stone Age. Except of course, we got the Pigs," he said, referring to the platoon's eight-wheeled armored fighting vehicles.

"So, what did you think of the colonel's briefing?"

"I think she told us too damn much."

"Why, Gunny, don't you ascribe to her philosophy? 'An informed Marine is a dangerous Marine.'"

Gunny shrugged and glanced over at Daniel. "Most of the time, maybe. But this? Mysterious mountains appearing from nowhere? Huge alien creatures ripping up the jungle and kidnapping an entire village? Different but still weird aliens slicing a Brazilian marine unit to pieces?" He shook his head. "To me, in this case an informed Marine is a scared Marine." He looked down and said in a voice that barely carried over the wind, "I know I am."

"What would you want her to do? We need to have information on what we face. You know we'll be the first ones in."

"Hell yeah! Of course, we will. We're Armored Recon. Oorah!" He met Daniel's eyes again. "I've seen a lot…been through a lot, in this job. I always get scared. That's part of it. But not like this. I'm not scared for me so much, but for the platoon. Our men have minimal jungle training, and we're going up against… Hell, against space monsters? And with what? On top of no communications and no GPS, we won't have air support or drones."

The sergeant's brown eyes looked beyond Daniel into the far distance. "All this crazy shit…and just us. Out here alone at the point of a long skinny stick, poking into some damn strange shit. Like I said, I don't like it."

Daniel remained silent. Gunny turned back around and the two men leaned on the railing together. Behind the ship, a long line of frothing white water faded into thick brown water. Beyond the river stretched the vast green vista of the Amazon rainforest.

6 David Makes a Catch

The fishing turned out to be poor for the rest of the day. After the monkey, nothing but trees came off the conveyor for the next three cycles. And not a one of them bore fruit or nuts. David would have to pack up soon. They only had two knives, and Paula would need the one he carried to prepare supper.

Paula had taken over the job of full-time cook, mainly because of her knowledge of local plants and animals, but also because she was really good at making decent meals out of strange combinations. On two separate occasions, she even saved them from being poisoned. Once Paula recognized a red fruit Alessandra pulled from the vat as strychonos, which contained strychnine. Another time, David brought in some berries. They turned out to be from a plant the local natives used to make blow dart poison. Even Josh respected her, or it seemed that way. He never yelled at her or swatted her rump with the stick like he did the others.

At least David had snagged the monkey. This might appease her. Sometimes she was almost as mean as Josh. It would've been nice to pull in some bananas or breadfruit; that would mellow her out. But such delicacies didn't seem to be in the cards…or in the pit, as the case may be.

As the vat finished emptying, he decided to give it one more cycle. Ever since he'd saved little Pedro's life, he'd been making progress with Paula. She hadn't been berating him much lately. Every little thing he contributed seemed to help. Now if he could only find a way to get Josh off his back as well.

The conveyor squalled to life, making him jump, but less this time than usual. He'd been here for a couple of hours now. Even the damn jarring squeal lost its impact over time.

The top of a rubber tree appeared and made its way toward the pit. More of the same species followed until it appeared as if a whole grove of them came down the belt. Wherever the gatherers were doing their thing today, there were a of lot of rubber trees.

The vat filled at a rapid pace as more of the seventy-foot-tall trees tumbled in. *Crap. Oh well, looks like more of the same ol' same ol'.* It appeared he wouldn't need to use the sledge today. He only had to carry the monkey.

It took about eighteen revolutions of the winch to roll up the rope. Josh insisted it be stored this way to prevent tangles. David could crank the winch at a respectable pace considering his injured arm, although he was slower than any of the others. So, it took several minutes for the last few feet to climb onto the spindle. He stopped turning the crank with a sigh of relief, then turned to pick up the monkey. Before his fingers closed on it, however, a long green and black camouflaged bundle tumbled off the end of the conveyor.

What the hell? He straightened and hurried over the low wall to search for the object in the mass below. No luck; he couldn't see anything. Whatever the green thing had been, it'd sunk out of sight into the vegetation. Frowning with frustration, he looked up in time to see a second bundle crest the conveyor's end and fall. The bundle hit with a crisp rustle of jostling leaves and disappeared.

It looked like a body. But why would a body be wrapped in camouflage? There was some white webbing around one end, but not very much. He found it hard to imagine stopping in the middle of a bunch of gatherers to wrap up a body. If you had the capability to move, you'd be running, not wrapping.

Another oblong greenish form tumbled off the belt. Then yet another appeared, and another, and another. The first three smashed straight down into the depths of the pit. The last bounced off a thick broken branch and slid down a wide tree trunk. It came to a stop near the edge of the pit about a third of the way around.

Shit! Too far from the winch. How bad did he want it? Good question. But…there must be a lot of stuff down there worth having. The material around the thing by itself would be gold. *What if it's a body?* A shiver of revulsion made David swallow hard . *Damn, damn, damn. It's got to be a body*. Well, there was only one way to find out. Whatever the thing in the pit might be, it represented an opportunity too big to pass up.

David nodded to himself, set his jaw, and ran to the winch. He unlatched the locking pin and began unwinding rope as fast as he could. When it reached the end, he snatched out the knife and cut it free of the spindle. Snatching up the rope, he hurried back around the pit to get above the bundle. While on the move, he tied one end of the rope around his waist. He finished as he approached the spot and began swinging the grappling hook to get ready to throw. He reached the wall, cocked his arm, and then hesitated.

The pit was a little over half full. Trees once again made up the bulk of the objects tumbling off the conveyor. Small trees. But still…If one fell this way and landed on the rope, it would pull him into the pit. *This is crazy. What the heck am I doing?*

A shudder of fear at the idea of going in ran through him. He started to untie the rope but hesitated again. With his injured shoulder, he couldn't pull the bundle up with his arms alone. There was no way to tell for sure, but the things seemed heavy based on how they crashed through the tangle of branches. He needed to use his legs and body together to have a chance. That meant keeping the rope tied around his waist.

Not too long ago, he'd seriously considered killing himself by jumping into the pit. After all, his father had killed himself when David was a kid. This kind of set a family precedent in David's mind. When he first got to the mountain, times had been very bad. It should have ended for him in the pit. But Josh saved him.

Afterward, everyone in the small camp seemed to hate him. In despair, he decided to end it all and get out of the game. It sounded like a good plan at the time. But after staring into the vat for a long time, he decided he wanted to live. This drove him to the conclusion he needed to become a better, more responsible person.

Things still sucked. But not so bad as before. And since he decided to live, the thought of getting pulled into the smelly green hell below scared the bejeezus out of him. Vivid images came to mind about being trapped while waiting to drown or get chopped to pieces. And now here he was, standing on the edge of oblivion with a hook and a damn rope tied around his waist.

A loud crunch came from the center of the pit, making him jump. His head snapped around toward the source of the noise. A Brazil nut tree over a hundred and fifty feet tall tottered in the middle of the vat. Leaves, woodchips, and dust fluttered in a haze around the trunk. The material inside the vat shook and smaller trees began sliding from the central pile toward the edge.

A scraping sound came from below, and he looked down to see the rubber tree holding the bundle slip downward about four feet lower before lurching to a stop. The bundle slid along the trunk a considerable distance, bumping into a pair of jagged stumps. It teetered there, close to falling off. The stumps still had small leafy tendrils which partly obscured the bundle. *Can I even hook it without knocking it off?*

"Grow up and be a man," he muttered. That's what his sister always told him. His eyes swept the chamber and the horror it contained. *How much more grown up do I have to get?* Although he was firmly committed in his resolve to become a better person, this was pushing self-improvement pretty darn far.

He shook off the thought and muttered to himself, "Okay, be a man. Make Sally proud. Just do it...just do it... just..."

"Raarrgh!" The scream burst from his throat as he cast the hook over the edge. Surprisingly, the scream seemed to help. "Aaargh," he yelled again as the rope whisked through his fingers. Before the hook reached the foliage, he slowed it by increasing his grip on the line. His heart began to beat so fast it felt like a rock drummer set up shop in his chest.

More loud crashes came from the center of the pit. But he refused to look, focusing his attention on the bundle and the descending grapple. A lifetime of seconds later, the hook reached the bundle and slid past. There wouldn't be but one chance at this. He jerked up on the rope with all the strength of his right arm, hard enough to stress his back and send a painful jolt through his injured shoulder. But the grapple bit into the material and the rope grew taught.

"Yes!" he shouted.

Now, how the heck was he going to pull it up? It turned out to be as heavy as he feared. With only one arm, he'd have to rely on his legs. But the walkway was only thirty feet wide and the bundle fifty feet or so down. This meant he couldn't get it out just by walking backwards. The distances didn't add up.

A shadow passed over him, but he refused to look up. He hunched a little in nervous anticipation. Following the shadow came another loud crash that made him jump. Another Brazil nut tree nearly two hundred feet tall, rightly called the King of the Forest, tumbled into the pit. It splintered the smaller trees as it struck and send wood slivers flying. Some pelted his face, making him blink.

Everything in the pit shuddered as the tree toppled over. For a few seconds, the tower of wood headed straight for the bundle below him. He reached for the knife to cut the rope but as the tree fell, it began to twist. With a crunch, it smashed down twenty yards to his right. More trees tumbled down behind it, spreading out as they slid down in a flurry of wood and leaves. Any one of them would pull him into the pit if they hit the bundle a solid blow.

Desperation proved to be inspirational. Pulling the rope with his good arm, he rotated his shoulder into it, then turned all the way around, using his body as a makeshift winch. This caused the rope to dig into his hurt shoulder. Pain sizzled though his whole left side. But he ignored it and repeated the process again. The pain intensified, and he stopped. After a few gasping breaths, he resumed, getting into a rhythm. Pull, turn, quick pivot; pull, turn, quick pivot; pull, turn, quick pivot. At last, the bundle came within a few feet from the top. He prayed for traction from his rubber-soled shoes and began backing up. The rope looped around his upper body made movement awkward. He felt like a mummy with a bad body wrap in search of a victim.

Once his feet slipped, and the load almost pulled him off balance. If that happened, his next stop would be in the pit. The rope around his chest and gut made breathing difficult. He panted from exertion and a fair degree of fear as he struggled back inch by inch. At last, the camouflaged bundle crested the wall and fell onto the walkway. David fell backward onto his rump. But he'd done it. He stared at his prize as he tried to catch his breath. Overhead the conveyor stopped, and the hiss and gurgle of flowing fluid came from the vat.

It is a body. Again, he wondered who wrapped it up. Whoever this person was must have been dead before the gatherers found him…or her. The camouflage material appeared to be nylon and had several dark stains visible. Most likely blood.

This must be a soldier from a nearby battle. If so, it must have not have gone well. For sure not for the person in the bundle. *Is there somebody out there attacking the mountain*? Maybe, just maybe someone was coming, though he didn't really believe it. Even if they were, it wouldn't be for the small group trapped in the mountain. No one even knew they existed.

The idea of touching the body now that it lay in front of him made his stomach quiver. However, there must be something usable here, even if only the cloth. There was only so much you could do with webbing, wood, plants, and animal skins. Steeling himself, David unwrapped the rope and crawled over to the body. He knelt beside the camouflaged form and pulled the knife from his belt.

It took him a couple of minutes to work up the courage to open the bundle. To take the knife and cut open the covering went way beyond his comfort zone. He considered going for Paula and

Alessandra but decided against it. Paula still thought that overall, he was pretty worthless. She believed he used his hurt arm as an excuse to get out of work. If he went to her now, she'd probably yell at him and tell Josh what a wimp he was. Then Josh would yell at him too. No, it would be better to do this on his own.

Sally always preached about taking responsibility and showing initiative. This made him wonder if she'd be proud of him right now. A warm glow filled his chest. Actually, she would be; he knew it in his heart. After a few breaths, the smile faded. Most likely she died when the helicopter crashed in the jungle. He'd seen one airplane shot down and heard about several others. Everything was getting shot down. It sucked. Now that he truly appreciated everything his sister tried to do for him, she was gone. His chest felt heavy as he looked at the knife. His eyes began to water. He wiped them dry and moved to the legs of the corpse.

The knife had a keen edge thanks to Josh's ceaseless sharpening. Even so, the webbing was more like strong plastic than spider silk and cutting through it proved to be tough work. Luckily there wasn't much of it, just a few bands around the body's feet and thighs. The material underneath the webbing was composed of thick nylon. This material must have been part of a tent or tarp. He found the edge and carefully began unrolling the body.

As he worked, the smell got worse. This was something he would not have thought possible, as the smell in the vat room already reeked. However, the smell from the green cocoon was a concentrated vileness that managed to surpass that of the chamber. Maybe in part because he'd grown accustomed to the smells coming from the vat. Regardless, when he pulled open the material to reveal the body of a young soldier, he almost vomited. Then he saw maggots crawling across the man's face, and his stomach spasmed. He half-crawled, half-jumped to the low wall surrounding the pit and puked. He retched until it felt like the lining of his stomach would tear loose from his guts.

A last convulsive heave brought up nothing but pain. He sat down, leaned back against the low wall and shook his head. "No way," he muttered. His breath came in ragged pants as he fought off the urge to start vomiting again. His eyes remained locked on the body as he slowly recovered. *I don't think I can do this.* But somewhere inside, he knew he would. *If not me, then who?* Alessandra? Little Pedro? Josh would no doubt do it. But David didn't want to suffer the crap Josh would give him. Upon reflection, that would be harder to endure than being sick.

"Oh God," he said with soft groan. Being responsible sucked.

He swallowed hard and forced himself to move back to the body. It helped to breathe as little as possible. When he did inhale, he sucked air in through his teeth. It helped some, but his stomach tensed with the threat of cramps with every mouthful of the foul stench. It took all of his willpower to touch the soldier again. After a few minutes, his face screwed up with determination, and he went back to work.

The soldier looked serene for the most part, as if dying didn't bother him very much. He appeared to be about the same age as David. His complexation was a light brown, and he had dark eyes and straight coarse black hair. The man had a small frame and couldn't weigh over a hundred and forty pounds. All these traits were common for people from central Brazil.

The soldier wore a belt connected to a harness. Both of these were covered with pouches of different sizes A large knife in a green sheath on the belt caught David's attention right away. A gem amongst the gold. David never appreciated the value of a good knife until he came to live in the cave. They used them for food prep, cutting kindling, working the webbing into ropes and so on. Right now, they only had three. Josh had carried two when he got captured, including a big survival knife and the six-inch skinning blade David had now. The third was David's, a small pocket knife given to him by his father. They used it for cutting fruits and vegetables.

The harness the man wore was a state-of-the-art, military load-bearing setup. A great find all by itself. In addition, it had a medium-sized pack with a built-in water bag. A tube ran from the bag to a clip on the right shoulder. It would be a big help carrying water to camp from the underground stream.

David forced the dead man into a sitting position and unfastened the plastic latches on the harness. He tried to be gentle, but the task required him to give the nylon belts several hard tugs to get it over the soldier's shoulders. Luckily, the urge to vomit weakened as he worked. But there was still a hard lump in his throat. Part of it came from disgust. But also, he felt guilty for taking the man's things. He knew this was a dumb way to feel. The guy was dead and all. But it made David feel like a thief.

At the same time, he felt elated to have such treasures to take back to the group. Just a quick examination told him the pack and pouches contained food bars, extra clothes, a sewing kit, a mess kit, a first aid kit, and more. These would be a major boost for all of them. He took the harness, pack, and water rig and placed them beside the monkey.

A large, blood-encrusted hole in the middle of the man's shirt made it plain what killed him. David had no idea what made the hole. Whatever it was had been very violent. David decided to leave the clothes alone. It felt shameful enough to be robbing the dead. Leaving the soldier naked seemed to be going a little too far. He did take the boots and empty the man's pockets, however. The side pockets on his pants were full of more breakfast and candy bars.

There was no ID; most likely it'd been taken by whoever wrapped up the soldier in the green material. Funny since the other stuff had been left behind. Why would someone take the time to wrap the body, take the ID, and leave the equipment behind? Had they been in a hurry? Maybe the soldiers had been in the middle of a battle. He shrugged. No way to know.

"I'm sorry," David said when he had finished removing the man's boots. "We really need this stuff. Thank you." That didn't seem like enough to say, but he couldn't think of anything else. Finally, he whispered, "God bless you."

What now? Put him back in the pit? NO! The thought sickened him. He would never feed a person to the damn gatherers. But he had to do something. As the rot progessed, the smell would be even more overpowering. The body needed to be buried. But where in the cave or tunnels would be a good place?

The floor of this chamber was solid stone, so he couldn't do it here. The cave where they camped had sand, but David didn't want to bury him there. The idea of having a dead body that close to camp gave him the willies. Maybe one of the tunnels? Josh said they were all caved in. David never ventured down any of them himself, but that seemed like the best bet.

He stood and went over to a large pile of webbing by the dome wall that was a byproduct of their fishing the pit. He gathered up several large pieces, took them to the soldier, and carefully wrapped him up in them. With the webbing wrapped around the body, the smell got much better. Though still hampered by his injured shoulder, David managed to drag the body over to the sledge. Thankfully the small soldier wasn't very heavy.

The sledge wasn't very big though. It was yet another of Josh's crude but effective constructions, comprised of logs and sticks bound together to make a small platform. About four feet long by two wide, it sat on wooden runners that'd been polished smooth by numerous trips across the stone surface of the chamber. David rolled the body onto it. This left the soldier's feet resting on the ground, but there was nothing he could do about that. Then he secured him to the sledge with a few more strips of webbing and placed the monkey on top.

The sledge rarely saw a load as heavy as this. David picked up the rope harness and looped it around his chest. He gave it an experimental pull. It took a bit to get it moving, but then the sledge moved with the customary grating sound of wood runners on the stony floor. Thankfully, after he got it moving, it didn't take all that much effort. That was good. Reassured, David leaned into the makeshift harness and began dragging the load toward the tunnel that led out of the chamber.

7 Sally Morgan Meets General von Jaeger

Julio led them to a large tent with two soldiers standing guard outside. The man on the right nodded and pulled back a mosquito net covering a narrow opening. As they started to go inside, Sally noticed Julio hang back.

"Aren't you coming?"

"Oh no, not me," said Julio. "That's for you and officers, not the likes of a lowly private." He waved to one of the few trees left in the wake of the camp's expansion, a large kapok tree with a crazy array of exposed roots. "I'll wait over there. Don't worry; I'll be here when you come out."

Sally smiled and said, "Okay. I'll see you then."

With a nod and a small wave, Julio headed for the tree.

They entered the tent and stopped just inside the rather murky interior. It seemed especially dim compared to the daylight behind them. A sunbeam from the opening cast a bright, dust-dappled ray that overwhelmed the few small lights inside. The air felt hot and stuffy. Two small, battery-operated fans whirred with a faint buzz, but their efforts to stir the air proved less than successful.

A dozen shadowy figures sat around a large table that took up most of the interior space. A few faces could be seen, lit by the flickering bluish light of their phones or computer tablets. Sally and her two colleagues stood frozen for several seconds as their eyes adjusted. One of the shadowy figures rose and headed toward them. As he approached, Sally recognized the tall, trim form of Colonel Marcus Antinasio.

"Greetings and welcome," he said.

"Hello, Colonel," replied Sally. She almost gave him a hug, but decided it would be inappropriate. While she considered him as close a friend as Julio, it just didn't seem proper. Especially here. Also, something in their relationship seemed more formal. Like they both wanted to be on their best behavior for the other person.

That's an odd thought. Maybe because he's Brazilian?

Marcus shook Dr. Allen's hand with a nod. They'd met several times and had established a decent, nonverbal rapport. Sally introduced the colonel to Paul and they also shook hands. Sally translated for them as needed.

Marcus said, "I've heard good things about the navigation system you developed. It's a big help for my patrol boats."

Paul beamed. "Thank you, colonel. But I had plenty of help, you know. The new guys from Manaus did most of the programming."

"I'm sure others helped, but the basic concept was yours. Good job."

Paul blushed. Before he could say anything else, another man emerged from the gloom.

The newcomer barely came up to Sally's eyes, which wasn't too unusual for a Brazilian. His uniform was bedecked with ribbons and fit him tight around the middle, making him on the heavy side for a military man. He had light brown hair and pale skin, a thin Van Dyke beard, and narrow set eyes. It made her think of a weasel. A fat weasel at that, considering his fleshy face and double chin.

Marcus gestured to the man and said, "May I introduce you to General Herman von Jaeger, the commanding officer of the Amazon Region Defense Forces?"

The general nodded regally and shook their hands. When he came to Sally, he grasped her hand by the fingers and squeezed almost to the point of pain. She felt an instant dislike for the man. His grayish blue eyes sat under suspicious brows. The smile seemed forced. "Greetings, Miss Morgan, I've heard a lot about you." The way he said the curt comment sounded more like a warning than a greeting.

Something about him put her on edge. She gave herself a mental shake and said, "Good to meet you, general."

She started to introduce him to her colleagues. But before she could say anything, the general placed his hand on her shoulder and gave her a not so gentle shove to one side. This shocked her into silence. *That ass-hat pushed me out of the way!?*

The general spoke in heavily accented though passable English. "Greetings, doctor, your reputation precedes you. I've heard you're well regarded in Brasilia."

Dr. Allen frowned at the general for a moment. He looked just as surprised as Sally at the push. Then he gave a slight shake of his head and said, "Thank you, general. You are too kind. Von Jaeger? Are you from Germany, by any chance? I have a good friend there by that name."

"Umm, no. My family came from there. But they immigrated to Brazil many years ago."

General von Jaeger and Paul exchanged greetings, and then the general glanced at Sally. His expression made her uncomfortable.

The general waved his hand at her and said to Dr. Allen, "So, am I to understand your…assistant… is going to do the presentation?"

Dr. Allen frowned again, obviously annoyed by the general's rudeness. He said in clipped tones, "Sally is not my assistant. In fact, she's the lead researcher for the study of the aliens. Due to her experience with them, she is without a doubt the world's leading expert. I believe we may need a new doctorial designation to cover her work. Besides, I'm afraid I don't speak Portuguese."

The general looked skeptical but said, "A pity. Well, we'll just have to make do. But the United States is sending Marines, and I have interpreters on the way. So, in the future, I would prefer you give the briefings in person." He did not wait for a response. "So, shall we begin?"

"Yes, certainly," replied Dr. Allen, his voice somewhat strained. He looked at Sally with an odd expression, then shrugged and gave a slight shake of his head to express his disbelief.

Forcing a smile onto her face, Sally gave a small shrug of her own in reply. She walked to the end of the table where a podium sat next to a large white screen. Paul loaded their data into a small projector while she looked at her notes and fidgeted.

General von Jaeger stepped in front of Sally and said, "All right, gentlemen, it is time to get started. Dr. Allen and his team have prepared an overview of the creatures' physiology for us. Regretfully he does not speak Portuguese, so his assistant will give us the presentation." Without even mentioning Sally's name, he waved her to the podium.

What the hell is this all about? Sally fought to control a surging wave of anger. To regain her focus, she gripped the edge of the table hard enough to turn her knuckles white for a count of ten. Then she relaxed, or at least tried to. She surveyed the room while the data finished uploading.

As her eyes adjusted to the low light, she made out the faces of a dozen people arranged around the table. There weren't any other women present. This didn't help her sense of unease.

Never in her life had she encountered such a total lack of respect. The current president of Brazil was a woman, for God's sake. Of course, the previous female president got impeached and booted out of office. Did that have anything to do with it? Or could there be some other reason besides her being a woman for his attitude?

Screw him, she thought. After everything she'd been through, she wasn't going to let a damn weaselly bigot mess with her head. She cleared her throat, tapped a button to bring up the presentation, and began.

"I believe most of you are familiar with the three different types of alien creatures we've encountered." She had to suppress a shudder as she pulled up the first slide and said, "The common term for this one is war demon."

On the screen, a picture appeared of the creature Patrol Boat Group 31 had carried out of the jungle. The six limbs caught the eye first. They made it look like a misshapen insect. On closer inspection, this initial impression faded. The demon had a mishmash of features that looked like a lot of different animals, though nothing terrestrial really came close.

Working on the alien had been one of the hardest things Sally ever faced. It'd been a challenge to maintain a calm, professional air. Her insides cried out for her to moan with fear. Even dead, the alien creature looked unnervingly menacing. It took every ounce of courage she could muster just to touch it the first time. Her very own personal D-Day. She still didn't know if working on the creature eased or aggravated her nightmares. Not that it mattered. Fear couldn't stand in the way of her research on the aliens…and how best to kill them.

The war demon's back legs were oversized and resembled those of a frog. The middle pair looked like they belonged on a lizard. But the front two appendages came straight out of a nightmare. One had a three-foot-long, sword-like claw at the end of a sinuous whip-like arm. In contrast, the other was shorter and much thicker, especially the misshapen forearm which ended in a large, clumsy looking, three fingered hand. This arm carried the creature's spike weapon.

The alien warrior's body was covered in overlapping scales, most of which had barbs of different lengths sticking from them. Large eyes dominated the head, but it didn't have a mouth, nose, or ears. Barbs, or maybe antennae, covered the skull as well. Many of these were longer than those on the body.

"The biggest discovery about the creatures is they aren't natural."

"They *are* demons!" said a hoarse half-whisper from the rear of the tent.

General von Jaeger leapt to his feet and growled in an angry voice, "Who said that?"

"Uh, my apologies sir," stammered a middle-aged officer, his form little more than an outline in the back of the shadowy tent. He leaned forward and one of the small, overhead battery-powered lights illuminated his worried expression. "I…I didn't mean to speak out. But…my God, how can they be anything else?"

Von Jaeger turned his glare on Sally. "Is that what you're claiming? That these…things are true demons?"

"No, not at all," said Sally. "I said they're not natural. They're…well, more like biological robots really."

Von Jaeger frowned and said, "Very well, you can explain that in a moment." He turned and addressed the others in the tent. "I am not pleased that this woman and Colonel Antinasio started calling these creatures…demons. But remember, his men were little more than policemen and prone to panic. I'm afraid now that the news channels have picked up the term, and we're stuck with it."

Sally clenched her teeth. She saw Marcus's face cloud with anger. His eyes blazed and he drew in a breath to say something but stopped. With an obvious effort, he relaxed and closed his mouth. His jaw clenched and his lips formed a thin, tight line. Tension ran through the tent like electricity

Paul and Dr. Allen couldn't comprehend enough Portuguese to understand the insult. But the tone of the comment, Marcus's and Sally's flushed faces, and the uncomfortable squirming of the others in the tent made it plain something had occurred. The two exchanged confused glances and began a terse whispered conversation.

Von Jaeger continued. "As for the rest of you, you're in command of real soldiers. Our country expects us to put a stop to these things and the destruction of our forests. We cannot allow stupid supernatural fears influence our men or our plans. Morgan, continue," he said.

It didn't seem possible, but Marcus's face turned a deeper shade of red and his eyes blazed hotter than ever. Sally stood in shock for several seconds as her anger boiled up once more. The man hadn't a clue as to what Marcus and his men…she, too, for that matter, had faced in the jungle. Seeing how von Jaeger's stupid statement impacted Marcus made it even worse. Sally's heart felt so heavy, it made her chest hurt. For a few moments, she seriously considered saying to hell with it and walking out.

"Well, get on with it," snapped von Jaeger.

Crap, she thought. *Calm down. So, he's an asshole. Let it go and stay focused. Do it for Marcus and the people of PBG-31 if nothing else.* Drawing in a deep breath and gripping the podium again to the point of pain as she slowly exhaled helped bleed off some of the anger. Her heartbeat slowed, and she drew in another deep breath.

"Very well. As I was saying, the _war demons_ are not natural," she said, intentionally emphasizing the words. This caused the general to give a small start and made his weasel eyes smolder. She felt a twinge of satisfaction. *Yes, you ass, I did that on purpose.*

She managed to maintain a neutral expression and continued. "But they are not supernatural." She nodded to Paul, and he pulled up the next slide. It showed a cutaway drawing of the war demon with several areas highlighted. This included the three-clawed hand, the spikes around the head, the eyes, and a large part of the creature's back. Red lines of various thicknesses connected the highlighted areas.

"The creature is more of a cyborg, or an organic robot. By our standard of biological definition, it's not even alive, primarily because it has no reproductive organs."

"What, like an ant?" said an officer to her left.

"No, ants have sex organs, though most of them are sterile females. This creature does not have any at all. Also, it has no lungs and cannot feed itself. The stomach is more like a fuel tank from which they derive all their energy requirements."

Murmurs and whispers erupted around the tent. Marcus asked, "Does this mean they can travel underwater?"

"Well…I don't know. But it seems plausible. Although that would possibly interfere with their communications. So far, that fits with the current theory."

An officer near the head of the table said, "Communicate? You believe these things talk? Or use hand…uh, claw signals?"

Sally shook her head. "They almost certainly communicate by radio." This got another round of murmurs, but they soon subsided and she continued. Pointing at the highlighted area on the creature's back, she said, "The creature has an internal skeleton reinforced with a carbon fiber casing. It has a spine made up of long, heavy vertebrae, also reinforced. On both sides of the spine are electrogenesis organs. These are very similar to those on an electric eel, only more dense and larger. The power output must be quite high."

She nodded to Paul, and another slide showed the creature with the spine and organs removed. "Just below the electrogenesis organs is the brain."

More murmurs as the men digested the fact the creature's brain was not in the head. Sally nodded as someone commented that this would make the demons harder to kill.

"I can assure you, they are quite hard to kill, especially if they are coming directly at you."

Von Jaeger frowned and gave a small snort. He said in a contemptuous tone, "You need to stay on track. You were discussing their use of electricity?"

Damn, damn, damn. She glared at him, her look not the least bit neutral this time. She forced her face into a more moderate expression and said, "Many of the…war demons' nerves are encased in some kind of carbon fiber as well."

Jaeger's face clouded at her obvious dig, but he remained silent.

It made her feel a little better, if a bit foolish, that she was provoking the highest-ranking Brazilian officer in the area. Sally looked away and swept her gaze over the rest of the men in the tent. She said, "Paul thinks it is a graphene-based substance. We have no idea how this could be done. But it appears to strengthen the nerves to protect them from high current. Or to possibly act as a shield from other electromagnetic sources. Maybe both."

Sally traced the red lines indicating the nerves on the screen. The thickest nerve bundle went to the head. Another thick strand led to the arm with the three-fingered hand. Other red lines connected to some of the spikes protruding from the creature's back and shoulders. These connections were much thinner.

"The head is the obvious center of its sensory system, but we don't believe it perceives the world as we do. There are no cones or rods in the eyes for one thing. It cannot smell or taste. It has no ears, though it may detect atmospheric vibrations through the eyes or antennae."

"What about their weapon?" asked an officer near the head of the table. "I've heard it fires some kind of spike."

Sally asked Paul to pull up the weapon page. A cutaway of the thick, short front arm appeared. "The weapon is as odd and alien as the rest of it. First, they grow the ammunition in their arm."

More whispers and a low whistle. Paul pulled out three mottled black and grey rods. They were about half an inch in diameter but of different lengths. Paul handed them out to be passed around the room. The cutaway showed the red lines of the reinforced nerves going to the tips of the three fingers. The rods were packed together in the creature's oversized forearm. A ruler at the bottom of the image indicated the rods varied from about an inch to almost a foot in length.

Marcus took one of the rods and examined it carefully. His face showed a mixture of interest and disgust. "How are these launched? Magnetism?"

"Unlikely. The rods have a very low level of ferromagnetic attraction. Actually, we have no idea. Paul believes they may use a gravity pulse, like they did for landing their mountain. But we don't have any way to test it. On the plus side, we don't believe these rods could grow very fast. So, they should have a limited number of shots. This may explain the method of attack they seem to favor. Based on our limited contact, they charge in firing spikes until they close and then leap at their enemy and start slashing with the sword-claw."

Marcus was a dim shadow in the low light, but his eyes were visible. Rather than blazing with anger, they appeared a bit distant. She wondered if he was remembering the battle against the demons in the forest. He passed the rod to the officer next to him and asked, "What's the best way to kill them?"

Sally locked eyes with him for a moment. Memories of the horrors they'd shared flashed into her mind, almost as if they were transmitting thoughts across the table. She nodded and he nodded back, acknowledging that he, too, had the battle on his mind. Both of them would be forever scarred by the experience. His question was of great importance though—to her and every soldier who might face a demon.

Von Jaeger glanced back and forth between them and smirked. Was it her the general hated? Or was it Marcus? *Or maybe both of us?* Regardless, something was going on here beyond the usual interactions with a mere bigot.

"Paul, please go back to the first slide," she said in English. When the image of the war demon reappeared, Sally continued in Portuguese. "First of all, you need bigger guns with more penetration. These things are very tough, especially if they are approaching head on. It is better to hit them from the sides, especially here." She pointed to the area between the middle set of legs and the front arms. "This area has thinner scales and a lot of blood flows through here. In fact, it has two hearts, one on each side of the spine. Hitting either one can give you a fairly quick kill. Also, the brain is just beyond that."

From the darkness, a voice asked, "Is it true you killed one of them?"

Sally nodded. "I was very lucky, but yes, I managed to kill one." She pointed back at the area just in front of the middle legs. "I hit it in one of its hearts as it turned on me. As I said, it was very lucky."

Marcus said, "There was no luck in you standing your ground and firing the shot."

Von Jaeger said, "That's enough. We've all heard about Miss Morgan's exploits. If a woman killed one, how hard can it be? Continue please."

This meeting felt like a personal assault. She noticed Marcus glaring at the general and hoped he wouldn't say something to get in trouble. Tension and silence oozed through the tent yet again. Just being around the general gave her a nasty, sticky feeling. *How did someone like this get put in charge of an army?*

"I said continue," repeated the general. "We do not have all day."

The rest of the meeting passed in a bit of haze for Sally. She gave the speech, but a part of her mind stewed in anger. For a few moments, talking became difficult as she fought back rage and, to some degree, tears. She would not let this asshole see her cry. *Damn him.* It wasn't like she was bragging about killing the thing. In fact, it was a memory she would gladly do without. But these men needed to know what they faced.

She hurried through the rest of the material, telling of the similarities between the war demon and the small scout demon creatures Marcus's men had also encountered. She said that without a specimen of the big harvesters, they could only guess about them. However, it would appear they were like living bulldozers. Reports varied, but they ranged in size from twenty to twenty-five feet tall. Their bodies were shaped like centaurs with four legs and an upper body with two arms. Supposedly they were powerful enough to tear trees out of the ground and capable of shooting white webbing from their mouths to snare pray. Reports from survivors said that the bulk of the destruction at Rio Estrada had been done by harvesters.

The general remained silent throughout. But his expression made her feel like a bug on a plate. As she finished, one of the officers near the head of the table asked, "What about less conventional means to kill them? Like chemical, biological, or nuclear weapons?"

Sally grimaced since she knew what that would do to the forest, if not the creatures. She prayed it would never come to that. But who knew?

"That is unknown at this time and impossible to determine. They do not breathe, and their scales are not particularly porous. This means the standard methods of getting chemical or biological agents into their bodies wouldn't be very effective. On top of that, their metabolism is very different from ours. So, we have no way of knowing what might work, even if we could get it inside them."

"And radiation?"

"Well, a nuclear weapon would be effective in terms of heat, energy and shock waves. Although most likely not to the same degree it would be on us. But as to how susceptible they are to radiation..." She shrugged. "There's no telling without studying a living specimen."

Another buzz of conversation circled around the table. Von Jaeger cut it off. "Gentlemen, there is little point in pursuing this topic. The use of such weapons would have to be approved at a much higher level than is sitting in this room. I cannot imagine turning loose nuclear fire in the middle of the Amazon, in the very heart of our country. This threat will need to be met by our brave men thrusting with courage into the heart of the menace."

That seemed an odd way to phrase fighting the creatures. Although, no odder than anything else about the man, she supposed. Sally waited for several long moments, but there were no more questions. With a relieved sigh, she sat down.

Von Jaeger stood and said in English, "Thank your team, Dr. Allen. This has been most informative. I look forward to…reading more on these creatures in the future."

In Portuguese he said, "We do not know what these creatures, these…aliens want." He said this last bit with a spiteful glance at Sally. "But we do know what they're doing. They've had a disastrous impact on our country. As you know, we're mobilizing our armed forces. But it is a long, slow trip up the Amazon. Nevertheless, the first two regiments are arriving now, with more to follow. In addition, ships conveying United States Marines will arrive in Manaus in the next few days. Our first task will be to secure the site of the lost village of Rio Estrada and the riverbank to the east and west of it.

"I'm confident we'll soon receive orders to put an end to this threat. I've conveyed to high command that we're ready and willing to attack these creatures. Then we'll drive them back to their mountains. I expect all of you to begin making plans to support such an assault. We'll discuss options in the morning."

He looked at Marcus with through squinted eyes and said in a gruff tone, "Antinasio, stay behind. We need to talk. Everyone else…Dismissed."

Marcus stood and came over to where Sally, Paul, and Dr. Allen were gathering their things. His mouth smiled, flashing bright white teeth. But the smile didn't reach his eyes, which looked a bit vacant and far away. A man with a lot on his mind. In a voice that sounded more than a little tense, he said, "Would you three be willing to wait around a bit? I'd like to thank you for your help with a nice lunch. My mess sergeant is very good; I believe you'd enjoy it. Also, I have a small matter I'd like to discuss with you."

Sally relayed this to her two companions. Dr. Allen wasn't enthused.

"Uh, well, I don't want to insult him. But the last hour of listening to people talk who I couldn't understand was enough for me. I would really prefer to go back to camp and get some work done."

"I'm in," said Paul. "I could use some decent food, and I can understand more than I can speak. By the way, was that general as big an asshole as I thought he was? My God, but…well, he just didn't seem happy with you at all."

"No, he wasn't happy," said Sally. "But I don't understand why he's so hostile." She shrugged. "Okay then, just two for lunch?"

Paul and Dr. Allen nodded in agreement, and she relayed this to Colonel Antinasio.

"I understand," he said. He nodded to Dr. Allen and shook his hand. "Julio is waiting outside. Tell him, and he will arrange an escort for the doctor and then take you to a canopy where we'll have lunch. If you'll excuse me, I believe the general and I have some unfinished business." His smile faded into a grim line, and he turned and sat back down at the table.

Sally noticed von Jaeger watching them, his expression neutral but his eyes shone with…well, she couldn't tell what. Certainly not with love and admiration. She returned his gaze with cool indifference. They seemed to have a growing mutual disrespect for one another.

"Come on," she said to the two men. "Let's get out of here."

The two men nodded and followed her outside to find Julio.

8 David Buries the Soldier

David paused when he reached the nexus of tunnels midway between the vat chamber and the cave where they set up camp. Nine passages met here, including the one behind him. Directly across the large, high ceiling chamber was the rough-hewn cave opening that led to their camp. The other passageways had well-formed arched ceilings and flat floors. But the one to the cave was more of a crack in the wall and seemed to have been created by nature.

At one time, in one of his mellower moods, Josh pointed out lines in the cave wall and said they indicated it'd been underwater at one time. Also, that the stalactites and stalagmites in the cave were created by dripping water over millions of years. The rest of the tunnels in the complex making up their prison had been carved out of the mountain.

David once more considered taking the body to camp but dismissed the idea. The passage to their cave twisted back and forth, and in a few places, large rocks made for a tight passage. Normally this wasn't a problem with the sledge. But the body weighed a lot more than the typical loads they used it for. Trying to get it over and around some of the rocky stretches along the way would be a different matter. The cave wouldn't be a great place for him anyway. It was pretty big, but even so, who'd want a corpse buried in the back room of their house.

This left seven other passageways to consider. Two of them had rubble visibly blocking them close to the entrance, so those were out. That left five, which all looked the same from here. Josh said each of them had been blocked off with piles of rubble. *But some must go further than others.*

David never had a desire to go down any of them. Hopefully one would have some place he could bury the soldier, or if not, at least get the body far enough away from their camp that the smell wouldn't reach them. With luck, he'd find enough dirt or loose stones to cover the soldier. In addition to stopping the smell, it seemed the proper thing to do.

But which way? The idea of dragging the body up and down the various passageways wasn't very appealing. It would probably be best to leave him here and go check them out beforehand. David heaved the sledge over to one side of the chamber and pulled off the makeshift harness. It had started out being easy to pull, but the load grew heavier the farther he walked. He stretched out his back for a moment and turned toward one of the tunnels.

Josh stood staring at him from the entrance to their cave. The big man's sudden appearance startled David and made his chest clutch. Josh always made him nervous. Finding himself unexpectedly on the receiving end of one of Josh's glares made him even more so. Josh had served in the Green Berets and CIA and was a very dangerous dude. A tiger in a world of dogs. In the small domain of the trapped survivors, he was a tiger in a cage of sheep.

At a guess, Josh was in his early forties. He had an odd build with legs too short and arms too long. David stood a little over six feet tall, and Josh didn't even come up to his chin. But what he lacked in height, he made up for with muscle. His arms were nearly as big around as David's legs, and his chest would make any powerlifter envious. Not that this bulk slowed him down or inhibited his fluid movements. He kept his reddish-brown hair cropped close, revealing a few knots on his large head. The same color hair, and almost as thick, covered his entire body. The first time he saw Josh was at a distance. David had been in shock at the time after being captured, and mistook the long armed, short legged man for an ape.

Whenever Josh looked at him, it gave David the sense of being a death row convict unworthy of clemency. A suspicious evaluation to determine if your ongoing existence was worthwhile. If you failed his judgment, Josh would eliminate the problem, permanently. David didn't know that Josh would kill him for being too big of a burden. But something told him that if the circumstances were right, he very well might. David knew that if anyone in the cave would fail to measure up to whatever standards Josh set, it would be he. Not a good feeling.

Josh's intense gaze left David and swept over the sledge. He walked over to it with his typical fluid grace and looked down. He gestured to the material rolled up on top of the body that had been wrapped around the soldier. "Brazilian issue camouflage. Probably a one-man tropical tent." Josh looked at David. "Soldier?"

David nodded.

Josh knelt down and examined the dead monkey and various items David had taken from the body. "This is a good find," he said. "So, what're you doing? Planning on burying him?"

David nodded again. "I was hoping to find a place in one of the tunnels where... you know? The smell won't be so bad."

Josh peered up at David with dark brown eyes that sat narrow and deep under a heavy brow. He rumbled, "It would've been easier just to toss him back into the pit."

David squirmed a little under the concentrated scrutiny, but he didn't look away. "Yeah, but...it didn't seem right. I...I'm not feeding them damn things if I can help it. I for sure ain't feeding them a person."

Did Josh's eyebrows twitch up a fraction of an inch? That was odd. After staring at David for a few seconds, the older man stood and gave a thoughtful nod. "Right enough," he said. "Come on. I know a place."

He reached for the harness, but David pulled away and put it back on. "I can do it. I...well, I pulled him up and brought him this far. It just seems like it should be my job to see it through."

Josh's eyebrows definitely rose at that. He looked thoughtful for a moment, his expression much less threatening. Then his usual scowl returned, and he pointed to the opening to the right of their cave. "That one would be best," he said. He stood, turned and walked to the tunnel.

With a grunt, David got the sledge moving. Once in motion, it wasn't so bad, although pulling it put a constant strain on his calves and the back of his thighs. In a few minutes, the strain began to wear on him. The tunnel had a slight downward slope, but not enough to help much. The runners grated and scraped behind him. David clenched his teeth and trudged along behind Josh, concentrating on putting one foot after the other.

The tunnel looked much like the one leading to the vat room. It had the same flat floor and arching ceiling studded with rods and pipes. About a third of the rods blazed with the ever present electric-blue light. After walking for a while, one notable difference between the tunnels became apparent. This one was much longer. And as they descended, it made a gradual turn to the left.

After they traveled a hundred yards or so, he started breathing heavily. After another hundred, he started panting. Sweat ran down his face in small rivulets. *How long is this damn tunnel anyway?* He began to regret not letting Josh pull the sled.

His labored gasps must have caught Josh's attention, because he turned and frowned back at him. "You need help?" he asked.

Despite his regret about not letting Josh help, he shook his head. Even with the growing weariness in his legs, pulling the soldier out of the pit made him David's responsibility. "No, I can make it. How much farther?"

"Not far," Josh said and resumed walking down the tunnel.

After what seemed much further than 'not far' to David, the left curving passageway changed direction into a tight right-hand turn. From there, he could see that it opened onto a large dimly lit space. A very big space, in fact.

The far side of the chamber's ceiling had collapsed. A pile of rubble sloped down at a steep angle from high above. Boulders and small rocks littered the floor with mounds of dirt and bent twisted rods scattered in between. The cave-in must have destroyed many of the glow rods as darkness hid behind every outcrop and boulder. Shadows lined the far walls.

This must be the place. Relief filled him. Dragging the loaded sledge for several hundred yards had been a lot tougher than he expected. The experience gave him a great appreciation for the inventor of the wheel. With a sigh, he took off the harness and let it drop to the floor.

At one time, the ceiling must have been a high dome, very much like…No, exactly like the vat chamber. Now that he had a few moments to take it in, he realized the room had once housed another blender. *How many did the gatherers have making their disgusting soup? Thank God, this one lay in ruin.* The blending pit in the center was almost completely clogged with rocks, dirt, and broken lengths of pipe.

Josh's voice echoed with an eerie tone in the large silent chamber. "Over there," he said, pointing at a pile of rubble to the left of the entry tunnel. Near the bottom of the debris pile, pipes and boulders had interlocked, making an overhang with a small shallow cave underneath. Smaller boulders, rocks, and dirt sat in loose clumps above it. "We can push that loose stuff down to bury him."

He walked over and grasped the soldier's shoulders. This time David didn't refuse the help and picked up his legs. They carried the web shrouded form over to the space and laid it down. The little cave was about three feet wide and ten feet long. It would be a perfect resting place.

Josh loosened the webbing around the man's chest and head and fumbled inside. He pulled out a chain with a dog tag on it. It made David feel stupid and a little sheepish. He knew soldiers wore them, but it didn't occur to him to look.

"One tag's missing, so he's been registered as dead in their books. *Corporal Jef Barros*, *Corpo de Fuzileiros Navais, Médico*. He was a medic for a Brazilian marine unit. I don't suppose you found a medical bag in his things?"

"I don't think so."

"Pity." Josh rolled the body over so that it nestled in the back of the outcrop. Then he stood up and stepped back. Still looking at the body with a solemn expression, he said, "You got any words?"

The question confused David for a moment. "Words?" Then he realized what Josh meant and nodded.

After a few seconds of thought, he said, "I'm sorry you died. Since you're a soldier, I hope you killed some of them. Whatever they are and wherever they're from, they've invaded this land with ill intent. I pray you made yourself an honor guard with their dead. Also, thank you for what you brought to us. I hate that your death was the price, but we promise to make great use of your things. We need everything we can get to stay alive. God bless you. Amen."

"Amen," Josh said with a slight nod. The big man turned to David with yet another odd expression on his face. The usual glower was gone. His eyes looked like someone just presented with an unexpected puzzle. After a moment, he turned to the wall of rubble and walked over to the undercut. He spent a few moments examining the boulders and rocks above it.

After gently poking a few places, he shook one of the medium sized boulders. Then he gave a slight nod and said, "Get back a little. Some of these rocks might roll a little."

David pulled the sledge away from the sloping wall of debris. As he did so, Josh pried several rocks free and dropped them in front of the makeshift tomb. Other rocks started to shift and with a rumble began to slide down. Josh leaped back out of the way. With a loud hiss of moving dirt and thumping impacts of stone, the mass picked up speed. Dust filled the air, and both men coughed and choked while scrambling further back from the small avalanche.

The dust cloud cleared enough to see that the Brazilian soldier had been well and truly buried. The rock and dirt rubble now extended a good ten feet farther into the chamber than before. The sight made David smile. It felt good to deny the gatherers the body. By doing so, he'd won a victory. A small one but still a victory.

The smile faded a few seconds later as an antennae laden head with malevolent eyes and a dark hole for a mouth appeared out of the swirling dust. The head was bigger than a basketball and looked small compared to the body supporting it twenty feet in the air.

"A gatherer!" he yelled, backing away with his heart pounding in his chest.

Josh spun, grunted, and drew his pistol. The two retreated until they stood just inside the tunnel leading back to the nexus. The dust continued to clear. Soon they could see that the body below the head and shoulders was buried in rubble.

"It ain't moving," Josh said, taking a few steps forward. "I think it's dead." He returned the big handgun to his holster.

The fear clutching David's chest eased, and he took a step forward to stand beside Josh. The dust cleared, leaving tendrils of gray drifting across the chamber. Dirt and debris covered most of the gatherer. It must be dead. The head, left shoulder, arm, and part of its broad chest protruded above the mound. The scales and what flesh could be seen had a withered, dried out appearance. It gave the impression of having been there for a very long time.

Josh walked to the creature, and after a moment's hesitation, David followed. Dead though it may be, it still looked dangerous…and evil. Why it looked evil was hard to say. Most likely because he'd seen these things destroy an entire village and kill a lot of people, including a friend. Or maybe it was the huge eyes with their downward sloping scaled brow. Regardless, the term evil seemed to fit pretty damn well.

"Well, now we know they can die," Josh said. He placed one booted foot on the pile of rubble and stepped up with care. The shale-like dirt shifted a bit under his weight but held. Thus encouraged, he eased up the pile toward the gatherer. "Guess they ain't supernatural demons, anyway."

"I thought you already said they weren't demons," David said.

Josh stopped climbing and glanced down. "No, I said not to call them that. I didn't want to make 'em seem special." He looked back, his expression for once not threatening, almost sheepish. "It's just better to know for sure. That they can die, I mean. You know?" He resumed climbing, slipping several times, but soon reached the gatherer's head.

Once face to face with the creature, he pulled out his big survival knife and poked at it. "Man, this thing is pretty tough. I'm going to stay here for a bit, see if I can learn anything." He turned back to David and gestured to the dead man's equipment. "Why don't you take that stuff on up to the others and go through it? Should make 'em happy."

David nodded and loaded the sledge back up. Now that it was nearly empty, it would be easier to pull. But he dreaded the uphill trip to their cave with his already tired legs. After slinging the harness over his shoulder, he began trudging up the tunnel. The sledge followed with the usual grating sound of wooden runners.

"Hey! Morgan," Josh yelled from the wall.

David looked up and found the older man staring down at him with a thoughtful expression.

"You done good today," he said and then turned and resumed poking at the gatherer.

David's feet did a little stutter step from surprise. *Did Josh actually say something nice?* Could he've imagined it? But no, Josh said it for sure. David's heart felt suddenly light. A complete one hundred and eighty degrees from when the shadowy gatherer form emerged from the dust until now. With a broad smile on his face, he turned and headed up the tunnel. The sledge didn't seem heavy at all.

9 Colonel Antinasio and General Jaeger

After the tent emptied, von Jaeger said, "So, Antinasio. That's your expert? I'm not impressed. You're not to invite her to give any more presentations."

"General Fernando put me in charge of setting up a research facility and dealing with the Americans. Miss Morgan is by far the most qualified scientist available."

Von Jaeger sneered. "Ah, yes. Fernando, your mentor. He's just a stupid old man. Why the Joint Chiefs put him in charge of research is beyond me. It's an affront to my authority as theater commander."

Anger already burned inside Marcus from the general's treatment of Sally. The high command was a political mess, mostly caused by the stupid games being played by von Jaeger and others of his ilk. This last comment about a man Marcus knew to be one of the best leaders in Brazil was too much. His chest burned as the heat from mounting anger flared to an unprecedented height.

"I imagine the Joint Chiefs wanted at least one competent leader involved in this," Marcus said in a cold voice. *Damn. That wasn't the right thing to say.* He had to get his emotions under better control. Bracing himself, he waited for von Jaeger's explosion.

Rather than an explosion, the other man's response came more as a slow burn. "That old man will not be around to protect you forever…colonel." Von Jaeger made the last word sound like an insult. Marcus was the youngest person in a decade to hold the rank. Von Jaeger had fought vehemently against the promotion.

"Regardless of who's in charge of research, I'm in charge of this operation," said von Jaeger. "That woman…that, girl is not welcome at any more staff meetings. If you cannot find someone else, you will meet with the North Americans yourself and convey the information. Better yet, just provide a written report. I only allow you to attend staff functions because the President of the Senate asked me to. But I'm under no obligation, and you're no longer welcome."

Jaeger stood and began pacing on the opposite side of the table. "It still shocks me that the President agreed to let the North Americans take the lead in this. Yes, we no doubt need the United States. They have capabilities we don't for dealing with this crisis. But it's inexcusable to give up potential world-altering technology so easily."

Marcus said, "Well, with the destruction of the University of Manaus, there was little choi—"

"No! That is no excuse." Von Jaeger leaned on the table. "It's a bribe to get them to help, nothing more! It is the essence of weakness. This is what comes of having a woman president. You'd think people would have learned after the disaster of the last one."

Marcus held his tongue. He'd been a junior officer when Brazil's first lady president, Dilma Rousseff, was impeached. The military had always been very political, but it'd grown worse every year since then.

Two powerful factions in the government worked against each other as much as with. A never-ending story worldwide when it came to politics. But things always seemed more volatile in Brazil. General Fernando led the supporters of the current president, Emmanuelle Coriz. It's a bad sign for your country when individual military officers' loyalties start to be tabulated. But this faction included the Navy high command and many of the army's leading generals.

The opposition's leader was Geraldo Viegas Ancaar, President of the Senate and an outspoken critic of everything the current president did. Political maneuvering kept him in power with deft applications of money and influence. He was von Jaeger's patron, but the two made a clumsy pair for leaders of such a powerful political organization. In Marcus's opinion, both were far more ambitious than smart. It seemed very likely the two were puppets for other, more intelligent leaders in the shadows.

"Will that be all, general?" said Marcus in a tired voice.

"No, that's not all." Von Jaeger pushed off the table and began pacing again. "The defeat you and your men suffered was humiliating enough. But your reports about the battle have made a hero of this girl, and that is even worse. I don't like it one bit." He stopped pacing and turned to glare at Marcus. "An American girl rescues a Brazilian marine? My lord, your report almost makes it sound as if she saved you all. Unlike you, I have no joy in the humiliation of my county."

"I only reported the facts."

"Well, I want you to un-report them." The general changed his tone, sounding suddenly friendly. "Come on, colonel, you must realize how this makes our country...our armed forces look. Things are getting crazy in Brasilia… around the whole country, for that matter. And with people trying to come to terms with… Well, whatever all this is," he said with a wave in the direction of the mountain. "We need to boost their confidence in our men and our leaders."

The man's sudden ingratiating tone went beyond insulting. Marcus would have to be a bigger fool than the general to be taken in by it. With a shake of his head, he said, "I'm afraid I cannot do that, general. I believe in telling the truth and letting people make of it what they will."

Von Jaeger slammed his fist on the table and yelled, "Get out! Leave! I'm done with you."

The timing of the alien crisis couldn't have been worse. The divisions in the government might make it impossible to take effective actions. The stupidity of the situation made Marcus's chest and stomach burn.

Marcus stood up slowly while staring at the general with a calm expression. Refusing to hurry, he fixed his gaze on the general's eyes and took his garrison cap from his belt. The general's face grew redder as Marcus moved with unhurried, deliberate motions. Keeping the precise, easy-going pace, he put on his cap, set it in place, and performed a crisp salute. He dropped it without waiting for the general to respond. Then he pivoted on his heel and strode from the tent.

10 Sally Agrees to Help PBG-31

Julio led Sally and Paul to an awning that looked like a camouflaged version of a standard camping enclosure. It had mosquito netting for walls with two fans inside creating a nice, inoffensive breeze. The shaded space felt pleasantly cool after the stuffy confines of von Jaeger's tent. The company improved considerably as well. It was wonderful to see Julio. The small private seemed to have come out of the jungle in much better shape than Sally, both physically and mentally. It was refreshing to be around his constant enthusiasm. Sally wished she could be so lighthearted again.

On the downside, the three-way conversation flowed with all the awkwardness Dr. Allen predicted. She had to frequently stop to translate for Paul. He didn't understand enough Portuguese to follow along very well, and she had to fill in a lot of holes. Julio told them that his family in Manaus were doing well, but the city itself was still in shambles. Also, there were a lot of rumors about the Navy crews that made him very angry. But before they could go into details, Marcus entered the enclosure.

"Greetings," said Marcus. "Sorry to keep you waiting. Julio, would you please tell Sergeant Lupe that we're ready for lunch."

"Yes, sir," Julio replied and hustled out of the canopy.

Julio's zealousness continued to be a cool balm for Sally. She smiled a full, genuine smile, a rare thing for her since the helicopter crash. "Does he run everywhere?"

Marcus managed a small chuckle. "Pretty much. I hope he can keep up that attitude; it's a real boost for the men." In a softer tone, he said, "I fear we may need it in the days ahead."

Marcus waved for them to sit down. The table was set with a white linen table cloth and four place settings of nice, if not fancy, tableware. An ice bucket with two bottles of wine sat in the middle.

"*Isso...umm, é muito... legal?*" Paul said in a clumsy attempt to compliment how nice the table looked. His mouth looked almost comical as he struggled with the strange words.

Marcus said in English, "Thank you very much."

Sally looked at him in surprise. "I didn't think you spoke any English?"

Marcus grinned and shook his head. In Portuguese, he said, "No, just 'thank you very much' and 'no, I don't speak English.' Not to be cruel, but it sounds as if Mr. Sanders has similar limitations with Portuguese."

Sally smiled and nodded. "Pretty much. Although he can understand a bit more if we speak slowly in formal Portuguese."

"Well, 'a fair amount' may be optimistic," said Paul in English. "But you guys go ahead; I'll listen and see if I can improve. Don't bother stopping every two minutes for me. You can fill me in later."

"So, what's this about needing Julio's good attitude in the days ahead?" said Sally.

"Well, it's something that's not widely known. Although it's not technically a secret. But as you're now contractors to the Naval de Brasilia, I suppose you can be told. You must hold it in confidence until official channels decide to communicate it, however. There are concerns in government about starting a panic."

Sally relayed this to Paul, who nodded in agreement.

Marcus poured some wine and cleared his throat. "Over the last month, Patrol Boat Group 31 has been working with special forces to gather information on the creatures and their mountain. How many of them there might be, how much jungle they've cleared, etc. It hasn't gone well. So far, of ten separate attempts, only four have returned. Over seventy men are missing, and many of the ones who managed to come back were wounded."

Sally clenched her wine glass so hard, she was lucky it didn't break. "War demons," she said in a low voice. It was not a question.

Marcus nodded. "Indeed. They are the main threat. But there are also the scout creatures. One patrol was inundated when several hundred fell on them from the trees. There were eleven men and only one escaped."

"*Morte por mil cortes*," muttered Paul in a near flawless accent.

Marcus looked at him in surprise. Paul shrugged and said in English, "Death by a thousand cuts. I downloaded a story about feudal Portugal to help me learn accents. It was gruesome, but not as bad as this. Ten men out of eleven killed by creatures no bigger than this plate? I understood that well enough. I almost wish I hadn't."

Sally translated the last for Marcus, who looked grim. "It's an apt description." They sipped at the wine while contemplating being cut to pieces by hundreds of small, sharp claws.

After a few moments, Marcus cleared his throat again. "From the patrols that did return, we've learned a few things. First, we've identified two more groups of harvesters ripping up the jungle. They work like ants with lines going back and forth between the mountain and forest. Each group is estimated to be between fifteen and twenty thousand harvesters."

Sally gave a low whistle and took time to relay this to Paul. He grunted in surprise.

"Also, there are some reports of another type of creature. It is even bigger and seems to perform as a transport like a truck. It has six legs and is supposedly twenty to twenty-five meters long, though the men who saw it did so at a distance. They weren't positive of its exact size."

Sally liked the metric system for research, but had a hard time visualizing in it. She did a quick calculation and came up with seventy to eighty feet. *Bigger than a whale, or a brontosaurus for that matter. Damn.*

Marcus looked past them and said, "Ah, I believe lunch is coming."

Sally turned and spotted Julio and a tall skinny soldier carrying some kind of small table. On it were several covered serving pans. The other man's insignia indicated he was a sergeant. Marcus stood and held open the mosquito netting for them. A wonderful odor followed the table into the canopy, even with the fans blowing.

"Miss Morgan, Mr. Sanders, I would like you to meet Mess Sergeant Philip Lupe. He's in charge of our company kitchen and is a fantastic cook."

If not for Marcus's introduction, Sally would never have believed the sergeant was a cook, much less a good one. *Aren't they supposed to be on the heavy side?* This man looked like an escapee from a concentration camp.

"You do me honor, sir," said Sergeant Lupe. "Please be seated. The food is best when it' s warm." Julio hesitated and Lupe said, "You too, Julio. The colonel told me you were eating also."

Julio looked unsure, almost embarrassed.

"Sit," said Marcus. "We discussed this earlier. Philip can serve us."

"Uh, yes sir." Julio's face turned red, but he looked pleased. Sally knew the young marine worshipped Marcus. He sat down while maintaining a stiff, upright manner. Then he took the napkin from the table and placed it in his lap with almost comical formality.

Sally's heart grew a bit warmer. Julio's focus on being proper reminded her of a puppy trying to please its family. It was sweet, but she also felt a bit sorry for him. It was tough having lunch with your hero.

There was another reason for the warmth. Julio's obvious admiration for the colonel reminded her how much she admired him too. It felt good to have lunch with Marcus, which surprised her. There was something about him. Something that made her feel…well, if not safe, maybe safer. It was strange. She considered herself a fiercely independent woman. But he'd earned her respect during their time in the forest. Here was someone you could count on, even lean on in tough times. With almost everyone wounded and bleeding, including himself, he'd found ways to lift their spirits. There was no doubt in her mind that he was a leader of rare and special ability.

And yet, the unwelcome memories of the forest kept the warmth in check to some degree. Facing the war demon had been the most terrifying thing she'd ever done or could ever imagine doing. Dark thoughts started to invade her mind. *No, I will not think of that. Lunch, think of lunch, of food, of anything, just not…that.*

A touch on her arm startled her but helped break the spell. "Are you okay?" asked Paul, the concern in his hazel-green eyes obvious, even though the hideous black glasses. "You went pale all of a sudden."

"Uh, yes. Yes, I'm fine. I just…" With a shake of her head, she managed to banish the dark thoughts back to a protected corner in her soul. How much longer could she keep things bottled up? *As long as I can*, she answered herself. *As long as I need to.*

She gave Paul a reassuring smile. "My, doesn't this look wonderful?" she said, nodding to the food.

"Uh, yeah. It does," he said, his eyes lingering on hers, the concern still there. Turning to Sergeant Lupe, he said, "Um, *Os fedores de alimentos… delicioso*."

Sergeant Lupe's thin dark face looked shocked. Sally, Marcus, and Julio burst into laughter. Paul looked chagrined. "What did I say?"

"You said, 'The food stinks deliciously,'" Sally said when she could catch her breath. The darkness around her heart lifted, at least for now. Laughter, as always, proved to be an effective medicine.

"Oh, sorry," said Paul with a crooked smile. "I guess I should keep my mouth shut."

"Please don't," said Sally, still chuckling and wiping moisture from her eyes. "That was actually wonderful."

Paul nodded and smiled at her. Was there a pleased expression there as well? Had he done that on purpose? Maybe. Paul could be very perceptive at times.

Lupe smiled once he realized his cooking hadn't been insulted. He began dishing out food from the covered pans. He put a plate in front of Sally that any Brazilian steakhouse would be proud to serve. There were two kinds of smoked beefsteak and some braised lamb. On the side, a medley of fresh vegetables and a serving of fried breadfruit. The sergeant uncorked some red wine and offered it to each of them in the manner of an expert sommelier. He even let Sally taste and approve it before pouring. When he offered some to Julio, the young man just shook his head and took a sip of water. Lupe corked the wine and stood back, waiting for them to taste the food.

"Wow," said Paul. "This is awesome."

Sally said, "Sergeant Lupe, you have a true gift. Thank you very much."

The sergeant beamed with pride. "Thank you, Miss Morgan. It's an honor to be able to cook for you." To Marcus he said, "If you will excuse me, sir?" Marcus nodded and the sergeant turned, pushed aside the netting, and walked out of the canopy.

"Well, I certainly wasn't expecting this," said Sally. "Is this a perk for being on the general's staff?"

Sally must have said the wrong thing. The corners of Marcus's mouth pursed into a deep frown. He gave an emphatic shake of his head and said, "I'm not on the general's staff." He smiled, but it looked forced. "And this isn't usual fare for any of us, I assure you. When I told Philip that I wanted to invite you for lunch, he was very enthusiastic. It's you. Your bravery and strength captured the hearts of my men."

Sally blushed. It amazed her how the Brazilian soldiers kept putting her on a pedestal. She said, "I'm the one with the captured heart. After all, you and your men rescued me from the jungle."

His smile broadened. "It's every soldier's aspiration to rescue a beautiful maiden from danger."

Sally thought the flush on her face must be bright red by now. But although Marcus's comment embarrassed her, she was also flattered. Some of the warmth painting her cheeks came from another small ember glowing to life in her.

Today had been a good day. Not only had she smiled some real smiles, she'd actually laughed a few times. The anger toward General von Jaeger may have even been good too, in retrospect. It was downright healthy compared to most of her feelings of late. This new spark was quite different from those other emotions though. Being called a beautiful maiden was corny and a bit silly, of course. But still, it made her feel… well, feminine. It felt surprisingly good.

"What's up?" said Paul with a smile. "You look happy. And a bit smug."

"Oh, uh, he just said it was his honor to rescue me from the helicopter."

Paul gave a wry look. "You promised to tell me about that, you know."

"Yes, I know. But not now, okay?"

"Of course," said Paul. "But later."

She nodded, though her eyes narrowed with a look of warning.

Marcus said, "How is your injury, by the way?"

She touched her side gingerly where she cracked some ribs during the helicopter crash. "A little stiff at times, but much better. How's your chest?"

"Only a scratch," he said, dismissing the bone deep slash he'd gotten from a war demon. "I hardly notice it."

Julio stopped eating, and his usually jovial face looked grim. This discussion no doubt kicked up a few bad memories for him as well. He'd lost several good friends that day.

To change the subject, but also because she wanted to know, she said, "Don't answer if this question seems improper. But is General von Jaeger hard to deal with?"

Marcus snorted and then gave a soft chuckle. "Well, as a matter of fact, yes. But as you mentioned, it would be improper of me to speak of it. Though I do need to tell you that future briefings will take place at your compound."

Anger brought fire to her chest. The man was truly a weasel. "Wow. It's because I'm a woman, isn't it? That's disgusting."

"Regretfully, I think that's part of his issue with you, but maybe not for the reasons you believe. Or not completely." He shrugged and said, "I think he has something against the United States as well. His political faction is constantly saying your country looks down on Brazil. Especially our military. For him, having an American seen as a hero for Brazilian soldiers is humiliating. Doubly so with the hero being a woman."

"Hey. Did he just call you...*herói*? A hero?" Paul's eyes mirrored his confusion, though they were also tinged with admiration.

Her expression must have been fiercer than she intended because Paul's eyebrows shot up and he flinched back. "Uh, yeah, later," he stammered in a low voice.

Sally gave a half smile and a slight shake of her head. Then to Marcus she said, "If what I did was heroic, it was no more so than what dozens of the others did that day."

Marcus nodded. "True. And I have written commendations for every one of them. They are seen as champions of the people. Most are working to help calm the people and get things back to normal." He said in a lower voice, "Those not still in the hospital."

Sally sighed. "To many of those, I'm sure. The only reason I'd want to go Manaus right now would be to visit them. But it's good to hear you recommended them all for commendations, that seems appropriate. Umm, you mentioned that things are bad?"

Marcus gave a small snort; it was unusual for him to show negative thoughts. "Here or in Manaus? The city is like a war zone. Which I guess it is, in fact. Thirty-two commercial jetliners and fourteen smaller aircraft crashed into the city in less than eight hours. The latest death toll estimate is over forty thousand. Even after six weeks, much of the city is still without power or clean water."

"Julio mentioned some of that. Do you have family there?" Sally asked in a soft voice that caused Paul to look confused again. It had to be frustrating to only understand every few words.

"Yes," said Marcus. "My parents and three of my brothers. They live just outside of town and were spared any harm, thank God."

"You mentioned things being bad here?" Sally said.

"Well, not bad yet, but soon possibly. As with the patrols, this is not ready to be communicated. This goes for you as well, private."

Julio nodded, as did Sally, who relayed it to Paul.

Paul said, "Well, that's no problem. I can't understand enough to keep up with what you're talking about anyway. But I'll promise for later." He met her eyes. "For when you tell me what the hell this is all about."

"Fair enough." Turning to Marcus, she said, "We'll keep it confidential until we hear something official."

"Okay, I'll accept that. As I mentioned, we've lost a lot of men, very good men, and we've learned little. However, reports from some locals indicate that a new column has started on the far side of the mountain. Maybe two of them." Worry showed in his deep brown eyes.

A knot formed in Sally's gut. "So, they're expanding? And it sounds pretty darn fast, at that."

"It seems so, though we don't know anything for certain. I told you of the patrols. But aircraft tried to scout the creatures as well. There've been many attempts. More than five hundred people have died trying. But none got closer than two hundred miles from the mountains. Over four hundred attempts were made by Brazil, the United States, Mexico, and Japan. Fighters, bombers, and drones…even a few missiles. In ones and twos and in waves. It didn't matter. Many were built for stealth, but that didn't help either. All were shot down far from the mountains."

Sally relayed this to Paul, who gave a low whistle.

Paul said, "I've heard the aliens have four platforms, big ass rocks actually, orbiting Earth. They're situated so that at least one is above the horizon in sight of their mountain at all times. Most of the planes and attempts to launch new satellites were shot down with high power lasers from these. Ask him if he's heard anything about that."

Sally asked Marcus, who nodded.

He said, "Yes, it's generally believed most of the aircraft have been hit with lasers a lot more powerful than any developed to date. But they also have some kind of hypervelocity weapon launched from the mountains. These capabilities make me fear General von Jaeger is badly underestimating them."

Sally knew there'd also been attempts to contact the creatures. But no responses ever came back. Yet another failed effort to understand the aliens and their ultimate objectives.

The harvesters landed their granite mountains in the middle of the Amazon and began shooting down every plane for hundreds of miles around. Soon after, they began harvesting the forest. Now they seemed to be ignoring the outside world completely. How much of the

Amazon would they take? Would they stop and leave at some point? Or keep growing and growing until they encompassed the world?

It was quite obvious how dependent the world's militaries were on aircraft these days. Besides the mysterious weapons of the harvesters, without air transportation it was very difficult to get men and equipment into the area to oppose them. And what if the military did manage to mount a defense of the forest? Would the aliens just move their mountain? Could they? If so, there were a lot of remote and inaccessible locations around the world. Several still in the Amazon Basin region.

"Well," said Marcus, breaking into Sally's thoughts about how scary the world was becoming. "Do you remember when the officer implied the creatures are actual demons from Hell during our meeting?"

"Yes. The general didn't like that much."

Marcus nodded and continued. "He's not the only person to harbor such fears, not by a long shot. I'm concerned a lot of my men are scared the creatures are from Hell as well."

"That's easy to understand," said Sally. "Some of the scientists back at camp mentioned such fear as well. If people dedicated to science are having doubts, it isn't a surprise other folks will."

Marcus's dark brown eyes seemed to focus on something far away. "To be honest, I wonder myself at times. I'm a bit of a fallen Catholic and not very devout, but…but I find myself praying more of late. Your report today was a great help. It's good to hear they're more like robots than…well, creatures from Hell."

"Because we understand how they are put together and that they come from space? That doesn't mean they're not demons," Sally said in a soft voice. "I struggle with some of this myself. I believe in a loving God, albeit one that operates far beyond our level of understanding. Dark times tend to breed dark thoughts. But it's hard to reconcile a loving God with what's happening here."

Marcus gave a mirthless chuckle. "Mankind has struggled with such thoughts throughout history. Some say we're being tested."

Julio looked thoughtful. Paul was looking back and forth between them with annoyance. He could understand enough to know they were discussing God, Hell, and demons. But not enough to understand the direction of the conversation. She knew how he felt about it, though. There had been a lot of similar discussions back at camp. He'd always expressed frustration with those who argued the creatures might be supernatural. No doubt his list of questions for her were growing fast.

Sally said, "But in the end, what does it matter? The creatures are here. The forest and most likely the entire planet are in grave danger. We must stop them. It doesn't matter their origin or possible theological motivations."

"Yes, of course," said Marcus. "I feel the same way. In fact, that is the main reason I asked you to lunch today. Or at least part of the reason."

Sally forced a wry smile. "I suspected such a wonderful meal had to come with a price."

"I've always thought that before asking a favor, it's best to have some good food," Marcus said with a grin. "At the very least, it doesn't hurt. As for my favor, I'd like you to make presentations to my troops about the harvesters."

Sally blinked in surprise. "Why me? I don't know much beyond what I covered today. I'm sure some of your people could do it."

Marcus's expression grew serious. "Despite General von Jaeger's bluster, the men are scared. And who can blame them? The general is a politician and a bit of a romantic. His idea of war involves soldiers made of steel marching off to battle and glory." He looked in the direction of the command tent and gave a shake of his head. "I'm confident he's never done it himself though."

Marcus pushed his plate out of the way and leaned forward, placing his elbows on the white tablecloth. "I'm proud of my crews and my marines. They're good and brave men and women. But we've never faced anything remotely like this. It's difficult enough to go into combat with an enemy you understand. But if you think you're fighting creatures from Hell…?" He shook his head. "I'm not confident they'll fight if it comes to that. And I fear we may need to fight in the near future," he finished softly.

Pushing back from the table, Marcus stood and began pacing, his eyebrows knitted tight together and his mouth a tight line. "In war, it's vital to have faith in the person next to you—that they'll stay by you, watch your back, and do their part. This belief is more important than any weapon or tactic. Right now, I fear such belief is weak. If one person breaks and runs, then panic might ensue. This could cause the entire unit to fall apart. If that happens, many would die for no purpose. Panic and fear have lost more battles, and lives, than any other factor in war.

"As for why I'd like you to give the presentation?" His face relaxed as he sat back down and poured more wine. "You've got three qualities that would be quite valuable."

Sally picked up her glass and met his eyes. "I'll bet two of them are that I'm a woman, and I killed one of the demons."

Marcus raised his glass to her. "Yes, those are two. However, they are not the most important reason. The most important thing is the respect you've earned from my people. You held your ground, you fought, and you won. After the battle, you faced the hardships of our march out of the forest as well as any. That is an example my men need, regardless of your gender. I want you to cover the material you shared today and tell about your actions during the battle. I want you to ease their hearts about fighting demons."

She considered ways to say no, but for some reason couldn't find one. At least none that weren't pretty lame. In desperation, she said, "You don't need a helpless woman telling these macho men how to slay a demon."

He looked at her intently. "No one in my command would consider you helpless for a moment. Every one of them knows how brave you are. And I'm not above using your gender to shame the…how did you put it, 'macho men,' into bravery. I'll use whatever it takes to shore up their resolve to fight."

The passion in his voice surprised her. She hadn't talked about any of this since they escaped the forest. Most of her thoughts revolved around David or about the work studying the demons. When she did think about it, mostly she remembered her own terror. Never anything heroic. But the way he said it…Something in his voice made her feel proud.

"What about General von Jaeger?" she asked. "I don't think he'd have much respect for what I have to say."

Marcus gave a small snort and then shrugged. "Well, that's his loss. You may not have noticed the difference in our uniforms, but he's an army general, and I'm a marine. I'm not in his direct chain of command. He's the area commander right enough. However, I decide how to motivate my crews and marines. Besides, I've had more than a few army officers ask about you. They may sneak a few men in to listen also."

Sally didn't want to do it. No way, no how. And yet…did she really have a choice? If it would help Marcus and the men who rescued her, how could she say no? Besides, it might aid her in letting go of her own grief and guilt. Something that might help occurred to her.

"What about Julio? He was there too and did everything I did. I'd prefer not to do this alone."

Julio was smiling at her and nodding with enthusiasm.

A suspicious feeling came over her. *Uh oh, I believe I've been set up.*

"Certainly. That is an excellent idea," Marcus said with a sly smile. "Actually, he's already volunteered. I asked him not to discuss it with you until I had a chance to ask you."

Despite her discomfort, Sally managed a dry chuckle. "Oh, so that's how it is. Okay, I'm in. I'll give it a try if you think it'll help."

Marcus's incredible white teeth flashed. "Excellent. We'll try not to let it be too onerous. You should be able to address my men in two small groups."

They spent a few minutes discussing details about when and where to hold the sessions. It would take Sally a few days to gather her thoughts and materials, not to mention her courage. They decided she and Julio would meet in two days to practice, then do the first presentation early the next week in the base's mess tent.

After the details were set, Marcus said, "Sorry to have to cut this short. But I have a meeting scheduled with my officers. Feel free to finish the wine. Julio will escort you to the gate." He stood and the others followed suit. Reaching across the table, he took Sally's hand and said, "Thank you very much for agreeing to talk to my men. I truly believe it'll help them prepare for what's coming."

"I owe you and your men a great deal," said Sally. "It's the least I can do."

Marcus squeezed her hand. It felt warm and tough. Not calloused, but not too soft either. A very nice hand, thought Sally as warmth radiated up her arm. The feeling surprised her. Their eyes locked, and he held her hand for a second longer, then gave it another squeeze and let go. He shook Paul's hand and then clasped Julio's shoulder. "Take good care of her, Private."

Julio stood up straight with his chest out, smiled, and said, "Yes, sir. I will, sir."

Then the tall, slender Brazilian strode out of the tent. Sally glanced at her hand. What had that been about? She'd been very impressed with Marcus in the jungle and really admired him, but this was…different. She shook her head with a frown and looked up to find Paul looking at her with a peculiar expression on his face. His eyes always appeared a bit too big when viewed through his thick glasses; now they seemed intense. Something strange just happened, maybe was still happening, based on Paul's odd look. Crap, she didn't have the emotional bandwidth to worry about it right now. Her head and heart were messed up enough already.

"Um, okay then," she said in English. "I believe I've had enough wine. Are you okay with heading back?"

Paul shook his head as if breaking out of a trance. "Uh…Yeah, sure."

Julio took the cue and smiled with a quick nod. He went to the netting and held it open, then began talking very fast. "Thank goodness you're going to do the presentation. The colonel said he wanted me to do it. But I said, 'Miss Sally would be even better than me.' Then he said, 'Well, I thought of that, but she's really busy.' So, I said, 'Miss Sally would do it if you asked her.' And sure enough, you said yes. This is exciting. I've never spoken to a group before. It'll be so much better to have you there. After all, we went through this together and it only makes sense."

Julio's tirade of enthusiasm returned the smile to Sally's face. It faded after a few moments, though. Agreeing to the presentations for Marcus was the right thing to do. It might even be good for her. But the idea of doing the talk disturbed her at a deep level.

Silence interrupted her thoughts. Julio had stopped talking. She looked over to see him watching her with an expectant expression. "I'm sorry Julio, I was thinking about what happened in the jungle. Did you ask me something?"

"Uh, it's nothing. I was asking about the presentation. But we can talk about that in a couple of days," he said, looking sheepish. "Guess I was getting a little ahead of things."

Lines appeared around his eyes as they took on a haunted expression, very out of character for him. It gave her a glimpse into how he might look as an older man. "Do you think about it much? About what happened?"

"Actually, I try not to."

Julio nodded, his face still old and haunted. "Yeah, it was pretty bad, wasn't it? That was the most scared I've ever been. Should…should I tell about that part too?"

The question surprised Sally. She hadn't considered describing her feelings. "Well, Julio, now that you bring it up, yes, I believe you…we should. They may have to face the creatures also. It might be good for them to know you can be scared, so scared you can barely think, and still fight them."

Julio looked around the camp. "Yes. Yes, you're right. That'll be hard, though."

"Yeah, it will. But it may be the most important message of all."

Julio nodded, but didn't say anything more. They walked in silence for a several minutes. Before long, the main gate came into sight.

As they neared the gate bunker, Carlosa's brother Raoul came out to meet them. With an almost reverent expression, he handed her a chain with a small gold cross on it. "Please take this," he said in response to her confused expression. "It was my grandmother's. I know it's not much, but my family isn't well off. It would mean much to me…and momma and Carlosa. Just a small token of our thanks."

The words formed in her mouth to say she couldn't accept it. But they died when she met the young soldier's eyes. Almost on its own violition, her hand reached out and took it.

"Thank you," she whispered.

"No, Miss Sally. Thank you," he said in a hoarse voice, "Please wear it in good health and may God protect you."

Sally felt tears come to her eyes. *Damn it, all I seem to do these days is cry.* But she managed a toothless half-smile and fastened it around her neck. She and Paul said goodbye to Julio and the men at the gate and left the military enclosure.

After passing through the strip of trees dividing the two camps, she turned toward the river. Paul hesitated and then followed. Her mind whirled. Would she be able to sleep tonight? Doing the presentations would force her to think about things she'd been avoiding. Could she face the guilt?

Colonel Antinasio's faith and Julio's joy about working with her felt good but misplaced. Add to that Raoul's gratitude and the soldiers' admiration…everything conflicted with how she felt about herself. She hadn't done anything special. She just lived while those close to her died. No, nothing special at all.

She stopped walking at the edge of the mudflat. A shudder passed through her. Paul put his arm around her. She knew he felt a lot of guilt also about David's disappearance… *Face it, his death.* She let the arm stay in place and leaned into him. It felt comfortable and familiar.

From here, the shattered remains of Rio Estrada could be seen—mostly just a few piles of rock sticking up above the ridgeline. Small tombstones marking the spot where her brother was taken. Beyond that, the imposing monolith of the White Mountain thrust skyward. *Is David there? Could he be alive?* She sighed. *No, don't even think along those lines.* It only dragged out the pain. She and Paul stood together, staring across the river for a long time.

11 Nelino in the Jungle

Nelino hated the rainforest. Funny, he didn't used to feel that way. From the boats, it was often a beautiful, almost magical place. The allure faded quickly when carrying a heavy load through a labyrinth of giant trees. Frequently tripping over roots and vines in the dim light didn't help his disposition. Neither did the heat, humidity, and a never-ending onslaught of insects. At least they didn't have to hack a path through this part of the forest. The foliage under the trees was actually pretty sparse. Not that it made for easy going, by any means.

They moved through a section of the forest where most likely no human had ever trod. Deep shadows lived under the triple layers of growth that comprised the jungle canopy. Direct sunlight rarely reached the loam under their feet. On occasion, when one of the forest giants fell and opened a path to the sky, a few scant rays might touch the ground. But the surrounding plants quickly filled such voids.

In the low light, only the nearest trees could be seen with enough detail to make out the texture of their bark. Beyond two dozen meters, the tree trunks became dark shadows against gray gloom. A few meters more, and it became impossible to separate the shape of an individual tree from the shadows around it.

The one good thing was they hadn't seen any more demons. Of course, that was a very, very good thing. It gave Nelino a reason to hope his prayers to see his wife and children might be answered. But they still had a long way to go.

Nelino swept the ground on the other side of a twisting buttress root with the walking stick he'd picked up before stepping over. For some reason, lancehead vipers liked this part of the forest. Three had been spotted over the last hour. More than enough to be concerned about. The super aggressive lancehead killed more people than any other snake in the Western Hemisphere, so their presence in the area couldn't be taken lightly. The frequent, twisty roots and deadfalls were their favorite hiding places.

Nothing moved in response to his prodding, so he stepped over the root and began picking his way forward again. Buttress roots meandered across the ground in every direction. He grew up with trees so equipped and didn't give them much thought. But tourists always marveled at the elaborate root systems of the larger trees in the Amazon. Due to their height and the shallow topsoil, the trees needed them to stay upright, hence the name buttress root.

But for someone picking their way along without the benefit of a path, they should have been called pain-in-the-ass-roots, Nelino thought. Near the trunk, they could be up to twenty feet high. They sloped down from there to perfect ankle-high tripping hazards. In many places, the roots from one tree overlapped those of another. The massive roots contributed a lot to making a maze out of the forest.

Sergeant Araujo walked a half-dozen paces ahead. He held up his hand in a clenched fist signaling to stop. Nelino copied the signal as he'd been taught for the people behind him, and everyone came to a halt. Araujo's attention was focused on something, most likely the soldier walking point. After a moment, he nodded and gestured to the left. Nelino repeated the motion for those behind and resumed following the sergeant as they headed out at an angle to their previous course.

Nelino checked his navigation tablet and saw this wasn't the direction they needed to travel. Something must be blocking the way ahead. In a few minutes, he saw a long dark wall appear out of the shadows. A toppled tree—a wimba tree, by the look of it. This tree must have made considerable noise when it fell, whether anyone was there to hear it or not. It must have been nearly two hundred feet long. Large dead branches had been sheared off the other trees that surrounded it, adding to the imposing barricade. Yet another detour on a trip filled with them.

Annoying, but he relaxed a bit. It didn't appear to be serious trouble. Since the light through the canopy stayed about the same, the tree must have fallen a while ago, long enough for the surrounding trees to fill in the sky around it.

According to Nelino's tablet, over the last four days they'd covered a grand total of seventeen kilometers from where they abandoned the boat. He had little doubt they'd walked triple that distance as they meandered back and forth through the forest. Although walking wasn't really the proper term for their slog. At this rate, maybe he should worry more about dying of old age than the demons.

A huge tangle of twisted and broken branches marked the end of the dead tree. A few paces beyond it, the group turned back toward the south. But they didn't travel far before Araujo held up his fist again. Then he waved his hand for them to hunker down. Everybody squatted, looking in directions the sergeant had assigned them earlier. This way, they had eyes covering every direction. He looked back and motioned for Nelino to come join him.

Nelino rose and crept forward. As he neared the sergeant, he noticed the forest ahead appeared much brighter. *Light? Yes, a lot of light.* The brightness covered a wide area. It appeared a large clearing must be ahead of them—a much bigger clearing than you'd expect from just a felled tree.

He reached the sergeant and knelt beside him. "Clearing?" he asked.

Araujo shrugged. "Looks that way. It must be really big, though. I expect Ankara will be reporting back in a moment," he said, referring to the corporal scouting ahead.

Even as he said it, the soldier appeared out of the gloom. He hustled over and dropped to one knee beside them. "No immediate threats in sight," he reported. "But the jungle ends about a hundred meters ahead."

"Ends?" said Araujo.

Ankara nodded. "Nothing but dirt for about two kilometers. I didn't step out of the tree line to see how far it extends east and west. But it looks like the cut the harvesters made to attack Rio Estrada, only bigger."

"Crap. Well, I guess we better move up and check it out," Araujo said. "Ankara, go keep an eye on our back trail. We don't want anything sneaking up on us while we figure this out."

The corporal nodded, stood, and glided back the way they'd come. Nelino noticed he didn't use a walking stick. The man moved with an easy grace around and over the various roots and occasional low light ferns and in seconds disappeared from sight.

Nelino frowned. "What's there to figure out? We still need to go south."

"Yeah, but open country isn't our friend. Let's go see what's what, and then we can discuss options."

Nelino nodded. Araujo stood and signaled for the group to advance.

The cut was as Ankara described it. Two kilometers didn't sound like much. A very short distance for a patrol boat. But looking across the wide expanse of dirt to the tree line on the other side of the cleared space, it seemed very far.

"So, what do you think?" Nelino said to Araujo.

"I don't know. I wonder why they cut these long strips? You'd think they'd go after the closest trees first."

Nelino bit his lip and winced in pain. It still hurt where he'd bitten through it. On the plus side, it made the burning cut across his cheek hardly noticeable. He let out a sigh after a moment and said, "Doesn't really matter, does it?" He leaned around the buttress root of the kapok tree where the jungle stopped in a neat, straight line. "You can see all the way to their mountains from here. How far away are they? About thirty kilometers or so?"

Araujo lifted his tablet, sighted the camera on the tallest peak, and nodded. He snapped a picture and made some entries. "Thirty-two kilometers. You're a good guesser. This cut gives us the chance to get some really good fixes on the main peak. At least that should help the eggheads calibrate the navigation system." His face screwed up in a funny scowl while he worked the tablet. After a few moments, he stepped cautiously around Nelino and examined the cleared strip in the opposite direction.

"According to this, there's a fair-sized river that way. Maybe we should work our way down this cut and see if it ends before we hit water. Then we could cross undercover." He stepped back into the shadows of the trees and said, "Any chance of seeing a boat?"

Nelino looked over at Gasquey, who was kneeling beside him. "What do you think, Chief?"

Her face was haggard and drawn after four days in the jungle. Nelino assumed his own looked much the same, if not worse. But she was holding up well enough. After all, none of the boat crews spent much time on jungle training. Trekking through the jungle was something the Navy avoided if possible. Which made sense as their careers revolved around being good on boats, not sneaking through the trees. So up until now, whenever he asked her opinion she'd reply, "I'm way out of my element here, sir." But rivers were her business. She knew the waterways of the central Amazon better than anyone.

"I don't know. Let me see your tablet." They had two. Nelino handed his over, and she began scrolling the screen around. "Hmmm. Well, spotting a boat's not really likely around here. Not this time of year, anyway. This river looks big on the map, but a lot of it flows through marsh lands northwest of here that aren't passable right now. However, the water due west of here," she pointed down the cut away from the White Mountains, "is deep along this stretch. It would be tough to cross carrying all this gear."

"Well, if this cut runs all the way to the river, at least we'll be a few kilometers farther from the mountains. We might as well check it out," Araujo said.

"Why not just cut across here?" said Gasquey, taking off her cap and wiping her brow. "Surely the demons can't see us this far away."

"Who knows what they can do?" he replied. "Besides, you're assuming they're just sitting in their mountain. Open country like that is always a danger zone." He plucked at his camouflaged shirt. "This green stands out pretty good against the soil out there."

Nelino looked at Gasquey's fatigues, then at the churned orange soil beyond the tree line, and nodded. The sailors wore camo much like the soldiers, except they wore black baseball caps while the soldiers wore bush hats. They would look like flies on a plate in the open.

He said, "Yeah, that makes sense. I'm tired of walking, but better to take as few chances as possible."

The chief nodded. "Yeah, well, as I've said before, this isn't my line of work." She sighed. "What's a few more kilometers more or less?"

Nelino looked up at the sky and said, "This is a good place to put the tablets out in the sun to recharge for a bit. We'll rest an hour and then head west. If this cut reaches to the river, we'll decide what to do from there."

The others agreed and shrugged out of their packs. Nelino and Gasquey looked noticeably more worn than the soldiers. But he felt they were doing pretty well considering their lack of training. By now, the two groups had forged a bond born of mutual suffering. The soldiers had even seemed to develop a high regard for Gasquey. She carried as much gear as anyone and did so without complaint. That was good. Working as a team was the only way they might get through this.

The faces of his wife and kids floated in his heart's eye. He blinked as his vision suddenly blurred. Had he been reported missing yet? Did she know? *Please God. Please help me get back to them.* Then, with a soft sigh, he pulled out two granola bars and sat down on the damp loam for a cold meal and a little rest.

12 Sally and the Fire

Thick, ropey vines entangled Sally's arms and legs. They pinned her tight and made struggle fruitless. She watched in horror as war demons dragged David away. His face showed pain and intense sadness as they cut him into red chunks with their long sharp claws. Nearby, two blood-soaked Brazilian marines stared at her with vacant and dead, yet somehow accusing, eyes.

Myra, her best friend, appeared and floated over to David, shook her head, and then glided over to Sally. One of the apparition's eyes hung out of its socket, leaving a black hole against her already dark skin. The other eye glared with the threat of terrible retribution. Her dead friend's mouth opened, and the inevitable scream of despair reverberated through Sally's soul. She jerked awake.

"Stupid monkeys," mumbled Sally.

Her nightmares had gotten marginally better over the last few days. But a troop of howler monkeys had taken up residence at the edge of the forest. Now, the little buggers screamed her awake every morning. For some reason, her subconscious started channeling their mournful howls into her dreams.

Different characters from a rotating cast of the dead performed the scream, though of course it always sounded the same. Howler monkeys were notorious for their loud, woeful cries. David and Myra almost always played center stage during the strange productions from her subconscious. But Keith, Paul, and the two Brazilian marines who died in front of her in the forest showed up from time to time. And on occasion, even barely remembered faces from Rio Estrada had supporting roles. The brain could be a strange place.

Ironically, the daily ritual helped her heal in a way. Instead of waking up with a feeling of guilt-laced terror, she was starting to feel…Well, just plain pissed off.

She blinked sleep from her eyes and looked over at the assault rifle hanging from the center pole of her tent. For the umpteenth time, she considered using it on the monkeys. The thought died even as it formed. There was no way she could actually do it. She just didn't have the heart to blow away dumb animals for merely greeting the dawn, no matter how obnoxious the noise.

Unaware of their ongoing temptation of fate, the monkeys gave another chorus of sad hoots. This made it obvious her sleep was done for the day. With a soft grunt, she hoisted herself off the thin pad on top of the aluminum-framed cot. After a good stretch, she put on a pair of khaki shorts and a purple polo shirt with the university logo over the left breast.

Coffee. I need coffee. For the moment, this one thought overwhelmed all other intellectual capacity. The goal set, she ducked out of her tent into a damp, dripping morning. At least it wasn't raining right now. This was the dry season, but it still rained a fair amount. It tended to be wetter here in the dry season than many places at their wettest. Despite the pitter patter of dripping water around her, the humidity felt a bit lower today.

The mechanical roar of a powerful engine drew her eyes to the far bank. Across the wide expanse of water below the camp, a barge with an excavator perched near the bow kicked up brown water. The big, rusty shovel sliced deep into the orange soil of the ridge just upstream from the Rio Estrada docks. The monkeys howled even louder as though arguing with the machine, a debate with a lot of noise but no substance. Sort of like politics in the United States. Despite her lack of caffeine, the thought made her smile.

Julio told her during one of their practice sessions that the floating docks wouldn't support armored vehicles. Several barges loaded with them were on the way and should arrive soon. A landing area needed to be cut out of the bank for them to land. Then a road would be plowed up to the ridge on the north side of the river.

The sight made her uneasy. It felt like the digging machine was poking into an oversized hornets' nest. In a way, this description fit too well. The thought that they might stir up the demons sent a shiver down her back. No doubt the aliens in the White Mountains were aware of the activity. She wondered what they made of it and how they might react.

The pull of caffeine could not be denied, pulling her attention back to the Big Tent. It wasn't really the biggest tent anymore, but everyone still called it that, even new arrivals, although they had no idea why. The name had been appropriate when the Americans first arrived in the Amazon. The Big Tent had been their central meeting area and served as their mess hall. So much had changed since then, not much of it good, in Sally's mind.

If anything, the Big Tent appeared a bit pathetic compared to the new ones set up by the Brazilians. These tents were bigger and of a uniform, crisp, olive-green color. The Big Tent had faded to a near gray and was patched in several places with mismatched green squares. Dr. Allen said it looked like a reject from a MASH rerun, a reference to some old TV show he still raved about. Sally hadn't ever seen it, but Allen said it was really funny. But as sad as the Big Tent looked, it kept the rain and sun off, as a tent should. And the familiar shape and color felt reassuring—a link to a more normal time when her brother had been her biggest worry.

Inside, Dr. Allen, Paul, and three Brazilian scientists sat at one of the six large tables. Dr. Allen wore long khaki pants and a blue button-down shirt. The others were dressed much the same as she in shorts and polo shirts. The Brazilian shirts were light blue with an insignia depicting two rivers joining into one, the symbol for the Manaus University.

A pile of papers sat in front of Dr. Allen. It took her a moment to realize it must be a newspaper, though an odd-looking one. The Brazilians were trying with marginal success to explain what it said. However, their command of English was only slightly better than Paul's Portuguese.

The newspaper captured her attention to the point she almost forgot to get coffee, though only for a second. Sanity prevailed, and she headed for the table holding two large urns. Neither held decaf. Coffee was the fuel of research, and no one in camp would touch anything other than full octane. She poured herself a cup and mixed in her preferred ratio of cream and sweetener. After the first sip, her curiosity about the paper returned.

Until now, Sally had not seen a real newspaper since she was a little girl. But with electronics screwed up in the area, the printed pages were a welcome sight. Information about the outside world had been hard to get lately. This paper was a bit different from the ones she remembered. It'd been printed on legal-sized notebook sheets folded in half along the short side, making a small book. No doubt it was due to a lack of the old-style paper used when newspapers had actually been printed.

Dr. Allen looked up with grim eyes as she approached. "The whole world's gone crazy," he said, shaking his head.

Paul nodded in agreement. Dr. Sandra Birkheuer, the lead Brazilian scientist, sat beside him. A slender woman in her mid-thirties, Birkheuer understood English far better than she spoke it. She relayed the comment to her companions, and they gave solemn nods.

The paper's name was *Diario do Amazonas*, meaning *The Amazon Daily* in English. This was a news website she was familiar with. Apparently, they used printing facilities in Manaus to cobble this edition together. The folded legal-sized paper made for a small front page. Headlines conveying dire news fought for the limited space. This left little room for the actual stories on front. Most of the real information was inside, making the paper rather on the thick side. Just scanning the headlines made it easy to understand the solemn expressions around the table. Three of the headlines were especially troubling. Cold chills ran through her despite the warm coffee.

Latest Death Toll in Manaus Reported at 135,250

Russia Disputes Alien Attack. Blames U.S.A. for Satellite Destruction

China Blockades Taiwan. U.S. Carrier Task Forces in Route

"Oh my God," said Sally in a soft, strained voice. The Manaus death toll was three times what she last heard. The number tore at her heart. But it wasn't very surprising based on the few reports they'd seen previously. Some neighborhoods hadn't even been searched yet, although by now the only thing left to look for was bodies. There was little doubt the death toll would continue to climb.

The rest, however…Crazy? Stupid? She found it hard to frame logical thoughts around what all this meant. A few dozen miles from here sat a terrifying, planet-wide threat. And a bunch of stupid ass people wanted to go to war with each other. Robert's statement about the world going crazy didn't even begin to cover the insanity on the page before her.

"So…" Her voice caught as she struggled with what she read. "So, no more Marines are coming?"

Dr. Allen shrugged. "It doesn't say. But probably not as many as should come."

Paul slammed his fist on the table and barked, "Damn it! Colonel Antinasio said those things are expanding faster than ever. If we can't stop them soon…" He met her eyes and shook his head.

"But how can...?" Sally couldn't quite get the words out. She swallowed hard and said, "How can they be so dumb?"

Paul snorted. "I don't know. It's insane. I feel like I'm in a crazy story called, *What if They Threw an Alien Invasion and Nobody Came.*"

Dr. Allen shook his head and said, "One of my favorite authors summed it up best. He said, 'Never underestimate the power of human stupidity.'"

Sally wanted to cry, but refused to give in to it. If she had to take her rifle and go fight these sons of bitches herself, then by God she would. There was no way she would let her brother go unavenged if she could help it. "Well, for now we–."

"Fire," came a panicked scream from outside. "Fire. The tents are on fire!"

Everyone exchanged confused, startled glances.

"Fogo?" said Dr. Birkheuer in a stained voice.

Sally nodded as Paul and Dr. Allen exploded into motion. She and the Brazilians did likewise a second behind them.

"Paul!" she yelled, reaching for the fire extinguisher that hung on the nearest tent pole. He turned, and with one fluid motion, she snatched it up and flung it at him. His arms came up just in time to catch it. The impact staggered him, but he held on. With a grim nod, he turned and hurried out of the tent. Sally ran over to the next pole, grabbed another extinguisher, and followed him out.

The Big Tent entrance faced a large central space. The other tents were arranged in a crescent on the opposite side. Only two of them were currently in use. The others were empty shells waiting for more equipment and personnel. The tent farthest left was a mass of flames. Greedy tendrils of fire reached for the one next to it, though it was not burning yet.

Shock and dismay stabbed at Sally with enough force to a stop her for a moment as she stepped outside. The blaze before her was the main lab. Their specimens, data…everything was in there. "Oh my God," she cried, her voice lost amid a rising chorus of panicked screams and shouts. Several people were sitting on the ground not far away. They were being tended to by other team members.

One man was using a fire extinguisher to shoot foam at the burning tent. It didn't seem to be helping. Paul ran up and grabbed his shoulder. Then shouted something lost in the din while pointing at the next tent in line. The man nodded and he and Paul began spraying it with foam. By now, several small holes smoldered on the side facing the fire, emitting thin wisps of smoke.

Sally pressed her lips together with the realization the main laboratory was gone. The next tent in line contained the physics lab. It had a lot of special equipment Paul built to analyze the signals coming from the mountains. Also, the navigation system updates and the alien biological circuits of the war demons. There was still a chance it could be saved. She ran to join Paul and other man in spraying fire retardant on the side of the forty-foot-long tent.

The heat from the fire made her sweat profusely, soaking her hair and shirt in seconds. Dark smoke, flecked with angry red sparks, raced upwards from the heat of the fire. The smoke quickly cooled, causing it to stop rising and mushroom out in a wide circle over the camp. The dark cloud cast a shadow over the area. *How damn appropriate is that?*

The smell of burning plastic and other, less identifiable chemical odors filled the air. There was also the scent of burnt alien flesh. Funny how much it smelled like any other roasting meat. The odor made her stomach knot up. She tried to thrust such thoughts from her head but didn't have much luck.

The alien tissue specimens were in a small prefab building used as a makeshift refrigerator inside the lab tent. They stored them in a cold room mostly out of habit, as no one had any idea what temperature would be best to preserve them. None of the specimens Sally put in culture dishes and tested at various temperatures decayed much. Earth germs apparently had no appetite for the strange flesh. She tried feeding a mouse, a small lizard, and a frog with meat from the demon, and all of them died in short order. The creatures' metabolism was as alien as everything else about them.

Sally believed the proteins in the cells had been bioengineered at a molecular level, possibly even down to the quantum state based on how they bonded with the graphene encased nerves. Now their samples, except for one small alien scout and the weapon arm from the war demon, were gone. The arm wouldn't be of much use for her protein studies. Paul's team had already stripped away the muscles, so the only thing remaining were the nerves, bone, and a few synthetic nodes. It would be a miracle if she could get enough material from those to conduct experiments with.

The smell of burning diesel also fuel hung heavy in the air. The odor probably came from the contents of the war demon's stomach. The creature they brought out of the jungle had a vile concoction in its gut like kerosene laced with acid. There had been nearly five gallons of the stuff stored in a red metal drum in the lab. Another crucial loss in their studies.

Her extinguisher sputtered and spat out a few last white globs. *Oh my God. Where are there more?* She turned and started to run for the next tent beyond the physics lab, but stopped when she heard the roar of a motor.

A camouflaged six-wheel ATV carrying four Brazilian soldiers rushed into the camp and slid to a stop. The ATV pulled a trailer behind it, carrying a large tank. The men leapt from the vehicle and snatched up the hoses coiled neatly on the side of the vehicle. Seconds later, they began spraying fire retardant. Two streams arched out at the burning tent and another at the top of the weapon's lab. The volume from each hose was many times what the small extinguishers could put out. In a few moments, the fires stopped, though smoke and steam filled the air.

Dr. Allen stood in the middle of a small worried group of dirty sweaty people. They all wore shocked expressions. Nearby, some of the team tended to three dazed people sitting on the ground. Fortunately, none of them appeared to be in too much distress. Several emotions played across Allen's roundish face, bewilderment being by far the most prominent. He nodded to her as she approached.

"No one got seriously hurt," he said. "Thank God for that." Then he turned toward the smoldering wreckage of the main lab. "But the specimens, the data…"

"I know," said Sally. "The data should be backed up, or most of it anyway." Sometimes people got lazy about doing that. She'd most likely lost a few files herself, unless her laptop survived. The high level of electromagnetic energy coming from the mountain made wi-fi useless. To save information, they had to download it onto data chips and... Well, no excuses. Everyone, including her, had damn well better back things up from now on.

More revving engines drew her attention to the trail leading up from the military camp. A small convoy of five camouflaged ATVs appeared, each carrying four soldiers. Julio drove the one in front with Colonel Antinasio in the passenger seat. The next two were full of familiar faces from PBG-31, though she couldn't place names to them. However, the last two held passengers wearing uniforms with a noticeably different camouflage pattern on them. Could these be U.S. Marines? Since they were due to arrive this week, that seemed like a good possibility.

She brushed her hair off her face and found it to be soaking wet. Then she noticed her perspiration saturated shirt. It was plastered to her body in a way that made her suddenly self-conscious. Of all the days not to wear a sports bra. The thin lacy thing she had on now would have been okay in the lab, but not soaked in sweat after fighting a fire. In this heat and humidity, her underwear got nasty pretty quick, and she just hadn't found time to do laundry lately. Oh well, just a bunch of important people arriving unexpectedly. *Shit, shit, shit.*

She prayed General von Jaeger wouldn't be among them. The thought of him smirking at the burnt tent and her drenched, clinging shirt sent a spike of anger through her. With a deep breath, she set her shoulders and walked toward the newcomers while recalling a favorite saying of her mother's.

"Oh well, what'cha going to do?" she'd say after some unexpected or embarrassing event. Momma never got rattled by what the world threw at her—a trait Sally tried hard to imitate, though not always successfully. A wry smile crossed her lips.

The ATVs stopped and people started piling out. Marcus came around his vehicle and joined Julio in staring with worried intensity at the smoldering tent. The other soldiers looked around as though searching for an enemy. Her shoulders relaxed a bit when the weasel-like face of von Jaeger was not among them.

"Are you okay?" Marcus said as she approached. "Anyone hurt?"

"No, we're good." She turned and looked at the tent. "At least physically."

Julio relaxed and gave her a reassuring smile. "Any idea how it started?" he said.

Sally let out a small sigh and shook her head. "One of the people who were in there might know something. I haven't had time to check into it."

Marcus nodded and gestured to the tent. "Serious loss, I suppose."

"The worst, other than somebody getting hurt. Nearly all our specimens and files were in there. Hopefully most of the data is backed up."

"Umm, the presentation is tomorrow evening. Should I cancel it?"

Julio gave a start, and his smile faded.

Sally hesitated, then said, "No, it'll be all right. The material I prepared is in my tent, so it won't be a problem. If its as bad as I fear, I may not have much to work on anyway."

Marcus nodded, but before he could reply, the people wearing different uniforms approached. A green American flag was embroidered on their shoulders, and U.S. Marines was over their left breasts. So, that answered the question of who they were. Julio glanced at them nervously before giving Sally a nod and going over to join some of the other marines from PBG-31.

A very fit, middle-aged woman with brownish-blonde hair led the small group. She looked like someone who ran triathlons for fun. This was a sport Paul loved and Sally admired, but considered it a tad crazy. From the woman's walk and bearing, there was little doubt she was in charge. Just behind her towered a large man with Asian features. The other two were less distinctive—a very slim, young, freckle-faced man and an equally young and studious looking dark-skinned woman wearing black framed glasses.

Marcus nodded to the Marines and said, "Sally Morgan." He gestured with his hand, palm up to the older woman. "Colonel Ames." His eyes made it plain it was up to them from here, as he didn't speak English.

The two women shook hands, and Ames said, "Greetings, Miss Morgan." She turned to the large Asian man and said, "This is Lieutenant Johnson, commanding officer of our Armored Recon Platoon." Sally shook hands with him, and Ames went on to introduce the black woman as Lieutenant Carol Woods, her administrative assistant, and Warrant Officer Andrew Webb, her translator.

Ames turned back to her and said, "So, you're Sally Morgan. I was hoping to meet you."

"You were? Umm, okay," Sally said, not really sure how to respond.

"Why, yes," she said with a smile. "Your exploits are all the news in Manaus. They are calling you the Demon Slayer. It sounds very heroic."

Sally pursed her lips. "Umm, well." She could feel her face turning red. *Exploits?* Well, everything she'd been through could certainly qualify as exploits, although that sounded rather flippant for such terrifying and deadly experiences. But in the news? She noticed the young Marine repeating their conversation to Marcus in Portuguese. He had a large smile that showed off his incredibly white teeth against his caramel colored skin. His good looks and obvious pride at Ames' complemint made Sally feel...odd.

She nodded toward Marcus. "The colonel and his men were the heroes, ma'am. If not for them, I might have died in a wrecked helicopter. At the very least, it's unlikely I would have made it out of the forest."

"Yes, I have heard of Colonel Antinasio as well. Although I must admit, the reports have been mixed."

She looked him up and down with an appraising eye and said to her translator, "Please tell the colonel that I consider myself a very good judge of character. After meeting you and seeing how well your boats are run, I believe the good reports over the bad." She waited for the interrupter to finish translating, then continued. "I know we're guests in your country, Colonel. And I'm sorry if I offend, but we've gotten conflicting directions from your government ever since we arrived. I must say, it sounds like you have more than a little political infighting going on here. Not a great situation, considering what we may be facing."

Marcus's smile faded into a grim mask. He said to Sally, "Please tell the colonel I'm not offended. We have a sad situation both in our military and at the capital. Ever since the impeachment of President Rousseff, our country has been in turmoil. There's a strong push underway for a return to the autocratic ways led by an aristocracy. The old families would like to see their titles restored. They claim it would make Brazil strong again. Sadly..." He stopped and frowned. "Uh, excuse me. I shouldn't express my personal beliefs on the matter. But yes, we do have a divided government at the moment."

Ames nodded. "I appreciate your honesty, sir. I suppose we'll just have to work around it." She gestured toward the remains of the lab tent and said, "So, what happened here?"

Dr. Allen and Paul walked up before Sally could answer, and Ames turned to meet them. After introductions were exchanged, she repeated the question.

Dr. Allen said, "We don't know, other than we obviously had a fire. It's a bit of a mystery."

"Please let me know what you find out," Colonel Ames said. She nodded back toward the base. "My executive officer and senior company commander went on to meet with General von Jaeger. We need to go join them. But I wanted to see what was up with the smoke before going to his command trailer." She zeroed in on Dr. Allen with piercing eyes. "Is there anything we can do to help?"

Dr. Allen looked thoughtful for a moment, then glanced at Sally and said, "Well, we need more samples. I fear the war demon and two of the scouts were destroyed."

Sally shook her head. "Robert, you don't know what you're asking. It's not like they can just go snag some of the creatures like that," she said with a snap of her fingers.

"Um, sorry," Dr. Allen said.

Ames shook her head. "No, it is quite all right, doctor." She indicated the tall Asian with a wave of her hand. "Lieutenant Johnson here will be undertaking some scout missions for us. If a situation arises that does not entail undo risk, I'm sure he'll do what he can."

"It would be my pleasure," said the lieutenant.

"Thank you," Dr. Allen said, giving Sally a bit of a smug look.

His smugness didn't bother her much. He was a good boss who always supported her. But then, neither Robert nor the lieutenant understood how tough the task might be. She just prayed no one would get killed 'collecting samples.'

"Well, we're late," Ames said. "Colonel, are you coming?"

Marcus shook his head. "No, ma'am. Umm, I wasn't invited," he replied through the interpreter.

Ames looked surprised for a moment and then nodded. "I see. Well, I guess I better go meet the general. He sounds like an interesting man."

Sally almost wished she could go too. It would be good to see the look on the little weasel's face when he met the American commanding officer. No doubt it would be a very interesting interaction.

As the Marines walked away, Marcus said, "I may not be invited to the meeting, but I do have other things to attend to. I will assign some men to help clean up." Something caught his eye in the direction of the civilian camp. "And…I believe we may want to post some guards as well, just as a precaution."

"What? Why?" said Sally, turning to follow his gaze.

The smoke started to thin, but still made an impressive cloud over the university camp. Below the ridge, in the direction of the civilian camp, a sizable crowd had gathered to stare up at the commotion on the hill. Off to one side, a little apart from the bulk of the mob, stood about a dozen people in robes.

She recognized the man who gave the sermon down by the river. He still wore his dirty robe or one very like it and carried the staff with the lopsided M. Beside him stood a woman dressed in similar garments—the one who pointed them out last week. The man appeared to be above the cares of the world, although his eyes had a crazy look, one being open wider than the other. The woman stared up at them with a little smile on her face that looked a bit smug. Was she focused directly on Sally? Something about her seemed familiar beyond last week's interaction. Where had she seen the woman before?

"Do you think any of them had something to do with this?" Sally asked. The woman must have noticed them looking because her head jerked down and she pivoted abruptly to look out over the river. Being the only person with her back to the scene at the university camp made her stand out more than staring did. It looked suspicious. But arson?

Marcus shrugged. "I'm just not taking any chances. There are some strange rumors going around about people wearing that crooked M symbol. Of course, we have lots and lots of strange rumors floating around right now. Still, this is one we may need to heed. I should have posted some men here earlier."

"Who are you guys talking about?" Paul asked, peering down

the hill. "That crazy preacher and his gang? Does Colonel Antinasio think they had something to do with this?"

"I think so." Sally switched back to Portuguese and said to Marcus, "That woman looks familiar. I think she may have done some odd jobs for us over the last week or so."

Marcus focused in on her. "From now on, I don't think you should allow outside helpers in the camp. Things keep getting more and more crazy. Best to play it safe by limiting access as much as possible."

"There are several people who helped us set up the camp. They've been around for some time. What about them?"

He frowned. "Like I said, there are a lot of strange things going on. Do you really need their assistance?" Then he shrugged. "Just be careful. This Church of the Mountain is new and seems to be growing. God alone knows why. It's up to you if you need the help. But keep them away from the labs. Okay?"

Sally relayed this to Dr. Allen, and Paul and they both nodded with solemn, thoughtful expressions. The Church of the Mountain? That must be what the M on the staff was about. Did people actually want to sabotage them? She sighed. As if they didn't have enough to worry about already.

13 David Runs the Vat

Low, hushed voices woke David. He dreamed he was living in the middle of a nightmare, and it took a moment to make sense of his surroundings. The fog cleared with the painful realization he did live in a nightmare—an even worse one than his dream.

His subconscious kept trying to convince him that real life wasn't real. Things came further into focus as he blinked the sleep from his eyes. The shadowed blue light, slight vibration of the ground, and faint rumble of distant machinery aptly demonstrated where he was. He sighed. Disappointment greeted him most mornings, or what passed for morning in the unchanging light of the cave. Even bad dreams tended to be better than his current reality.

Across the fire, Alessandra and Pedro were having an animated, whispered conversation. Alessandra put down a hair brush and began braiding her shoulder length black hair. Her dark eyes twinkled as her delicate mouth lit up in a smile at something Pedro said. With her slim build, David had originally thought her to be much younger than he, but it turned out she was several months older.

They spoke in Pedro's native Yanomami dialect, although David heard an occasional word in English. The boy had been part of a small tribal group who moved to Rio Estrada during the rubber plantation days. Some said they were abducted and forced to live there. He was a small, skinny boy of about ten. Alessandra was the only one who understood him, and she'd been teaching him English, which he was eager to learn. They spent a fair amount of time playing connect the dots in the sand. The young boy loved playing connect the dots.

The group had organized itself around the fire in a lopsided circle. David slept in a small hollow by a large boulder which reflected the fire's heat back at him. He had almost half the circle to himself. The other four survivors split the remaining space. They didn't exactly shun him, but he did feel like the odd man out. Alessandra and Pedro often huddled together.

Paula and Josh each had hollows pressed into the sand about ten feet away. They slept close to each other, but not touching, not that David had seen anyway. Was it his imagination, or were they sleeping closer together now? *Hmmm, maybe.* They tended to talk to one another more than the others, but not a whole lot more. The group spent a lot of time in silence. Each of them, even Josh, carried wounds to their hearts and souls. And they still suffered from shock. Except maybe for Josh, who maintained an aloof, stony demeanor that only Paula managed to crack, and that rarely.

Pedro stood and walked over to David, which was a bit of a surprise. The young boy looked painfully skinny and still limped from the wound in his calf. But he'd made remarkable progress considering how close he came to dying less than three weeks ago. He carried a six-inch-long stick with ten thorns tied to it in a neat row. "Dots?" he said, holding up the stick with a smile.

This was the first time he had invited David to play. David shot a puzzled glance at Alessandra and found her smiling back at him.

"I think he's getting tired of beating me," she said. "He's got a real eye for the game."

"Sure, why not?" said David.

"Su'ra, why not'a?" the boy said with care and nodded. "That yes?"

David smiled. Something he didn't do much these days. "Yeah, that means yes."

The boy looked puzzled for a moment, then said, "Yes," with more assurance.

Alessandra said, "Stick to simple words and avoid slang, and he'll understand you better."

David nodded and watched the boy with interest. Pedro used the side of the stick with no thorns to sweep a section of sand about two feet across, making a flat square. Then he flipped the stick over so that the thorns faced down and pressed it into the sand. This left a neat row of ten dots. He repeated this process until he created a grid with twenty dots on a side. Then he sat back and waved at the grid with an expectant smile.

"Okay," David said. He made a line with a small stone connecting two dots.

Pedro responded quickly. To each careful move David made, Pedro smiled broadly and made his move almost instantly. It was a little unnerving. The game looked simple enough, but Pedro apparently had some kind of strategy. Somehow his moves kept forcing David to be on the defensive, and the boy began claiming multiple boxes. In short order, the game was over. Pedro won by an almost two to one margin in closed boxes.

David looked up to find Alessandra looking down at them. Amusement shone in her large, dark eyes. "I told you he was good."

"No shit," said David.

"No shit," Pedro repeated. "Again? Dots?" His eagerness would have been puppy cute if he hadn't just kicked David's butt so badly.

David resolved to do better and nodded. Pedro brushed the area flat and laid out another grid. When he finished, David gestured for the boy to go first, but Pedro said, "No, no. You."

With a shrug, he made his first line. As before, Pedro grinned and made a quick move in response. The puppy-dog cute smile began to look more like that of a shark. David concentrated on each move. It helped, but not much. Pedro seemed to know in advance what move David would make. Pedro won again, though it was a little closer this time.

"Again?" Pedro asked, the puppy dog earnestness returning.

David started to say yes but was cut off with a gruff bark from Josh. "Enough. Time for PT."

Josh's voice came from closer than David would've expected. He looked up to find him and Paula standing with Alessandra. Had they been watching? It was odd to have everyone on his side of the fire. It seemed even odder for Josh to wait until they finished the game before announcing time for physical training, if that was indeed what he'd done. Upon reflection, it didn't seem likely. Josh was like a force of nature that moved on its own implacable schedule. Waiting for anything didn't fit his style.

David almost groaned but suppressed it. Moans and groans tended to draw unwanted attention from Josh. Pedro hopped up with a faint wince and limped with determination toward the tunnel that led to the vat room. The little guy insisted on being included from the first time he managed to stand. His leg had to hurt. But he ran, or rather walked as fast as he could, the same number of laps as everyone else.

And if there was a person Josh would have excused, it would've been Pedro. Josh still gave him a light swat with the stick when he passed. But instead of bothering the boy, he smiled up at Josh, taking no offense at all. In fact, he seemed pleased to be included in the ritual. This ongoing enthusiasm was the one trait of Pedro's that annoyed David, although not very much. The boy was hard to dislike.

The two-a-day workouts were getting a little easier to take. David's arm kept improving, but he still used the sling. His endurance improved, and he could keep up with Paula, Pedro, and Alessandra. Josh only passed him once or twice a session and didn't hit him nearly as hard with the damn stick. However, getting whacked on the butt was still a humiliating experience that David dreaded.

Typically, when the group entered the vat chamber and started running, David would get behind Josh and do his best to keep up with him. Inevitably, he'd tire and slow and Josh would lap him, clump up from behind, and smack him on the ass. He did the same to the women, though not as often or hard. And for some reason, it didn't seem to bother Alessandra and Paula much.

When they first began the twice a day runs, the women giggled sometimes when Josh smacked his butt. Mostly likely because by the sound, it was easy to tell who got the hardest whack. Or maybe they thought David was just being lazy and deserved it. The spanking ritual bothered him even more because he believed they still snickered at times. It took him back to being bullied in high school. Girls had always giggled at him then too.

They got to the chamber and stretched out. In a few minutes, Josh set out. His combat boots made a distinctive clump-clump sound as he ran. David fell in behind him and began to chug along at his usual plodding and gasping pace. Josh ran like some kind of machine, maintaining a steady, ground-eating stride.

Josh almost lapped him before David finished his fourth lap. In short order the distinctive clump, clump, clump of Josh's boots on the gritty surface announced his approach from behind. David hated the sound almost as much as the squalling conveyor. Despite the sounds from the vat, David could hear the thudding boots the whole time they ran. It marked Josh's steady progress around the pit and announced the approach of another imminent butt slap.

Today, it triggered an unfamiliar sensation in David. Instead of dread and resignation, something new washed over him. Anger. Anger and a burgeoning determination not to get hit today filled his chest. He clenched his teeth and picked up the pace. The tempo of Josh's clumping boots also increased. *The son of a bitch is trying to run me down.*

David pulled his arm free of the sling and shook it out. *Ouch.* But it didn't really hurt that bad. It throbbed with a soft, dull ache. With the arm free, his balance improved and the slight pain helped to keep him focused. With both arms in motion, he got into a better rhythm. He found himself going faster with little more effort. Still, the sound of Josh's boots thudded closer. David ran even faster, pushing himself. Josh sped up as well. On and on David ran.

He passed Alessandra, Pedro, and Paula. All three watched him chug by with surprised expressions. However, even running as hard as he could and with his heart hammering in his chest, Josh pounded along right behind. Time lost meaning, and he passed the women and Pedro again as if in a dream. He'd never managed that before, but didn't think about it. His sole focus was on staying away from the stick.

At last, exhaustion almost made David's legs buckle and forced him to slow to a half-jog, the best pace he could still manage. His breath came deep and fast from exertion. He'd given it all he had and failed. Anger burned deep in him as he clenched his butt. He gritted his teeth in frustration while waiting for the stinging blow, but nothing happened. After a moment, Josh pulled up beside him, breathing a bit fast for the first time David could remember. Josh studied him for a moment and gave a small nod. Then he flipped the stick into the vat and continued running beside David.

The move surprised David so much his feet got crossed and he stumbled a few steps. Josh hesitated to allow him to regain his footing and catch up. A wave of euphoria started in David's chest and rushed up through his head as the two continued to keep pace side by side. *Josh threw away the stick?* They jogged on around to the tunnel entrance. Alessandra, Paula, and Pedro were already there, watching with big smiles on their faces.

In the mad dash around the vat, David had completed an extra lap without even realizing it. The women and boy cheered as Josh and David approached, although Pedro looked a bit uncertain what the excitement was about.

For David, this was better than the day he graduated high school. It might well be the best day of his life. Well, at least since the time before his parents died. Josh smiled at him when they stopped. Not much of a smile, just a slight twitch at the corners of his mouth. But it was a vast improvement over his usual glowering expression.

After a moment, however, the smile faded and Josh growled, "Enough of this crap. Time for calisthenics." His face softened a fraction as he looked at David; then he smiled a sardonic grin. "Looks like you're getting a little motion in that arm. That's good. But I doubt you'll enjoy building it up." Then he turned and started up the tunnel.

Josh's grouchiness couldn't dampen the good mood fostered by the disposal of the stick. With smiles on their faces, the rest of them followed him to the exercise area. Paula patted David on the shoulder and Alessandra winked at him. David truly felt like he belonged for the first time. Strange, before coming to the Amazon, he'd led a soft and easy life and yet hated it. Now he lived in a nightmare world and found a glimmer of happiness, or at least a warmth in his heart he'd lost a long time ago.

The warm sensation seemed contagious. From the looks of the others, they felt it too. Not only were they healing inside and out; the little group just took a major step toward becoming a team.

14 A New Day in the Mountain

Beyond the tunnel and small open space where they camped, the cave split into four branches. It made David think of a deformed hand with the group's firepit at the palm and four smaller caves stretching out as fingers. A small stream ran through the left two fingers near their tips. On the far left, the stream entered the cave near the ceiling and cascaded down a series of ledges. This was where they drew drinking water from.

It also made a pleasant place to go think since the sound of running water masked the sounds of the blender. David had spent a lot of time there in the first few weeks trying to sort himself out. He still came there from time to time just trying to escape the melancholy fill of the cave complex. The blue light rods sparkled like sapphires off the bubbling water. In conjunction with the myriad tinkles and splashes, it was very soothing.

In the same cave, about twenty feet downstream from the cascades, the stream flowed into a small pool before flowing out again. This area was used for bathing, if scrubbing yourself with cold, wet sand could be considered as such.

The water continued underground and flowed into the adjoining cave. This was the smallest of the four fingers, and the group used it for relieving themselves. The next finger over had a rocky floor and opened out into a small chamber. This didn't see much use except for storing extra meat, vegetables, fruits, and nuts preserved by Paula. The finger on the far right had a floor covered with deep sand. Josh had designated this area for exercising.

After their run, he led them to the exercise chamber, which was roughly twenty yards wide by forty deep. The space was mostly clear except for a handful of medium to large boulders scattered around the sandy floor and several floor-to-ceiling rock columns. The light from the ever-present electric blue rods cast odd crisscrossing shadows around them.

Josh had built makeshift exercise equipment for strength and agility training. There were several branches with rocks tied to them for barbells, a few crude benches, and a wooden frame lashed together with webbing for pullups. It reminded David of stuff from an old Flintstones movie he'd seen as a kid.

 The feeling of teamwork following Josh's surprise move of tossing the stick into the pit faded, but something still felt different to David. But when they entered the chamber, they went back to their usual subgroups and routines. Paula and Alessandra went to one side of the chamber and began lifting weights together. Pedro followed Josh to the logs where Josh helped the boy with stretches and exercises to strengthen his leg. David went to an area in between and began fiddling with another set of weights.

His arm felt stiff but didn't really hurt much. At least not unless he tried to move it beyond certain limits. He did a few curls and squats, but they didn't feel like they helped much. Josh finished instructing Pedro, then walked over to where he did his own workouts. This area had by far the biggest barbells and strongest bench. The man could lift some serious weight.

Would Josh give him some pointers? The thought of asking sent a quiver across his shoulders. He'd never talked to him except when Josh asked a question demanding to know something. And that happened very rarely. Not to say Josh didn't speak to him, or rather at him from time to time. But mostly the older man tended to glare a lot. The judgmental stare that made David feel like he was unworthy all the time.

But David had promised himself to be a better person, someone his sister would be proud of. And Sally wouldn't be intimidated by someone giving her a dirty look. She always said not to be afraid to ask for help. That not asking was both dumb and showed more weakness than one realized. With that in mind, he set his shoulders, and walked over to Josh.

Josh took off his shirt and started doing one-armed pushups. Scars crisscrossed his chest and arms, white lines across freckled skin underneath a mat of red hair. After popping off a dozen or so with his right arm, he switched with a quick fluid motion to his left, never breaking stride. He seemed to have muscles on top of muscle, connected with a thick network of veins. When he finished, he hopped up to his feet and looked at David, his expression neutral. Not that it helped much. Josh looked intimidating even in his sleep.

David wanted to turn away but forced himself to hold is ground. "Uh, could you…I mean, would you show me some exercises for my shoulder? Uh, please?"

Josh's eyes softened and the corners of his mouth quirked up a bit, but only for second. Then his face went back to neutral. "Sure," he said. "I ain't a physical therapist, but I got some on the job training, so to speak." He looked around the exercise area and nodded toward a large boulder. "Over there."

At the boulder, Josh took his arm and, with surprising gentleness, moved it up and around. Each time David winced or grunted, he would halt and move the arm in a different direction. After a few minutes, he stopped and nodded.

"Did you feel any popping or grinding sensations?" Josh said. David shook his head.

"Good. I think stretching and strength training will do the trick." Josh spent the next few minutes having David face the boulder and use it to for leverage to put pressure on his shoulder at various angles.

"Do it until hurts a little, but don't get carried away. Hold for a count of ten and then relax. Do five reps on the positions I showed you. I'll check back on you in a little while, and we'll see if we can work in some weights."

To David's shock, Josh patted him on his uninjured shoulder with a nod and faint smile, then went back to his own exercises. Yes, something had definitely changed. At least in his relationship with Josh.

Everyone settled into their own little world after that. David did the stretches and thought a lot about Sally. Sometimes about the destruction of Rio Estrada and Heather, the girl who died in his arms just before he got captured. She'd been one of the few people in camp who treated him like a person instead of an oddball. He'd seen a lot of terrible things that day. But the image of her head smothered in webbing while she suffocated before his eyes still haunted his dreams...although it competed with nightmares of a gatherer scooping her up right afterward, and then spearing her limp form on one of the long sharp spikes on another creature's back. That was how the aliens carried off their plunder.

He knew the others had similar bad memories. Maybe even Josh. Alessandra's whole family had been killed before her eyes. So, had Pedro's mother. Paula escaped her home as the monsters destroyed it, but her husband did not. At least she'd been spared seeing him impaled like the others had.

Alessandra lay on a medium-sized boulder with one of their makeshift barbells over her chest. Paula stood at her head and watched as the girl lowered the thick stick to her chest and then back up in smooth motions. Pedro was nearby doing some leg exercises Josh had shown him, and David worked on his stretches.

Except for soft grunts and sharp inhalations, they worked out in silence. They rarely talked when gathered in a group like this. Paula and Alessandra whispered between themselves at times, but only in short sentences about what exercise to do next. Their hearts were getting better, but not healed. Today they seemed a little looser, no doubt a carryover from Josh throwing away the stick. But everyone remained lost in their own individual worlds.

A loud fart cut through the silence, and they all looked at Pedro. The boy was pulling his injured leg toward his chest. His expression of chagrin transformed a second later into a loud giggle. Alessandra burst out laughing, followed by David and Paula. Even Josh chuckled for a while. The laughter trailed off but left smiles in its wake. It surprised David how good the laughter made him feel. From the expressions of the others, they felt the same way.

Everyone went back to their workouts. David's heart felt considerably lighter. They always say laughter is the best medicine. Regretfully, it isn't always a long lasting one. But as his thoughts began to turn back to Sally and how much he missed her, someone began to whistle.

The tones were clear and beautiful. He turned and saw the whistling came from Josh. Despite doing one-armed curls with a weight David couldn't have handled with both of his, the tune came out smooth and nearly flawless. *Sittin' on the Dock of the Bay*. It'd been one of Sally's all-time favorites. David was only dimly aware his jaw dropped open.

Josh stopped and looked around at the others, his face returning to its more accustomed scowl. Everyone had stopped working out to stare at Josh with shocked expressions.

"What're you looking at?" he growled. "You never heard anyone whistle before? Get back to work. Just be glad I ain't singin'. The beauty'd probably break your heart."

They grinned at one another and got back to their exercises. Josh began whistling again. The sound made David feel lighter inside again, like a booster shot to the laughter. He'd learned the words to this song long ago. The warmth continued to grow in his chest and David began to sing.

Josh looked at him with raised eyebrows but kept whistling. It felt good to sing. Besides video games, it was one of the few things he'd enjoyed in his old life. In a moment, Paula joined in. Alessandra and Pedro started to tap the beat on nearby rocks and for a few minutes, the exercise area was filled with the sounds of Otis Redding. They sang it through twice before Josh stopped them.

"Okay, that's enough of that. This is exercise time, not a concert. I'll whistle some more, but the group renditions will have to wait until…" He looked thoughtful a moment. "Say, after supper."

Everyone smiled and began to exercise with renewed vigor. Josh whistled a few more tunes while he went through his own routine.

David felt really good. First, the birth of a team in the vat room. Now hope, along with music, echoed through the cave.

15 Nelino and the Open Land

The marsh before Nelino looked foreboding. In the wet season, with the water twenty feet or so higher, it would've been better. At least in appearance. Then only the largest trees would be visible poking out of the water. They'd make leafy green oases scattered across a water desert. For now, it was a land of mud, tall grass, jutting logs, and God alone knew how many snakes and caiman. Regardless, it didn't matter much. It was an impassable barrier for people on foot.

Such difficulties apparently didn't stop the demons. The wide path of cleared land they'd been following continued straight as an arrow out into the marsh. The churned orange soil transitioned into roiled dark mud stripped of organic material. No trees, grass, logs, or even dried out, dead water plants existed for as far as they could see.

Some small animals and insects might have moved back into the area since it was cleared. Although, there couldn't be much there left to draw them. The mud would mire down anyone trying to cross it. How the demon harvesters managed cross it, much less work it, to clear the land was hard to imagine.

"Crap," Araujo said, kicking a dirt clod at the edge of the cleared land. "I was really hoping we wouldn't have to cross this."

"At least it doesn't look very far," Nelino said.

Araujo snorted. "The heck it ain't. Not only are we going to be exposed the whole way; it sucks to walk through that," he said, waving his hand at the cut. "Have you ever walked across a plowed field? Luckily, it's not real muddy right now. Then it would be even worse. But still, it wears your legs out fast."

Nelino remember playing in a tuber field when he was a kid. And he remembered having to lift his feet high and be ready for the dirt to crumple and shift when putting them back down. Every step took twice as much effort as on regular ground. The stretch of churned earth between here and the next tree line was a lot like that, maybe even worse as it had been torn into larger clumps. A lot of the clods were knee high, and the group would have to go around them. Big enough to be obstacles, but not really big enough to hide behind. It would be a long afternoon.

He turned to Gasquey and said, "How are you holding up? Feel like crunching dirt clods?"

"Sure, sounds like fun. Yeehaa," she said in a flat tone and cinched up her pack. "Let's hit it."

Araujo smiled at her and said, "You know, you're completely undermining everything our glorious little general said about women in the military."

Gasquey gave him a wry smile. "Yeah, that's the whole reason I'm here. Didn't you know?"

Araujo's smile widened and he chuckled softly. "Well, normally I'd send out a scout. But I don't want us getting too far apart through here. Spread out and keep your intervals. I'll take point for this stretch. I crossed a lot of plowed fields when I was a kid. It'll be like old home week for me."

However, his grin faded into a grim line and his eyes narrowed as he turned and walked out of the tree line. His first step made a distinct crunching sound. They were lucky it hadn't rained much the last couple of weeks, so the topsoil was dry. It turned out to be a small consolation.

The ground proved to be just as hard on the legs as Araujo predicted. The top crust of the clods crunched down when you put your full weight on them. It was a bit like climbing stairs that gave way just before stepping up. Then you had to lift your foot high to get it out of the resulting shoe-shaped crater. The heavy loads they carried made it difficult to balance, adding to the strain. Nelino felt like he teetered on the brink of falling every few steps. They moved slower than ever, yet he started panting from exertion before they covered a hundred meters.

The special forces men spent a fair amount of time training on crossing difficult terrain. Several of them offered to help carry his or Gasquey's packs. He would've been tempted, but after she refused the first offer, he felt obligated to do the same. *Stupid macho bullshit*. But then, he was a typically stupid, proud male. On the other hand, after

Araujo's compliment, Gasquey may have been pushing herself further than made sense as well. Nelino supposed neither sex was immune to doing dumb things solely to impress others.

A little over halfway across, even the soldiers began to struggle, with the possible exception of Sergeant Araujo. The man must have had an enormous energy reserve as he took little half-hops from clump to clump as though he enjoyed crushing them beneath his boots. Maybe it was just a special technique he knew. If so, there was no way Nelino could copy it. His legs had no hop left in them.

The sergeant kept pulling ahead. After turning and observing them lagging, he paused and looked them over. With a frown, he stopped and held up his hand. "Okay boys…and girl," he finished with a grin at Gasquey. "Let's take fifteen. Make sure you load up on fluids."

Moans of relief emanated from soldiers and sailors alike, accompanied by the crunching thumps of dropped packs. Next came a chorus of soft sighs as everyone slumped on top of them. Everyone sat down but Araujo, who dropped his pack, but stood gazing up the cut toward the White Mountains. He pulled out his canteen and took a long draw, then frowned and lowered it, peering intently off into the distance. After a few moments, he relaxed and drank again.

Did he see something? Nelino tensed. *No. He'd say something, not relax. Wouldn't he?*

The ominous twin peaks were over thirty kilometers away and still towered over them. After studying the cut between the tree lines for a few moments, Araujo finally dropped to one knee and replaced his canteen. However, his eyes kept sweeping the terrain between them and the mountains. Seeing the sergeant rest helped ease Nelino's tension.

Then Araujo leaped to his feet and snatched at a pouch on his belt. He pulled out a pair of small binoculars and focused them up the cut. His shoulders slumped, then squared back up. By now, his behavior had everyone's attention.

"Okay. Fast travel. Cut the luxury goods and move."

The sergeant had helped Nelino and Gasquey pack for just such a situation. 'Luxury goods' included tents, ponchos, cooking utensils, and extra food carried in their main packs. The 'fast travel' command meant to dump them and carry just the supplies on their belts and combat harnesses. It meant that from here on out, they would truly be roughing it. Something bad must be coming their way.

No one asked any questions, not even the sailors. Araujo wouldn't have given the order if there was any time to waste. In seconds, they set out at an awkward jog.

"War demons. About thirty. Heading this way. Fast," Araujo called out in clipped sentences as they moved. "Maybe ten kilometers. Get to the tree line. Pray to God we can lose them."

Fear was a powerful motivator. Terror even more so. But it could only drive a person so far. Three-fourths of the way to the tree line, Nelino's legs began to cramp. He fought through it, running despite the stabs of agony by sheer will. For the longest time, the trees didn't seem to get any closer.

The ground crunched and shifted under his feet as if the land had become malevolent, trying to turn his ankle. Something whizzed by his head, and someone cried out in pain. One, then two rifles began firing with systematic, short bursts. The shots sounded in even-spaced cadences, the mark of trained shooters. Then another rifle roared in a long chatter of sustained fire. Nelino hesitated and started to look around.

Sergeant Araujo yelled, "Keep moving, keep moving."

Someone yelled, "Go! Go! Leave me. I'll provide cover fire."

"Goddamn it," shouted Araujo. "Get to the tree line! Now!"

Nelino obeyed, knowing he was as out of his element as Gasquey, not even sure if Araujo was yelling at him or someone else. One rifle continued firing. There was an explosion, then silence. The only sounds were horse panting from people running for their lives and the sound of crunching dirt.

His slow progress toward the trees seemed surreal. He was Alice in her Wonderland, where running only kept you from going backwards. Then a towering jatoba tree suddenly loomed in front of him. He plunged past it into the forest, ran about ten more meters, and dove behind the exposed roots of a large mahogany tree. With awkward fingers, he began fumbling with the unfamiliar rifle. The cold plastic banged his cheek as he jerked the weapon butt up to his shoulder.

Looking down the barrel, he twitched it back and forth, searching for something to shoot.

Araujo jumped down beside him. How the man found him was a mystery. The sergeant pointed directly away from the cut and said, "Fifty meters that way. Find cover and wait. Move!"

Nelino moved. It felt very scary to leave the cover of the giant tree, but he had no doubt Araujo knew way more about staying alive out here than he did. He ran for a count of fifty, added five more for luck, and took cover in small cluster of palm trees. Silence settled over the forest. Nelino carefully put the rifle on safe, fearful he might shoot one of their own people due to his hyped-up nerves.

A shadow moved to his right, and he jerked the rifle around. Thank God, he'd put the safety on. The form was human, and it wasn't until he realized this that he noticed his finger was knuckle white on the trigger.

"Over here," he called out in a loud whisper. The other person jumped in surprise and swung their own weapon his way before lowering it and hurrying to join him.

He recognized the soldier as the man drew closer, Corporal Manuela Xavier. The man nodded and took a position behind another palm tree a few meters away. One by one, three other soldiers appeared, then Araujo and Gasquey. Nelino let out a sigh of relief at the sight of his shipmate and did a quick count. Seven. That left one man missing.

"Antonio?" Corporal Xavier asked. His voice made it clear he already knew the answer.

Araujo shook his head, and everyone's shoulders drooped. "Got hit. Died brave," he said softly. "Kept firing to draw them in to him, then set off his claymore. He shredded one, maybe more."

"What about the rest of the demons?" Nelino wasn't sure who asked, but it was a damn good question.

Araujo looked puzzled and shrugged. "They're clustered around his body, just sitting there. Say a prayer they don't change their minds anytime soon. We need to fast travel that way," he said, pointing deeper into the forest.

"Claymore?" Gasquey asked Nelino in a low voice.

"A mine," Xavier said, tapping a small, curved rectangular box on his side. "C-4 explosive driving 700 steel balls. We all carry one for…Well, whatever. Just depends, I guess."

Everyone stood silent for several seconds, digesting what Antonio had done for them.

Araujo broke the silence. "Move, people. We don't want him dying for nothing."

Nelino forced himself to his feet. Everything hurt, even his teeth for some reason, probably from clenching them in fear. And he'd thought the physical training requirements for sailors to be bullshit. Never again. Now he wished he'd trained to be a marathon runner. It still took all his will to make his legs start moving, though once in motion, it wasn't too bad.

I guess you never know how far you can push yourself until you have to. Please God, help me find the strength to keep moving. It looked like he still had a lot of pushing to do as they set out. In a few seconds, they began weaving through the forest at a rapid clip, tired legs and all.

16 Sally and Julio and the Presentation

The lowering sun sat near the horizon when the soft purr of a well muffled ATV reached Sally. A few seconds later, a four-seat camouflaged vehicle came into sight. Julio drove, his face lit by a dazzling smile. Marcus sat beside him. The vehicle pulled up in front of the Big Tent where she stood waiting.

"Hi, Sally," said Julio with his typical boyish enthusiasm. "Ready to go?"

"All set," she said, climbing into the back. The seats faced the opposite direction, so she sat sideways to talk.

"Greetings, Sally," Marcus. "I really appreciate you doing this. A lot of people have expressed interest."

"You won't believe all the people who showed up," Julio said.

"Really? I thought it was just your men, Colonel."

"Yes…Well, do you remember Sergeant Lupe?"

"After that wonderful meal? How could I forget?"

He smiled his dazzling smile. Again, it surprised her how handsome it made him look.

Marcus said, "I believe you are his personal hero, and he's been talking up the presentation to the other mess sergeants. He almost makes it sound like you should be on Broadway."

Sally frowned. "We haven't even done one yet. How can he say that?"

Marcus chuckled, but then took on a slightly contrite expression. "I told him to hold it down when I heard about it. But the word's already out. We changed the location to the largest tent available at the request of the Officer of the Mess. It seats about five hundred."

"Wow," she said. "That's a lot of people." She wished she'd dressed up a little more. Her yellow button-down shirt with the university lion crest and knee topper shorts felt a little too informal for this.

"That's nothing, Miss Sally," said Julio. "That's just how many can sit inside. They had to roll up the sides so more people could see you."

"Us, Julio. Remember? I'm not doing this by myself, you know."

"Oh, I know. It's just that…Well, no one's coming to see me."

"Don't sell yourself short," Marcus said. "You killed a demon too. We didn't do nearly enough of that that day."

Julio blushed, but didn't say anything.

They got to the gate in the log and earthen berm surrounding the base. Beyond, there was more open space than the last time Sally visited. Several units had already been relocated to the other side of the river. But it was still a substantial base with a maze of tents, large and small. After passing through the gate, Julio swung the ATV onto a wide avenue that bisected the camp. He drove a short distance, turned right, and then up a slight rise. As they crested the small hill, Sally let out a gasp.

The large mess tent would do a small circus proud. But it was nearly lost in the sea of humanity surrounding it. There had to be several thousand people there.

"All this just to hear a speech?" Sally said in a small voice.

"I guess you haven't seen the newspapers," Marcus said. "Remember Carlosa?"

"Of course," she said, pulling the small gold cross from under shirt. "His brother gave me this."

"Ah, yes, Lieutenant Pinheiro told me about that. A nice gesture. Good of you to wear it tonight. I will be sure to tell Corporal Bustani. It will make him happy."

"I always wear it," she said with a sudden hitch in her voice that forced her to clear her throat a couple of times. "In remembrance of Carlosa and those other boys. And…other things."

A twinge of pain crossed Marcus's eyes, and he nodded slowly. "I understand. Well, Carlosa was interviewed by several news organizations. The way he tells it, you were an avenging angel sent to deliver him that day. Not in those exact words, mind you, but that's pretty much how it came across."

"You've got to be kidding," she said, her face warming considerably.

"I thought you knew," Marcus said, a note of apology in his voice. "The news has spread all over camp. Most likely all over Brazil."

""Colonel Ames mentioned something about a story in Manaus, but I never imagined… Well, wonderful, that won't be hard to live up to," she said, shaking her head. "And now I get to make a speech."

The ATV pulled up to one end of the tent where a small stage and podium had been set up. Julio turned around and beamed even brighter, which Sally almost found hard to believe. "Yeah, it'll be great." It appeared her sarcasm was lost on him.

With a sigh, Sally got off the ATV and stood studying the layout. Julio was supposed to go first, so where should she wait?

A green canopy with mosquito-net walls sat behind the stage. The late afternoon sun hit the netting in such a way as to obscure what was inside. Marcus and Julio headed toward it and she followed. As they approached, a section of the mosquito-netting parted and Colonel Ames, Lieutenant Johnson, and Warrant Officer Webb came out. All were smiling, and Ames extended her hand as she approached.

"Hello, Miss Morgan. Good to see you again." They shook hands.

"Please, Colonel, call me Sally."

"Sure. I'm Linda," she said. The two groups took a few moments to exchange handshakes. "Just wanted to come by and check out your presentation. Any chance you'd give one to my people later? In English, of course," she finished with a smile.

"Umm, why don't we see how this one goes first?" replied Sally.

"Oh, I'm sure it'll be fine. I want my folks to hear about facing these things firsthand." She turned to Julio, glanced at her interpreter and then said, "Please tell the corporal that I heard he has a good story too. Would he be willing to talk to my people as well?" Her eyes shifted to Marcus. "Provided his senior officer approves."

After Webb translated, Marcus turned to Julio and said, "It's all right with me. Julio?"

Julio looked very young and unsure. He turned to Sally, who nodded encouragement. A crooked smile appeared on his face, and he nodded.

"Excellent," Linda said. "Well, we don't want to hold things up. I believe General von Jaeger is holding seats for us."

"Von Jaeger? Here?" said Sally.

"Yes, when my folks told me about the presentation, I told him I wanted to attend. He insisted on coming along." She leaned close to Sally and murmured conspiratorially, "He doesn't impress me much. But when in Rome and all." She looked at her two companions. "Gentlemen, I believe it's time to take our seats."

The other two nodded, said good luck, and followed their commander out of the enclosure and into the tent.

Sally, Marcus, and Julio ducked into the canopy, where an impressive array of finger foods sat on a small table just inside. Julio's eyes widened, and he headed straight for the table. Marcus cleared his throat, and Julio stopped like a chain was tied around his waist. With a slightly sheepish look, he turned to Sally and said, "Miss Sally, would you care for anything?"

Sally chuckled and shook her head. "No, not right now. Maybe afterwards. Please go ahead."

Julio looked at Marcus, who gave a slight nod, and Julio helped himself to a small plate.

Marcus pulled out a pocket tablet, glanced at it and said, "We're scheduled to start in about fifteen minutes. I'll go check to see if things are ready. Once we begin, I'll give a little background information and introduce Julio. When he finishes, I'll do the same for you. Any questions?" Sally shook her head and he said, Very well. Make yourself comfortable. And good luck."

From there, things moved in a blur. Sally sat down and began fidgeting. She'd never spoken to a crowd anywhere near this size. Plus, General von Jaeger was here. That pissed her off. She thought maybe she should focus on her anger, since it was better than being scared shitless.

She remembered hearing Julio's introduction. A rabbit meets a fox expression washed over his face. But then he steeled himself and left the canopy. The sound system was good, and her friend's voice carried clearly into the enclosure. His opening was shaky, but soon he picked up speed and did a really good job. The crowd clapped, and then Marcus introduced her.

Her own speech was even fuzzier. There were a lot of smiling faces. But more than a few looked at her like something found on the bottom of a shoe. Von Jaeger seemed to be trying to burn her out of existence with his eyes. In contrast, to his right Linda Ames smiled up at her encouragingly.

Sally started by describing the strange storm and how it impacted Rio Estrada. At first, it felt as every other word she spoke was either, "Uh," or "Well." However, as she got to the deaths of her best friend Myra and the others in the helicopter, the emotions of the past welled up inside her and whisked her back to that terrible time. Rather than giving a speech, it became a soul cleansing.

It had been somewhat the same when she wrote the speech, only ten times more so giving it. The terror of the battle, the deaths of those poor brave boys assigned to guard her, killing the war demon…All of it seemed to replay before her as she talked. The tension she felt eased as she neared the end and discussed the extraordinary leadership of Colonel Antinasio and the bravery of his men.

She completed her narrative with a description of the devastated wasteland that had once been Rio Estrada, and tears started to flow unbidden down her cheeks. She'd been taught that the best way to end a speech was with a call to action. For this speech, she made a passionate appeal to stand together and fight. The demons were the greatest threat humankind had ever faced, and it would take everyone working together to overcome them.

At last it was over, and she finished with an awkward thank you to the men of PBG-31 for saving her. Silence followed.

They clapped for Julio. Was I that bad? Run, run off the stage, a part of her said. But she stayed in place, gripping the podium, waiting for Marcus to come rescue her. An eternity of maybe four seconds followed, then a thunderous applause filled the tent and the area around it.

The noise snapped the spell and she saw the crowd, really saw it for the first time. Folding chairs filled the tent. Beyond it, people stood in disorderly rows. *A standing ovation?* Yes, from everyone but von Jaeger and the men sitting next to him.

He sat in the front row of seats to Sally's right with a score of Brazilian officers, who also remained sitting. A few of them clapped, but not for long after they received stern looks from the others. To the left of von Jaeger stood Colonel Ames and maybe a dozen Marines. They all clapped and a few cheered while beaming up at her. The sight reminded her of a State of the Union Speech in the United States, with the Americas cheering and the Brazilians looking stern and disapproving. At least it was only the Brazilians in the front row who looked so restrained, the rest applauded with almost as much enthusiasm as the Marines.

Before the applause faded, von Jaeger leaned over and said something to the officer to his left. Then he made a cordial nod to Colonel Ames to his right, stood and walked like a man with a mission out of the tent.

As he was leaving, Marcus hopped up on the stage and walked over to her with an extended hand. "Outstanding," he said, pumping her arm. "I knew it would be." He moved to the podium, and the applause slowly tapered off. He took on a somber tone. "As Miss Morgan said, 'We face a great threat, and we must work together to overcome it.' I want to thank the United States for coming to stand with us."

Sally noticed for the first time that the Americans in the front row all wore earbuds. Did they have a human translator, or one of the artificial intelligence translation bots that were supposed to be the hot thing in international travel these days. In the past, such devices tended to make a lot of dumb errors due to context or emotional overtones. She shrugged; it didn't matter. They seemed to understand what was being said just fine.

Colonel Ames nodded solemnly and stood to face the crowd. She waved, and this was greeted with another round of enthusiastic applause. If only such passion could be maintained when it mattered. Ames sat back down, and Marcus said a few things about moving assets across the river, then good evening to the crowd. There was another round of applause. It sent electric thrills up her spine and made Sally wonder if this was how politicians and rock stars felt. It was a bit intoxicating. Then Marcus turned and gestured for her to head to the canopy behind the stage.

Inside, Marcus beamed at her. "That was inspirational. Julio, yours too. Everything I hoped for and more. I think my people could eat demons for lunch right now."

Julio looked like he might float through the top of the tent. Sally felt an emotional tsunami rolling through her. The performance drained her to the core, but it had also been cleansing. She hadn't been sure at first, but maybe this would be good for her. The food on the table now looked very appealing, and a wave of hunger washed over her. She prepared herself a small plate and collapsed into one of the folding chairs set up along one side of the canopy—exhilarated, proud, a little shaky, hungry, and now very, very tired. What a ride.

The opaque quality of the netting reversed as the afternoon gave way to early evening. Julio turned on a small light suspended from the apex of the canopy. The mosquito netting began to prove its worth as insects started to cover the outside of it. It occurred to Sally that the inside light must have turned the interior into the proverbial glass house, and she sat up a bit straighter. It wouldn't do for people to see her looking weak after asking them to be strong.

After a moment's reflection, a soft chuckle escaped her. Damn, was she playing to her fans or something? In a way, she supposed she was. What a weird feeling. The price of fame. But what were the rewards? To build goodwill with the military and get a chance to repay the lost souls of PBG-31? Yeah, those were pretty damn good rewards.

Voices came from the darkness outside and then Colonel Ames entered. Sally started to stand but the older woman waved her back down and said, "Don't be silly. Sit, sit. I just wanted to tell you–."

The netting was thrown aside, and the officer von Jaeger spoke to after the speech burst into the canopy. He left the net open, careless of the onslaught of bugs it would allow in. He looked around with an air he evidently thought to be regal but just made him look like an asshole. Sally felt a slight impulse to stand again but suppressed it. She had an instant dislike for the man. A von Jaeger clone for sure, only taller.

"Sally Morgan, you are to report to General Herman von Jaeger immediately," the officer said, pronouncing the general's name and rank like the man was only one step below God.

The man's tone and order were a bit of a shock. Sally started to stand, but Colonel Ames held up her hand and eyed the intruder.

Ames said, "I don't know exactly what he said, but I sure as hell don't like the way he said it. Something about you seeing the general?" Sally nodded and Ames said, "Tell him you're a U.S. citizen and don't take orders from him."

The officer was looking back and forth between Sally and Ames. He seemed confused for a moment, then repeated his command for her to go see von Jaeger. Sally stood. "It's okay, Linda. In fact, we're under contract with the Brazilian government to do research, so in a way, I do work for him."

Marcus stared down the officer with a cold expression. "We get the message, Santos. Can't you see she's eating? She'll go when she finishes."

Colonel Santos bristled, but didn't say anything. He sniffed as if the people around him were not worthy of his concern, turned on his heel and left the tent. Julio hurried after him and pulled the netting closed. Then he looked back at Sally with a worried expression.

Sally ate one more bacon-wrapped shrimp and said in Portuguese, "I guess I better go see what he wants. No point in pissing him off any more than I have to." Marcus nodded. "Can Julio show me how to get to his office?"

"Better than that, he can take you in the ATV."

Julio nodded and she smiled at him. She turned to Colonel Ames and said in English, "If you'll excuse me, Linda, I need to go see what this is all about."

"Certainly. And just so you know, if your arrangement with the Brazilians doesn't work out, I'd be glad to have you as a consultant on my staff."

Sally smiled. "That's good to know, ma'am. Now, if you will excuse me." The older woman nodded, and Sally ducked out of the netting followed by Julio.

The crowd had dispersed for the most part. As they approached the ATV, a tall, very pretty brunette woman wearing a tight blue dress better suited more for the city than the Amazon walked up to them. "Guten Abend, Frau Morgan." She frowned with slight shake of her head, then smiled. "Uh, good evening, Miss Morgan. May I talk to you, please?" she said in near flawless English.

"Not right now, I'm afraid. I'm on my way to a meeting. May I ask what you want to talk about?"

The woman handed her a card with a large DW printed on it with smaller letters underneath spelling *Deutsche Welle*, and under that Dagmar Halter. The woman said, "My name is Dagmar Halter. I'm a reporter for German International News. I really enjoyed your presentation and wanted to get some follow up information."

First fans, and now reporters. Sally's quiet life in science seemed to be headed in very different direction from how she'd always imagined. She said, "This isn't a good time. But you can come by our camp sometime tomorrow. It's on the tall hill just south of the river."

While they were talking, a tall blonde man walked up. He was dressed far more sensibly for the rainforest. Dagmar introduced him as her producer and cameraman, Udo Handloik. He said something in German and shook her hand.

"I know where your camp is," Dagmar said. "Tomorrow will be excellent, say, in the early afternoon."

Sally agreed and got into the ATV with Julio. "What was that about?" he asked.

"Reporters. From Germany."

He smiled. "You're going to be famous."

She shook her head and chuckled, leaning back as the ATV purred to life. Famous? Well, maybe, but first she had to get through this meeting with that little weasel von Jaeger.

17 Sally and von Jaeger

The drive only took a few minutes. Near the center of camp, they came upon the cluster of trailers housing the base's administration offices. Julio stopped the ATV outside the largest one, of course, and pointed to an elaborate sign. It was emblazoned with General von Jaeger's rank and name along with the title, "Commanding Officer," in Portuguese and English. Sally was half-surprised it wasn't lit up in neon.

"Well, here we are," Julio said. "I'll wait here for you."

"Thanks." Sally felt nervous and angry at the same time. Based on the smoldering glares von Jaeger gave her during the speech, she doubted this would a social visit. *Try to keep an open mind*, she told herself. *It doesn't have to be bad, does it?* At least she didn't see a squad of Military Police waiting outside. Hopefully not inside either.

Another, less ostentatious sign hung above the trailer's door. It said, "Base Administration. Commanding Officer." The door was unlocked, so she opened it and went inside.

Sally found herself in a plush outer office. A door across from her once again proclaimed the name, rank, and title of the occupant. As it was the only other door in the trailer, it seemed like overkill. The air was cool and dry, almost cold. It made her suddenly aware that her shirt was damp, not surprising as it had been a hot afternoon and being on stage before several thousand people would make anyone sweat a little. At least she had a decent bra on this evening.

A desk sat to one side with a uniformed woman looking at her expectantly. She was blonde, wore heavy makeup, and was quite pretty. While her attire could be considered a uniform, it didn't fit her as one would expect of a soldier. It was somewhat low cut and exposed the top of the woman's ample bosom. The anteroom felt more like the office of a spoiled, rich CEO than a military officer.

"Miss Morgan?" said the sergeant. "Please have a seat. The general will be with you in a moment." The woman then proceeded to ignore her by staring at the monitor on her desk.

There was a plush maroon couch and three matching wingback chairs in the anteroom. Sally chose one of the latter and sat down. And sat, and sat, and sat. Whatever was important enough for her to rush across camp was not so important the general couldn't keep her waiting. Poor Julio. She wondered if he was still waiting for her. After nearly an hour, a slight buzz came from the direction of the sergeant's desk.

"You can go in now," said the woman.

Sally stood, frowning, and walked to the door. She started to knock, but then thought, to hell with it. She opened the door and walked in. The inner office was even more opulent than the anteroom, with a carpet so thick and soft, it felt like she sank to her ankles. A tapestry covered the entire left-hand wall, depicting a medieval battle with nearly life-sized knights engaged in frozen combat. To her right were two glass cases displaying a wide variety of military artifacts, most of which appeared to be of German Nazi SS vintage.

"Miss Morgan. Please be seated."

It took Sally a moment to find the general; his less than impressive frame was swallowed by a huge desk at the far end of the room. He made no effort to rise or greet her other than telling her to be seated. With a frown, she sat down in one of two heavy wooden chairs in front of the desk.

Jaeger stared at her across a wide expanse of polished wood for several long moments, his eyes showing disapproval. For what, Sally couldn't imagine. She met his gaze with cool indifference, though her insides fluttered. The little jerk was trying to intimidate her, but why? Because he didn't like her speech? If so, why not?

Or did it have to do with her gender? Maybe a bit of both. She thought about the sexy, non-regulation uniform of the woman out front. That wouldn't go over in the United States these days, not in any circle Sally associated with. In Brazil? Well, some military units were integrating women better than others. Regardless, she refused to give him the satisfaction of looking away and maintained a steady, unflinching expression. She could stare at him as long as it took for him to explain why she was here. They could sit here and stare at one another all night for all she cared.

The general's look of disapproval deepened, and he made a small "humph" sound. "I was not impressed with the presentation concerning your supposed exploits during the skirmish in the forest."

"Supposed exploits?" She drew in a deep breath to quell her rising anger and said, "Regardless of what you call it, I gave the presentation about my time in the forest at the request of your officers."

"Yes, most notably at the request of Colonel Antinasio, who is not actually one of *my* officers. His men are outside my chain of command. However, the rest of the people on this base are not, and you're to stop all such activities. In fact, after tonight, I will have orders issued to have you arrested if you come onto this base again. And the new one across the river as well."

This threw her. "What? Why?"

"What you said in your little speech is against the official version of the battle. Antinasio's men were reported to have fled, and that's why they had such heavy losses."

"That...that's insane," she stammered. "That's not what happened at all."

"I'm not going to discuss it with you. Just heed my warning unless you want to go to the stockade."

Sally sat in stunned silence. It was plain von Jaeger enjoyed her shock and confusion. He probably took it for weakness.

"You know you're just a pawn in this, don't you?" he said.

The man kept saying things that didn't make any sense. "A pawn? For what, the fight to save the forest, maybe humanity?"

Von Jaeger snorted. "The creatures are a concern, certainly. But this…mountain thing, it can't take over the whole planet. They will be dealt with in due course. There are bigger issues at stake for Brazil."

Sally's mind spun even faster. This guy just did not process things the same way she did. How can they both be living through the same experiences and view things so differently? She slumped back into the chair.

This made von Jaeger's smile broaden. He looked like a caiman about to take down a small deer. "If you can see reason… Tell things a little differently to support the official story…" He leaned back, made a steeple of his fingers in front of his nose, and stared at her over them. Now he looked like a greasy used car salesman confident of closing a deal.

"The men like looking at pretty girls," he said. "It wouldn't hurt for you to make a few more speeches." His hand dropped, and he leaned forward. "But I'll not have your inflated story of Antinasio's men, who're little more than policemen anyway, disheartening my soldiers. If his men had been true soldiers, then I'm sure this fracas would've ended differently. I do not want a… a woman making heroes of some constables who got mauled by a bunch of animals."

Sally didn't remember getting up. But she found herself leaning over the desk, her hands flat on the cold, hard, wooden surface, glaring down at von Jaeger. "How dare you insult those men? You have no right…" She stopped. What could she say? His expression changed again as he looked up at her with eyes wide, a rabbit cornered by a hound, his bluster gone.

A flash of pleasure went through her at the fear in his eyes. *So, a mere woman can scare the crap out of our mighty little general.* The thought helped ease her anger somewhat, and she backed away and sat down without saying another word. There was no point in doing anything stupid. The man was hopeless.

Von Jaeger gave another small snort, and his features returned to an expression of contemptuous disapproval. "As I was saying, you are banned from the base and there will be no more presentations. And I'll be speaking to Dr. Allen about your behavior during this meeting as well."

Sally shook her head. Behavior? What the hell did that mean? No doubt he'd make it sound like she'd attacked him. Not that she cared. Robert had no more love for this asshole than she did.

"Whatever gives you a thrill, general. I get the message, no more presentations. Will that be all?"

"*No!*" It didn't seem possible for Jaeger to look any more annoyed, but he managed to do so. He glared at her for several long seconds, his face contorting as he struggled for words. Then in a very quiet tone he said, "We still have official… business… Regretfully."

He stood and picked up a large envelope with what appeared to be a small box inside. Shaking his head in disgust, he walked around the desk and flung it onto Sally's lap. The envelope was a standard shipper from *Brazil Correios*, Brazil's version of FedEx. "Take this to Antinasio on your way off the base. I don't know how you two pulled this off, but rest assured, if there was anything I could do to stop it, I would."

"Pulled off…? What are you talking about?" The undistinguished envelope gave no clue as to what it contained. This whole meeting just kept getting stranger.

Jaeger gave a loud, derisive snort. She'd never been in a conversation that left her so confused.

Turning his back on her, he said, "Get out of my office."

Sally was more than happy to oblige. She stood, gave him as contemptuous a look as she could manage, and strode from the office. Outside, Julio had his head on the steering wheel. As she approached he sat up, blinked sleep from his eyes, and smiled.

"Sorry you had to wait so long," she said. "I had to sit in the waiting area for almost an hour."

"No problem," he said. "I was getting a bit worried, though. May I ask what he wanted?"

Sally frowned in disgust. "Mainly to tell me I've been banned from the base."

Julio's eyebrows shot up, but before he could say anything, she held up the envelope. "Also, apparently to be a delivery person for this. I'm to give it to Colonel Antinasio."

Julio looked stunned, and in a worried voice said, "Banned? Why?"

Sally started to tell him what the general had said about PBG-31, but hesitated. There was no point in hurting his feelings.

Julio must have sensed this. "Is it because of the stories the army is spreading about us? About us being cowards? I heard the general made it the 'official' version."

Sally nodded, and the young private looked grim, a most unusual expression for him.

"Yeah, the colonel warned us about that. He said it was about politics and not really about us. There's some kind of fight going on between the leaders of the army and navy, higher up than that actually."

"Yes," she said with a scornful glare at the trailer. "He wants me to change my story."

Julio nodded thoughtfully. "And you refused? That might cause some trouble."

Sally laughed. "It already has, I guess." She shook her head and said, "But I wouldn't...couldn't say you and PBG-31 are cowards."

He managed a slight smile, looking grateful and uncertain at the same time.

Sally held up the envelope. "So, let's drop this off with the colonel, and then you can take me home."

"I think Colonel A is hosting an officer's mess this evening. He doesn't usually like to be disturbed when he does that, unless it's really important."

Sally looked doubtfully at the envelope. How important could it be? Most likely a formal order banning Sally or something. But what was the bulge that felt like a box? Should she open it? No, that didn't seem right.

"Would you please give it to him in the morning, then? I think that would be okay, don't you?"

"Sure." Julio took the envelope, and his smile returned. "You don't think it's a bomb or something, do you? They say the general is out to get the colonel."

Sally laughed. "Let's hope not. That would take political infighting to a whole new level."

Julio's mouth quirked downward. "I guess we won't be doing any more speeches then."

"I guess not," she said with a sigh, then waved toward the university camp. "Well, I guess I better get off base. Would you please take me home?"

"Sure, it'd be my pleasure."

18 Sally and Paul

After Julio dropped Sally off at camp, she was surprised to find Paul fidgeting outside her tent. His eyes cut away from hers almost as quick as they met, looking down and to the side like a shy teenager. But his smile was genuine enough.

"Could I talk to you for a moment?" he said.

She was still wound up tight after her encounter with General von Jaeger. But Paul was an old friend. She forced herself to relax. "This sounds serious." He didn't reply. After a short, awkward silence, she said, "Of course."

What could he possibly want? For some reason, she felt suddenly uncomfortable. Probably just lingering tension over her talk with the general, she told herself.

If possible, his expression regressed a few more years, from teenager to a child with his hand in the cookie jar. His expression was pained as he glanced around and dug one foot into the dirt, adding to his little boy look.

"Uh, well. Could we go for a walk, maybe?"

"Okay," said Sally, although she had a tense feeling in her chest. Paul was as self-assured a man as she'd ever known. This shy boy routine didn't fit him at all. She'd never seen him be so…tentative. Only one topic came to mind that would make him act this way—deep personal feelings. *But why now?* They'd had a thing once, but… Well, it hadn't so much ended, as just faded away.

As they walked across the camp, Sally said, "Paul. Why now?"

Her question obviously caught him by surprise. "Uh, what do you mean?"

She gave a small chuckle. "Come on, Paul. I know you better than that. You want to talk about where we left things. Right?"

Paul laughed. "Am I that transparent?"

"Not usually. But then, usually you seem to operate in another world."

He nodded. "Yeah. True enough. But so, do you. Is that what happened between us, we just operated in different worlds?"

"I wondered about that…once," she said in a low voice. "I think we were just too busy to find time to be together."

He sighed. "Yeah. And I guess that says something about our feelings, doesn't it?" He cast a sidelong glance at her. "At least at the time. But what about now?"

Sally pondered the question. He was much like her in many ways. Both loved science. Both were dedicated to things they believed in. Both were extremely curious about the world and wanted to make it better. Why hadn't they found more time for each other? He was certainly good looking enough, once you got past his ugly glasses, ruffled hair, and sloppy dress. He'd won numerous triathlons and had a six-pack that would turn any woman's head. No words came, and the silence dragged on.

He gave a sigh. They'd reached the edge of the compound and headed down the hill toward the civilian camp. The smells of a dozen different types of cuisine drifted up toward them. Fires and torches lit the area with a cheery yellow glow. Several types of music fought for dominance, though none achieved it. It made for an odd blend with reggae, rock and roll, and local rhythmic drums growing louder and then fading from different directions. She hadn't taken time to go, but several staff members reported the local nigh life to be quite vibrant in the burgeoning town.

"There's something else I wanted to say," he said, his voice heavy and sad. "I'm..." He sighed again and continued, "I'm so very sorry about David. I..."

"Stop it!" Sally barked. "Just stop. Please." She turned and took his left hand in hers. "I don't blame you, okay. David was not your responsibility. You got him safe to Rio Estrada. There's no way you could have known..." She shook her head, unable to finish the thought.

Paul's eyes looked angry and concerned at the same time. "I could say the same to you. I've seen you around camp. You're tearing yourself up over this. Over David and Myra both. Why can't you turn it off so easily?"

She dropped his hand and looked away. "That's different."

"No, no it isn't. None of us have much control over what we feel guilty about, no matter what we tell ourselves." He smiled, but it looked strained. "So, I'll feel crappy about things if I damn well want to, okay?"

This brought a genuine chuckle from Sally. "Fair enough. They always say misery likes company. Is that why you felt this sudden need to talk?"

Paul pursed his lips in thought. "Honestly, I don't know. I began having thoughts about us not long after we got here. I just... Well, it seemed sad the way we just drifted apart. I really care about you."

Sally nodded. "I care about you too. But...I don't know. Things went from hot and heavy to cool and distant. Now...now it's different. A different kind of caring."

"I'll take that," he said. "For now. Would you be open to...maybe...maybe spending a little time alone? Just talking? Over dinner or something?"

After a moment she said, "I might."

The quiet stretched again as they walked. Once, it would have been a comfortable silence; now it felt strained. *Funny, silence is silence. Just a lack of sound. So, how can it feel different?* But it did. A matter of perception.

They reached the bottom of the hill and entered the crazy network of paths that made up the civilian camp. The camp and all of its diversity, strange groups, and odd mixture of construction stretched unheeded around them. Sally thought of Marcus. What about her feelings for him? That was an avenue she had no idea how to travel, or if the ever-proper Brazilian even wanted to. Or if she wanted to, for that matter.

Another possibility now presented itself with Paul. But what the heck. Paul was already a known variable. She almost laughed as the thought came to her, but suppressed it for fear of offending him. A known variable indeed. Was she so much the scientist? Life didn't readily fit such notions. Marcus was beyond analysis, in a way. That was part of his appeal.

For that matter, it seemed strange to even be having these thoughts and feelings, especially now, with the future so full of uncertainty. Yes, life did not follow the same methodological structure as science. Part of her wished it did. But then, mystery was one of the things that lent spice and meaning to life.

She noticed Paul glancing at her with apprehension. It couldn't have been easy for him to ask such a question. It showed a level of interest she wouldn't have thought he possessed. That said something, didn't it?

"Okay," she said. "But…let's take it slow. All right?"

"Of course," he said, the relief in his voice obvious. "We can just talk and see where things might go."

"See where things might go," Sally repeated softly. There never was a way to know where life might go, or when it might end, for that matter. The last six weeks had taught her that, if nothing else.

"Let's head back, okay?" she said. "It's getting late."

He nodded. They turned around and started walking up the hill. Neither talked on the way back, but the silence felt a little less strained.

19 Daniel and LAV patrol

"Listen up, Recon!" shouted Gunnery Sergeant Stevens to the camouflaged men and women standing before him.

First Lieutenant Daniel Johnson watched the scene from the turret of his mottled green and black Light Armored Vehicle. While t he official designation for the vehicle was a LAV-25, but a lot of Marines called them "pigs," or "old pigs." It was as much a term of endearment as one of disparagement. Everyone was highly aware that the machines were older than anyone in the platoon, including Gunny. And with the sergeant being thirty-five, most of them considered him to be older than dirt. Of course, the pigs had gone through extensive upgrades over the years, but they were still made of old metal.

"Oorah!" chorused the platoon in response to the gunny. Except for Private Blevins who answered, "Sooooiie, Pig!" Gunny gave the young Marine from Arkansas a tolerant look that nonetheless said, "Watch it." He didn't like people stepping too far from convention in his platoon.

Whispered discussions ceased as the camouflaged forms turned to face the dark-skinned, ramrod-straight sergeant with prematurely graying hair. The Marines stood in a loose, half-moon formation in front of the platoon's armored vehicles, their attention focused on the senior sergeant.

A smile forced up the corners of his mouth despite his best effort to maintain a professional demeanor. From the hatch on top of the nine-foot-tall vehicle, it was easy to assume an outsider's perspective of the Marine antics and think they were a bit silly. But by God, they got under your skin and were very effective at promoting a strong sense of teamwork. You had to hand it to the Corps; they were damn good at what they did.

Gunny spoke in a loud, clear voice. "All right, Recon. We've been here a couple of weeks now and haven't done much except piss off a bunch of fishermen. Well, today is the day you start to earn your pay." He nodded up toward Daniel. "The LT already went over the mission, but just in case some of you were sleeping, I want to reinforce a couple of points. Besides, I know how much you love to hear my voice. I didn't want to short you on my inspirational leadership."

A few faint groans came from the platoon, but most of them smiled.

"Our first mission objective is to scout and observe. This means avoiding contact. If any of those things head our way, we will endeavor to evade them. If we are faced with nonlethal aggression, do not respond. Do not fire unless fired upon. Unless, of course, the lieutenant or I begin firing first. Any questions about that?"

There were none, so he continued. "Our second mission objective is to gather data via your assigned team instrumentation packages. Follow your procedure, and we should be good. But don't get too focused on your equipment. Poke your head up every minute and scan your environment. In other words, keep your eyes open.

"Keep in mind it's really muddy out there. Traction will be an issue. Drivers, keep an eye on your intervals. I don't want us bunching up or stringing out." He met the eyes of each of the platoon's four drivers, holding his gaze briefly until they nodded their understanding.

"Finally, no radio communications means everyone must stay doubly alert. I can't call you. And if I have to ram someone to get their attention I will be severely pissed off. Got that?"

The platoon gave a collective nervous chuckle and everyone nodded.

"All right, Recon!" he bellowed. "Semper Fi! Saddle up."

"Oorah," the platoon chorused and began scrambling into the surrounding vehicles.

Gunny walked past Daniel's LAV . Their eyes met, and the older man let his carefully masked tension show for just an instant. "Ready to go poke 'em with a stick, sir?" he said with a small smile.

Daniel nodded. "At least it's a sharp stick," he said, patting the fifty-caliber machine gun in front of his hatch.

"Stay sharp," Gunny said. Daniel watched as the sergeant strolled leisurely to his own LAV and with slow, unhurried motions climbed up the armored side to stand atop the turret. Feet braced, he gazed over the platoon as the men and women began settling into their positions.

Private First-Class Mark Fletcher, Fletch to his friends, climbed up the front of the vehicle, nodded to Daniel, and dropped into the driver's hatch in front of the turret. A second later, the big diesel engine roared to life.

Corporal Sharon Bennett, the vehicle gunner, vaulted onto the turret and then slid through the gunner's hatch to Daniel's left and into her seat with one fluid motion. The other four Marines of his team entered the LAV through the back hatch and settled into the troop compartment below.

He could hear a click as the others plugged their helmets into the vehicle com system. They used the wire backup since even inside the LAV, the interference from the mountain overrode wireless communications. Once everyone verified they were hooked in, he said, "Okay, Fletch, are you ready to kick this pig?"

"Foot's back and ready, sir."

"You know where we're going, right?"

Fletch almost sounded hurt. "Gunny would kick my ass if I didn't."

"Then wake me when we get there," Daniel said with an exaggerated yawn.

"Yes, sir. And may I say, sir, your leadership is truly inspiring."

Daniel smiled. The two had a running joke about Daniel's lazy habits. "They sent me to school for that, you know. Delegation's the key. I got very high marks."

Corporal Bennett groaned and Daniel glanced over at her. She stood in the gunner's hatch shaking her head with a wry expression on her face. "Can't you guys come up with another topic to beat to death?"

Daniel felt a little sheepish. This had been going on for a while. Maybe it was time to find a new line of humor to help ease the tension.

Gunny gave Daniel a thumbs-up and slid down into his own command hatch.

Daniel made a final adjustment to his helmet mic and said, "Okay, Fletch. Kick this pig!"

"Aye, sir. Kicking the pig," came the reply. The LAV's diesel engine roared and the eight-wheeled, boat-shaped LAV kicked up orange and red mud from all its tires. It slid sideways a couple of feet, lurched, and began gaining forward momentum. It reminded Daniel of a car skidding around on a road covered in ice. This bode ill for the speed and maneuverability they normally counted on. It took noticeably longer than usual for the formation to reach the agreed upon cruising speed of twenty miles per hour.

The vehicles spaced out, and the platoon assumed a diamond-shaped formation with Gunny's Battle Pig Three on the left flank and Daniel in Battle Pig One on the left. Battle Pig Two took the lead. The gunners were up top, searching in all directions with binoculars along with the vehicle commanders.

About twenty miles ahead rose the twin peaks of the White Mountains, which towered over them even at this distance. The closest peak was by far the larger—a monolith of white granite. Where parting clouds allowed, shafts of sunlight made the granite shine. It even sparkled here and there where the light glinted off pockets of quartz, like some kind of bizarre gothic temple.

However, on closer inspection, the white granite had a dull, dead look when not in the direct sunlight, like old bone. There were dark openings boring deep into the stone like open eye sockets. Miles upon miles of potential hiding space holding...? Well, that was sort of what they were here for, wasn't it? No one had any idea what was really going on around the mountains. And today's mission took them on a leisurely drive around the base of the thing to see what happened. *Oh joy.*

The day before, Daniel spent several hours staring at the mountains. Sometimes he'd feel a twinge of panic from just thinking about them and how they suddenly appeared from one day to the next. It was akin to being told the Grand Tetons or Mount Rainer had only been there a couple of months. The scale of what he saw challenged his mind to accept that it hadn't been there for a billion years. And as the LAVs rumbled on, the mountains rose ever higher above them.

Daniel glanced left at Gunny, who was staring at the mountain as well. The sergeant seemed to sense his gaze and glanced his way. He held up his right index finger and poked his left hand. Daniel nodded in reply. *Yes*, you were *right about being on the end of long, skinny stick. But seeing it is something else. We never imagined we'd be sent to poke something like this.*

The route to the mountain lay along a six-hundred-yard-wide, fifteen-mile-long swath of destruction that had once been forest. It connected to a three-mile-wide strip of cleared land surrounding the mountains and a two-mile half-circle of cleared and churned land that had once contained the thriving frontier village of Rio Estrada. On a map, the half-circle looked like a huge animal rose up from the river, took a bite out for the land, and swallowed the town and surrounding trees.

All that land, not to mention the homes of over two thousand people, had been stripped down and cleared within a matter of hours. This might have been a little easier to believe than the appearance of the mountains themselves. But it was still unpleasant to consider. Just how many of those things from the mountains would it take to do that?

"This camouflage sucks, sir," Bennett said. Her tone sounded condemning even over the earphones.

"We discussed this, corporal. We followed the manual and used the standard camo for the Amazon region. Since we were headed to a rainforest, it seemed the best option at the time." He turned and gave a shrug. "What did you want us to do?"

"I know, but it's freaking me out heading toward that mountain with us looking like green bugs on an orange napkin."

"I know what you mean," Daniel said. "This thing has all of us a bit freaked out."

The land left in the wake of the harvesters was stripped bare of every living thing all the way down to the root systems of the trees. The orange soil so common in the area had been thoroughly churned up and was crisscrossed with deep furrows. Despite this being the middle of the dry season, enough rain still fell to leave the landscape an orange, muddy mess.

Daniel had to admit the four vehicles waddling up the torn track couldn't have been more visible. But their paint was back on the Wasp, of course. He'd submitted a requisition for brown and black. Hopefully it was on the way. But that didn't do much good for them right now.

The Recon Platoon came to the end of the slash and entered the large open space between the base cliffs and the jungle. They turned right to follow the tree line and shifted the formation with Gunny's LAV in the lead.

Across from them was a sheer gray and white wall. Reports said it was nearly three thousand feet tall and ran all the way around the base of the mountains. From this distance, he had to crane his head back to see its jagged top.

A few places along the wall had crumbled, scattering boulders across the field below. This left white and gray shapes thrusting upward from the orange soil like weird oversized houses. The platoon now moved into truly alien territory. Daniel felt his attention torn between searching the terrain ahead and staring at the towering megalith to his left. Anyone, or any *thing*, watching from the mountain couldn't help but see them. Daniel wondered what they thought about the four armored vehicles churning through the mud.

After about twenty minutes, a line of lumbering shapes came into view. Even though they were still over a mile away, there was no doubt what they were. Colonel Ames and her staff hoped they would encounter a band of the harvesters working on the forest. It looked like that part of the mission was a go. Gunny glanced back and held up three fingers, indicating he planning on stopping in three hundred yards.

Daniel gave him a thumbs-up. "Okay Fletch, Gunny's going to stop up here in a minute. Steer us a couple of degrees to the right, and we'll take station on his flank."

"Roger that," replied the private.

"Sergeant Packard," Daniel said. "Are you guys ready down there?"

"Aye, sir," replied the deployment team leader. "We're geared up and ready."

A few minutes later, the LAV slid to a stop. "Brakes set," snapped Fletch.

"Clear to deploy," Daniel said.

"Deploying," said Packard. A pair of clangs came from below as the rear hatches swung open followed by the rustle of fast moving men and women.

Each vehicle carried a team of four Marines assigned to perform different tasks. Daniel's team set up long range telescopic cameras. Gunny's team fanned out to help keep watch, and the other two teams set up equipment to analyze the interference, test air conditions, and make long range sound recordings.

The scientists are going to go ape shit over this. This was way better than expected. Daniel lifted his binoculars and watched in fascination as the massive, six limbed harvesters worked. They reminded him of ants as they came in a long line from the mountain, grabbed something, and immediately began walking back. They didn't really look comparable to insects though. More like misshapen centaurs that combined an oversized elephant and King Kong, only with spiky scales all over. But they worked similar to ants. Daniel gave a nervous chuckle. *Twenty-foot-tall ants. That's a pleasant thought.*

They cleared away the forest at a steady pace. Each of the harvesters was as powerful as a bulldozer, and there were thousands of them. The elation at coming across the creatures at work faded as he considered how much damage they were doing. Even at this distance, the air reverberated with the sounds of breaking wood, roots being ripped from the earth, and the fainter cries of terrified monkeys. Daniel felt a spasm in his stomach followed by a constant tightness as he watched.

It was somewhat of a relief when a shout came from the left. Daniel glanced around and spotted Gunny standing on his turret, pointing towards the mountain. His face looked as strained as Daniel had ever seen it. He was pointing with an exaggerated motion downward and to their left rear.

Whatever had Gunny upset must be coming from the bottom of the mountain wall. With a grunt, he levered himself out of his seat, climbed onto the turret, and trained his binoculars where Gunny pointed. The relief he'd felt was short-lived.

Tendrils of mist drifted across the base of the mountain, making it difficult to see details. Even so, he spotted what appeared to be a dark, pulsating mass flowing out of a dark crevasse in the mountain. From time to time, a misshapen dot would flash into view when it leaped high enough to be picked out from the surrounding horde. Despite the South American heat, a finger of cold traced up his spine.

Oh, my God. War demons. Thousands of them. These were the creatures that overwhelmed the Brazilian marine company. Thousands and thousands and thousands. His mind couldn't move past that for a movement. After a full minute of staring at the growing army, he shook his head. *Okay, enough of that. Time to get going.*

Lowering the binoculars, Daniel glanced over at Gunny, who gave a grim nod. Daniel nodded back while whirling his index finger over his head. "Mount up!" he yelled.

Gunny began repeating the call to mount up. Others did likewise, and in a few seconds the order echoed around the platoon. The area around the LAVs became organized chaos. In less than a minute, the Marines broke down their equipment and began scrambling into the LAVs.

While they were loading, Daniel looked for the best route to avoid the aliens at the base of the mountain. So far, the demons—and he felt sure they were war demons—hadn't started toward the recon platoon. But his gut told him that wouldn't last. Their sudden emergence couldn't be just a coincidence.

It would be best if they could just drive directly away from them. But the jungle formed a thick wall of vegetation in that direction. The LAVs wouldn't be able to weave their way through the maze of trees and fallen logs very far before being forced to stop. Or at the very least, to go so slow as to make little difference. There wasn't any option other than returning the way they came.

Daniel said into his vehicle microphone, "Fletch, once we get moving, angle toward the jungle. Run right along the edge. Stay as far away from those things as possible."

"Yes, sir."

When the last of the teams were aboard, the four LAVs turned and started back toward the Brazilian position. As before, progress was slow as the vehicles spun and slipped, fighting for traction. Traveling in the shadow of the trees at the forest's edge, they covered about half the distance when a group of several hundred demons separated from the main body and headed directly toward them.

"Crap," Daniel muttered. Apparently, whoever or whatever was giving orders to the demons had a different idea about making contact than Daniel's superiors did.

Swallowing hard, he motioned to Gunny and the other vehicle commanders to string out so their weapons would have unobstructed fields of fire. There was no telling what the creatures' objective might be, but Daniel seriously doubted it was anything good, and he had no intention of taking any chances. As the platoon formed a line, each vehicle's turret swung about to face the advancing aliens.

Daniel ducked into the turret and saw Sharon checking the feed mechanism of the 25mm chain gun that was the main armament of a LAV-25. She gave him a thumbs-up and said, "Good to go, sir." Daniel nodded and stood back up.

In addition to the chain gun, the LAV had two machine-guns—a medium one mounted coaxially alongside the main gun in the turret and a fifty-caliber mounted on top by the command hatch. The top mount could be fired from inside by remote control, but most of the vehicle commanders preferred firing them directly when practical. Only if they came under fire would they duck down and use the small screen and control stick inside the turret. Even though the Marines were from the video game generation, the gun monitors had a limited field of view that seemed claustrophobic. It was easy for a commander to focus on it and lose track of the overall situation.

Daniel kept one eye on the advancing creatures while he checked the feed on the machine-gun, making sure the ammo belt was in place and a round chambered. The other commanders did the same.

Daniel made exaggerated motions, pointing at his chest. The others nodded, understanding they were not to fire until he did. Then the platoon settled in to wait for the leaping, oddly shaped war demons to close the distance.

"Will you look at those sons of bitches move!" said Sharon over Daniel's headphones. "They must be doing forty miles an hour."

"Yeah," said Fletch. "The mud sure doesn't seem to bother them much. Do you think they're going to attack, LT?"

"Looks like it," replied Daniel. "If they keep coming in, we're not going to wait to find out. We'll open up on them at 500 meters if they don't stop."

He picked a particularly large clump of churned earth as his mark and set the gun to track on it for a reference point. *Okay, time to duck.* The Brazilians' commander, Colonel Antinasio, said the creatures began firing at his men from about three hundred meters. The colonel seemed competent enough despite the rumors, so Daniel trusted the statement. The demons were still twice that distance away, but why take chances? As he turned to signal, a clang came from the turret and something plucked his sleeve, just above his vest. It left a burning sensation behind. They were under fire!

Crap! Dropping into the turret, he scrambled to the controls for the machinegun. That spike had come from way farther than three hundred yards. Thunks, bangs, and clanks, the beginning of a hail storm of death, began rattling off the LAV's armor. No sign of any penetration, though. *Thank God for that.*

"Everyone okay?" he said into his headset. Everyone reported they were.

The crosshairs in the center of the small screen on the weapon console were still centered on the clump he'd marked. The demons were almost there, but not yet. He spared a second for a quick glance out the rear periscope.

Battle Pig Four followed them and had a blood-splattered form still outside the commander's hatch. It had to be Sergeant LaToya Washington. Blood covered her abdomen and flowed down the side of the turret. From here, he couldn't tell where she'd been hit, but it was bad. He kept expecting someone to pull her in, but she stayed slumped across her machine-gun. As he watched, her body jerked as something slammed into her.

"Oh, my God," croaked Daniel, feeling helpless. Without radios, he couldn't call the other LAV. The crew must be too focused on the demons, waiting for Daniel's signal to fire. They probably had their eyes glued to their screens.

In frustration he yelled, "What the hell are you doing over there! Get her in, get her in!" No use. They must not even know she wasn't inside.

The gun monitor screen caught his attention. The demons charged past his mark and were closing at terrifying speed. Daniel's head twitched back and forth for a second in indecision and then settled on the weapon screen. *Now! We have to fire now!*

He grabbed the pistol grip control beside the screen and pressed the firing button. The machine-gun above erupted with a muffled popping roar that sent vibrations through the steel turret. When the auto tracker ID'd a target, it would highlight it for human input. With a touch of the fire button, the gun would lock it in memory, track it, and fire in order of selection. With practiced hands, the cursor flowed across the screen, fast, smooth, and accurate. Tap, the system locked on a demon. Tap, Tap, Tap, and the gun above fired the first burst while Daniel locked in the next three targets. A killing machine for the video game-age.

There was no point in picking more targets; it took the gun time to identify the specified demon in the shifting mass and swing to engage. Deadly, but slow. Too damn slow. Against human attackers who tried to hide and take cover, the system was without peer. Against this strange, alien charge, the precision killing wasn't as effective.

The demons were less than two hundred meters away as the line of Marine LAVs poured out streams of fire and steel to meet them. The chatter from his gun was augmented by the pom, pom, pom of the autocannon chain gun. Each shot from the 25mm cannon sent an explosive shell into the mass of charging monsters. From below came the chatter of battle rifles as the Marines in the troop compartment opened fire through the side gun ports. Acrid smelling smoke filled the cabin.

To hell with individual targeting, the damn things were too close to miss. He turned off the auto tracker and began sweeping the gun back and forth across the front ranks of demons. The other commanders followed his lead and the effect was telling. The combined fire from the Battle Pigs smashed into the aliens, grinding their charge to a halt, but only for a few moments. Then the demons scattered left and right with bounding leaps, making them more difficult targets.

The sound of impacts on the hull swelled suddenly, startling him. The creatures must be concentrating their fire on his LAV. He swiveled his head about anxiously, expecting to see a hole appear in the turret any second, but the armor held. However, a scream of agony came from the compartment below as a bolt flew in through an open gun port.

Then the sound of impacts abruptly stopped as the demons swarmed onto the LAVs and began bashing at the vehicles with their claws. The LAVs lurched from side to side as other war demons tried to flip the wallowing vehicles by throwing themselves under the wheels.

They were now too close to shoot. Dark shapes moved across Daniel's vision screen; a glimpse of a claw or oddly shaped leg were all he could make out as the creatures clambered over his vehicle.

Despite the microphone, Daniel yelled needlessly over the din. "Sharon! Swing the turret around and see if you can use the coaxial to clear them off the other LAVs."

Sharon nodded and swung the turret to face the vehicle behind them. Daniel saw with relief LaToya's body had been pulled inside and the hatch was shut. Sighting back at the trailing LAV, Sharon fired off a burst from the medium machine-gun. A demon twitched and fell away from the score now swarming over the other vehicle. She began picking off more of the creatures with carefully aimed fire. Daniel didn't dare use the fifty-cal to clear the demons off; it might punch through the thin armor on the side of the turret. He tried to target those beside it instead.

Two dark shapes flashed by Daniel's screen. Then his gun monitor jumped, and he lost sight of the other LAV. His screen now showed nothing but blue sky. A moment later, the whole turret lurched violently with a metallic groan, sending Sharon flying sideways. Her helmet bounced off the armor with a clunk, and she grunted in pain. Daniel was also tossed about as the turret began jerking back and forth, the rotation system moaning in protest.

"Son of a bitch!" yelled Sharon as she grabbed the breech of the chain gun for support. "They're going to fry the motor."

Daniel's screen became a blur of frenzied motion. Despite seeing nothing but sky, he began firing randomly in the hope of driving off the demons. But the bullets flew off harmlessly into the orange wasteland. A metallic screech came from above. His screen went blank and the weapon refused to fire anymore. As the turret continued its wild gyrations, he and Sharon could only cling to their seats and pray.

A different, more rhythmic series of metallic thumps clanged on the turret, and the motion suddenly stopped. Sharon and Daniel looked at each other in surprise.

"Get on the coax," said Daniel excitedly. "Get 'em off the other LAVs."

The young woman nodded and grabbed for the machine-gun grip. "It's Gunny, sir! He pulled up beside us, and the guys in the troop compartment took out those bastards."

"Let's return the favor, Sharon. Keep pouring it on."

Sharon got off a few shots before three more war demons leapt up and grabbed the long barrel of the chain gun.

"Hang on!" yelled Daniel as the turret began lurching back and forth again. "Crap!" How were they going to get rid of these things?

Smoke swirled through the cabin as the battle raged, and his eyes and throat started to burn. Another scream came from below as a demon spike found a target. More clangs rang across the turret, and again the motion stopped. Sharon leapt back to the gun, but now the turret moved very sluggishly. The rotation and elevation systems hadn't been designed for the kind of abuse they'd just taken.

"Damn it," she yelled, slapping her palm against the gun. "I can't get it to come around." Cursing, she continued to work at the turret controls, getting mechanical groans from the drive motor and gearbox in response.

With his video out, Daniel looked through the periscopes mounted around the command hatch. The next LAV in line had nine demons scrambling over it, smashing at it with their claws or rising up to fire their spike weapons. Three of the creatures industriously jerked the turret back and forth. The large vehicle lurched sideways and tilted precariously for a moment as more of the demons tried to lift if from underneath. The driver barely averted disaster by jerking the wheels back and forth, and sent the LAV crashing back down on all eight wheels.

From below came the stuttering roar of the platoon's machine-gun firing through the rear port. The creatures grasping the other LAV's chain gun jerked as purplish fluid erupted from their scaly backs before tumbling off the LAV onto the ground.

"All right!" he cried, slamming his fist onto the console in excitement. Someone below was thinking.

With its machine-gun free, the other LAV began firing at Daniel's vehicle. He ducked reflexively as bullets clattered and whined off the turret, adding to the bangs, clunks, and scrapes already threatening him with major hearing loss.

With a grinding pop, the turret suddenly turned smoothly. "Frickin' A!" shouted Sharon. Seconds later, she fired off a burst at the other LAV.

With the LAVs supporting each other, the number of attacking demons thinned quickly. Daniel could not believe his troops were actually shooting at one another, but it seemed to be working.

Suddenly the pounding stopped. Daniel saw the remaining demons leaping off the LAV behind them and bounding back toward the mountain. When he believed they were far enough away, he cautiously opened his hatch and saw that fewer than thirty survived the fight. A few bursts of fire erupted from some of the LAV chain guns, sending streams of cannon shells after them, to no effect. Then, only the sound of laboring motors could be heard.

Looking back down the line of LAVs, Daniel saw they were covered in dents, broken equipment, and purplish splatters of demon blood. More than a few had dead war demons draped on them. But all his Pigs were still there, continuing their wallowing gait over the muddy ground.

From the screams he heard earlier, he was certain there were casualties to tend to. But his command had survived the attack, that was the main thing. He sighed and wiped sweat from his face. They would have to tend to the wounded as best they could while on the move. There was no way he was stopping until they got back to base.

Off to the right, framed by the menacing white mountain, was Death Pig Three. Gunny stood in the commander hatch, looking up at the towering peak and shaking his head. After a moment, he turned and his eyes locked on Daniel. He smiled and held up his right index finger and then thrust it into his palm.

The stick poked and didn't break. That's what Gunny was signaling. Daniel gave him a thumbs-up.

Lifting his binoculars, he zeroed in on the base of the mountain. The rising sun had burned off most of the mist. The large, dark split in the side of the mountain where the demons emerged could be seen better now. The light revealed more war demons sitting motionless in front of the sheer walls at the base of the mountain. Thousands…tens of thousands sat there, seemingly content to ignore the lumbering LAVs.

One dead for sure. He prayed they hadn't lost anyone else. Was it worth it? They proved the LAVs could stand up to a demon assault. It didn't sound like much. Not worth Sergeant Washington's life. At least, not to him. But higher ups put a different value on information than grunts in the field. It was the reason there were scouts. Sometimes good people got hurt; sometimes they died.

Please God, let something we did today do some good.

The White Mountains were part of something bigger than any of them, anyway. Some said they were a miracle and others a sign of Armageddon. The science folks said they were aliens, but the awe-inspiring scale of the towering mountains still gave one pause.

Why in the hell did they attack us? And why with so few?

Those questions were way above his pay grade. He had a feeling a lot more people would die before this was over. With a sigh, he ducked back inside the lumbering, sliding LAV to check on his people. It was best to let the brass worry about the motivations of the demons; he had enough on his hands for now.

20 Sally, the Reporter, and News from Manaus

Paul stepped through the mosquito netting that served as a door for the Big Tent. His entrance caught Sally's eye. It made her happy and nervous at the same time. Yesterday, she wouldn't have given it a second thought. Funny how one little conversation could make life more complicated.

He blinked as his vision adjusted after the bright noon sun outside. He spotted her eating lunch and said, "Hey, Sally. Thought you'd be here. There's someone to see you."

"Expecting company?" Dr. Allen said from across the table.

Sally shrugged and then remembered that she was. "Oh yeah. A reported asked to see me last night after the speech. But I had that wonderful meeting with von Jaeger and forgot. I told her to come by today."

Dr. Jane Powers and Dr. Sandra Birkheuer were at the table with them. Both frowned in disapproval at the mention of the general. "I can't believe he banned you from the camp," said Dr. Powers. "The man must have a screw loose."

Dr. Birkheuer, whose English was improving daily from working with the Americans said, "Screw loose? Mean crazy. Yes? He worse dan dat. He evil."

Paul looked impatient. "Well, what should I tell this lady?"

Sally glanced around the table and said, "Just send her in." To the others she said, "Is that okay? She said she just had a few questions." They nodded, and Paul ducked back out of the tent.

The reporter followed Paul into the Big Tent, glanced around, spotted Sally, and nodded. She wore far more sensible clothing than she had the night before—green shorts, a brown bush shirt, and a wide brown felt hat. Except for the hat, her clothes looked much the same as the scientists around the table. Her chestnut-brown hair trailed out from under the hat in a tight braid. Regardless, she was still a striking woman. Trailing behind was her producer. The man was handsome enough but seemed to fade into the background. Sally wondered if that was the mark of a good support person for such an obviously dynamic lady.

"Hi," said Dagmar. "Thanks for agreeing to see me."

"Sure," Sally said and made introductions. "Do you mind if I finish lunch? We got behind in the lab."

"Certainly, please do." The reporter and her producer sat down. "Did you hear about the battle?" Dagmar said. The shocked expressions of the people around the table provided answer enough. "Some American recon vehicles got into a firefight with the demons."

"What!" Dr. Allen said, then shot a guilty look toward Sally. He obviously remembered his request for samples to Colonel Ames a few days ago.

The reporter nodded. "It sounds like a major victory. General von Jaeger made a statement saying our fear of the creatures are overblown. Scores of demons were killed with only one fatality. Several Americans were wounded, though." She looked at Dr. Allen. "They recovered a lot of demon bodies as well. I heard your team needed more specimens to work on."

Dr. Allen looked sick. "Someone died getting samples?"

Dagmar looked confused. "Not getting samples, not really. According to the official news release, the patrol was sent out to take pictures of the harvesters at work. Also, to help update data for the new navigation system. The demons attacked them on the way back to base."

Allen didn't seem to take much comfort from this. With a guilty look at Sally, he said, "Excuse me, I…I have to take care of something." He stood, threw away what remained of his lunch, and hurried out of tent.

"Was it something I said?" Dagmar asked, the skin around eyes wrinkling in concern.

"No," Paul said. "Don't worry about him. He's a very busy man."

"So, what did you want to talk about?" Sally said.

"Several things, really. I want to know more about what led you to being in the jungle, the work your team is doing and..." Her blue eyes bore into Paul with a smoldering look. Paul's eyes widened slightly. "I want to know what inspired you to come up with the navigation idea. From what I've been told, it's genius. And it will be invaluable in the fight against the aliens."

Paul looked uncomfortable and for some reason looked at Sally. *He's worried I'll be jealous. Am I? Maybe. A little.* One more thing to think about.

"But first, have you seen the latest from Manaus?" she said, pulling out one of the thick, legal-sized newspapers. "The world is going nuts. And there's a story about the boy you rescued from the demons too."

"I heard about the story last night, but I haven't read it." Sally gestured toward the paper and said with a smile, "It seems like you're bringing more news than you're collecting."

"Well, I'm in the information game. I find that if you give in good faith, you often receive the same."

Dagmar spread the paper on the table and everyone crowded around it. It was an English version of the same newspaper they saw before the fire. This one had yesterday's date, and the top story was the crisis in the China Sea brewing between China and the United States along with Taiwan, South Korea, and Japan. This really upset Sally. Not only were a bunch of asshole politicians using the crisis in the Amazon as an excuse to promote their own agenda, but the fact that an alien horde was rampaging through the rainforest was not even the top story. Not by a longshot. Some of the other headlines were pretty disturbing, though.

Big City Food Shortages Grow Critical

Drivers Desperately Sought for Defunct Self-Driving Vehicles

Paul tapped on the story. "Yeah, with GPS out, most automated vehicles would be screwed. The delivery services must have been trashed. What a mess."

Dr. Powers pointed to the next headline. "Is this like those nuts we have here?"

Mountain Worshippers Claim Responsibility for Attack on Vatican

"Who knows?" said Sally. "Regardless, these folks seem more and more dangerous."

Paul pointed to a picture of a young man with a prosthetic leg working with someone wearing scrubs. "Carlosa Bustani Recovering from Ordeal in Forest," he read. "Is that the boy you saved?"

Sally nodded. It was great to see him doing well, if having your leg amputated could be considered as such. A beaming, older woman who looked a lot like Carlosa stood nearby. Probably his mother. Sally smiled, feeling warm inside. It made her proud that she'd helped save the boy.

"You weren't kidding about the world going nuts," said Paul. "Well, nothing we can do about it here." He looked at Dagmar shyly. "So, what did you want to know about the navigation system?"

Again, Sally felt a slight, odd sense of jealousy mixed with humor. What did she really feel for Paul anyway? No doubt she cared about him. But as a lover, or more as a brother? Of all the crazy times for such thoughts and feelings to come up. Just biology, she supposed, although she wanted to believe the affairs of the heart went deeper than that. The whole girl-boy thing was just so complicated. She shoved the feelings aside. It would work itself out over time, one way or another.

"Oh, before I forget," Dagmar said. "Colonel Antinasio asked me to give you this." She handed Sally a small envelope.

Sally frowned and opened it. Inside was a handwritten note inviting her to a celebration dinner with Marcus and some of his men. The note went on to say she should feel free to invite two others if she would like. The final line said not to worry about being banned from base, that PBG-31 would handle that.

Sally read the note to Paul, who looked as surprised as she felt. "So, what do you think?" she said. "Want to come along? If Sergeant Lupe cooks, it should be pretty good."

He looked thoughtful and then nodded. "Maybe. If I can get my hands on one of those translator apps the Marines were using at your speech. It would be good to understand a little more of what's being said."

"Good idea. See if you can get two of them. I'd like to invite Dr. Allen." She folded the paper and pondered what the, 'PBG-31 would handle it,' line meant. Were they going to sneak her on base? Also, the note didn't specify what they were celebrating. *Oh well.* Good food was reason enough to go. The stuff they had here was okay, but a bit bland.

"Will you be seeing the colonel anytime soon?" Sally said to Dagmar.

The reporter nodded. "Yes, that's why I agreed to play messenger. I have an interview with him in the morning."

"Great," Sally said. "If you don't mind, would you let him know that I'll attend. And possibly Paul and Dr. Allen as well."

Dagmar nodded. "My pleasure." Then she turned to Paul said, "Now. About this navigation system."

21 Nelino and the Monkeys

Three days and nights in the rainforest with no tent, no ground cloth, and no netting led to a lot of insect bites. Nelino only had a few more squirts of bug repellent left, and then he would really start getting eaten alive. Food concentrates were running low, so they were on half rations and he was constantly hungry. Every suspicious shadow or strange sound, which pretty much described every aspect of the rainforest, made him flinch and kept his nerves wire taut. To top it off, the lack of sleep turned his eyelids into extra grit sandpaper. Ah, the joys of roughing it in the Amazon.

However, despite the bugs, hunger, and constant plodding through God-awful country, he felt they were doing pretty well. They hadn't seen any more demons, and they were still alive. All things considered, being alive made up for the other stuff.

The best part was they should reach the Jauaperi River sometime tomorrow. If Petty Officer Lisboa and Jobim made it back to base with the wounded, and pray to God they had, then with luck they'd spot a patrol boat. Thoughts of taking a hot shower, getting into clean clothes, and using an actual toilet nearly replaced his desire to see his wife and kids. Not quite, but almost.

This little adventure certainly reaffirmed his career choice. Life on a boat was far better than running around the forest on foot. And while the special forces men were better trained for this than he and Gasquey, they looked pretty worn out themselves. No amount of training could make such conditions easy, no matter how much pride they took in it.

"Okay, let's stop here and eat," Araujo said with a wave of his hand. The command interrupted Nelino's fantasies of family, fresh clothes, and a comfortable bowel movement. Not that he minded. Sitting for a bit sounded really good about now.

Nelino picked a log from some fallen forest giant that didn't look too rotten, sat down, and pulled out half a granola bar to chew on. He suppressed an urge to take his boots off. His poor toes squished every time he wiggled them. But early attempts to soothe them had taught him it didn't really help. There was nothing to dry his feet with and putting sodden socks and wet boots back on felt worse than just leaving them on to begin with. *Ahhh, dry socks.* He bit his abused bottom lip and nodded. Something else to fantasize about.

Gasquey sat down next to him and dug out a small packet of trail mix. Seeing it made Nelino's mouth water. Damn, a stupid bag found in any vending machine, something he wouldn't even consider buying on an ordinary day, now had the appeal of a prime steak.

"Tomorrow? Don't you think?" she asked.

Nelino nodded as he finished the last nibble of granola. "Yeah. And dear Lord, am I ready to get back on a boat."

"Uh huh," she grunted in agreement.

There was little talking and what there was took place in hushed tones. The forest seemed muted as well, like the animal life was sparse in this region, or hiding. This made him nervous. Had the animals cleared out because of the demons? It would be a wise move, but surprising if they'd developed a fear of them so fast. A lot of animals in the Amazon clung to their territory right until a bulldozer cleared the land out from under them, a sadly familiar sight when one spent as much time chasing down illegal loggers in the backcountry as he had.

The few conversations underway came to an abrupt halt when Araujo held up his hand and went, "Shh." Everyone froze, listening with the ears of the hunted.

A soft swishing came from the east, something odd moving through the jungle. *Is there a hint of clicking to the sound? God. please let it be the wind.* Maybe the clicking was just branches knocking together. Nelino looked overhead at the soaked and dripping tree limbs. *Not bloody likely.* A cold tingle ran up his back.

Araujo's head snapped around, and he stared into the depths of the forest intently. After a few seconds, he leapt to his feet with the quickness of a jaguar.

"Time to move, people!" he barked in a hoarse whisper. After a quick look around to orientate himself, he pointed. "That way, fast-travel."

Gasquey crammed the last of her trail mix into her mouth. Not even a mysterious threat could dampen her hunger. Despite his fear, Nelino wished he had some trail mix himself. He feared he might need the energy. Within seconds, the group was rushing through the twisted confines of the forest like eels around fallen logs, over three-foot-tall roots, and dodging thorny vines. Before this adventure, Nelino could never have imagined moving through the jungle so quickly. Still, the clicking rustle sound gained on them. It was as if they were running from the wind.

"What is it?" Gasquey panted softly.

Nelino shook his head. "Something bad. Probably those damn scout demons."

"Oh, Lord," she said, and put on a burst of speed. Impressive. She was one fit sailor. Of course, part of her speed no doubt came from being scared shitless. Well, he was scared too and managed to pick up his own pace.

It took a lot of focus to fast-travel through the forest. The special forces were trained for it. While the group traveled, they had tried with some success to teach the basic techniques to Nelino and Gasquey. Run, leap, twist, and jump over logs and various obstacles spread across on the forest floor. It wasn't so much running as hurdles mixed with a weird dance.

Gasquey mimicked the movements of the special forces men with smooth, athletic grace. Nelino did better than he could have imagined. He'd done fairly well at keeping up during the march. But now, with everyone running for their lives, he fell behind.

Whatever nightmare behind them was making the clicking sounds, it gained steadily on him. At this rate, he'd be the first to learn what it was. An honor he would gladly forego, as it would most likely mean his death. But then, that was the luck of the draw, wasn't it? The rule of the jungle. Run slow, be the first to die.

The worst thing about dying would be never seeing his wife and kids again. They'd had such big plans for the future. Now she'd have to do them without him. *Camila, my dear Camila. I'm trying. Dear God, please understand how hard I tried.*

Someone screamed, either in agony or fear a short distance ahead of him. *Ahead? No, it couldn't be.* Another scream, then shots rang out from the same direction. What the hell is going on? The clicking sound now came from all around. *Had they been chased into a trap?*

A misshapen object dropped to the ground in front of him—a shadowy shape the size of a badger with a ridiculous number of legs and scaly skin. It landed with a soft thud directly in his path and promptly scurried toward him. Nelino jumped over it with a dexterity born of desperation. One of the creature's arms lashed out at his leg. It was tipped with a three-inch-long claw that cut a slash in his pants. Then he was over it and left the small deadly creature behind, at least for the moment.

Araujo's voice echoed out of the trees. "Run, run for the river!"

Despite his fear, Nelino paused to look around, trying to determine which way to go. With the others out of sight, he'd lost his bearings. *Which way is that damn sound coming from?* Everywhere, it seemed. He fumbled out his tablet with nervous hands and glanced at it. The device determined his location and gave him the direction to the river. *That way! To the south.* For a moment, he almost dropped the precious tablet, but managed to jam it back into its case on his belt as he stumbled along. Then he got back into fast-travel mode and picked up speed.

Unaware he was doing so, he began encouraging himself under his breath. "Run, run like a deer," he gasped in a half-whispered. "For... your wife, for...your kids."

A movie stunt double would have gawked at the moves the short and somewhat stocky Nelino pulled off rushing headlong through the forest. A hand on a waist high log, and he vaulted over it. Then reacting before he could think, he pivoted, jumped, and partly flipped over a buttress root that reached nearly to his chest. That led to a dive and roll under some vines and back up in an instant, sprinting flat out.

How the hell did I do that? It doesn't matter. Run.

It couldn't last. Nelino wasn't fit enough, not for this level of exertion. Few in the world were that fit. A small root got him. After a leap and a spin, a move he would never attempt in any other situation, his foot came down on a long, snaky kapok root, and twisted. Pain shot through his ankle and he tumbled, falling hard. Mud, and moss, and luck kept him from breaking an arm or rib. *Get up,* his heart cried. *You've got to run. Run.*

His abused body refused to obey, and not just because of the ankle, which was bad enough. There comes a point where a person's reserves come to an end. He'd reached that point. He sometimes wondered how far someone could push themselves. Now he knew. *I want to live, to go home.* But his body said, *Sorry. No more. Done in. Time to rest.* But to rest was to die. *I don't want to die.* He began to crawl. It was all he could do, but it beat just lying in the mud waiting for the end.

The small root that tripped him continued to rise out of the ground and became part of a fifteen-foot-tall buttress root at its host tree. It joined a dozen others to make a small fort of living wood at the base of a towering kapok. This tree had more big buttress roots than most, telling him this was a huge and ancient tree.

Nelino dragged himself between two of the largest roots and found a space where they flared in such a way to make a good hiding spot. He braced his back against the tree and pointed the rifle back the way he'd come. The shadows in the maze of curved wooden walls felt comfortably safe. An illusion. The clicking noise was close and getting closer.

All the sounds from his companions stopped. No more screaming, no more shooting. The only sound he could hear was the strange clicking and rustling. Now that he stopped moving, it seemed to come from his left somewhere. *Did everyone else die? Who screamed?* He hoped it was one of the special forces men and not Gasquey. Not that he'd wish harm on any of them. But she'd been a friend for a long time.

He clutched the gold cross his wife gave him when Saline, their first child, came into the world. During her labor, his wife had hidden it in her hand. A few moments after Saline's birth, she gave it to him saying, "You're a father now. This is for guidance on how to be a good one and protection so you can be." He'd worn it ever since.

A screeching bark came from close by. The shrill yet gruff sound made him jump. It came from overhead and to his right. He craned his neck around, fearfully expecting to see some new horror already in the tree. But no, not a horror, a monkey.

Is that a spider monkey? Spider monkeys were pretty common, but this one's call sounded different. Its voice was deeper in timbre than he would expect. It sat on one of the lower branches, dividing its attention between him and the approaching rustling and clicking. In addition to having a lower voice, the monkey appeared considerably larger than usual as well. The light gray fur was different too. A new subspecies maybe? The rainforest hid many secrets. Could this be a previously undiscovered type of primate?

"Hey! Run, you stupid monkey," he said as loud as he could in a horse half-whisper.

The monkey stared at him for a moment, then back at the approaching sound. Nelino felt both stupid for trying to warn it and sorry that it didn't understand. *Is that a baby on its back?* Yes, a small fuzzy head poked up and looked quizzically over her shoulder. A mama monkey, then.

Wait, beyond it was another, even larger one sitting on the same branch. Then he spotted several more above the first two. Must be a whole troop. All of them bigger than usual. These were similar to the white-cheeked spider monkeys typical of the region. Like spider monkeys, these had the odd, seemingly stretched out arms and legs with an extra-long prehensile tail. Their size and gray color set them apart, though. They appeared at least twice as big as any he'd ever seen before.

After seeing the first few, he got better at spotting them. Spider monkeys tended to travel in groups of thirty or so. However, way more than that occupied the tree above. He noticed more in several of the trees nearby. There had to be several hundred on the branches around him.

My God, I've never seen so many together. Why? Foraging for food for such a large group must be tough. The one with the baby emitted another chittering howl, and the others began answering. It fast became a deafening chorus.

Wait, did the mama monkey have a rock? Yes, she indeed held a rock firmly in her right hand. The larger one beyond her carried a thick stick like it was a club. In fact, all the monkeys he could see held rocks or sticks. Spider monkeys were quite intelligent and known to use small sticks to fish for bugs, or to scratch themselves. But these seemed to be carried as weapons. *Are they here to fight?* Surely not… And yet...?

The thought sent a chill through him, both from wonder and fear. Not fear for himself—it was plain their rage wasn't directed at him—but fear for the monkeys. These appeared to truly be an undiscovered subspecies and must be incredibly rare, despite the size of the group around him. Had they banded together to defend their home? He'd lived in the Amazon his entire life, and never heard of any kind of monkey behaving this way. But as crazy as the thought was, it appeared to be true. This made Nelino very sad. Because if that was the case, they would most likely be slaughtered. Poor, stupid, brave monkeys.

The approaching noise grew louder, sounding like a clicking wave flowing through the treetops. There must be thousands of scout demons, if that was indeed what made the sound. Whatever they were had boxed them in from two sides. He felt sure it had to be scouts…or something worse.

The monkeys went into a frenzy, screaming and bashing their sticks and rocks against the broad limbs of the kapok tree. The sound was primitive and loud. A sound of defiance signaling their willingness to defend their home.

Nelino pressed his back against the trunk and clutched the little cross white-knuckle tight. Fear seemed like such a puny word to describe how he felt. Plus, it was only one component in a torrid mix swirling through his soul. Despite the fear, he felt proud of the monkeys. It seemed unlikely they stood a chance. But still, they demonstrated something noble in what they were trying to do.

A host of dark, multi-legged shapes flowed onto the limbs above. The monkey with the baby looked at him one last time. The eyes looked intelligent, afraid, and sad. She knew. She knew they stood no chance. Maybe he was humanizing her expression, crediting the simian face with emotions she didn't really have. But he didn't think so. She knew, but she still was going to fight. The monkey's expression hardened and turned fierce. She looked up at the approaching scouts. With one last scream, the momma monkey leapt forward, her baby clinging on for dear life. He lost sight of her after that.

All the monkeys leapt into action at nearly the same time, chasing down the large, spidery-alien scouts. The primates were in their element and swung through the trees with the same athletic grace of regular spider monkeys, despite their size. As they passed a demon, they'd smashed down at it with whatever weapon they carried.

Hitting the scouts like this appeared reasonably effective. Monkeys are very strong, and many of their blows landed with killing force, either smashing off limbs or spitting the creatures open. An ember of hope blossomed in Nelino's chest.

But sometimes a monkey would just snatch one of the scout's legs and fling it out of the tree. This didn't work so well. Unless the scout crashed into the tree trunk or large branch on the way down, they merely plopped down onto the soft loam of the jungle floor. The soft impact didn't seem to faze them, and they promptly headed back up the tree.

The ground soon became littered with the writhing, multi-legged demons. This made Nelino nervous as hell, and he pressed himself harder against the tree. Not that it did him much good. Fortunately, the demons had no interest in him at the moment. The buttress roots around him seemed to ripple from all the small, dark bodies scrambling back up it. His ember of hope cooled to stone.

The monkeys couldn't sustain their early success. Scores of demons were smashed, bitten, or flung out of the tree. But in the end, they never stood a chance. Each demon had one arm equipped with a two- to three-inch serrated claw they used with fearful efficiency. In the trees, sooner or later one of the primates would swing toward a limb covered with the aliens and had its hands slashed or fingers amputated. If they fell, they died. When one of the monkeys fell from the tree, they almost never got back up. If they did, they never made it back to the tree. The monkey's fur protected them a bit, but on the ground, they quickly got swarmed. Within minutes, the number of monkeys had been cut in half.

It took several of the demons rushing past Nelino for him to realize that this might be his one chance to get away. They seemed totally preoccupied with the battle above. Maybe they didn't see him as a threat. He almost laughed at the thought because they would be right.

With a grunt, he rolled over and forced himself onto trembling legs. Despite protesting muscles, they held him up, which was a pleasant surprise. His ankle ached, but it supported his weight. After the first few hobbling steps, he found a rhythm and picked up speed. The rifle became a makeshift crutch in places, but after a few dozen yards, it got in the way and he slung it over his shoulder. He almost tossed it aside. But the weapon provided a small sense of security. Not that he kidded himself. If the scouts came after him, he stood no better chance than the monkeys.

The screams of monkey defiance faded behind him. He feared it was more due to their dwindling numbers than the distance he'd traveled. But the rustle-click noises didn't follow. The small demons were too busy finishing off the hapless monkeys, he supposed. The thought brought a hard lump to his throat, especially thinking about the poor mamma monkey going into battle with her baby.

Dear God, why have you let these horrors loose on our world? As usual, when desperate people ask such questions, there was no answer. At least not one Nelino could understand. *Is this some kind of test?* Again, no answer. Only those who claimed to speak for God seemed to get such answers. And when such people who claimed divine knowledge shared what they heard, their answers tended to be worse than none at all.

Everything hurt…legs, back, chest, and arms. The ankle worst of all. However, he'd nearly reached the point where the pain felt like an old friend. It occurred to him that his lip hurt like hell too, and it came as no surprise that he'd bitten almost completely through it. The cute little habit his wife adored would most likely lead to a rather nasty scar. Maybe he could grow a beard to cover it. Thankfully the navy still allowed such things.

Exhaustion forced him to stop sometime in the night. He didn't bother to look at his tablet to check the time. What damn difference did it make? Fear of insects, snakes, spiders or demons couldn't keep him from falling into a hard sleep, even if only for a few hours. He roused before dawn and used the tablet to verify the direction he needed to travel. His brain felt foggy, and he checked himself three times before setting out. South by southeast.

He picked a tree, stood, and staggered toward it. Once there, he checked the tablet, picked the next tree, and moved again. Tree by tree, he staggered through the forest, amazed at each stop to still be alive. One painful step after another, he headed toward the river and his hopeful salvation.

No sounds pursued him, though memories always would. A few hours after dawn, he reached the river. In the early afternoon, he spotted a boat.

Thank you, God. I will live to see my wife and children. But the others? Gasquey? Araujo? The rest? He bit his abused lip, and more tears flowed. Sorrow and extreme stress provided plenty of motivation for tears. They would no doubt continue to flow for a long time to come.

22 David and the Plumbers

As the days went by, David needed to tighten his belt notch by notch. His stomach began to harden under the daily sit-ups, and his muscles grew bigger and became more defined. The injured shoulder still ached a bit, but improved steadily. He could now do multiple pushups and five pull-ups. It was nothing compared to what Josh could do, but better than he'd ever done in his life before being abducted.

One day before PT, he noticed his pants sagging around his waist, despite his belt being on the last notch. He went to where the new knife was kept by the cooking fire and used it to cut a hole in it. As he finished and stood up to cinch it in place, Paula's voice came from behind him. "You know, we can't call you fat boy anymore."

Startled, he looked back in surprise and saw her smiling at him. Alessandra stood beside her and held up her thumb. "Looking good," she said with a giggle. The two women walked away, headed toward the stream in the back of the cave.

His face felt very hot. "Uh…thanks," he called after them. Alessandra gave a little wave in reply and kept walking.

Looking good, am I? His head felt light. After watching the two women disappear into the shadows of the tunnel, he turned and saw Josh looking at him with a slight smile on his face.

The small smile on Josh disappeared so fast that David wondered if he'd even seen it. "What're you looking at, fat ass?" he growled. "Get ready for PT."

David jumped in surprise. It'd been a while since Josh spoke to him like that. He snatched up the shirt he wore to run and began fumbling it on. *Wait.* Did he hear a soft chuckle? He glanced at Josh, only to find him glowering back with fearful intensity. David finished dressing and hurried toward the vat room.

David tried to puzzle through what just happened. *Josh had been smiling, hadn't he?* The warm feeling generated by Paula and Alessandra faded away as they gathered in the larger chamber and began running. David forgot about the compliments, though they did come back later in pleasant dreams.

Funny thing. As much as he hated running a few weeks ago, he enjoyed it now. Or would have if not for the depressing noises coming from the vat. Even so, he learned to tune the sounds and smells out to a large extent and get into his own little world while he ran. No one lapped him anymore, not even Josh. Although, to be honest, everyone now ran at a good pace and no one got lapped.

As they finished their laps, Josh waited by the exit, still running in place. Pedro, David, Alessandra, and Paula joined him in short order. With a nod, Josh led them at double time up the tunnel. This had become the normal way for the team to go from the vat chamber to the workout area.

Josh had developed a fitness plan for each of them. David was proud the women no longer considered him to be a fat ass. It felt good to know he was making progress. He could certainly see the results of the workouts on the others. Alessandra looked like an action hero, with well-defined muscles overlaying her slender curves. Paula, who was a little on the stocky side to begin with, now looked like a power lifter. Pedro was still skinny but had gotten noticeably stronger, and his limp disappeared. David knew Josh pushed them hard to be in shape for an escape attempt. But David still couldn't see how they could get out of the vat chamber.

When they reached the gym, Josh held up his hand. "I believe it's time to change up our workouts. You're making good progress, but we need to work on developing some different skills and do a little team building."

"So, no more weight training?" Alessandra said, sounding a little disappointed.

Josh's lips twitched in a near smile. "We'll still make time for weights, but I'm scaling it back some. Not as much bulk, more strength. This requires slightly different techniques. But first, we're going to do some training in hand-to-hand combat."

"Hand-to-hand?" David asked. "I can't see my best punch being more than a bee sting to a gatherer."

Josh looked annoyed. With an obvious effort at being patient, he said, "No, but what about one of those other things you described? That bear-sized one in the forest you saw just before getting caught." Josh shrugged. "Might not help against them either, but you never know. It's good to know how to punch. Besides, we ain't training for an enemy; we're training for a situation. Basic hand-to-hand is good for flexibility and helping you think fast on your feet."

Alessandra said, "Yeah, that makes sense."

Josh had them stand in front of him in a loose half circle. Since David salvaged the dead soldier's clothes, they had a little more to choose from for the workouts. Today, Alessandra wore camouflage fatigues with a black tank top. The soldier had been small and both fit her surprisingly well. Paula and Pedro both wore men's boxers and camo short-sleeved shirts, although Pedro had to hold his boxers up with a belt of webbing and the shirt reached almost to his knees. David wore his usual shorts and a blue polo shirt. Each of them looked confused as Josh began his instructions.

"So, put your feet like this," Josh said, angling his body with his left leg ahead of the other and his knees bent in a slight crouch.

The others mimicked his stance with varying degrees of success. Pedro took up the stance with his face screwed up in an exaggerated fierce mask.

Josh's eyes swept over them and he sighed. "Well, we all gotta start somewhere."

He went around correcting their stances, then showed them how to make fists and hold their arms. Once he was satisfied, or as satisfied as he ever got, he started teaching them what he called 'forms.' It wasn't what David expected when Josh said they were going to learn hand-to-hand combat. The forms seemed closer to dancing than fighting, but Josh was in one of his no-nonsense moods, so he kept his mouth shut.

Pedro, however, kept adding his own moves once Josh set him in a form. He kept throwing crazy punches or awkward looking kicks. Josh watched with strained tolerance through several rounds of this, then went over and stood very close to him. The boy looked up with hopeful eyes tinged with unease. Josh stared at him for a moment, shook his head, and wagged his finger in the boy's face. Pedro nodded and stopped doing the comic book fight moves. He focused on each stance from there on with a laser intensity and began mimicking Josh with admirable precision.

They continued working forms for the next half hour or so. It surprised David how much effort it took to hold them and move from form to form. Finally, Josh called a halt.

"Well, not terrible for your first day, but not good either. This takes concentration and thinking in advance as I call each station out. I expect better next time," he said. "Okay, to finish out this morning, we're going to do a little team building." He pointed to a large boulder on one side of the workout area that stood almost twenty feet high. "We're going to climb that rock. The objective is to get everyone on top with only what we have on us. Alessandra, you're in charge."

She looked confused. "Me? I don't know how to get us up there."

Josh looked patient for a change. "That's the point of the exercise. To figure it out as a team. The leader doesn't need to know the answer. Your job is to lead the discussion, gather ideas, and bring some order to whatever is decided."

"So, why don't you just lead us?"

Josh shook his head. "Not this time. You're all too dependent on me as it is. I'll follow orders, but it's up to you four to come up with a plan."

Alessandra looked at Paula, who shrugged and said, "Don't worry, we'll figure it out."

Alessandra nodded and her face became more determined. "Okay. Well, let's start by going to the boulder."

Everyone looked at Josh for affirmation, but he shook his head and gestured toward Alessandra. Then he walked over and stood by the boulder.

Paula said to Alessandra, "We could get you and Pedro up pretty easy, and maybe me."

Alessandra shook her head. "But we'd never get David and Josh up there. No, we need to get Josh up first. He's the strongest. He could help pull the rest of us up. How about we start with David at the bottom and Paula on his shoulders? I can boost Josh up and he can climb up to Paula and see if he can get up on the boulder from there. But first, everyone take off your shoes."

There was a brief chorus of "Sure, OK, and why not," from the others along with a flurry of shoes being removed. Josh complied but remained steadfastly silent.

David leaned against the boulder and made a stirrup with his hands for Paula. She stepped into it and climbed up onto his shoulders. The old shoulder injury gave him a slight twinge, but not enough to be a concern.

"Okay Josh, your turn," Alessandra said.

She got down on her hands and knees in front of David, and Josh stepped up on her back. David crossed his arms to make a foot rest about chest high, grunting a little as Josh climbed up. Paula bent over slightly and locked her fingers together to form a stirrup. Using these steps, Josh managed to clamber up onto Paula's shoulders. This left Josh's outstretched hands just a few inches short of reaching the top of the boulder.

"Crap," said Paula. "Not tall enough."

"Me, me," Pedro called out, hopping up and down and waving his arms.

"Tell him we're trying to get Josh up first," Paula said.

"Josh first, yes," Pedro said. "Stand on me." The boy made a muscle with his arm. It looked pretty skinny to David.

"Josh. Do you think you could stand on Pedro?" Alessandra said.

"Maybe," he replied noncommittally. "At least for a second or two."

David's legs could feel the stress, and he wondered how Paula was holding up. Leaning against the rock took some of the strain off, but there were a lot of people on his shoulders by now. Alessandra lifted Pedro and he climbed up behind Josh, both of them now standing on Paula's shoulders. David could feel her legs quivering slightly against his head.

Pedro and Josh carefully shifted around until Pedro's knees were on Paula's shoulders. Josh climbed on top of Pedro and then jumped. The sudden leap made the other three shake and shift with a nerve-wracking swaying motion. Then the weight was gone, and Josh scrambled up onto the boulder. Pedro stood and Josh reached down and pulled him up as well. Everyone but Josh gave a slight cheer.

"You ain't got it done yet," Josh said in one of his gruff tones.

Alessandra frowned and then nodded. "Hop down, Paula," she said. As the older woman did so, Alessandra called up to Josh. "If we get David up, can you lift him the rest of the way?"

He looked around and shook his head. "The rock slopes upward going back. There's nothing to anchor to, and I'd probably slide off."

Alessandra quirked her mouth to the side in a small moue and her nose wrinkled. She glanced at the other two with raised eyebrows

David said, "How about we get Paula and you up there to help anchor him? Then maybe you guys can pull me up."

"Yeah, good idea. But I think we can improve on it," said Alessandra.

She went to the rock and braced against it. "David, you get on my shoulders, then Paula, you go on up."

David looked her slender form up and down and said, "Are you sure about this?"

She nodded and made a stirrup out of her hands. David looked dubious but did as she asked. He jumped and tried to put as little of his weight as possible on the stirrup. She grunted but held as he stood and leaned against the rock.

"Turn around to help Paula," Alessandra said between clenched teeth.

David made an awkward turn and leaned back against the rock. "Okay, Paula, now you."

Paula cocked her head to one side and gave a half shrug. She stepped onto Alessandra's hands and then, with David's help, scrambled onto his shoulders. From there, she could reach Josh, who pulled her up with ease.

"Can you hold him, Paula?" Alessandra called out.

There was a pause. Then Paula said, "I think so. There's a crevasse not too far back. Pedro can hold onto it, lock legs with me, and I'll hold Josh."

David heard Josh give a dubious grunt. "But...uh, crap, okay. But if you let go, I'll be doing a serious face plant."

In a moment, Josh reached down for David's arms. "I don't think I can pull both of you up. No leverage," he said.

"Just get a grip on David, and I'll climb up," Alessandra said.

Josh nodded, his expression neutral.

David reached up and found Josh's hands. They clasped each other's wrists firmly.

"Okay," said Josh. "Do whatever you're going to do."

"All right, here I come," she said.

Alessandra grasped David's ankles and pulled herself up, let go with one hand, and grabbed his belt. Then she slithered up, wrapping her legs around him like he was an oversized rope. In a moment, her legs wrapped around his waist and her eyes stared into his.

"Hi, there," she said in a husky, breathy voice.

"Uhh, hello," said David, his own voice a bit breathless.

"Just be a minute," she said, and kept climbing. Her chest, stomach, hips, and legs slid over his face. It made him feel strange and tingly all over. Strange, but very pleasant. A few seconds later, she called down, "Made it. Now, all together…Pull!"

David slid up the wall, the rock scraping his back, but not enough to do any serious harm. He went faster and faster and with a final surge, felt the ground slide firmly underneath him. They were all on top.

"Yayy!" yelled Pedro. The others joined in, even Josh. They danced across the top of the rock like a wild Amazonian tribe doing a jungle ritual.

After a few seconds, however, Josh held up his hand and everyone settled down.

"Well done," he said. "But there was an easier way. You guys need to discuss other options before taking on something like this in the future. Don't jump on the first idea someone comes up with."

Paula glanced at the other team members. "What do you mean?" she said, looking a bit defensive.

Josh smiled and gestured at David and Alessandra's waists, then pointed at his own.

"All three of us have belts that could have been linked together into a serviceable seven to eight-foot rope," he said. "You could have used this to help pull someone up, and it would have been a bit safer than the little climbing stunt we just did."

They looked at one another, their enthusiasm slightly subdued.

"Also," Josh continued. "Where's everybody's shoes?"

Everyone looked down in confusion. Their footwear was in a neat pile at the bottom of the rock.

"Not a deal breaker. We go barefoot half the time anyway. But you've got to think about your next move, not just the immediate objective. If this were for real, we'd have to go back for them or go on without 'em."

Alessandra's head dropped, but Josh put his hand under her chin and lifted it back up. "None of that, now. You did very well. Better than I expected for your first time." He stepped back and said, "I proclaim this exercise a success. All cheer Alessandra."

And they did.

That evening…or at least what passed for evening, Alessandra led Pedro to one side of the fire. With no clocks, their schedule tended to follow the sleep patterns of Josh more than anything else. The bluish light always stayed the same, and there were no outside indications of time. But it felt like evening to the small group, as it was the time right after their last meal of the day supper.

Pedro kept flicking his eyes over the others, then looking down and digging his foot in the sand. *He's nervous.* David didn't think it possible. The boy usually only displayed enthusiasm for any and all situations.

"Pedro's been working on something that he wants to share with the team," Alessandra said. With that, she waved her arm toward him with a flourish.

Pedro's face went from nervous to a darker shade of brown. But he stopped digging his toe in the sand, and then smiled shyly. He pulled out a piece of bamboo with holes cut in it. The boy wet his lips, put the bamboo to them, and then began to blow through it.

A beautiful and familiar melody filled the air. It sounded very familiar to David. *What is that? Bye, Bye Miss American Pie?* Sure enough, after the first refrain, Alessandra began singing. They'd been singing regularly since Josh first started whistling for them during workouts, but this was the first time with musical accompaniment. The song had been another of Sally's favorites. The music and Alessandra's contralto voice nearly brought tears to his eyes. It sounded wonderful.

After a few moments, Josh began humming along to the melody. Soon, Paula began to sing as well. It amazed David they all knew the words to old song. He joined in and their rendition sounded fantastic, at least to his ears. And what other judge mattered?

The song was both joyful and sad. The last stanza about the Father, Son, and Holy Ghost catching the last train for the coast left David with a melancholy feeling. But not in a bad way. Everyone must have felt it because they sat in silence for a long moment. Pedro cast worried glances around the campfire.

Alessandra broke it with loud clapping and said, "Bravo!" The others quickly did likewise and Pedro darkened again, but with a big smile on his face.

After a moment, he looked at Alessandra. She nodded, and he began playing an upbeat tempo melody David didn't recognize. Alessandra came up to him, curtseyed and held out her hand. David drew back in confusion.

"Dance with her, you idiot," said Josh.

"Oh," David said. He smiled and took her hand. He'd never danced before and felt stupid. But Alessandra was patient and began teaching him steps that matched the music. She must have been working with Pedro for some time.

Paula stood and held her hand out to Josh. His expression made David feel a bit better about his own confusion.

Alessandra laughed and said, "Dance with her, you idiot."

Josh cast her an angry look. But only for an instant. Then he laughed too. "Very well, my lady," he said as he stood up.

After the first few hesitant steps, the women managed to teach David and Josh some simple moves. Soon they were dancing a Brazilian jig that involved lots of twirls and spins. They danced through three songs in a row before stopping to rest. That was the excuse Josh gave, though he was the only one not out of breath. But no one objected, and they spent the next few hours teaching Pedro new tunes while whistling and singing in accompaniment.

The group sang every night now. Pedro's flute just added to the mix. The songs no doubt would have sounded terrible to an outsider. Most likely their hobbled together lyrics would drive the original composers to tears. But the songs sounded and felt good to them. In fact, if not for the fear of the gatherers hanging over them, David could almost be happy here. But the gatherers were there. And the worry over how long they had before the creatures might come for them weighed in the back of everyone's mind.

The next morning, Josh growled, "Okay, boys and girls, up and at 'em. PT in ten minutes."

Another typical day…unless it was night. Regardless, David pushed himself up and hurried back to the small cave that served as their bathroom to relieve himself. Alessandra and Paula followed him, but they went to the right side of a large boulder and David went left. No one set it up this way; they just fell into it. Made sense, he supposed. Boys on one side. Girls on the other.

When he finished, he noticed his belt was a tad looser. He'd have to cut another hole in it soon. Amazing how quickly the weight came off with a healthy diet and regular exercise. Not that the exercises Josh had them doing would be considered regular, except maybe for Green Berets or pro football teams.

Back home, his diet consisted mainly of cheeseburgers, french-fries, and Cheetos. The food he ate now was all fresh meat, fruit, and vegetables. But none of it would have been found on a typical dinner table in the United States. It consisted of monkeys, tapirs, bananas, breadfruit and such. If not for the constant fear of death from alien monsters, this place would have made a good fat camp.

Alessandra and Paula were waiting for him when he came out from around the rock. Nice of them. With no time-keeping devices, Josh's ten minutes was kind of arbitrary. It really meant you better not be the last one ready to run, or not by very much. They both smiled at him, and the three headed for the vat room together.

Josh and Pedro were waiting by the banked fire pit. Based on Josh's expression, he felt they were pushing his ten-minute time limit, but he didn't say anything. Pedro was hopping up and down like a puppy eager to go. Josh looked down at the boy and a hint of smile quirked the corners of his mouth, but as usual, it didn't last long.

Pedro bounced over to David and said, "Run wit you?"

"Sure. Pedro, you don't have to ask," David said. The boy did it every time they ran. The boy had an obvious crush on Alessandra. But he seemed to see David as a bit of a big brother. Maybe because David played dots with him the most.

"Don't?" Pedro said in a hurt voice. "No run?"

David smiled and said, "No...I mean yes. Run with me."

The boy brightened. As they ran, he liked to try out new English words Alessandra had taught him. It was often pretty comical.

They left the cave, entered the nexus of tunnels, and took the one leading to the vat chamber. Pedro said, "Check 'er titties?"

David almost stumbled in surprise. Alessandra was wearing her bra, and a pair of fatigue pants from the dead soldier's backpack. The bra was pink and made of thin material. It didn't hide much in the cool cave complex. The women had made it plain that this was Brazil and such dress was entirely appropriate and the men better not stare or make any remarks. But Pedro's question was the last thing David expected the boy to ask.

Alessandra saw his expression and giggled. To Pedro she said, "Not titties...play." To David she said, "Titties means play in his language. I taught him to play checkers last night to give dots a rest. He's taking to it really fast."

"Oh," David said, embarrassed that Alessandra knew what he'd been thinking. "Uh, okay." He said to Pedro. "After lunch?"

Pedro nodded and started to say something else, but he stopped with a funny look on his face. "*Quiie lea motti poa poah?*" he said to Alessandra.

She stopped walking with a confused look. Then she nodded. "*Quiie lea posti poa.*" She looked at the others and whispered, "Something's not right."

"What's the–?" David began, only to be cut off when Josh put his hand over David's mouth. Josh pointed to his ear while shaking his head.

"It's too quiet," whispered Paula.

They were about twenty yards or so from where the tunnel exited into the vat chamber. It was very quiet, too quiet. None of the normal squeaks, hisses, crunches, or rumbles of working machinery could be heard. After weeks of being besieged by the grisly sounds of the giant blender while they ran, the sudden silence seemed more ominous than the growl of a hungry leopard.

"Wait here," whispered Josh. He drew his pistol and crept forward. The pistol looked big even in Josh's oversized hand. David had watched him clean it and marveled at the size of the bullets, each being bigger than his thumb. But compared to the size of a gatherer, it didn't seem nearly as impressive.

Paula and Alessandra both pressed up close behind David, one on each shoulder. Even the tension coursing through his body couldn't mute the electric sensation caused by feminine bodies pressing against his back. What would have been pleasant felt strange considering the situation. He stepped forward to reduce the contact. In response, they stepped up. This prompted him to move forward again. Before David knew it, they had inched to the chamber entrance.

Josh reached the pit and looked down. Then he frowned back at them and gestured with his head toward the vat.

David edged up to the low wall with Paula, Alessandra, and Pedro. They looked down and saw a large Jatoba tree jammed behind the blades of one of the big, propeller like cutters mounted to the wall. The vat was less than a quarter full, and the material didn't have the fine milkshake consistency it normally achieved.

Josh gave a small grunt. "So, the bastards have plumbing problems."

David looked at him with puzzlement in his eyes. "Okay. But if they have plumbing problems, where's the–"

"*Ni ki la fuge! Ni ki la fuge!*" Pedro exclaimed, pointing toward the end of the conveyor, his face twisted in fear.

"Plumber," finished David. Dread filled him as his eyes followed the boy's trembling finger. A tree sitting near the end of the unmoving conveyor lurched forward, stood poised for a moment, and then toppled into the vat with a plop.

"Back to the tunnel!" Josh said in a harsh, urgent whisper. "Now!"

The others didn't hesitate. The group scrambled toward the tunnel as something moved in the shadows where the conveyor entered the chamber. As they crowded into the passageway, David saw another shape move and then a third.

Pedro clung to Josh's leg with fierce determination as occasional shivers racked his body. Josh held his pistol in one hand and stroked the back of the boy's head with the other. He said in a whisper, "They ain't gatherers. It's something different. I guess plumber fits well enough."

A rounded shape like a large beetle emerged from the shadows. It paused at the end of the conveyor as if to survey the chamber below. The creature, or plumber, was about the size of a large bear. It looked very different from the gatherers who captured him, although there were traits that made them seem related. The scales were larger and, instead of spikes, had holes from which objects protruded. The head was where it most resembled the big gatherers. Both had big eyes, no mouth, and a cluster of spiky antenna on top. It looked like a bug with six limbs, but with four legs and two arms they carried low in front. One arm ended in a large, powerful looking claw and the other in an almost delicate looking hand with four long fingers.

Alessandra and Paula huddled behind Josh at the tunnel opening. David fidgeted and craned his neck to look over the top of them. He wanted to run, but to where?

"Shoot, shoot it!" Alessandra screamed suddenly, no doubt remembering the horror of seeing her family dragged away from the church.

"Quiet!" hissed Josh. "If I shoot, it could bring a whole damn army down on us. Just be quiet and watch. If it comes this way, we'll run down the tunnel."

David said, "Shouldn't we hide? Go back to the cave?"

Josh shook his head. "If we saw them, they probably saw us. Even if we could hide," he pointed at the vat, "we'd have to come back here for food. Plus, that conveyor opening is the only way out. Now be quiet!"

The creatures showed no interest in them. They didn't react to the humans at all. One of the plumbers descended on a slender white cord from the conveyor until it was even with the catwalk. Then it flipped another line ending in a four-sided hook, much like their fishing grapples, over the low wall and pulled itself over to the side. A few seconds later, it scrambled onto the walkway.

A series of crunches and cracks came from overhead as an even larger shape moved out of the shadows. There was no problem identifying this one. One of the twenty-foot-tall, spike-covered gatherers walked ponderously down the conveyor and stopped. The two plumbers worked around it for a moment and then the gatherer stepped off the conveyor. It dropped a short distance and jerked to a stop, suspended by several white cords. Then the monster slowly lowered out of sight into the pit.

Were two plumbers strong enough to winch it down? That seemed unlikely but who could know? The gatherer had to weigh ten tons or more. This made David think there might be more aliens up in the shadows.

Alessandra started to shiver and whimpered quietly. Paula held her and cooed soothing sounds. David fully sympathized with Alessandra. It took more than a little effort not to moan himself. Seeing the fearful monster brought back a lot of very bad memories. Everyone's breathing but Josh's sounded loud and ragged as they watched the strange creatures invade their small world.

The plumber down on the walkway scuttled around to a point just above the jammed blades. It stood less than fifty paces from where they huddled in the tunnel. Josh fidgeted with his pistol but didn't raise it.

The beetle-like creature placed the bladed hook on the low wall, then climbed over and into the cauldron. After a few minutes, the other two slid down the ropes used to lower the gatherer. They disappeared below the low wall.

Josh eased Pedro off his leg and gently pushed him toward Alessandra. Then he edged forward and looked down. After a moment, David and Paula crept up beside him. Alessandra stayed in the tunnel, one hand pressed firmly to her mouth with Pedro's arms wrapped around her waist.

The plumbers' only interest was in the damaged blades. Most of the gunk in the bottom of the pit had been drained away, leaving about six inches of slime behind. The plumbers sloshed through this goop to the gatherer. It bent and scooped up two of them. With no apparent stain, it lifted one in each hand up to where the tree was jammed behind two of three blades attached to the big cutter, almost thirty feet up the wall.

Each plumber held a small, black box that emitted electric blue flashes. With each flash, pieces of the tree fell away. In a few minutes, the blades were clear. The plumbers then used a different device on the blades themselves. These also looked like boxes but emanated a constant beam in a different color bluet. Whatever the boxes were, they softened the material. After a few moments, the gatherer put down the two smaller creatures and reached out its massive arms to bend and straighten the blades.

Then the gatherer picked up the third plumber who'd remained motionless nearby and held it up in front of the cutter assembly. This one used a different gizmo that looked like a ray gun from an old science fiction movie on the blades. The ray gun thing shot out a dazzling bright red beam, too wide to be a laser, but it made David think of one nonetheless. It played the beam up and down the straightened blades for several minutes. Then the beam stopped and gatherer put the plumber down.

The big gatherer made a fist and smashed it into the material. No longer soft, it emitted a metallic boom. Evidently this meant it was fixed, since all three plumbers went back to their ropes.

Josh shooed his small flock back to the tunnel. The plumbers scrambled up their lines, went back to the conveyor, and disappeared from sight. The large gatherer stayed in the pit.

This time, the five of them crept forward as a group to the edge of the vat and looked down. The gatherer stood motionless in the muck at the bottom.

"What's it doing?" whispered Paula.

Josh shrugged and shook his head.

They fidgeted for fifteen minutes, talking in terse whispers about why the gatherer might have remained in the pit and what they should do about it. Then, with a squeal that was much quieter than before, but still loud enough to make them jump, the conveyor started back up. Trees and other debris rained down on the creature. It didn't move or show any sign of concern.

They're going to chop up one of their own?" said Paula in disbelief.

The gatherer remained motionless and emotionless, standing still as stuff piled up around it. Soon it was buried. The vat continued through its normal cycle, filling with flora and fauna from the Amazon. The viscous, sweet-smelling, syrupy fluid rose up the sides, and then, with a series of powerful lurches, the pit spun up like the giant blender it was.

"That's just too weird," said David over the roar.

"It just didn't care," said Alessandra, her eyes narrowed in confusion. "It just stood there and let itself get chopped up."

Anger flushed her features, and she turned to Josh. "I don't understand why you didn't shoot them. Now when they go back to the boss, they'll come searching for us."

Josh shrugged. "I guess that's a possibility. Of course, then I'll have lots of opportunities to shoot. I learned a long time ago that once you start pulling the trigger, things tend to take on a momentum of their own. By not shooting, I kept our options open in case they don't report us."

"Let's get away from the pit," yelled Paula. "It's hard to hear in here."

Stepping away from the wall blanketed the noise considerably.

Paula turned to Josh and asked, "Why do you think they wouldn't report us?"

"Just a hunch," replied Josh. "They didn't seem too excited to see us. If I was a maintenance worker and saw a bunch of strange creatures hanging around a machine I was working on, I would've run for help right then. These things acted pre-programmed or something."

David looked into the chamber and said, "So you think these plumbers just do maintenance; they don't care or react to anything else."

"Are you two saying those things are machines?" asked Alessandra skeptically.

"No," said David. "But they could be very specialized, like biological robots, or drones. That might explain why that one just sat there in the vat waiting to be blended."

"Like an anthill?" asked Alessandra.

David nodded. "Exactly, like an anthill. Of course, we need to learn more, but that might be sort of what they are."

Alessandra shook her head. "What difference does it make? They're still demons to me."

Josh frowned at her. "Gatherers. Not demons." Then he smiled. "It might make a big difference. The more we understand them, the better chance we have of figuring out how to get out of here."

He stepped to the tunnel mouth and looked up at the conveyor. "I sure wish they left those ropes. It's going to be tough to get up there."

Turning, he placed his hands on his hips and barked, "All right, kids, you don't get out of PT just because of a little excitement. Hop to it. And start thinking about how we can get up to that conveyor."

The rest of them looked dubiously up at the belt protruding into the chamber thirty feet above their heads. The only space where it was open was the last twenty feet, right over the middle of the vat. David traced a line from there down to the churning mass in the pit and shuddered. A fall off the end of the belt led to either a long drop to the bottom, or a short drop into a brown soupy whirlpool. Neither was a pleasant prospect.

"We can't get up there," choked David. "No way. And even if we did, we'd never be able to outrun the conveyor."

Josh looked annoyed. "Not with that attitude. You never know what you can do, but you always know what you can't do."

"Huh?" said David.

Josh just shook his head and pointed down the catwalk. "Run," he said.

David started running.

23 Sally, Marcus, and the Survivors' Dinner

The note from Marcus said Julio would pick her up in front of the Big Tent at 1900 hours. Or rather, 7:00 p.m. as she preferred to think of it. So, she stood at the designated place by the designated time.

Paul hadn't been able to get his hands on the translator app he wanted, so he and Dr. Allen decided not to come. At least, that's what Paul said. *Did Paul have something set up with Dagmar?* And why did Sally keep thinking about that? She was the one who wanted more time, and more time meant...Well, more time. So, should she expect him to just sit in his tent waiting for her to decide something? *No.* But a small part of her, the mean part, wanted exactly that. For the millionth time, she wondered why the whole girl-boy thing was so confusing. A constant storm of trials and tribulations from inside and outside your heart and head.

While she waited, she began worrying over what she wore. More silliness really, but a source of apprehension nonetheless. The invitation said casual. But what did that mean for a Brazilian marine unit in the middle of the Amazon? She'd chosen a pair of modest length shorts and a white button-up shirt—simple and cool and, in her mind, casual. But everyone had their own thoughts and their own perceptions. If only she had access to the internet, maybe it could have given her some clues. She forced these concerns from her head with her mother's old mantra, 'Oh well. What'cha going to do?'

The soft purr of an ATV was what allowed her to actually banish such crazy thoughts. Her favorite Brazilian private was at the wheel, beaming at her as usual.

"Hi, Sally," Julio said. "All ready to go, I see." He looked past her at the Big Tent. "Is anyone else coming?"

"No. Dr. Allen and Paul both had other duties." She climbed into the passenger side of the ATV. "So, what are we celebrating? Marcus...Uh, Colonel Antinasio's note wasn't very clear."

Julio's already bright smile went up a few watts in power. "All sorts of things, really. Lieutenant Pereira returned from his mission, for one thing."

Joy so strong it sent a pleasant warmth through her chest and arms. "That's wonderful. I was really worried about him. Wow. Just, wow." Nelino had been with the group of marines who met them after the battle with the demons and helped her and Julio pull Carlosa out of the jungle. He'd been missing for nearly two weeks, but now he was alive and back in camp. The happy news continued to warm her as they drove.

"Well, that's worth celebrating all by itself. But what do you mean by all sorts of things?"

"Lieutenant Viana is also back from convalescence leave," Julio said happily.

"More great news," Sally said. The warmth in her chest spread further. Jeronimo Viana was Julio's commanding officer and had led the men who rescued her along with Marcus. He'd been hurt during the battle but still managed to go get help. This celebration sounded like it would indeed be wonderful. Her concerns about clothing vanished. These men wouldn't give a damn how she dressed after what they'd been through together.

"Also," Julio said, "did you hear about the battle?"

"Um, you mean the American armored recon unit? Will there be Americans there?"

Julio nodded. "Colonel A. invited them to tell about the battle. They're supposed to have some news for you." He looked over at her from the corner of his eye, his expression suddenly sly. "There's one more thing too. A surprise."

"What?"

He shook his and said, "I can't tell you. Colonel A. will be mad that I even said as much as I have. Besides, here we are."

"Here?" Sally said in surprise. They were nowhere near the main gate. The ATV rumbled along the west side of the earth and log berm that surrounded the camp. They approached a canopy like the one she waited in before doing her presentation, only much larger. It had been erected next to the berm overlooking the river.

"Well, you know, the general banned you from the base. So, we brought the base out to you," Julio said with a chuckle.

The evening was warm, with low humidity by Amazon standards. Julio parked a short distance away from the canopy, and Sally could see perhaps twenty people inside through the netting. Lieutenant Nelino Pereira and some people she didn't know were entering the pavilion-like tent ahead of them. As they dismounted, a Humvee pulled up nearby and Colonel Ames, Lieutenant Johnson, and Warrant Officer Webb climbed out.

"Why hello, Sally," Colonel Ames said with a warm smile. The Marines began walking alongside them toward the canopy. "Big night, eh?"

"Sounds like it," she replied. To Lieutenant Johnson she said, "I heard you had a firefight with the aliens."

The young officer nodded gravely. "Indeed," he said. "Now I understand why people started calling them demons. If I hadn't seen a presentation on the telemetry data, I'd be inclined to see them that way myself."

"There's been some discussion on calling them something different," Colonel Ames said. "But the news outlets in the region have started calling them that, so I guess the name's stuck." She looked at Lieutenant Johnson. "Sounds like it might fit them pretty well anyway."

"I think so," said Sally. "The name of the big one fits too, harvester. I hear they have at least four columns tearing into the forest right now."

Ames nodded grimly. "And we thought humans were hard on it. We estimate they're destroying a thousand acres a day. And we still have a long way to go to get enough troops to have a decent chance to stop them. But our patrols have had some success. Lieutenant Johnson and his people got you some samples."

Sally nodded with grim eyes. "Yes, I heard. But at a cost."

"Sergeant LaToya Johnson. A good soldier, a better woman. God rest her soul," Ames said softly. Then louder, "But a higher cost for the demons. They must have lost at least a hundred."

"Damnedest thing though," Johnson said. "Only a handful came at us. At least, compared to what waited around the mountain. I don't think they were trying to take us out as much as learning what we could do."

That's a sobering thought. "Marcus mentioned something similar after our fight in the woods," said Sally. "They could've finished us off if they wanted to that day." A sigh escaped her. "One of the many disturbing aspects of the battle was that two men came up missing, despite the fight being in a rather limited area. I still hope they just ran away. Couldn't blame them if they did. But…well, most think the demons took them."

Silence settled over the small group for a moment, most glancing into the dark in the direction of the alien mountains.

"There's just so much we don't know about them," Ames said. "That's why we're counting on you and your team." She stopped suddenly and turned toward Sally. "What's this bullshit about you being banned from base?"

Sally shrugged. "General von Jaeger feels like I'm a bad influence on his men."

Ames snorted and resumed walking. "The man is a little twerp."

Sally chuckled and said, "Yes, ma'am. Actually, that's one of the nicer things I've heard said about him."

Ames laughed. "Well, I'm trying to be political." She didn't comment further as they walked the last few steps to the flap in the netting and went inside.

Nelino Pereira stood with several marines and sailors from PBG-31 just beyond the entrance. One man in the group wore fatigues slightly different from the others. Nelino caught sight of her from the corner of his eye and turned with a broad smile. "Hello, Miss Morgan. It's good to see you again."

She gave him a quick hug and said, "You too. Please, call me Sally." After a quick, appraising look at the Brazilian sailor, she said, "My, you've lost weight. And I see you injured your lip."

Nelino looked embarrassed. "Uh yes, my lip is my own fault from a stupid habit I'm trying to break." He gestured toward his midriff. "As for losing weight, that comes from spending a few days in the forest running for my life."

He turned to the woman and man he'd entered with. "I would

like to introduce you to Chief Petty Officer Mericea Gasquey and Sergeant Cyro de Araujo. They shared my fun experience."

She shook hands with both noncoms and said, "I've heard the patrols were encountering a lot of aliens. How…how bad was it?"

"Pretty bad. We lost some good people."

The next half hour passed in a bit of a daze. Nelino told about his experience, beginning with the loss of the first patrol boat, then about his own boat being sunk and the desperate cross-country hike with the commandos. The monkey battle fascinated and sickened her. Possibly a whole subspecies of an unknown advanced primate, wiped out. Another crime to lay at the feet of the creatures. Nelino finished with a recount of his rescue and the joy of finding four other survivors already on board, including Gasquey and Araujo.

"I'm so sorry about your people…your friends," she said, her eyes going to each of them. "But it's great to have you back. Don't be surprised if folks want you to start making presentations now."

Sergeant Araujo slowly shook his head. "No, Miss Morgan. Some of our party killed of the demons, but they didn't make it out of the forest. I only wish I had, at least one." He met her eyes and said, "I have a newfound respect for your accomplishments and will gladly work to dispel the stupid rumors about you among my comrades in the army."

The man's earnestness surprised her. "Uh, well, thank you. I wasn't aware there were stupid rumors being spread about me."

The man gave a grim smile and nodded. Before he could say anything more however, a large, dark skinned man walked up. Sally smiled up at him, and Lieutenant Jeronimo Viana smiled back. His arm was in a sling, but overall, he looked much better than the last time she'd seen him.

"Hi, Sally," he said.

She gave him a hug, which seemed to surprise the big man. It was a bit funny. Before her experience in the jungle, Sally had never been much of a hugger. Of course, she'd developed a special bond with these people.

"Jeronimo. It's great to have you back. You look great."

He smiled. "Well, considering the last time you saw me, I'd

been tossed about like a puppet by a war demon…I cannot take that as too much of a compliment."

Before they could talk more, three loud pings resonated from Colonel Antinasio tapping on his glass. Talking in the enclosure drifted to a rapid stop.

"Could everyone please take their seats?"

She made Jeronimo promise to talk to her before leaving, and he agreed.

Sergeant Lupe came up to her with a wide smile on his face. Instead of fatigues, he wore white from head to foot, including an apron and tall white chef's hat. He looked every bit the head chef of a four-star restaurant. "Miss Sally, it's so good to see you again. I believe we have your favorite tonight, I hope you like it."

"My favorite? Why…how could you possibly know that?"

The tall, slender cook nodded toward Julio. "He found out for me. It's braised steak bourgeoise with buttered asparagus and cheesy potatoes, right?"

"Oh, my Lord, yes," Sally said, dimly remembering telling Julio how much she loved steak and cheesy potatoes and how long it'd been since she'd last had it. *That little devil.* "My mouth is watering already just thinking about it," she said.

The sergeant looked very pleased. "I only hope my preparation is to your liking. Now, if you'll excuse me?" With a nod, he turned and hurried away. Sally noticed that another tent was set up behind the canopy and assumed that to be his kitchen for the evening.

Sally looked around for her seat. There was a rectangular table set up with a podium at one end of the enclosure and six round tables that filled most of the rest of the space. Placards were placed at each seat. In front of the placards was some of the fanciest china and gold dinnerware she'd ever seen. They'd really gone all out. The effort put into setting this up outside the camp touched her deeply.

"Miss Morgan. Sally. Over here."

She turned and saw Marcus gesturing to a place next to him at the podium. *On his right?* That would be the guest of honor seat. *Her?* Was this for her presentation? That really seemed a bit much. With a shrug, she headed for the seat indicated by Marcus.

All the soldiers wore standard camouflage fatigues, which eased her fears about what she was wearing. She'd seen pictures of military dress attire and knew it could be rather formal and impressive. It would have been intimidating to be amidst a roomful of people dressed like that while wearing shorts. As people took their seats, she noticed there were two other civilians present.

One was Dagmar's producer cameraman, Udo, who also wore shorts, topped by a black dress shirt. As usual, he managed to blend into the background. He moved around the tables, unobtrusively taking pictures.

Then there was Dagmar herself, who was dressed in a stunning, tight fitting, sleeveless red dress. The front was cut low and drew the eyes of every man in the canopy. Come to think of it, she managed to draw Sally's eyes as well. The reporter was a beautiful woman, tall, chestnut-brown hair, and slim in all the right places. At least Sally didn't have to worry about Paul this evening. She felt a little ashamed for feeling that way, but she couldn't help it.

Marcus greeted her with a bow and an elaborate wave toward the seat beside him, along with one of his dazzling smiles. "Welcome, Sally. So very glad you came. Sorry no one else from your team could make it."

"Too bad they didn't know there would be other people who speak English," she said with a nod toward the Marines' table. She noted it had two empty seats. "I'm sure they would've reconsidered if they had. It's confusing for them when they're the only non-Portuguese speakers. By the way, thank you so much for setting this up outside the base. I can't believe you went to all this trouble."

"Actually, Sergeant Lupe made the arrangements. The man has a magic touch that extends beyond food. I predict he will own a very successful restaurant one day. Please, have a seat. They should be ready to serve in a few minutes."

She looked at her place and then eyed him with suspicion. "So, I'm the guest of honor?"

"Ah, you noticed that, did you?" he replied with a sly smile. "Yes, you are." He held up his hand. "No questions. All will become clear after dinner."

Sally gave him a smile somewhere between bemused and tolerant as he pulled out her chair. As soon as she sat, the dinnerware before her caught her attention again. The wine glasses and water goblets were rimmed in wide gold bands. The dinner plate was gilded as well with an elaborate crest in fine gold leaf. The silverware was, well gold…goldware. White clad men began serving soup in elaborate gold-rimmed bowls.

"Wow," Sally said. "This is some really fancy dinnerware."

Marcus focused on it and his eyebrows arched slightly, as though noticing if for the first time. Before soup was placed on the plate before him, he picked it up and turned it over. "Waterford 1933," he read aloud. "Yes, this is indeed very fancy."

Soup was placed before Sally. She looked up to thank the server and saw that it was Corporal Raoul Bustani, Carlosa's brother. He beamed at her as he stepped back. "Thank you, Raoul," Sally said. "How's your brother?"

"Getting along very well, Miss Sally," he said. "The new prosthetic leg is working great."

"Wonderful," she said.

As he turned to go, Marcus said, "Corporal, please bring Sergeant Lupe out to see me when it won't interfere with dinner. Thank you."

Raoul nodded, his smile fading slightly. With another nod to Sally, he hurried toward the kitchen tent.

After a delicious French onion soup, Raoul retrieved the bowl and served a lettuce wedge with blue cheese dressing. Another of Sally's favorites. She couldn't recall ever discussing this with Julio, so maybe it was just luck. After the salad plates had been removed, the main course arrived. The steak and sides were among the best she'd ever tasted. Sergeant Lupe was indeed an amazing cook. Not long after, Raoul and Sergeant Lupe entered the canopy and headed for the main table.

"My compliments to the chef," Sally said as the two men approached. "This is the best steak bourgeoise I've ever tasted."

Lupe beamed and nodded acceptance of the compliment, then turned a worried eye on Marcus. "Raoul said you wanted to see me,

Colonel?"

"Yes. First, excellent meal. You have outdone yourself."

"Thank you, sir."

Marcus gestured toward the dinnerware, his face becoming stern. "Where exactly did you get this?"

"Um, well sir, there's a market in the civilian camp now that has pretty good prices on meat and fresh veg–."

Marcus held up his hand with another stern look. "Not the food. The plates and glasses and…" He held up a gold fork. "These."

"Well, sir," said the sergeant. "You said you wanted to celebrate, so I thought a little something special was in order."

Antinasio frowned. "Yes, that's all well and good. But it's not what I asked."

Lupe fidgeted. "Um, well sir, let's just hope General von Jaeger doesn't have any unexpected dinner plans."

"What! This is stolen from the general?"

Lupe looked crushed. "Oh, no sir. Not stolen. We merely borrowed a few things from his mess sergeant. He assured us the general wouldn't miss them. He's a friend of mine, and when I explained to him Miss Sally Morgan was coming for dinner, he insisted." He leaned in closer to Marcus and said, "Not all the army guys are assholes…sir."

Antinasio looked doubtful for a moment and then shrugged. "Well, I suppose we should finish quickly in that case." He smiled and said, "At least if we're going to the stockade, we shall have a superb dinner first."

"Yes, sir," Lupe said, obviously relieved. "Thank you, sir."

As the chef walked away, Marcus said, "I told you he had skills beyond cooking. Regardless of what he said, pray the general doesn't find out."

Sally laughed. "In a way, I almost wish he would. Not to get you in trouble. But anything that annoys that man would please me a great deal." Marcus laughed and nodded in agreement.

During the meal, Marcus talked of his family in Manaus and about the destruction to the city. The whole country was in turmoil, economically, politically and even religiously. Every facet of society was fighting one another over what the demons were, what they represented, and what to do about them. From what little his family heard about the rest of the world, Brazil wasn't alone in this regard. The most amazing thing to both him and Sally was the Russians, along with various groups worldwide, who insisted the whole thing was a hoax of some kind.

As she finished eating, he said, "If you'll excuse me." She nodded, and he picked up an unused spoon and carefully tapped it against his water goblet. The various conversations underway beneath the canopy tapered off.

"Thank you," he said. "I've asked for dessert to be delayed. Colonel Ames and her comrades must leave for a briefing with our good general and wanted to be part of our little celebration."

Webb translated this to Colonel Ames, and she said, "Thank you for your consideration, Colonel. And for this excellent meal." Webb relayed this, and a round of *viva* and *aqui* echoed around the room.

Marcus nodded in response and then said, "First, I want acknowledge and thank the U.S. Marines for being with us in this fight. I have good news. Another Marine Expeditionary Unit, the 23rd, is on the way. Due to aircraft being useless around the White Mountains, this unit has unloaded its aviation assets and is now carrying an extra load of armored vehicles. As Lieutenant Johnson and his men demonstrated, these are highly effective against the war demons."

There was a polite round of applause. "In addition, Brazil's own amphibious assault ships have cleared the Panama Canal. They will need to swap out aircraft for tanks as well, but should arrive in two weeks." Another round of clapping, including a few cheers from the marines of PBG-31 in attendance. "Other nations, most notably Australia, England, Germany, and Italy, have also promised to send forces."

Things are looking up, thought Sally. *If only that nonsense in China would settle down, maybe people would come together to face the real menace.* Something inside her questioned this, however. The world always seemed to find new ways to demonstrate that it was full of crazy people.

"Now, down to the business of the evening." He pulled out five small boxes from under the podium. "Lieutenant Viana, Lieutenant Pereira, and Private Arente. Please come front and center and stand at attention."

The three men did so at once, Julio looking apprehensive. *Ah, so he didn't know about this part.* It seemed Marcus had secrets within secrets.

"By recommendation of commanding officer Colonel Marcus Antinasio of Patrol Boat Group 31 and approved by General Juan Julis Fernando of the *Corpo de Fuzileiros Navais*, let the following be known. These men are hereby recognized to have performed as sailors and marine of distinction and exhibited outstanding leadership in performance of said duties. By this order, Senior Lieutenant Nelino Pereira is hereby promoted to captain. Lieutenant Jeronimo Viana is also hereby promoted to captain."

Applause filled the netted canopy. Sally couldn't think of any more deserving people. Maybe that special forces sergeant who Nelino said saved his life, but of course he was outside Marcus's chain of command. *I wonder if he's in hot water now due to his friendships within PBG-31?*

"In addition, Lieutenant Viana has been awarded the Blood of Brazil Medal for wounds sustained during combat with the alien creatures now designated war demons, place of origin the White Mountains, a recognized enemy of Brazil."

Marcus came around the podium and presented Nelino with one box, shook his hand and whispered into his ear. He then moved to Jeronimo and gave him three boxes, also whispering into his ear. Jeronimo nodded, stepped forward, and pivoted neatly on his heel as Marcus stepped back with a sharp, formal step.

The new captain stepped up, pivoted, and came face to face with Julio. He said, "By recommendation of his commanding officer Lieutenant Jeronimo Viana and approved by Colonel Marcus Antinasio, let it be known. Private First-Class Julio Arente is hereby promoted to corporal for recognition of outstanding bravery and leadership during battle with said war demons, an acknowledged adversary of Brazil." Jeronimo handed one of the small black boxes to the beaming and very proud young soldier.

There was another chorus of applause and handshaking all around. Marcus said, "Please be seated, gentlemen. There'll be time for more celebration later. We have more business and are working under a bit of a time limit."

Julio walked away in a slight daze while staring into the box he'd been given. He looked as if he couldn't believe what it contained. In a few moments, the three men resumed their seats.

Sally smiled broadly at the three Brazilians as they walked away. She felt very happy for them but felt puzzled about the dinner. They deserved the promotions. *So, why am I sitting in the seat for the guest of honor?*

Marcus stayed on the guest side of the head table and picked up the final box from beside the podium. He turned toward Sally and said, "Salina Isabella Morgan, would you do me the honor of standing?"

Sally blinked at the use of her official first name. No one had called her Salina since her mother died. Suddenly nervous, and not sure why, she swallowed and stood.

"Miss Salina Morgan is under contract to the government of Brazil for research into quantum biological remedies to soil issues in the Amazon Basin Region. Based upon official reports submitted by Lieutenant Jeronimo Viana, she has hereby been nominated by General Juan Julis Fernando of the Corpo de Fuzileiros Navais for special commendation. Reports submitted by Lieutenant Jeronimo Viana of same said organization have been substantiated by Private Carlos Bustani, Colonel Marcus Antinasio, and Private Julio Arente, and approved by the Joint Chiefs of Military Affairs for actions pertaining to and immediately following combat with harvester war demons, a recognized enemy of Brazil. By this order, let all men and women know that the appropriate commendation has been determined to be the Naval Medal for Distinguished Services. This is the highest award Brazil gives to non-military persons for acts of heroism above and beyond the call of duty in service to our country."

Sally stood stunned, not sure whether to smile, laugh, or run. Instead, she stayed at the table, her expression no doubt as confused as her insides. Marcus opened the box he held and pulled out a red and blue ribbon from which hung a square silver cross with a small central disc. He stepped forward and carefully placed the ribbon over her neck, leaving the metal itself dangling between her breasts. He then stepped back from her in three measured, very formal steps.

He stopped and came to ramrod straight attention. "Company...attention!" he barked. As one, everyone in the canopy stood up. She noticed Sergeant Lupe and Raoul were inside by the opening to the kitchen.

"Present...arms!" The military personnel saluted her, including the Americans. Dagmar and Ugo just stood politely and watched. "Order...Arms!" Everyone dropped the salute, and then Marcus smiled and said, "At ease. As you were."

He stepped forward and shook her hand. "Congratulations, Salina. Do you mind if I call you Salina? It just sounds, well to me, more comfortable."

She nodded, still dazed. "Marcus, I...I don't understand. There were others–"

"No," he said softly, but with enough force to cut her off. "No, there weren't, not really. You were the only civilian. You picked up a rifle, killed a demon, and saved a young man's life. So, don't say there were others." His smile broadened and his eyes grew mischievous. "Besides, you said you wanted to annoy the good general any way possible. Believe me, this really, really annoyed him."

Sally chuckled and shook her head. "Well, in that case–"

"Excuse me, sir," Nelino said. "Are you going to allow anyone else to shake her hand?"

Marcus turned with a wry expression. "I see now that you've been promoted, you're going to become insufferable. And by the way, it's even more important now to work on that lip chewing habit."

"Oh, I don't know, sir. After what I went through, I believe it might bring me luck."

Marcus laughed and turned back to Sally. "If you'll excuse me? As you can see, your fans await."

A line had indeed formed behind Nelino. It felt silly reaching across the table, so she worked her way down to the end and the line shifted accordingly. Again, time passed in a blur. The only conversation that stuck with her came with Colonel Ames.

"Congratulations, young lady," Ames said. "From what I've heard, this honor is well deserved."

"Thank you, ma'am. I wish I felt as confident as you. I just did what anyone would do. I think I just got very lucky."

"Oh, no doubt luck played a hand," she replied. "Or God, for those of us so inclined to believe such things. Regardless, it took a lot of guts to keep going in the face of one of these…monsters?" Ames said with a nod to Lieutenant Johnson at her side.

The lieutenant nodded back with a grim set to his mouth. "That fits them, ma'am. Never believed I would ever see anything like 'em."

The American colonel said, "I would like for you to come give my leadership team a briefing. Not just your story so much, though I want them to hear how you killed one of these things, but what we know so far. I'll set something up for early next week. Lieutenant Johnson here will be dropping off three of the creatures his people killed to you early tomorrow, by the way."

"I'll be glad to," Sally said. "What about General von Jaeger banning me from Brazilian bases?"

Colonel Ames snorted. "Drop your contract with the Brazilians. I know you feel a debt to these men here tonight. But things are screwed up in their upper command. I'll sign you up as an American contractor, and that'll be that."

Sally considered it. "Well, maybe. Let me discuss it with Colonel Antinasio first. As you said, I have a debt…a huge debt to him, and his men. But if I can't help them due to this thing with von Jaeger, then I'll most likely take you up on that."

"That's all I can ask for. But please try to make it to the meeting. A lot of things are in motion. For now, I'll plan on you coming. And if you don't feel that working for me is the right thing to do, I'll understand. Also, if for some reason you can't make it, let Lieutenant Johnson know when he stops by tomorrow."

Sally nodded agreement. After a final round of congratulations and goodbyes, Colonel Ames led her small procession out of the canopy. Sally sighed at their retreating backs. It was good to have options but fighting an alien invasion shouldn't be this complicated.

The celebration wound down pretty quickly after that. People had plenty to do besides engage in mutual admiration. Sergeant Lupe began directing a mixed crew of marines and sailors in breaking down the tables and chairs. By tomorrow, it would be difficult to tell a party ever took place here.

Sally and Marcus walked over to the small table set up as an open bar. Nelino and Jeronimo were already there with Julio. The two officers seemed to have taken it in their heads to get Julio drunk, a project they would no doubt regret come morning. However, instead of being a riotous endeavor, they seemed somewhat somber. Sally felt the heavy mood settle around her as well. Too many people they knew had died. From the look of things, more would likely die in the near future. A sure damper for any party.

"Colonel Ames has offered me a contract working for her," Sally said in a quiet voice. "I told her I wanted to discuss it with you before deciding."

Marcus pursed his lips and nodded. "I think you should do it. I can write something up dismissing you from your current one."

"Are you sure? I really like working with you and PBG-31. It's just...well, you know, von Jaeger and all."

Marcus snorted. "I fully understand. Besides, I believe we're going to be redeployed back to Manaus in a couple of weeks. Von Jaeger seems to feel we soil his command."

"What! You're leaving?" The news cut her deeper than she would have imagined. "I'm...I'm truly sorry to hear that."

"We're not too happy about it either, especially with a full brigade of Brazilian marines on the way."

"Well, that makes my decision an easy one. I'd appreciate it if you'd write up the contract termination." Saying it made her heart hurt, and it hurt enough already. The loss of David and her friends flooded back to her. Now she would be losing these friends as well, though at least she'd know they were safe, or as safe as anyone in a world gone insane.

They drank in silence for several long moments. "Sir," Nelino said. "May I make the toast?"

Marcus nodded, his expression a mix of grimness and sadness.

Most toasts didn't make people look like that. She wondered what to expect. Even Julio had a haunted look very uncharacteristic for the young man. The other two also wore serious faces.

Sally hadn't been drinking much, and her glass was empty. Nelino waited until she poured a small amount of wine into it, then said, "To lost friends, comrades, and brothers. May their spirits always guide us."

Marcus, Julio and Viana repeated the words. It was like a kick to Sally's heart, making it lurch in her chest. The perfect words said at the worst time to hear them. Tears cascaded down her face, which surprised her as much as the men around her.

"Oh my God," she choked. "I…I need some air. Sorry." She turned away from them and hurried out of the canopy.

Once outside, she half-walked and half-jogged toward the river. There she stopped, bent over, and gulped in air to try and stop the flood of ghosts invading her head. A few words, all it had taken were a few unexpected words. Now the demons of her soul resurged with new strength, hammering her carefully constructed defenses to dust. The heavy weight of guilt landed on her shoulders like a physical force, causing her legs to buckle. She slowly kneeled at the edge of the water as her knees gave way.

The tears became blurred visions of David and Myra with accusing faces. "I'm sorry, I'm sorry," she said to them. "I didn't want you to die. Oh God, I'm so sorry."

"Salina?" Marcus said, his voice sounding concerned and very far away. "Miss Morgan, are you okay?"

Blinking in a vain attempt to clear her tears, she looked up at him and shook her head. "No, not really." Looking out at the river, she said, "Sometimes I don't think I can take it anymore."

Antinasio didn't say anything. He came over and sat down beside her. Just having him nearby was comforting. It helped pull a few of her thoughts away from the overpowering sorrow in her heart. And the guilt. Oh God, the guilt.

"So much for being the tough, brave demon slayer," she mumbled between sobs.

A quiet, mirthless chuckle escaped him. "Not at all. In fact,

Jeronimo and I were discussing how tough you are earlier today."

"Tough? Me? I've barely been holding it together since we left the jungle. The work helps, helps a lot. But I have horrible nightmares."

Marcus handed her a clean cloth napkin. She took it with a weak smile and wiped her eyes.

He said, "We all have nightmares. But that doesn't mean you aren't tough. Did you know that of the forty-eight men who survived the battle, you, Julio, Jeronimo and I are the only ones still in camp?"

She looked up and shook her head.

Nodding he said, "Of those not physically wounded, six men had such severe anxieties, they had to be hospitalized. Many of the others are in Manaus undergoing some type of psychological therapy. Jeronimo did likewise while he was there. As for Julio and me... we spend a lot of time with the chaplain. All of us need help to cope with what we went through. So yes, you're pretty tough."

He placed his hand on her shoulder. It felt warm and soothing. "The chaplain said something to me that I didn't understand at first. But after a while, it began to make sense. He said, 'Don't let your guilt stand in the way of your grief.'"

Sally's face hardened. A spark of anger flared in her chest. She shrugged off his hand and said, "What do you know about guilt? I was responsible for my brother's and best friend's deaths. If I'd just stayed at camp, they'd be alive."

A flash of anger leaped to Antinasio's eyes for a second in response, and then he slumped. The man of iron who held together a bunch of battered survivors after a soul shattering defeat and then led them out of the jungle melted before her eyes. His head dropped between his knees, and he locked his fingers on top of his head.

"I led fifty-eight men to their deaths," he said softly. "Many of them, I knew for years. I knew most of their parents, wives, and children. I had to write...write so many letters." He looked up, tears brimming in his eyes. "So, yes, I believe I understand something about guilt."

Sally looked at him for a moment and then nodded slowly. "Yes. Yes, I guess you do." She leaned her head on his shoulder and said, "So, does this mean you're as messed up as I am?"

He gave a snort. "Maybe. But if being messed up is what you are, then I can only hope to be so."

He put his arm around her shoulders, and they both stared out at the river. After a few minutes, he straightened, rolled his neck as though working out a kink, and said, "I believe the party is pretty much over. Julio is too drunk to drive, I fear. Do you want me to take you back?"

Shame at having run out on the toast stabbed at her, but only briefly. She realized that if anyone could understand how she felt, it would be those in the tent. Warmth crept through her chest at the thought. Nodding, she pulled away from him and said, "Yes, but first let's go finish that toast. I feel I was rude."

"See? Tough as they come," Marcus said. They both stood and began walking to the canopy.

When they arrived, Julio, Nelino, and Jeronimo looked up with concern. She managed a weak smile and said, "My apologies, gentlemen. I… I just needed to get some air." Walking over to the small table, she picked up her wineglass and held it out toward them. "To lost friends, comrades, and brothers. May their spirits always guide us."

Marcus picked up his drink, and they raised their glasses to hers and then drank. As they finished, a warm glow from more than just the wine came alive and coursed through her. Realizing that she was not the only one carrying a burden of sorrow and guilt made her feel…not so alone. This was the best night she'd experienced in a long time. The powerful feeling of comradery was no substitute for losing David and Myra. But she realized that here was a band of brothers with whom she was very proud to belong.

"Gentlemen," she said. "Thank you so much for being such good friends." The genuineness in her voice both pleased and embarrassed them. They looked like shy little boys for a moment.

"The pleash-ure ish ours, Miss Sally," Julio said, his voice a bit slurred, though his tone sounded sincere enough. The others nodded in agreement.

"It's getting late," Marcus said. "I think it's time to bring the evening to a close."

"Osh-kay, I's ready go," Julio said, blinking his eyes as though trying to get them to focus.

"That's okay, corporal," Marcus said. "I'll take her. You need to get to bed."

"Uh, yesh shir," he said, still blinking his eyes too fast and looking confused.

"Don't worry, sir," Jeronimo said with a chuckle. "We'll get him to his tent. See you in the morning." He took one of Julio's arms and Nelino the other. "This way, corporal," he said. "And if you feel like throwing up, you better give us some warning."

Sally and Marcus walked to the ATV, climbed in, and headed back to the university camp. "I'm very sorry to hear you'll be leaving soon," she said.

"Me too." He looked over at her for a moment, then back at the trail. "For many reasons."

The way he said this sent a small shiver through her. There was no doubt she cared deeply for him, and he was very attractive. But was there something more here? In other circumstances... Well, that was wishful thinking. And now he was leaving, or soon would be.

"Um, Salina, I want you to know that I care very deeply for you," he said, mirroring her thoughts. "Maybe when things calm down, you could come to Manaus? I would love to show you around." He snorted softly and said, "What is left standing, that is. But it's a very beautiful city."

"I would really like that," she said. They neared the camp, and she suddenly wished the ride were longer. She took his hand, and he looked at her in surprise. "I care very much for you as well. I was thinking similar thoughts, but the timing..."

"Yes, it's very bad, isn't it?" he said. They pulled up in front of the Big Tent, and he turned and took her hand in both of his. The warmth she felt earlier turned into fire.

"Crazy, isn't it?" He said, gazing deep into her eyes. "To meet someone that might be...well, someone very special, in the middle of all this...mess."

Sally sighed and nodded. She gave his hand a final squeeze and said, "So when things calm down, we have a date, right?"

"Indeed," he said as his dazzling white smile lit up his face. "Good night."

24 David and Team Work on Escape

"So, let me get this straight," David said while warming his hands over the fire in the cave. "First we build a winch. Then we use it to haul up trees to build a framework on both sides of the vat. Then, we build a suspension bridge over the conveyor."

"What's a suspension bridge?" asked Alessandra.

"Basically, a rope bridge," said Josh. "Or more likely, probably just a rope."

"Whew, sounds like a lot of work to me," said Paula.

Josh shrugged. "Yeah, but unless someone has a better idea..."

"What about when we reach the conveyor? Won't we just get carried back into the vat?"

Josh frowned. "Well, that's a possibility. We'll deal with that once we get up there. Maybe we can disable the blades again to give us time to get away before the plumbers come."

Alessandra looked up thoughtfully. "What about those pipes and things on the ceiling? Couldn't we just build a ladder, climb up, tie off some ropes from the pipes and then do the same on the other side? Then pull the ropes up to build your bridge?"

Josh looked surprised. He tilted his head to one side for a moment and then nodded. "Well, from the mouth of babes. That would be a hell of a lot easier. Guess I was overthinking it."

"But still dangerous as hell," said David.

Paula laughed. "Like staying here is healthy? Besides, we can rig a safety harness to the rope. It should be a snap."

Alessandra looked over at the ropes they used to pull things out of the vat and shook her head. "Well, we'll need more rope, stronger rope."

"And some food and a way to carry more water too," said Josh. "No telling what we'll face once we get out of here. All right, after P.T. tomorrow, Pedro and I will work on a ladder to reach the pipes above the catwalk. You guys," he pointed to Alessandra and David, "start making rope. Paula, you work on food and a way to carry water."

Everyone nodded, even Pedro. While his English had improved a lot, he probably understood little of what was being said. He was just always proud to be part of the group.

"Once we get up to the conveyor, I'll scout around and we can figure out what we need to do to keep from getting carried back. Not much more we can do till then. Right?"

The other four looked at each other and nodded again.

"As long as we don't get any unexpected company," said Paula in a low, soft voice.

It took three days to make enough rope to span the chamber. David considered this to be pretty fast considering Alessandra had to weave three hundred feet of rope nearly an inch in diameter. Once she completed it, the group went to the blending chamber to test it.

The rope was heavy, and it took considerable effort to get it in position. David, Alessandra, and Paula went clockwise around the pit with one end and tied it to a thick pipe. Josh and Pedro took the other end in the opposite direction and secured it around another. Then David, Alessandra, and Paula hurried around the vat and joined them. The five of them pulled it as tight as they could and tied it off. The rope cleared the wall, but still drooped a little in the middle when they finished.

"Well, it handled all five us pulling on it as hard as we could," David said. "That's a good sign, right?"

Josh shrugged and gestured toward their test logs. They had tied three of them together, that weighed more than double what Josh did. David followed and the two men walked to the bundle. Alessandra tied several loops of one of their fishing ropes around the logs.

"Ready?" Josh said.

The others nodded and Josh and David lifted the heavy logs up to the main rope. Alessandra and Paula fastened ropes around it so that it hung underneath it. The weight of the bundle pulled the main rope almost down to the floor. David and Josh lifted it back up and as a group, they moved the bundle of logs over the low wall so that it rested on the edge of the pit.

"Let's do it," Josh said, taking the smaller line from Alessandra. He walked a third of the way around and began pulling their test logs across. As soon as the full weight was on the main rope, it began creaking and popping.

The logs didn't make it far. After about fifteen feet, there was a soft pop as the main rope broke and the logs plummeted into the pit. They hit one of the blades below with a clang and a spray of splinters.

Josh gave David and Alessandra a look that made them both blush and squirm.

"Uh, sorry," said Alessandra. "Maybe it needs to be thicker?"

"Do ya think?" replied Josh.

Alessandra and David went back to braiding. Thankfully they'd salvaged the rope so they didn't have to start from scratch.

While the rope was being refurbished, Josh and Pedro built a ladder made of a mahogany log with stout sticks lashed to it for rungs. Their challenge was getting it into a position to reach due to the curve of the dome. But by tying rope loops to pipes and other protrusions, they managed to climb up about thirty feet and secure cords that could be used to pull up the larger rope when it was ready. They then did the same on the opposite side of the conveyor. Josh and the boy both seemed very smug with their accomplishment.

David and Alessandra spent a lot of time together working on the rope. David mostly just pulled or cut the white material into strips and held them so they wouldn't tangle while Alessandra braided. It amazed him how quickly her fingers moved.

The next day, he noticed her looking at him intently. She did this even though her fingers continued to work with machinelike efficiency. He smiled and then blushed and squirmed as she continued to gaze at him.

"If we get out of here," she said suddenly, "what are you going to do?"

"Do?" he said, frowning. "Why, I guess I'll go back to Huntsville. Probably go to college."

She looked down, her fingers a blur of twisting and turning. After a moment of silence, David said, "Well, what're you going to do?"

She shook her head, and said in her somewhat stilted formal English, "I do not know. My family, my house..." She looked at him again. "Everything is gone."

"Oh," said David quietly.

"Do you think I am pretty?" she asked, catching him by surprise.

"Uh, yes, very."

She continued looking at him, then with her head tilted slightly to one side said, "Your sister, you think she is dead?"

A lump suddenly appeared in David's throat, and he nodded.

"I am sorry to upset you. But," she drew in a deep breath, "I like you very much. Could I come back to America with you?"

David's eyes felt like they were trying to pop out of his head. "Uh, to visit?"

"No, to live. Maybe I could go to college with you?"

He shifted uncomfortably. "Uh, I don't know. Why?"

She lifted her head high. "Well, my parents and I saved enough money for me to go to college in Manaus. But now I want to get as far away from here as I can. I speak good English, so why not? But I will need a sponsor."

"I suppose the States would be far away from here. But I don't even know what I'm going to do yet. How can I plan for both of us?"

She looked up at the ceiling of the cave. "If I... if we make it through this, I believe we could make it through anything." Her expression hardened and for a moment, her eyes burned into his. "And you would not have to plan for me; I can plan and do for myself!" Her intense expression softened. "But it is difficult to get into your country. As I said, I need a sponsor and a good roommate for going to school."

All well and good. But why had she asked if I found her good-looking? Don't make anything of it, he chided himself. *She just wants to be away from this damn mountain. And who can blame her?*

David shrugged and said, "Let's work on getting out of here. If... I mean, when we're out, we can talk about it then."

She nodded slowly, though her eyes said he might hear more on the subject sooner than that. *What's with that gleam in her eye, anyway?* Was this about going to the United States, or was she flirting with him? He couldn't remember a girl ever giving him a look like that, and he squirmed a little. However, pleasant tingles crept across his chest...and other places. He tried unsuccessfully to suppress a pleased smile. As they worked on in silence, he noticed she had a pleased look as well.

Later that evening, Josh had them take turns counting as the pit filled, blended, and emptied. This would be their only way to time the blender's cycle since they didn't have any clocks. They did it dozens of times and averaged the results. Paula was the least consistent with the group average, followed by Pedro and David. Alessandra and Josh got close to coming up with the same numbers on a regular basis. Using their averages, the team decided they had a minimum count of eighteen hundred. The count was often longer, but no one was willing to chance it. Their plans revolved around executing their escape in stages within this timeframe. Alessandra and Josh became their official timers.

The next day, they stood at the edge of the pit, watching with eager anticipation as the rope creaked under the weight of three large logs. After a few minutes, the rope gave no sign of failing, and Alessandra beamed with pride. "I told you that would work," she said. "It just needed a tighter, thicker braid."

"I sure hope you're right," Josh said. "Well then, it looks like we're a go. Let's get this strung up, and I'll get my stuff ready. After we sleep, I'll go up and scout the conveyor."

Everything felt strange the next morning. For the first time since they'd been imprisoned in the mountain, Josh didn't call for them to do PT. Instead, they only went through their martial arts forms to stretch out. After weeks of routine, it felt weird, but made sense. They might need to use their muscles to the extreme, and it'd be best to be well rested, especially Josh.

After they ate, Josh loaded up his gear and they headed for the vat room. After a quick nod and confident smile, he climbed the ladder to where the heavy rope was secured thirty feet above their heads. The conveyor was running, but they knew from experience that it wouldn't for much longer. The pile of trees and white bundles of plants and animals were almost halfway up the pit. Josh wanted to reach the belt right after the belt stopped.

He hooked a safety line over the rope and, hanging down like a giant sloth, went hand over hand to the conveyor. A smaller cord trailed out behind him to could pull over his supplies. They wanted to minimize the strain on the rope as much as possible. Alessandra clutched David's arm nervously, and they held their breaths as Josh worked his way out over the vat.

The rope sagged under his weight and started to bring it down to the top of the conveyor's arched opening. The further he crawled up, the lower it hung. As he closed on the conveyor, it dipped below the open arch just as a large tree emerged from the mouth in the dome's wall.

"Oh my God," Paula said. "It's going to hit the rope."

Josh was still twenty feet from the edge of conveyor. One of the tree branches snagged the rope and held on to it like a malevolent prankster—a bad joke with potentially deadly consequences. Josh and the rope were dragged toward the end of the belt.

"Oh no, oh no, oh no," Alessandra muttered in a quivering voice.

The tree reached the end of the belt and tumbled, pulling the rope down. The group gave a collective gasp, but Alessandra's careful braid held the rope sprung free. Josh bounced up and down for a few moments and everyone held their breaths, expecting it to break. After too many long, breathless seconds, the bouncing slowed to a stop. The rope held.

He looked back down at them, shook his head and blew out his cheeks, and gave a small wave. Then he pulled himself the rest of the way to the edge of the conveyor. As he got there, the belt lurched to a stop. Alessandra took on a look of concentration and David knew she'd her count.

With the grace of the ape he resembled, Josh scrambled the rest of the way across and swung down onto the thirty-foot-wide belt. David, Paula, and Pedro gave a small cheer. Alessandra remained silent but her lips moved as she kept up her count. Josh gave them a smile and thumbs-up.

"What's your count?" Josh called out. Everyone knew the question was for Alessandra.

"Eighty-seven," she responded.

Josh nodded and hurried to the far side of the conveyor. Once to the edge, he jumped up and grabbed the sagging rope. With a quick slash of his survival knife, he cut it in two. The far side fell into the pit, and Pedro ran around and began pulling it up. Josh hurried over to their side of the conveyor and climbed up to a rod they'd selected earlier set high and to one side of the conveyor opening. He quickly secured the rope to it and gave it several hard tugs to make sure it would hold. With a grace that didn't match his bulk, he swung his legs twice and dropped back down, landing with a quick roll that finished with him back on his feet.

He then grabbed the thin line secured to his waist and pulled his supplies over. With smooth efficiency, he gathered up a white bundle prepared by Alessandra and slung it over his back. Then he took six gourds full of water and arranged their carrying cords so they crisscrossed his chest. The Brazilian combat harness with the integral water bag had been too small to fit him. But Josh had two canteens along with the pistol on his wide web belt.

Once he had the load settled, he called out, "Count?"

Alessandra yelled back, "Three hundred fifty."

Josh gave them another thumbs-up, turned, and disappeared into the shadows of the conveyor tunnel.

David could hear Alessandra continue to count in a soft whisper. After Josh disappeared, she said, "Well, that took a count of four hundred." She looked down into the cauldron, which had begun filling with liquid while Josh climbed. "He should have about fourteen hundred counts left before the belt starts back up. I sure hope this works."

The others nodded solemnly in agreement.

25 Josh on the Belt

After he waved to Paula and the others, Josh turned and surveyed the interlocking branches before him. "Damn," he muttered. Then he started counting under his breath starting at five hundred. He didn't want to take any chances.

Pulling out his survival knife, he began hacking his way through the mess. Each individual limb parted easily enough before the keen blade, but the sheer volume made for slow going. After cutting his way forward for a count of one thousand, he paused and glanced back at the opening, which was disconcertingly close. His mouth screwed up in annoyance. "Damn."

He hacked with more vigor. When he reached a count of fourteen hundred, he reached a section of the conveyor covered with white bundles and only a few trees. Wiping sweat from his brow, he looked back. The end of the conveyor was out of sight, but only because of the foliage in the way. He could not have come more than fifty feet. This wasn't going at all as he had hoped.

With fewer trees and debris piled on the conveyor, he made good progress from fourteen hundred to seventeen hundred on his count and covered about a hundred yards. He felt he was counting too fast and wanted to go further but decided not to push his luck. The conveyor had always stopped for a count of at least eighteen hundred. That seemed to be the minimum time for the vat to go through a cycle. And though it usually it took a little longer, it wasn't a bet he could afford to lose. Trying to outrun the belt while fighting his way over and through the gatherers' plunder would be a very bad idea.

Alessandra had come up with an idea for traveling on the conveyor. Taking the bundle off his back, he pulled out the hammock she made for this and looked over the numerous rods and pipes above the belt. He spotted a large, black conduit running parallel to the wall. Satisfied this would do the trick, he went over and tied the hammock to it using bowline knots that should be secure yet easy to untie. After he had it in place, he scrambled into it. There was an additional rope attached to the middle of the hammock, and he tied this around the pipe as well. Finally, he secured his meager supplies of food and water to smaller pipes above him. He checked his knots by giving them several sharp tugs. Then he bounced up and down a few times. Everything held, so he settled back to wait.

The hammock had worked well back in the cave, but now came the ultimate test. Time passed slowly while he waited. Then he heard the soft screech of the conveyor as it lurched into motion. In moments, the belt began rushing underneath the hammock at a disconcerting speed. It would be difficult to outrun even if the way were clear. He let out a grunt that turned into a long sigh at the thought of being swept back into the pit.

A shadow passed over him, and he looked up just as a large tree riding close to the wall slammed into his shoulder. It squeezed him against the wall of the tunnel, and the rough bark ground across his body. Several groans escaped his lips as the tree scraped off some skin. Then it was gone. The hammock was torn in several places, as was his hide, but at least the ropes held.

He craned his neck to look up the tunnel. No other large, wall-hugging trees were in sight. *Thank God for that.* He grimaced as the hammock made contact with a patch of raw, bleeding skin. There was nothing he could do about whatever might come. But if a big enough tree hit at the wrong angle, it could get very bad.

Several more trees brushed by and one hit pretty hard, but nothing like the first time. Finally, the conveyor squeaked to a halt. He began counting under his breath as he worked at untying the bowline knots. They came loose as they should and he hopped down, folded the hammock, and headed on up the belt.

He was luckier this time and didn't encounter any large intertwined jumbles. However, there were still plenty of obstacles to negotiate. Piles of brush, a large dead tapir that looked like a cross between an overgrown rat and a pig, and lots of white bundles littered the belt. No people though. That was a good thing.

As he weaved his way through the maze, he kept up his slow, measured count—not the best time keeping system, especially when you were nervous. And Josh was very nervous right now. When he reached fifteen hundred, he decided to stop. He examined the walls and spotted several likely looking rods protruding about four feet above the belt. This time, he peered ahead to see if anything obvious would hit him. Regretfully, he couldn't see far enough to determine what might pose a threat. With a sigh, he pulled out the hammock and tied it up again.

During this stop, he was hit several times by large piles of web coated bundles, which was nerve wracking but didn't hurt, though one of the bundles left a disgusting, smelly smear down his back. Then one medium-sized tree came into view. It had a lot intact roots, and one scraped by hard enough to hurt, but didn't do any serious damage. Overall, much better than the first time through. If only his luck would hold. After what felt a very long time, the belt came to a halt. Again, he untied himself and resumed picking his way deeper into the mountain.

Three more times he repeated traveling forward as fast as possible, stopping to tie up the hammock, suffering through various collisions, untying, and pushing on. During the third stop, a particularly large tangle of trees came grinding down the tunnel and a jagged, broken branch gouged into his left shoulder, driving a six-inch sliver of wood under his flesh. He began to wonder if he would survive this trip. Pulling the blood-soaked shard from his skin, he patched the wound with a strip of webbing as best he could and pressed onward.

A rough six-foot-wide opening on the left wall of the tunnel came into view, and relief washed over him. It was about two feet above the belt and looked as if something had smashed through the wall, though no rubble or debris could be seen.

Under other circumstances, he'd have approached it with extreme caution. However, his count was at sixteen hundred, so he hurried forward and peeked around the corner. Seeing nothing of immediate threat, he stepped up onto the foot-wide ledge bordering the opening, and squatted down.

The opening sat near the top of a huge, dim cavern. The further reaches of the space were obscured by swirling mist. A wide ledge perhaps fifteen-feet wide ran under the opening about four feet below him, blocking the view of the lower reaches of the chamber. The familiar rods emitting electric blue light dotted the ceiling, fading away into the misty distance. What sounded like peals of far-off thunder echoed through the cavern, accompanied by faint flashes reflected in the fog. The sickly-sweet smell of baking cookies and death was very strong here. There was also a hint of ozone in the air.

Finding the opening was a very good thing. If nothing else, once the group got out, they could rest here before going on. They could even get food from the conveyor. Water might be a problem, though. The gourds Paula pulled from the pit and dried out worked okay, but it took four or five1 to hold a meaningful amount of water, and they were heavy and awkward to carry.

He paused at the hole for several minutes and considered his options. Stop and explore this walkway, or continue along the conveyor in the hope it would lead outside? The urge to stop was strong. Just being on the conveyor was nerve-wracking as hell. However, the conveyor seemed like the better choice for getting out of their prison without encountering gatherers. Or at least until he reached the end. Regretfully, everyone had either been unconscious or in such a state of shock, they couldn't remember much about their journey through the mountain. But one thing was sure; the belt brought them in so it had to lead out. With a sigh, he determined it best to keep going on up the belt.

Before leaving, he decided to rest a few minutes. He hopped down from the opening onto the walkway. The thunder was noticeably louder inside. It sounded ominous and provided a good reason not to stop here for long. After shrugging out of his bundle, he sat down on a smooth, dark gray surface and leaned against the wall. Across the walkway, blue flashes accompanied the thunderous booms, making odd shapes in the mist. *What could that be all about?* Curiosity almost made him change his mind about going on. But exploring mysterious things wasn't his mission. Finding a way out was.

The belt could still be heard behind him when it started up. While he waited for it to go through a cycle, he nibbled on some dried bananas, drank some water, and steeled himself to get back on the belt. The wound on his shoulder had soaked through his bandage, so he took time to change it out as well. But sitting here didn't feel safe, so when the belt stopped, he started his count. He hopped up, grabbed his bundle and then climbed up and back onto the conveyor.

As before, traveling along the belt was part scrambling through a maze and part chopping a path through interlocking branches. Along the way, he found fastening his hammock lower down the wall helped reduce impacts from trees. He also learned that instead of tying off to larger pipes, it was better to set up just behind them. That way, they helped fend off debris.

Five more times, he hacked or weaved his way forward for a count of seventeen hundred. Then he'd stop and set up the hammock against another onslaught from the conveyor. After it stopped, he untied and kept on. From when he started that morning, he estimated he must have traveled nearly two miles. Just as he was starting to wonder if this damn tunnel would never end, a new noise at the threshold of hearing drifted down the tunnel.

The sound was a low, rumbling groan, powerful enough to be felt as much as heard. The tone was of a resonance that vibrated in one's chest in a disconcerting manner. As he crept forward, it grew louder, sometime punctuated by a loud clang as if a great piece of metal had been struck by a hammer. The sounds held steady for several minutes as he struggled through a throng of interlocked branches. Nearing fifteen hundred in his count, he gave up, moved to the wall, and set up the hammock. When the conveyor started, the squawk and constant low squeals drowned out the strange noise.

Once the conveyor stopped, the sounds from up ahead seemed louder than before. Untying himself, he pressed forward with more energy, fueled by growing curiosity. Other noises joined the original vibrating rumble and loud clangs. Popping and creaking and even an occasional shrill scream joined the cacophony. *Is all that coming from the end of this damn thin☼ g?* The light began changing, becoming a more muted, softer blue. He began picking his way through the refuse on the belt with more care. The air smelled less of cookies and more of death. Josh couldn't decide if that was good or bad.

The vibrations from the low frequency moan expanded outward from his chest and made his whole body vibrate. It grew until it sounded like a factory from hell. The accompanying clunks and bangs added to the assault on his ears to the point of pain. He stopped long enough to cut off some webbing from a nearby pile and stuff it into his ears.

Damn, he'd lost count. Somewhere around a thousand. There wasn't much time before he'd have to erect the hammock, and he began to move quicker.

Pushing back a thick rubber tree branch, he finally saw the end of the conveyor. Or, not so much the actual end as where it began. But it was the end of this trip. His heart sank at the sight; there'd be no escape this way.

Just beyond the last intervening leaves of the tree, another vast chamber stretched before him. The belt ran into it, but dipped down and disappeared from view. A fine haze hung in the air, somewhat like the cavern he passed with the thunder. It muted the blazing electric blue light, easing the shadows and making it easy to see the activity below. It was not an encouraging sight.

He inched forward until he could see more of the floor below and let out a grunt of amazement. Thousands of monstrous gatherers were engaged in frenzied, seemingly chaotic activity. Across the way, probably a quarter of a mile, another conveyor dwarfing the one he stood on brought tons upon tons of Amazon life into the half-mile wide cavern. The rumbling groan came from there. The source of the loud bangs, clunks, and shrieks originated from gatherers frantically chopping limbs off trees, ripping them apart, or moving them across the floor.

Four other conveyors were visible, all of them as big or bigger than the one he was standing on. Everything falling off the main conveyor, which had to be over two hundred feet wide, was carried across the chamber in a smooth progression by the legion of gatherers. The twenty-foot-tall creatures appeared to work in a random fashion, sometimes carrying an object and sometimes passing it along like a bucket brigade. Regardless, material crossed the wide expanse in a smooth, efficient flow.

Swarming around the gatherers were at least three times as many smaller creatures. These looked a bit like the plumbers that fixed the vat. However, they had longer arms and more powerful looking legs. These picked up the smaller bits and pieces that fell as the larger gatherers worked. They then transferred the debris to the waiting conveyors. As with their bigger kin, sometimes they carried a load, and sometimes they passed it along in a chain. Despite scurrying amidst the larger workers' legs, often right underneath them, none of them got stepped on or kicked. At least not in the short time Josh watched.

All the creatures, large and small responded instantly when a smaller conveyor stopped or started, shifting the flow with a precision that belied the random appearance of their activities. Orchestrated chaos was the only way he could describe it. Large limbs were chopped, broken, or ripped from trees as they went, arriving at an exit conveyor trimmed to fit. Josh had wondered how the giant trees managed to fit through the tunnel behind him; now he knew.

It was obvious the small group couldn't escape this way. They'd never get across the chamber below. Turning, he began the slow trip back to the opening he passed earlier, though he didn't get very far before having to stop to hang the hammock. If there was a way out, it would have to be through the thunder cavern.

He considered riding the conveyor back to the opening but decided against it. There wasn't enough room for error. If he stumbled at the wrong moment, he might end up being swept into the vat. No, better to do it the hard way and not take chances just because he was tired.

Luck favored him. The belt didn't have as many tangles to hack through, and it only took four stops going back. Exhausted, battered and bleeding, he let out a sigh when he spotted the break in the wall. With newfound energy, and nearing seventeen hundred in his count, he picked up his pace to a half-jog to the hole. He didn't relax until he climbed over the jagged entrance and jumped through.

He dropped four feet onto the walkway, landing with practiced ease. This time he crept forward in a crouch to look over the edge. It appeared to be several hundred feet to the ground, though it was difficult to determine in the flickering haze. This chamber was nowhere near as well-lit as the last one. *Did something move down there?* It was hard to tell with the play of light and shadow.

Regardless, the ledge was deserted. It would do to give him a break from the physical and mental exertion of traveling on the conveyor. Based on the number of times the conveyor had stopped, he guessed it to be over six hours since he started his trek. He needed to rest without the constant fear of being swept off the wall and down the conveyor.

Something warm tickled the back of his arm, and he noticed blood dripping to the ground. The bandage he'd replaced on his shoulder was soaked through again. He sat down under the opening and removed it. Tossing the bandage over his shoulder onto the conveyor, he probed to see if any bits of wood might still be embedded in the wound. Finding nothing, he flushed it with water. David had packed some Jatoba leaves among the supplies, and Josh used these along with more white webbing to bind it. Hopefully it wouldn't get infected.

Once finished, he closed his eyes and leaned back against the cool stone. From the darker part of his mind came the thought, *someone with any sense wouldn't go back.* His chances alone were far greater than trying to get them all out. The conveyor squawked to life behind him, and he shook his head with a snort. *Hell, I could never do that.* The group was becoming a decent team, although not one he would've chosen under any other circumstance. But then, you played the hand you got dealt or folded. And he wasn't folding.

He moved his right arm carefully and winced. *Damn, I'm getting too old for this shit. If I get out of this, I need to seriously consider retiring.* This brought a faint smile to his lips. One of his longtime friends who'd been killed by the gatherers told him he always said that after a bad day. True enough.

For some reason, that made him think of Paula. Now, there was a woman with her head on straight. He smiled for a minute, thinking of the night she'd come to him and they'd snuck off to the cascades in back of the cave. He could do worse. Strange, this was the first time he'd ever considered retiring *with* somebody. Kind of gave the idea more merit.

Drawing in a deep breath, he blinked his eyes open. *All right, Josh, break time's over.* He stood and looked around the ledge. The urge to explore was strong, but the first step would be to get everyone out of the vat area. Then they could start searching for an escape route. It wouldn't do any good if he found a way out and couldn't get back to the cave. Take it one step at a time; that was the way to go.

While waiting for the conveyor to stop, a loud crackling boom, much louder than the rest, came from behind, making him jump. He turned and eyed the depths of the dim chamber.

"What the hell?" *Something strange going on down there.* The thought made him give a short bark of laughter. As if strange shit wasn't normal in this place.

The ledge followed the wall to his right, descending as it curved left, down, and away out of sight into the depths of the chamber. To the left, the ledge ended in a wall which protruded outward for perhaps a hundred feet. A dark, jagged crack that might be a passage was the only thing marring the wall's stone surface.

Turning right, he began following the path downward, peering into the shrouding mists for signs of movement. Before he brought everyone to the ledge, he'd better at least make sure it was reasonably safe.

Down, down, down the path he went as it sloped in a long shallow curve to the left. Soon, he could look up at the ledge where he started. He could also see past the wall jutting into the chamber. Beyond it was the dark opening of a large cave. A series of flashes accompanied by booms and pops lit up the inside walls. Both were noticeably more intense from this vantage point. But the angle of the opening kept him from seeing anything but rough-hewn stone. After a moment's hesitation, he continued. As he descended, more of the cave's inside became visible.

Outside the cave, the mist shifted, thickening and then thinning. Light from the blue bars didn't illuminate the space far below very well. A gray, shadowy form moved at the limit of his vision. He froze. There was just enough light to tell that something was there, but not what. After a moment, it faded from view. He knew better than to merely dismiss it as nothing.

With the constant thunder, noise wasn't a problem as he crept forward. Still, he moved as if it were, moving slow and scanning the path ahead, down and around. It probably wasn't smart to any further. *Damn, what an understatement.* But not knowing what might lurk here wouldn't be good either. *What the hell, you only live once.* He kept his back pressed against the wall as he eased downward. From time to time, he eased forward to peer down, but saw no further movement.

This place felt like the lair of some beast guarding the doorway to Hell. At least there didn't seem to be anything of immediate threat to the ledge above. Once more, he hesitated. Another rumble and series of bright flashes discharged from the chamber below, drawing his gaze back down. Curiosity tugged at him. *Just a little farther,* he told himself.

Moving slowly, staying close to the wall, he scanned every direction with each step, knowing he was pushing his luck, but drawn forward by an overpowering desire to know what was in the cave. Thunder and light assailed him as he descended. If there had been any wind, he would have thought he were sneaking up on a tornado. Crazy blue shadows jumped and leaped all around. The mist seemed on fire one moment, then faded into a faint blue glow the next. His every heartbeat screamed for him to go back.

But he was too close to stop now. Five more steps allowed him to see around the wall and into the cave. Wonder filled him when he realized the scale of it. Even in the dim light between blinding flashes, he could see that this chamber dwarfed the one where gatherers hacked up trees. The far side was lost to view, but even so, it had to be the largest underground space he'd ever seen. Through the mist, things moved. He squinted, trying to understand what he saw. The flashes stopped and the mists parted for a moment. The sight before him made his knees feel so weak that he leaned against the wall for support.

"No way," he whispered in awe. "No freaking way."

26 Mountain Worshippers

In the three days since the celebration and medal presentation, Sally's sleep had been better. Not that the medal had anything to do with it. She still didn't think she deserved it, although knowing the medal pissed off von Jaeger at least gave her some sardonic pleasure.

The best part had been the sharing of memories…and pain…with Marcus and the others. She still had nightmares, but they continued to lose power over her. Tonight, she dreamed of the fire that burned down the main lab tent. *Such a waste and so stupid. Why would anyone do such a thing?*

It almost seemed she could hear the voices yelling fire even now. *Or is that real?* Her brain struggled to sort reality from dream. Reality won when a jarring explosion of nearby gunfire shocked her into wakefulness. She shook her head, partly in denial of what she heard and partly to clear it.

The last vestiges of sleep fled as more shots rang out, followed by a blood-curdling scream of agony and fear. A scream very similar to what she heard in the jungle, the scream of someone on the verge of death.

She leapt out of bed, just as holes appeared by magic in a line across her tent, letting in small shafts of early morning sunlight. The windup clock by her cot exploded, and her pillow did a quick jig as foam flew in the air. She threw herself to the ground and curled into a ball.

Think, damn it, think! Don't just lay here. The camp was under attack. *Duh.* But not by demons. That was hard to process. Who the hell would attack them? Well, by God, she wasn't going to just lay here waiting to get shot. She uncurled and slithered over to the assault rifle given to her by PBG-31. It wasn't loaded. But she kept ammunition in a box under her cot.

She half rolled, half slid over to it and pulled out three clips. All she had on was her underwear and a t-shirt, so where could she put the extra clips? Inspiration led her to tie the shirt in a knot under her breasts and shove a clip in between them. It would have to do. She left the other clip on her bed and crawled to the tent flap.

One of the tents burned brightly—sadly, the Big Tent. Smoke filled the air. She lay at the entrance to her own tent with the rifle at her cheek. Looking down the barrel, she swept the muzzle back and forth in a slow arc but saw no one. The first shots had come from somewhere off to her left. Now, sporadic shots were coming from the right. T left side seemed most likely to where the bad guys were since that's where this nightmare started. Still crawling, she began making her way toward the right, praying she wouldn't get shot accidentally by one of the Brazilians guarding the camp. Of course, she didn't want to get shot at all. But getting hit by your own people seemed infinitely worse.

A figure burst from behind the Big Tent. From the left! She swung the rifle around, hand on the trigger, but paused. Could she be sure? Who was it? As bad as getting shot would be, killing a friend… She had enough nightmares about dead friends already.

Whoever it was carried a gun; she could tell that much through the swirling smoke. The figure stopped running and crouched down, then swung up the rifle and began firing toward Sally's right. The smoke cleared, and she saw a woman wearing a brown robe with a white cloth around her head. This was no friend.

Sally's heart climbed up and made an effort to block her throat. She tried to force her hands to stop trembling as she sighted down the barrel. Just like dad taught her all those years ago. Of course, that had been at a target, not a human being. Try as she would, her hands continued to quiver slightly.

Squeeze, don't jerk. Another lesson easier to think about than to do. Then the rifle bucked and her ears started to ring, though she couldn't remember actually hearing the shot. The figure in brown lurched and fell to the ground, clutching her leg. But the woman still held the rifle and used it to leverage herself back up, then pointed the weapon off to the right again.

"Drop it!" Sally yelled. *Drop it, please God, make her drop it.* The woman spun in her direction and fired. So, did Sally. This time, the rifle fell from the woman's hands as she dropped like a limp doll to the ground. Sally felt like throwing up. It took a strong act of will tot choke it back down.

The intensity of shooting from both left and right increased to a raging roar of cracking explosions. Sally swept the muzzle of her rifle to the left. She saw flashes in the smoke, but nothing she dared shoot at. She wasn't willing to fire as indiscriminately as these people were.

The firing suddenly slackened from the left, and indistinct crouching forms emerged from the smoke on her right. She started to jerk her rifle around but froze instead. Somehow, she knew this would be a bad thing to do at this point. The murky forms became more distinct, transitioning into those of a dozen Brazilian marines. Sally pushed her rifle away and held her hands up.

"Don't shoot, don't shoot!" she yelled.

But the marines were not as indiscriminate as she feared. They rushed by her with barely a glance. Regardless, Sally remained prone and away from her weapon. The marines disappeared into the smoke to her left, and another round of firing began—a few pops at first that swelled into a crackling roar lasting several seconds. Something whizzed by her head, and red dirt kicked up a dozen feet in front of her. Then silence, except for a constant ringing in her ears.

"Clear south!" a voice called out. "Clear!" another voice shouted. Then another, "Clear."

"Civilians, stay down," yelled another voice. "Raoul, check north."

"Aye, sir," came a crisp reply.

Thank God Marcus stationed them here. But how bad was it? Someone screamed after the first shots, probably someone from camp. Sally shuddered as an emotional surge of worry, exhilaration, and relief swept through her.

"Civilians, muster in front of the physics tent," said the same voice who'd told them to stay down. He spoke in Portuguese, so Sally called out the command in English as well.

After standing, she started to retrieve her rifle, but thought better of it. *Probably not a good time to be carrying it around.* The physics tent was to the left. *Oh, dear God, that was where the bad guys had been.* She began to get a very bad feeling. Hurrying in that direction took her past the woman she'd shot, and she paused.

The woman's body was on her knees with her head and torso folded backwards in an odd position. She wasn't young or old, maybe mid-thirties. The white band around her head had a crooked M drawn on it in fuzzy red lines. *Not these ass wipes again.*

Sally considered herself to be pretty spiritual and did not begrudge anyone their beliefs. At least not until whatever they believed prompted them to start hurting and killing. Any sorrow she felt over killing the woman faded as anger flared in her chest. She felt a sudden strong urge to kick her. With an effort, she suppressed it. With a disgusted shake of her head, she turned and jogged toward the physics tent.

For the second time in two weeks, smoke billowed over the university camp. Why the Big Tent? It lay on the opposite side of the small clearing in the center of camp from the physics tent. *Most likely a diversion*, she thought. The tent she headed for now wasn't burning, which she found reassuring. Dr. Allen stood in front of it with a growing number of researchers gathering around him.

Most of them were in varying stages of dress, or undress. She suddenly became conscious of her bare midriff, scanty underwear, and bouncing breasts in the tied-up t-shirt. She slowed long enough to pull out the spare clip and untie the shirt, which fell in a comforting drape to her thighs. Though she still felt exposed in the thin material, it was no worse than what anyone else wore. Not that anyone was paying attention anyway. They had far more serious concerns to occupy them right now.

The physics tent looked unharmed, but the scream had come from this direction. It could have come from either a man or a woman. Paul worked in this tent, and he tended to be an early riser. The thought added a bit more speed to her gait. The bad feeling grew stronger.

"Who screamed?" Sally said as she rushed up to Dr. Allen. "Is Paul okay? Is everyone okay?"

"Sandra Birkheuer is dead," Dr. Allen said with a sad, slow shake of his head. "Two of the Brazilian physicists were wounded, Manoel and Sergio. I...I haven't seen Paul."

Before she could ask any more questions, the officer in charge of the Brazilian guard detail, Lieutenant Mauro Pinheiro, approached with half a dozen of his men. With a few words and gestures, the marines took up stations around the civilians. Then he came over to Dr. Allen and Sally. His eyes looked strained and full of concern, and more than a small amount of shame.

"Greetings, Miss Sally," said the lieutenant. "Please give my condolences and apologies to Dr. Allen and your people. We never expected an attack of this nature."

"Sally," called a familiar voice. She turned find Paul running toward them. "Thank God you're okay."

Relief flooded through her. "I feel the same about you." The smile at seeing him unharmed quickly faded. "Did you hear about Dr. Birkheuer?"

He looked grim and shook his head. But her expression and tone must have told him. "She didn't make it, did she?" he said.

"No, she didn't. Manoel and Sergio are wounded, but I don't know how bad." She turned to Dr. Allen with the question in her eyes.

"Manoel got hit in the leg; with luck he'll be okay. Sergio...

Well, he has a chest wound. It looks really bad."

"Lieutenant, we have one man badly wounded," she said. "Can you get him to your aid station?"

"Of course." He turned and called, "Raoul." One of the marines, Carlosa's brother, turned around. The young man looked tense and very much on edge. "Go get our ATV. We have wounded, and there's no time to wait for the rapid response team."

Raoul nodded and ran toward the other side of the camp.

"He's just inside," Dr. Allen said, with Sally translating. "I hate to move him, but he needs more attention than we can give him here."

Lieutenant Pinheiro called for his team's medic. "Our corpsman has some plasma and drugs. Maybe he can stabilize him for transport." As he finished speaking, another marine ran up with a large bag sporting a red cross. The medic rushed past them and into the tent as the ATV came into sight.

The medic did a quick check and started an IV. Then he stepped back, and four marines carried Sergio to the vehicle and placed him on the back seat. As Raoul started the motor, three more ATVs roared into camp, followed by a larger, six-wheel vehicle loaded with marines.

Marcus and Nelino exited the second ATV in line. Marcus headed in Sally's direction while Nelino began positioning men in a wider perimeter around the camp. The ATV carrying Sergio pulled out, and Marcus watched it go with a grim expression. He also stared for a long moment at the shrouded form of Dr. Birkheuer laying just outside the physics tent.

He nodded to Sally and Dr. Allen as he approached and turned to Lieutenant Pinheiro. "Situation report please, lieutenant," he said calmly.

"Yes, sir. No military casualties. One civilian dead and two wounded, one very seriously. Six hostiles confirmed, possibly seven. Five hostiles terminated..." He looked at Sally and said, "One by Miss Morgan here."

Marcus glanced at her, and his left eyebrow rose slightly.

Pinheiro continued. "We have one wounded hostile in custody, waiting on interrogation. There's a good chance one got away to the south, based on three sightings at the end of the engagement."

The woman Sally shot caught Marcus's eye and he walked over to her, the others following a short distance behind. When he reached the woman, he knelt down, looked her over, and then up at Sally. "Is this one yours?"

Mine? What a strange way to put it. But yes, it's true, isn't it? Sally nodded, surprised she felt…nothing? No, that wasn't it. Her insides churned with a mix of emotions. They seemed muted, however. Was she becoming numb to all this? The one emotion that bubbled the closest to the surface right now was anger. Maybe she was reaching that point where she could be considered battle hardened. After all, she was no virgin to violent death anymore. *What will be the long-term cost of this on my soul?* No doubt, she'd be paying a price, whatever it might be, for a long time to come.

Marcus stared at the woman's forehead a moment longer, then reached down and pulled off the white strip of cloth tied around her head. The M on it wasn't done with a pen or felt-tip marker; it was blood. The symbol had been carved into the woman's forehead from the middle of one eyebrow to the middle of the other. The line in her flesh was still red with flecks of un-clotted blood dotting it here and there. The cuts must have been made very recently. A pre-attack ritual of some kind?

"The Church of the Mountain," Marcus muttered. "A whole new kind of crazy loose in the world. First, an alien landing and ongoing devastation of the forest. Now this. Hell, I'm not even sure which is worse right now."

He stood and looked down the hill toward the civilian camp. The university compound sat on the highest point on this side of the river. It had been erected before so many people moved in and had a great view. Although that might not be much of an advantage if people were going to start attacking it. The civilian camp had grown into a substantial town in its own right. By now, it must be twice as large as Rio Estrada had been before being destroyed. The camp was a maze of tents, shacks, lean-tos, and an occasional modular house.

Beyond the last of the construction at the far side of town and on the opposite ridge sat a large, multi-story, rough wooden structure— the Church of the Magnificent Mountain Holy Cathedral. A grandiose name for a big log building, but they probably thought of this as being sacred ground. And to their credit, it was by far the biggest structure in sight. That it stood on the opposite ridge from the university camp provided a degree of symbolism, though Sally was too numb to give it much thought at the moment.

Marcus tilted his head toward Lieutenant Pinheiro while keeping his eyes on the building. "What's the name of their grand pooh-bah or whatever they call him?"

"Shepherd of the Mountain. His name is Eduardo Chermont, sir."

"Yeah, that's him. You checked him out after the fire, right?"

The lieutenant nodded. "Yes sir. Used to be a street preacher in Sao Paulo. Constantly in and out of trouble with local law enforcement. He sometimes financed his ministry through pickpocketing and muggings. A real moral paragon. But what really got him in hot water was having sex with underage girls. Had a bit of a stable in his flock. One of them got jealous, or came to her senses, depending on which report you read. She turned him in, and he left town. There isn't a warrant for him, though. Most likely, he reached a deal with the magistrate or something."

"Send a squad to find him and take him to base. I'll want to talk to him."

"Yes, sir." Pinheiro turned and issued the order to some of his men.

"Now then, where is this prisoner of yours?" Marcus said.

"This way, sir," Pinheiro said. "He took a round in the leg. It seems to have lessened his religious fervor a bit."

"Reality will sometimes do that. All well and good to die for a cause, but to get hurt and caught?' He turned to Sally. "Would you care to meet our friend?"

The question surprised her, but it seemed like a very interesting encounter. "Yes, I believe so," she said.

She followed Marcus and Lieutenant Pinheiro to the side of the still smoldering remains of the Big Tent. It worried her to feel sadder over the loss of the tent than the woman she'd shot. The tent had been home for some time now, but still. *What kind of person am I becoming? God help me.*

The man sat on the ground with his hands bound behind his back. The left leg of his blue jeans had been cut away, and a bandage encircled his thigh. He wore a brown shirt and a white cloth tied around his head. A notable difference between his and the one worn by the woman was that the M symbol wasn't bloody. It appeared to have been drawn with a red marker. Two marines stood nearby with rifles at the ready. The man rocked back and forth as he stared fearfully at the approaching group.

Marcus whispered, "Let me do most of the talking. Unless you notice something really important. Okay?" Sally and Pinheiro nodded.

Marcus stood over the man and stared down at him with smoldering intensity. The man stopped rocking, but the fear remained, and he started to have little twitches in his head, neck, and chest. "You're a devil," he whispered.

Marcus nodded. "Indeed, I am, if believing the opposite of you is consider deviltry. For I believe that shooting unarmed civilians is not God's work."

"They…you keep the bodies of murdered angels here. And…and you violate the Lord's will with the devil magic that uses the holy signals for navigation. That's not God's will, or He wouldn't have destroyed the satellites. God's will is to punish man by depriving him of his evil technology."

"So, that's why you came. To destroy the samples and navigation system." He leaned closer to the man. "Who sent you?"

For some reason, this stiffened the man's resolve. He straightened and said, "God sent us."

"Okay," Marcus replied. "And is Eduardo Chermont God's voice—the one who conveys to you God's will?"

This obviously surprised the man. He sputtered for a moment, then said, "No. God speaks to each of us through our hearts. We act for love of the Lord."

"Uh huh." He turned to the others. "Well, that was easy. We know what they were after, though that was an easy guess. And we know this Chermont character sent them."

The man wailed, "Nooo! The shepherd didn't send us. We…we

come for God."

Marcus snorted. "The truly sad thing is that I think you believe that. And if that's the case… Well, we'll just have to see what the good shepherd has to say."

"The shepherd is coming here?" The man started rocking back and forth again.

"In good time. And I for sure want to get you two together," Marcus said. "After I've had a few words with him first." He gestured toward the man and said, "Get him to the base infirmary. Keep a close eye on him. I'd hate to have him kill himself or something stupid. I'll send for him later."

Then he looked at Sally. "Well, this attack puts us in a strange situation, besides the obvious."

"Obvious?"

"Dealing with our losses," he said with a wave at the smoldering tent nearby. "But if these lunatics are going to start shooting, this camp is not safe. If not for our friend General von Jaeger's order, I'd move everyone to the base."

"You think they'll attack again?" she said, glancing at the man on the ground.

Marcus shrugged. "We have to plan that they might. However, I can't spare enough men to guard this place effectively."

Sally noticed Dr. Allen and Paul standing a short distance away. Paul was probably trying to catch a little of what they were saying, though with his poor Portuguese, she doubted he would have much success. She gestured toward them and said, "This might be a discussion we need to involve them in."

Marcus nodded, so Sally called out, "Robert, Paul. You need to hear this."

Dr. Allen and Paul walked over, eyeing the man sitting on the ground warily. Dr. Allen said, "Sorry to be trying to listen in, but Paul thought he understood something about more attacks?"

"Yeah, Marcus was saying he doesn't have enough men to properly guard our camp. He could move you to base, but I couldn't go."

Dr. Allen said, "Well, Dr. Birkheuer happened to be discussing something along similar lines last night. Not the base, but back to their campus. She told me things are much better there now. With the new microwave transmission system about to come online, communications with the front should be readily available."

Paul said, "That's okay for the biological research. But the physics group needs to be closer to the White Mountain to adjust the nav-system. Also, we're getting closer to using their return signals to track the harvesters' and demons' movements. Large groups of them anyway."

After Sally translated this for Marcus, he nodded enthusiastically. "A tracking method? That would be a wonderful asset. But if you could come to Manaus when I leave, that would also be wonderful."

Paul's head came up at this and he looked back and forth between Marcus and Sally with a puzzled expression. *How much did he understand?* How much did she want him to understand? He must know that if she went to Manaus, any chance of rekindling their old relationship would have to be put on hold.

As for going to Manaus, that was very tempting. To work and sleep in air-conditioning, to have a real bed and an actual shower would indeed be wondrous. And to have Marcus nearby... Well, she still wasn't sure how to feel about that, but it would give her a chance to find out.

That brought her back to Paul. What to say to him? A hard certainty came to her that she'd have to tell him about her feelings for Marcus. Not fun. But he deserved to know. Telling him would really suck, but they'd had their time. It didn't work then. Why expect it to work now? Going to the city would force a decision that made her feel happy and sad at the same time. But now was not the time to bring it up. Later, when they were alone.

"I'll need to discuss this with Colonel Ames first," Sally said. "I told her I'd consider doing my work as part of her staff. If the bioresearch moves, though, it would make more sense to keep my current contract. I'm scheduled to meet with her next week. In the meantime, we might as well start planning to move."

Marcus nodded thoughtfully. "Yes. It will take a little time to make preparations anyway. I can provide additional security for another week or so to beef up defenses. Hopefully these…" He glanced at the man on the ground and said in a disdainful tone, "people…will find it difficult to get enough idiots to mount another attack anytime soon. But we can't count on that, of course."

After Sally finished relaying this to Dr. Allen and Paul, both men agreed. Dr. Allen said, "I hate to see the team split up, but it seems for the best. Communications should be good enough with the microwave relays that we can stay in touch and collaborate if needed."

Paul didn't say anything, but his eyes spoke his feelings. They held sorrowful hope, but it was plain he knew their future together had just become much less likely. He was a good man, and Sally hated to see him hurt. But that's the way life rolled, wasn't it? Once more, and not for the last time, she wondered why the relationships between women and men had to be so complicated.

27 David and the Escape Attempt

After a quick glance at the conveyor, David looked back in time to see Pedro jump two of his men and land in a king's spot. The little sucker set him up perfectly. Pedro had as good a knack for checkers as he did for dots. One of these days, they'd have to teach him chess. David had a feeling he'd be good at that too. Well, the game was all but over, so David sighed and said, "Surrender."

Pedro beamed at him in triumph. Not gloating. Pedro wasn't a gloater. He just had joy in the game and being good at it. "Again?" he said.

David nodded, but his heart wasn't in it. He could generally give Pedro a good game. However, trying to play checkers and keep watch on the belt overhead split his concentration too much. *When would Josh come back*? It had to have been hours and hours, although time could be tricky when you relied on your feelings. It was funny living in a world with no clocks. Most of the time, you didn't really notice. You got up when everyone else did. Ate, exercised, and did your business to the group's communal clock. But when waiting…

Well, that was a different matter entirely.

What if Josh doesn't come back? What if he fell and got carried back to the vat on the conveyor? Maybe they just hadn't seen him go into the pit? It was a chilling thought. What would it mean? It would mean they'd have to go on without him, for starters. It was kind of ironic worrying about the big ape after all the times David wished he'd go to hell. That seemed like a long time ago now. Well, the group would go on somehow. It wasn't like they'd have any choice.

Despite his focus on the makeshift checkerboard, Pedro still spotted the old soldier first. "Josh," he yelled, standing up and waving. "Josh, he ist backed."

Josh returned the wave, his face looking haggard and drawn even from thirty feet overhead. With slow, deliberate motions, he hooked his safety line onto the rope, swung his legs up, and began slowly inching his way across. Below him, the vat gurgled as it started draining.

"I get 'Lessandra," Pedro said. With another wave at Josh, who was too busy to notice, the boy took off at a sprint.

David went over to meet him. When Josh reached the ladder to the catwalk, he tossed his hammock bundle and empty water gourds down to David. *Was that blood on the hammock? On his shoulder?* Josh sighed as he stepped off the ladder onto walkway. His face did indeed look haggard. It must've been a rough trip.

Josh sat down with a slight thump and shook his head. "Man, I could sure use a beer." He managed a rueful grin at David. "That alone is enough motivation to get the hell out of this place. Besides the constant threat of dying, of course."

David had tried a beer once. It tasted like crap to him. Being only eighteen and a self-made social outcast, he hadn't had much opportunity to develop a taste for it. Regardless, he smiled and said, "Yeah. Too bad. We pulled some out of the vat while you were gone, but we just ran out."

Josh snorted. "Yeah, that's my luck."

Pedro returned with Alessandra and Paula.

Paula said, "You look like shit."

"Love you too, sweetheart," Josh said. "But I can't complain. I feel like shit."

"Rough trip?" Alessandra asked. Josh nodded and she said, "Do you think the rest of us could make it?"

Determination returned to his eyes. "Absolutely. It'll be a piece of cake. We're getting the hell out of here. I just wouldn't recommend any side trips."

David, Alessandra, and Paula looked Josh up and down. He was bruised, scraped and bloody. They exchanged uneasy glances. Obviously, not a one of them had his confidence about the ease of making the trip. But none of their eyes expressed any doubt that they would try.

David could now do ten pullups, something he'd never have imagined doing before this started. Heck, he'd never even done one before. Of course, Josh could do that many with one arm. Both Alessandra and Paula could do as well as David. And Pedro? Well, Pedro was a monkey. He could do them all day long without ever getting tired. Or so it seemed. Being able to do pull-ups and upper body strength would be a skill they'd need to attempt the escape.

It took Josh a little while to recover from his trip, but whether it was a few hours or several days was impossible to tell in the timeless world of their cave. Three sleep cycles went by, if that meant anything, so closer to four days than not. While he was recovering, they discussed and prepared for their escape. This consisted of two parts, The Climb and The Conveyor. That was the focus of their world now.

The Climb would be the process of getting themselves and their supplies up to the opening over the immense vat. This would have to done in stages due to the run and stop cycles of the conveyor. Just thinking about climbing on Alessandra's homemade rope sent shivers through David. But the task was made more complicated by the fact it had to done during the time it took to fill and empty the vat. And they only had Alessandra and Josh's counting to track it.

The Conveyor phase was focused on the trip up the belt to the hole Josh discovered. To help reduce the chance of being skewered by tree branches or roots, Alessandra came up with the idea of reinforcing the hammocks with bamboo strips. She couldn't go too crazy beefing them up because they had to be light enough to carry and easy to erect and disassemble quickly. But based on Josh's experiences on the belt, some kind of armor seemed in order. She'd already made the hammocks, and bamboo was in ready supply. David helped her work on them while Josh rested and they had them ready by the time he felt strong enough to travel.

Finally, the day came to make the attempt. Everyone was quiet after they woke up and during breakfast. It reminded David of their early days together. Once more Josh decided to forego PT, leading them through their fighting forms and a series of stretches instead. Once he determined they were loosened up, they gathered their gear and he led them to the chamber.

They lined up at the ladder with their assigned loads, in the order of how they would cross. This had been determined based on their weight. The theory was it would be best to put the most strain on the rope first, then the lighter loads afterward. This meant Josh followed by David, Paula, Alessandra and Pedro.

"Okay, this is it," Josh said, sweeping his eyes over his small team. "Take deep slow breathes. Keep your cool. Once you start, don't look down. It's just another exercise. Right?"

Everyone nodded solemnly. David just hoped he didn't look as frightened as he felt. Getting up to the conveyor would be the scariest thing he'd ever had to face.

He'd been terrified when the gatherers captured him during the destruction of Rio Estrada. But that had been more like a nightmare where he had no control over what happened. Once the creatures trussed him up and started carrying him to the White Mountains, his brain basically disengaged. In other words, he gave up. It took no conscious action on his part to do anything. No fears had to be faced and overcome. He just had to accept his fate and wait to die.

Climbing the rickety ladder and hooking one handmade rope over another to shimmy out over a two-hundred-foot drop was a different matter. Just standing at the bottom of the ladder made his throat tighten. But its thirty-foot height wasn't even that bad. It was situated safely over the wide walkway that went around the vat. Many of the team exercises Josh put them through had been as high.

But the rope crawl was a stomach-clenching proposition that had his knees trembling and heart fluttering. While Alessandra was weaving, and tying the line together, it wasn't something he'd even thought about. But now, whenever his to eyes followed the rope up the slight angle from the ladder to the rod projecting from beside the conveyor, he remembered every knot and twist. It looked like two hundred feet of a rather amateurish art project. Yet his life would depend on it. Not a fun thing to dwell on, but his brain wouldn't allow him not to.

After they each nodded that they were ready, Josh gave them a thumbs-up, turned, and began climbing. In a few minutes, he began inching along the rope until he hung suspended over the vat, just short of the conveyor belt, waiting for it to stop.

"Are you ready?" Alessandra said with a slight quiver in her voice. They definitely didn't want two people on the rope at the same time—one more detail to complicate the escape.

David swallowed hard and nodded. He'd studied Josh's movements intently in an effort to pick up any last-minute tips. They'd practice the rope-crawl many times, but never over a distance like this. Certainly, not with the prospect of instant death right below them. He checked the climber's seat that went around his waist and between his legs for the hundredth time. It was still tight, although he already knew this due to the uncomfortable pressure on his balls.

"The vat's nearly full. You better get in position," she said. "Good luck."

He nodded again, not trusting himself to speak. It only took a few seconds to reach the top of the ladder. Once there, he got his safety rope ready and watched Josh.

The conveyor ran somewhat quieter since the visit by the plumbers. It rumbled to a stop, and Josh swung down from the rope and landed lightly on the belt. He turned and gave David a thumbs-up. Not that he needed to. As soon as Josh let go of the rope, David began tying his safety line. His fingers felt strangely awkward as he made the special knot Josh taught them called a bowline. It was one that would hold, but could be easily untied. Once secured, he let the line and his climber's seat take his full weight for a count of thirty. Everything held.

He took in a deep breath and gave Alessandra a thumbs-up to signal he was ready. Then he wrapped his legs around the main rope and began to shimmy upside down toward the conveyor.

"Don't look down," Josh yelled.

Yeah, right. David had actually been doing pretty well until Josh yelled. Now he looked. *Crap!* The vat was half empty, and the goo-encrusted blades around the sides were emerging. They looked to be a very long way down. He glanced over at Josh and saw him busily attaching his hammock to the rods on the wall next to the conveyor opening. After that, he didn't look at anything but the rope overhead and his hands as they inched along it.

"Eighteen hundred," Alessandra yelled.

David kept his eyes on his hands. It didn't matter if the conveyor started; he would be on the rope through the next cycle. Paula should be getting in position by the ladder about now. The top of the dome was noticeably closer, and he looked ahead to see that he'd nearly reached his stopping point.

"Nineteen hundred," Alessandra called out. A few seconds later, the conveyor rumbled to life. That was actually a shorter cycle than usual and a firm reminder that their timing count max of eighteen hundred was a number to heed.

A piece of green cloth tied to the rope came into sight, and he stopped. Josh told him to trust in his harness at this point and rest his arms. It took an extreme act of will to release the rope. His heart thudded even harder and a shiver went through him as he let the safety rope take the weight of his upper body, although he kept his legs crossed over the main line. He hung there like a sloth forever while the vat filled with trees, carcasses, and white bundles. The time of this part of the process varied the most depending on the number and size of trees riding the conveyor.

Looking down at the vat became a little easier, and he watched it fill. Josh said there were four other vats like this running somewhere in the mountain based on the conveyors he'd seen. And what if there were even more? Maybe there was another giant processing room too. If so, the aliens could do a lot of carnage to the rainforest, even more than he first thought. How much damage would they do before moving their mountain? Assuming they could move it. It must not be easy. However, David felt positive these creatures came from space. And that led to the question, *are there more of them out there?* Well, he had enough to worry about just getting away from this batch without dwelling on that.

"Get ready," Josh yelled.

David pulled himself back up and grabbed the rope. Paula should be getting ready to hook up at the top of the ladder, but she'd wait until he was clear. Being on that damn belt would be weird. He prayed their math was good and the creatures would stick to the schedule.

The conveyor rumbled to a halt, and David hooked his left arm over the rope to free his hands. The bowline knot came undone easily, and he sighed with relief. It almost always did, but he'd screwed it up in practice a couple of times. And he hadn't been nearly as nervous then. Now he was suspended over the vat, relying totally on his own muscles.

With the safety line out of the way, David gripped the main rope with his hands and uncrossed his legs. He could see the top of a tree in the vat about fifty feet below him. But that leafy mass wouldn't slow him much if he fell. If that happened, the best he could hope for would be an instant death or to be knocked unconscious. Otherwise, he'd have to endure the wait of being drowned in brown fluid or bashed to pieces when the vat went into blender mode.

The conveyor was just below and to his left. He began going hand over hand and reached it in a few seconds. He began swinging back and forth to build momentum. During practice sessions, Josh had always told them, "Don't try to stick the landing; just get on the belt."

David mumbled this under his breath as he swung. "Get on the belt, get on the damn belt."

He swung longer than he should, longer than Josh ever let them in practice. "Don't do that!" Josh had yelled more than once. "It just wears out your arms. You have to pull up, swing, and release."

David could feel the strain on his arms sapping his strength. It wasn't far, just a couple of feet. He had to go and go now. Determination filled him, then fear, then... *What the hell.* He pulled up at the bottom of the next arc and let go, clearing the low wall bordering the conveyor by a good two feet. Time stopped for a long moment. Then he hit and rolled. Safe. At least for the moment.

Josh was beside him a second later, helping him to his feet. The man's ape-like face was lit up by the biggest smile David had ever seen on him. "By God, you did it," he said, sounding like a proud father. "I knew you could, but…"

"But you didn't know if I would?" David said.

Josh nodded. "You never know until the main event." He met David's eyes and said, "You done good. Real good."

Pride coursed through David. It felt nearly as good as the relief of still being alive after the insane stunt he just pulled. Of course, it couldn't really be considered too insane if it was your only chance to live, could it?

Paula was now on the rope, inching toward them. "Come on," Josh said. "You need to get your hammock set up."

David nodded and untied it from around his waist. It didn't have the bamboo armor yet. That would have been too chancy to carry and do the jump. They didn't need it right now. It wouldn't be until they began going up the conveyor that the bamboo would come into play.

The opening to the conveyor was a circular arch thirty-feet high and wide. Josh had set up some rope ladders and guide lines so they could secure hammocks out of the path of objects coming down the belt. David strung up his hammock on the curved wall. This would leave him dangling over the vat itself. He'd seen pictures of mountain climbers sleeping in similar arrangements on the internet. Never in a million years would he have imagined doing something like that. Not to mention his rig was a homemade affair made of braided alien fibers. The hammock took some careful maneuvering to tie up while clinging to the twisting rope ladder. He began to get nervous his fumbling fingers wouldn't be able to get it done before time ran out.

Alessandra called out, "One thousand."

Still plenty of time. He tried to convince himself of that anyway. As she called out, "One thousand four hundred," he got the hammock set and carefully climbed in. The ropes and knots held, but his heart still hammered at the thought of something slipping or breaking. The process of tying it from the unsteady rope ladder had been much more difficult than when they practiced on solid ground. He hoped it would be easier in the tunnel where they would have firmer footing.

Paula made it to the green cloth and hung there, waiting. Her part was a little different than David's in that she pulled a thin rope behind her. They would use this to pull their supplies up.

When the conveyor stopped running, she waited for Josh and David to climb out of their hammocks and hurry over to her. Then she tossed a weighted stone secured to the end of the line to David.

Pedro had already secured a modest-sized bundle to the main rope, and David began pulling it across with the thinner line. The bundle had yet another thin rope tied on back that Alessandra played out. It nearly reached Paula when Alessandra called out, "Seventeen hundred." David secured the line to the wall, and he and Josh hurried back to their hammocks. Paula and the bundle hung from the rope through the next cycle.

When the conveyor stopped again, Paula untied the bundled and it fell until the lines on each side stopped it. She unhooked herself next and did the tricky dismount, albeit with more grace than David. Josh pulled in the bundle and went to help Paula set up her hammock. David removed the bundle and tied the two lines together to feed it back to Alessandra. During the next few cycles, they used the small line to ferry bundles up to the conveyor carrying the bamboo armor, food, and water. Then Alessandra and finally Pedro crossed.

When Pedro flipped off the rope and made a graceful landing, everyone exchanged high fives. Josh said. "Okay, The Climb's out of the way. Everyone into your hammocks and try to get some sleep. Then we'll tackle The Conveyor."

28 David in the Mountain Heart

The trip up the conveyor went slowly. Josh pushed them hard. However, getting their gear and themselves through the frequent tangles of brush and debris proved to be a challenge.

The bamboo shields Alessandra developed were a great idea, but they were bulky to move. She'd done her best to make them easy to carry, but she had been limited by the available materials and the need to make them strong enough to be useful. They were made to fold up like curved, Japanese fans and only long enough to cover the head, shoulders, and chest. However, they seemed to snag on something every time the team came across more than a few small trees clumped together, which happened a lot.

So far, they'd gone through the process of stopping, hanging hammocks, huddling against the wall, and then repacking to travel seven times. Josh said it only took him five to reach the opening, and there was no telling how much further they had to go.

The eighth stop is where things went to hell. They set up per their standard lineup—Josh in front, then David, Paula, Alessandra, and Pedro. Josh said he wanted them in this order so that if something bad came, the larger people would take the hit and hopefully provide some protection for those on down the line. This wasn't just chivalry, though he may have had some of that in his motives. Josh had a softer heart than David would have credited him a few weeks ago. But he told them it wouldn't make sense the other way around because then anything coming down the conveyor would just bang the small person first and then the next bigger person in line. This seemed logical to David.

So far, there'd been some bumps and scrapes, but no serious injuries. In addition to the bamboo shields, Josh learned a few tricks during his scouting trip. He always tied his hammock behind a large pipe or where rods protruded the furthest from the walls. The rods were very strong. But even so, most of them were bent and there weren't very many useful ones to provide cover.

This time, several protruded out about a foot from the wall with some good places to tie up right behind. The group lined up and began getting their hammocks ready shortly after Alessandra called out, "Sixteen fifty."

Thanks to a lot of practice, they got their hammocks situated within a count of one hundred. Everyone was securely tied and waiting when Alessandra said, "Eighteen hundred." The conveyor lurched into motion and she called out, "Two thousand twenty-five." Pretty close to average.

David zoned out watching the conveyor zip by underneath him. By now, it'd become repetitious to the point of being a bit boring, despite the ongoing tension. Also, the greenish belt's motion was mesmerizing. This changed abruptly when Josh yelled, "Watch out. Brace yourselves."

David craned his neck to look up the tunnel and saw an ominous shadow coming at them. David double-checked his knots and hunkered behind his bamboo shield, trying unsuccessfully to make himself smaller.

A crunch came from just ahead, followed by a grunt. David glanced forward and saw a mass of leaves brushing along the wall sweep over the lead hammock. As he watched, the top of the tree began to rotate, pushing itself harder into the wall. The shadow loomed over him, and his bamboo quivered under a blow. He was thrust into the wall with painful pressure. He realized the tree must be turning and falling over as it moved. The pressure let up, and he started to relax.

A louder crunch followed by a scream came from behind. "Oh god, help muh–" Paula said, the last word cutting off abruptly.

David turned and looked back. The bamboo armor restricted his movement however and he couldn't see anything in that direction. He heard Alessandra grunt, and then Pedro emitted a small, sharp bark of pain.

"Sound off. Is everyone all right?" Josh yelled.

Their replies came together.

"I think so," Alessandra said.

David barked, "Okay."

"Yi," said Pedro.

"No," grunted Paula and moaned loud enough to be heard over the conveyor. "I…uh, got…hit," she gasped. "I…think it's…bad."

"Hang in there," Josh called back. "Don't move. "We'll come to you when the conveyor stops."

She didn't answer. Not good.

The conveyor ran for what seemed a very long time. David could hear grunts and snuffles coming from Paula's hammock, so at least she was still alive. Thankfully, no more trees came along their side while they waited.

When the belt stopped, everyone but Paula hurried out of their hammocks. Josh reached her first and knelt beside her.

"Where did you get hit?" he said in a gentle tone.

"In…my side. It came down from above."

David said, "I think it rolled. It pushed on me and when it went past, it must've gone over on her."

Josh nodded and eased Paula's shirt up. Her right side was covered with a large red welt, already turning faint purple in the middle. She gasped when he probed it gently with his fingers.

"I don't feel any rough spots, so hopefully there are no major breaks. There may be a fracture or two. How's your breathing?"

"Hard…to. Hurts…like hell."

Josh nodded. "Yeah, that's typical with a chest contusion. Do we need to rig a stretcher?"

Her eyebrows knitted together in determination. "No! I…can make it. Get me…up."

He looked at Alessandra. "Count? Sorry, I lost mine."

"Five hundred twenty-three," she said, her lips moving slightly as she continued counting.

Josh shook his head. "We'll need to stay here until the next cycle." He opened one of the pouches on his belt and took out a small bottle.

David recognized it as the one Josh took from him the first day they arrived. Josh told him his shoulder injury didn't merit using them, that the small quantity of medicine was all they had and must be rationed. Most of them went to Pedro while he fought a bad fever, so there couldn't be many left.

Josh shook the pills out onto his palm. It made a very small pile; David guessed seven or eight. Josh picked up half of them and put the rest back in the bottle. He pulled out his canteen and gave the pills to Paula, helping her lean forward to swallow.

"That should help with the pain and keep the swelling down. Rest for now." He looked at the others. "Split up her stuff. If you feel overloaded, let me know and either we'll redistribute or leave it behind. You know the priorities."

The other three nodded. The hammocks came first, or they wouldn't survive the next cycle. Then came water and clothing. Food they could get off the conveyor. However, the only water source they knew of was in the cave. And no one relished the idea of making a trip back there.

"I...I can handle the...harness," Paula said.

Josh looked into her eyes, and then nodded. The combat harness with a built-in water system David took off the Brazilian soldier was fairly heavy, but it distributed the weight very effectively. "We'll start out that way. But we need to minimize strain on you. Every extra motion or weight puts tension on your chest muscles, and that ain't good right now. So be honest, not stupid about it."

She still looked determined as she nodded agreement.

Alessandra took down the smallest of three sacks made of webbing hanging next to Paula. "Pedro, you think you can handle her clothes?" She repeated the phrase in his Indian dialect and he nodded. She did this almost every time she spoke to him to prevent confusion and help with his English.

Alessandra unhooked the two remaining bags with a soft grunt. Both contained gourds full of water and were heavy. "I can handle her hammock. You guys want to take one water bag each?"

David nodded and reached for one of the bags, but Josh stopped him and took both.

"I'll carry these and take point during the next stoppage," He looked at David with intense eyes and said, "You help Paula. We've got to get off this damn belt. I want to push hard, and it'll be up to you to help her keep up. Pick her up and carry her if you must."

Paula said, "I can–"

"Shut up," said Josh. "If you collapse, we've got to be ready. We'll need to go as far as possible."

Her eyes looked hurt at his tone, then softened as she realized he was right. She nodded.

"Eleven hundred," Alessandra said. It amazed David how she could talk and do other things while keeping a count in her head.

"Thanks," Josh said. "Okay, everyone get set. When the belt stops, we go."

The others nodded and went back to their hammocks. A moment later, the belt lurched into motion. What had begun to be boring was anything but as the belt ran beneath David. He kept craning his neck, trying to see what was coming. Thankfully, no more wall hugging trees approached.

Worry stretched the time and made it seem the belt would never stop. But finally, it did, and everyone hurried out of their hammocks except Paula. She did manage to get out on her own and started to untie it, but Alessandra quickly finished her own packing and helped her.

"One hundred fifty," Alessandra said as they set out. Almost double their usual time, but not bad considering Paula was hurt. However, it wasn't a good start for getting off the conveyor.

Paula only made a few steps before she reached up and grabbed David's shoulder. He stopped, but she gasped, "No, keep going. I…just need…to lean…on you." She kept walking, though he had to help her over any obstacle more than a few inches high. Her breath came in ragged pants, like a small, overloaded steam engine. She looked pale and her expression was one of painful concentration.

"I…can…make it," Paula kept gasping. "I…can…make it." David realized she was talking to herself more than him.

Josh led the way, kicking aside the worst of the debris. Alessandra followed and helped move limbs aside when they needed to make an easier path. Then came David with Paula leaning heavily on his arm. Last was Pedro, who danced back and forth and occasionally helped David get Paula over a large branch Josh couldn't move.

"Five hundred," Josh and Alessandra said in near unison. They were moving slower than ever. A herd of turtles would beat the crap out of them in a race. At six hundred, they saw a piece of webbing tied around one of the pipes.

Josh said, "This is where I stopped on the way back. But I was taking a leak when the belt stopped, so I left a little late. We can make it, but we gotta move."

The next hundred yards went okay. Not great, but nothing major blocked their path. "Eight hundred," came the count from the two in front.

Then they ran into a tight tangle of trees. At first, they appeared to be just another brush pile. Josh and Alessandra began hacking through it. Josh used his big survival knife and Alessandra the combat knife David took from the dead soldier. That's when things got nasty.

"Nine hundred."

Josh stopped counting. "Shit, give me the other knife," he said, reaching a hand out to Alessandra. She handed it over with a puzzled look on her face.

Josh used both knives like he was doing martial arts, turning into a living buzz saw. He slashed through thinner branches with the combat knife in his left hand, then hacked through thicker branches with two or three lightning-fast chops with the survival blade in his right. Alessandra fell back to help David move Paula.

She didn't call out a count for what seemed forever, and then she said, "One thousand fifty."

David wanted to yell that it had to be over fourteen hundred! But he was too busy helping Paula navigate the narrowing passage left in Josh's wake through the mound of tree limbs. The ends of the stumps were full of sharp points and splinters that repeatedly dug into flesh. Paula was crying and sobbing with every step, but made no effort to stop.

The way forward grew even smaller, a narrow green tunnel lined with sharp wooden spikes, the remains of Josh's onslaught.

"Twelve hundred!"

That couldn't be right. They'd been going through this stupid tree mound for much longer. But the training Josh put them through helped with more than just the physical conditioning. *Trust your teammates. Do your job. Stay focused.*

Despite Josh doing all the cutting, he got ahead of the others. Helping Paula hobble through was going much too slow. "Lay down! I'll pull you." She started to protest, but David turned her around and forced her to the ground. Then he grabbed her under her arms and started dragging her. The downside was he couldn't see where he was going.

Alessandra saw the problem and squeezed ahead. Balancing Paula's bamboo and webbing hammock under one arm, she grabbed David's belt and began tugging him through the cut. David let her guide him and began shuffling backwards, ignoring the frequent gouges from sharp sticks in his back and arms. They picked up the pace considerably.

"Fourteen hundred."

Crap! Now time was going too fast. *Had it taken that long to get Paula reoriented? Apparently so.* But they soon caught up to Josh, who was beginning to slow down.

"One thousand five hundred." Alessandra's voice cracked a little.

It was almost time to start tying up the hammocks. But in the narrow confines of the tree tunnel, there wasn't room. Would Josh stop and clear an area? Apparently not. But he did seem to find new energy and redoubled his efforts at clearing a lane for the team.

At one thousand seven hundred, they broke through. "There!" screamed Josh, his voice hoarse from exertion. "Just ahead."

David glanced back and nearly got his eye poked out for it. But he could see beyond the trees. There were still plenty of obstacles ahead but nothing like what they'd just come through. Did he see a dark spot on the wall? Could that be the opening? If so, it seemed frighteningly far ahead.

"Let me up," Paula said, trying to turn over.

David ignored her, picked her up, and cradled her in his arms. His injured shoulder hadn't bothered him in several weeks, but the sudden motion made it flare with pain. He grunted but kept going. Turning, he began lumbering up the belt after Josh, who was shoving debris out of their way with frenzied energy. Alessandra and Pedro ran ahead to help.

If Josh had been a buzz saw before, he became a bulldozer now. He put away the knives and scampered forward so low he was nearly on all fours, truly looking like the great ape David thought he was when he first saw him. Small bundles or piles he swept aside with his long powerful arms. Larger piles he plowed into like a football player, bowling them out of the way. Bit by bit, they neared the opening.

"Nineteen hundred," Alessandra gasped out. She and Pedro moved smaller objects out of the way like small whirlwinds traveling in Josh's wake.

Oh God, we've never pushed it this far. David's arms burned and his shoulder screamed at him to stop, to put down the painful weight. But he fought through it. He wasn't dropping Paula. He wasn't going to quit.

Paula's arms were locked around his neck as he stumbled forward. He could her grunting as he shuffled forward as fast as he could. David's expulsions of breath became a prayer to whatever Gods may control the conveyor.

"Please don't start. Please don't start. Please don't start," he huffed and puffed.

Then they were there. Josh leapt down first. Alessandra and Pedro stopped and danced nervously waiting for David and Paula. They helped push him up and over so that David half jumped, half fell through the opening, landing in a tumble with Paula. She cried out in agony as Alessandra and Pedro came right behind and landed on top of them.

They lay in a pile, panting like the exhausted animals they were. They listened for the conveyor to start. Instead, a peal of distant thunder made them jump. Josh had warned them about the thunder. But the crackling boom after the mad dash to escape the conveyor almost made David pee himself.

The others must have had similar reactions, but it triggered an incredible surge of relief. The next thing, they were all laughing. For several moments, they drowned out the odd booms of the cavern with sounds of mirth that bordered on the maniacal. Even Paula, who laughed and sobbed with pain at the same time as tears ran in rivulets down her face. Then, with the customary squeal, the conveyor began moving behind them. This brought the laughter to a quick stop. After a few seconds of listening to the booms and soft squeals of the conveyor, they slowly began to untangle themselves.

David's whole body ached, and he flopped over on his back. It felt wonderful to be on a surface that wouldn't lurch into motion at any moment and carry him to his doom. Never had cold, hard stone felt so good. They lay or sat, all of them gasping, in a loose circle, even Josh. Thank God for the training they'd done. David regretted every bad thought he ever had about Josh. He thought back about that last mad dash and shuddered at how close it'd been.

Pedro recovered first. Nothing surprising about that; the kid seemed to run on nuclear energy. He stood and walked over to the lip of the wide ledge overlooking the cavern beyond. Flickers of light noticeably brighter than the glowing blue rods silhouetted him and sent ghostly shadows back toward the group. There came an especially bright flash, followed a heartbeat later by a thunderous boom. It seemed as if a thunderstorm brewed just beyond the ledge on which Pedro stood. David could imagine a swirling tornado beneath the boy's feet. But he knew it wasn't a storm down there. It was something much worse.

Paula looked bad. Alessandra and Josh were kneeling beside her, trying to get her to drink some water. She managed a few sips, grimacing with each swallow. Her skin was pale, and David noticed her shiver from time to time. Not good. He heard Josh say something about making a stretcher out of the hammocks and bamboo.

David climbed to his feet and stretched out his back. Then he rolled his aching shoulder around to loosen up and make sure he hadn't reinjured it. Both hurt, but not so bad as to suggest it would be anything permanent. God, he hoped not. It looked like he would be needing both in the very near future if they had to carry Paula.

His legs felt a bit rubbery, but they steadied as he made his way over to Pedro. Despite the thunder-like peals, no subterranean storm could be seen from the ledge, just random blue lights blurred by mist stretching into the distance overhead. Below, a shadowy swirling murk of blue fog. The flickers of lightning and rumbles of thunder had an irregular pattern, growing in intensity, and then fading, only to swell again a few seconds later. A big blue Hell.

The poor light and mist hid the depths of the chamber. But it did reveal the ledge they stood on sloped down to the right and followed the wall in a wide left-hand curve. To the left, there was a gray white wall, like granite, with a large crack running up the face. It appeared large enough to enter at the bottom but quickly tapered to a hairline fracture about twenty-five feet up. This wall jutted out a hundred feet or more beyond the ledge and then stopped, blocking the view in that direction. All as Josh described it.

Paula's voice, strained but angry, could be heard over a lull in the thunder. "Get me up," she said. "I want to see."

"Are you sure about this?" Josh said. His concern was obvious as he looked down the sloping path. "You're banged up pretty bad, and I'm not wild about taking a chance on getting noticed."

David turned to see Paula grasp Josh's arm. "Yes, I am sure," she said. "I really want to see. If this thing is what we're up against, I...well, I just need to see."

He looked over at David. "How about you? You want to come? I'll need help with Paula."

The rumbling thunder shook David's confidence. Fear made a knot at the base of his throat and he swallowed hard, unsure if he wanted to. Paula's pleading eyes tipped the scale. He drew in a deep breath and let it out slowly, then went over to help Josh support Paula.

Alessandra had already told them she had no interest in seeing what occupied the cavern below. It was plain Pedro wanted to come. But after a sidelong glance at Alessandra he shook his head. The two watched as David and Josh put their arms around Paula and helped her to her feet. The three started to hobble down the sloping walkway. But before they had traveled more than a few steps, Alessandra rushed after them with Pedro right behind. She grasped David's arm and looked up at him with fearful, though determined eyes.

"If you go, I go," she said.

The comment surprised David. He wasn't even sure of the significance. Did Alessandra care that much for him? Since there were too many questions to risk saying anything stupid, he just gave a brief nod.

Pedro ran to Josh and wrapped his arms around one thick, muscular leg. Josh looked surprised, then befuddled, then slightly pleased as he wrapped one of his oversized paws around the boy's small hand, although he kept his other arm around Paula. They almost seemed like a family going on a picnic. The thought made David chuckle softly. A family picnic in Hades. But on second thought, it really wasn't that funny.

The path was steep, but free of debris and easy to walk on. They descended a couple of hundred feet before they reached the halfway point of the long curve and they could began to see around the protruding wall. Pedro let go of Josh's hand and fell in behind them. David was pressed into the side wall. Alessandra walked just behind him, one hand gripping his shoulder with pressure just shy of being painful.

"A little further should do," Josh said.

Paula gave a small gasp of pain and said, "Sorry, hurts worse than I thought. I need to rest a bit."

"Do you want to go back?" Josh asked.

"After all this? Hell no," she said, managing slight grin. "Just give me a minute."

The two men helped her to a small rock ledge, which she almost collapsed onto. David stretched again and eased to the edge for a look out at the cavern. The lip looked firm enough, and the team exercises had helped ease his fear of heights, but it paid to be cautious. An involuntary shudder ran through him at the sight. It looked very foreboding. Thankfully, from what Josh had learned on his expedition, they wouldn't have to go all the way to the bottom.

Paula recovered her breath and waved him back over. Josh and David resumed their positions, and the small group continued to edge down and around the ramp.

The sweet smell they now associated with the demons grew stronger as they went down. Before long, it even overwhelmed the smell of death and reminded him of chocolate chip cookies more than ever. They traveled far enough to get directly below the hole they entered through. As they walked, a two-hundred-foot tall opening into another chamber came into view.

Josh held up his hand, and they began to creep forward even slower. They moved in a tight cluster. David was surprised Josh didn't say anything about that. He generally didn't like them bunched together like this.

"Old habit," he'd usually say. "Makes it too easy for one grenade to take out the whole team." But for this, it appeared even he wanted the close contact of the others.

At last, they moved far enough around to through the opening. As the mist thinned, there was enough light to see the largest cavern yet. It stretched off into the distance for what had to be miles, although the scale of it made it difficult to tell for sure. The mist, while fainter, caused a painful glare each time one of the thunderous flashes lit up the air. This made David's eyes constantly fight to adjust to the light. Each flash was followed by crackling pops and bangs. A series of more powerful flashes ended in a chest thumping boom that made all of them jump. Then the lightning and noise would slacken as if gathering energy for another round.

At last his eyes managed to adapt enough to make some sense of what lay below. The movement David spotted from above was not the random motion of a few beings. Inside were thousands upon thousands upon thousands of creatures. What appeared to be the motion of individuals was the pulsations of multitudes as they jostled around and over one another. Like a living carpet, tightly packed gatherer of all shapes and sizes covered the floor as far as he could see.

The thickest mass was around and on top of a large hill that dominated the center of the chamber. Hulking gatherers, tool users, and... other things that none of them had seen before. One was the size of a tool user but had a long, whip-like claw that looked very dangerous. Another looked much bigger than a gatherer and must have stood fifty feet tall. But this last one was just a hulking shadow and too far away to distinguish details in the strange lights.

Their movements seemed to have no purpose. Why were they clustered together in this chamber like this? Feeding or fornicating, maybe both, for all he knew. Except for a few individuals, David couldn't tell where one creature ended and the next began. He remembered their discussion back when the gatherer had allowed itself to be buried and blended in the pit. The scene before him looked like something from a documentary on termites or bees. The idea they were in some sort of huge hive seemed more likely than ever.

The size, scope, and sheer numbers staggered the mind. There were hundreds of thousands of them, maybe millions. The sight made his mouth go dry.

The small group stared transfixed until a super bright flash followed by the loudest clap of thunder yet made all of them flinch and duck down. Alessandra and the boy both cried out in fear, pressing their hands to their ears. Despite the ringing in his head left in the wake of the blasts, David could hear her praying with fervent intensity.

Most of the thunder and lightning came from two, three-hundred-foot tall spires projecting from the hill up into the ceiling of the vast chamber. Both were studded with secondary spires of various sizes, sticking out all over in a random fashion like a child's attempt to draw a tree. Blue lightning played between these as well as the main spires, racing up and down constantly. Sometimes, small dancing threads of blue fire would leap along the ceiling and down the walls of the chamber.

There was one final, numbing crescendo that roared through the chamber, and then the discharges eased to merely intimidating once more. As the sound abated, David lowered his arms and blinked, trying to clear his eyes of splotchy afterimages. His ears rang, and he feared for moment he'd lost his hearing. Only the ongoing crackles and booms still coming from the towers let him know otherwise.

The icy chill climbing his spine earlier now became a blizzard. This, then, was Paul's electromagnetic pulse source. An EMP, the nuclear explosion level interference that disrupted radios for hundreds of miles. Of that, he had no doubt. David felt as though he'd just witnessed firsthand an atomic detonation and prayed they hadn't been bathed in a lethal dose of radiation.

He wanted to turn and run, yet froze in place, as if moving would take more force of will than his overtaxed brain could generate. The others looked as awestruck as he felt.

David tracked the spires down and around. Josh said the mother of them all lived here, but he couldn't see her. He looked near the bottom of the spires but saw nothing. As his gaze swept over the hill, nothing distinguished itself. Then he focused back at the base of one of the immense structures. *How's it anchored? What's it anchored to?* The spires widened out at the base. The flicking lighting made it difficult to trace the lines.

Then he saw it, and the blizzard chill became colder still, a cold that would rival the darkest depths of space. At first, his reasoning mind refused to grasp what his emotions screamed. But then he realized that before them was the potential new master of Earth's food chain.

For the hill itself was alive. As the multitudes of gatherers moved along the base of the mound, he saw it pulse and quiver. The spires were antenna, growing from a creature beyond gargantuan. It had to be over two miles long, and maybe half as wide. His dry mouth hindered his speech, but he managed to shout, "It's a queen! They are like ants. We are in a hive."

The queen didn't have any recognizable features one would expect of a living being. No arms, legs, eyes, or mouth. It was just one huge, slowly pulsing mass. He wasn't even sure of its color, though he thought it was mostly a bluish gray. But there was no questioning the entire hill lived.

David's desire to be away from this chamber came alive with vigor. He began backing up the slope, the others doing likewise. They'd seen enough. After a few steps, Alessandra let go of his arm, grasped his hand, and began tugging him upwards.

They climbed in a stupor. None of them said anything until they reached the ledge with the opening to the conveyor. Then Josh spoke.

"Well, are you happy now?" He had to be yelling to be heard, but his voice sounded muffled and distant to David's abused ears.

"Not particularly," replied Paula, sinking to the floor. The trip had taken a lot out of her.

"That's the Devil," breathed Alessandra. "We are in Hell." Her voice was tinged with hysteria. "How can we escape from Hell?"

Despite her pain, Paula rounded on her angrily. "We are not in Hell. None of those... those things are lost or tormented souls. They are just a bunch of freaks of nature, overgrown ants or something."

David had no idea what the creatures were, but he was confident they were much more than merely overgrown ants. However, he kept his mouth shut. Alessandra looked away from Paula, turned, and buried her face against David's arm.

Paula shook her head, then looked up at Josh. "Well, we are not going to get out of here that way. What now?"

Josh shrugged. "We know the conveyor is out unless we want to try sneaking across the chamber where they chop up the trees. So, we don't really have a choice but to check out this passage." He gestured to the crack in the wall to the left of the opening. "If it doesn't go anywhere...Well, we'll have to figure something out then."

David and Paula nodded in agreement. Alessandra just shrugged, her face still partially hidden by David's arm. Pedro nodded too. In fact, he'd probably learned enough English now that his nod had merit.

"Okay," Josh said, laying out Paula's hammock on the ground. "Help me get some of the bamboo laced through this, and we'll get a stretcher ready."

Paula started to protest, but Josh just stared at her for a moment. She looked at the others for support, but their faces held the same, 'don't bullshit us look,' as Josh. With a sigh, she leaned back in resignation.

They decided to leave two sacks holding water gourds hidden by the crack in the wall to save weight. Someone could retrieve them later. Even as tired as they were, no one wanted to rest in the cavern. For now, they just wanted to get far away from the thing below. After about fifteen minutes, they got Paula situated on the stretcher. David picked up one end and Josh the other. Josh nodded to Alessandra to go first. She'd recovered a bit and nodded back with renewed determination in her eyes. Then they walked into the passage with the hope it would lead to their salvation.

29 Sally Meets with Colonel Ames

"This is amazing," Dr. Allen said as his eyes scanned the half mile of water between the civilian camp and old Rio Estrada docks. At least a hundred watercraft of various shapes and sizes floated in between. "It almost looks like we could walk across."

It wasn't so much that there were more boats in the river than before. But most of the ones in view were much bigger. A couple would almost qualify as ships. Numerous barges waited for an opening at the docks or the landing area the Brazilian engineers had carved out of the hillside. Even the boats lined up for the floating platforms on the civilian side were bigger than usual.

Julio told her the two biggest ones that looked like ships were Brazilian river gunboats. So, technically they weren't actually ships. But they looked like ships to her and bristled with guns. Both looked very reassuring. Sally wished they could've been battleships.

The three researchers stood on one of the civilian docks as it bobbed gently from the wakes of all the boats. The three civilians wore U.S. Marine fatigues with no insignia. Colonel Ames said it would help clarify they were visiting her headquarters and not the Brazilians' if the question came up.

The silence stretched after Dr. Allen's comment, although he clearly expected some kind of reply. Sally and Paul stood on each side of him, staring out at the harbor. Dr. Allen cut his eyes back and forth between them, sensing something was up, but not sure what. *It's just as well.* The talk with Paul last night hadn't gone badly, but it hadn't been fun either.

She'd started off telling him that they'd had their time, and she felt it best they moved on. He had looked hurt, but not surprised.

"Yeah, okay," he said. "I…I had a feeling it was over. If only we'd put more time into this thing back…well, you know."

"Yeah, I know. Maybe it would've been different. We live in a very strange, new world now," she said, thinking that was the understatement of the decade. And even though she'd agreed it might have worked, she didn't really believe it. They'd gone down different paths because they wanted different things, pure and simple. It happened that way sometimes.

They'd promised to be friends, as most couples do when they break up. They also promised to stay in touch, no matter what. She was sure they both meant it. And like all ex-couples, they knew it to be unlikely. That was too bad. She really liked and admired Paul. And it was always possible their paths might converge again someday. Who knew? They did have a lot in common.

With only the awkward silence greeting his first observation, Dr. Allen must have felt compelled to say something else. "So, a Brazilian patrol boat is taking us to an American meeting? Doesn't that seem odd?"

"Yeah, sure does," Sally said, suppressing a sigh at his attempt to start a dialogue. Not that she had ill will toward him; she just didn't feel like talking. Besides, Dr. Allen already knew why they were waiting on a Brazilian boat. Colonel Antinasio was going to the meeting as well. In addition, the Marines relied on, or rather had relied on, helicopters for moving people around. Since any aircraft attempting to fly within three hundred miles of the White Mountain got shot down, they had a shortage of transportation.

Dr. Allen glanced at Sally and Paul again, then gave a small shrug. For the next few minutes, they stood in silence as boats and barges moved pulled into docks and churned across the river.

"There they are," Paul said as one of PBG-31's jet boats rounded a nearby barge and headed toward them.

"There's our ride, Miss Sally," Julio said, not understanding Paul's statement in English. He and Raoul were standing nearby in full battle harness, their rifles slung at their side. Ever since the attack, university personnel had armed guards if they left the camp area. Marcus wasn't taking any chances with the Church of the Mountain. Julio wasn't normally one of the guards. However, Colonel Ames wanted him to tell his story too, so it made sense for him to pull double duty.

"Yes, Julio, thank you," she replied. "You all set?"

The young corporal shrugged. "I guess so. It will be weird talking through a translator. Seems like they could read about the battle just as easy."

"I think Colonel Ames wants you there to answer questions, not just talk. Besides, it will be good to have you along."

The boat pulled up to the dock, and he just smiled at her in reply before hurrying to help catch the mooring lines. Marcus, Nelino, and Jeronimo were onboard, and they raised their hands in greeting. She noticed Paul giving Marcus a dirty look. Did he blame the Brazilian for her not getting back together with him? Well, there might be a little something to that. But Paul wasn't the vindictive type, though he might be jealous she'd be with Marcus in Manaus. And why did she even care? *Did I make a mistake with Paul? Crap, here comes that complicated thinking again.* She didn't even know her own heart; she should damn well stop trying to figure out other people's.

Once they boarded the boat and got underway, Marcus stepped down from the small bridge and greeted them. Paul loosened up and shook hands with him cordially enough. She knew Paul was too good a person to bear an unreasonable grudge.

"So, how did your meeting with the Shepherd go?" she said.

"About how I expected. He denied ever suggesting any violent acts. In fact, he vehemently condemned any such actions." Marcus looked disgusted. "The Church of the Mountain is only engaged in preparing the world for God's punishment, not actively supporting it. Or so he said, anyway."

"But you're not buying it?"

"No. Thing is, I got the feeling he didn't really either. I mean about God's punishment. There's something strange with that guy. Besides being a religious fanatic, I mean."

"Well, the packing is going well," Sally said. "I just hope Colonel Ames is okay with the move. I did promise to join her staff."

"Yes, but your work would suffer. The facilities you'll have in Manaus should be far better suited for studying the harvesters."

Any further conversation was cut off by the roar of three United States Marine hovercraft. Marcus had told her they were called LCACs, which stood for Landing Craft Air Cushion. Each of the large vessels moved with incredible speed. The three LCACs made floating, skidding banked turns as they went past and then headed straight for the area cleared by the Brazilian engineers. Just before hitting the shore, they flared backwards slightly and drove right out of the water onto land. Each carried several armored vehicles. Sally wasn't sure if they should be considered boats or aircraft. By the time the hovercraft settled and cut their engines, the patrol boat reached the Rio Estrada docks.

They docked without incident. No one challenged Sally for coming to the base, although several sailors working on the docks pointed at her or waved. She smiled and waved back. It made her feel a bit like a kid sneaking out of school, and she kept expecting someone would confront her for being on the base in violation of von Jaeger's orders. But no one did.

Colonel Ames's aid, Lieutenant Woods and her interpreter, Warrant Officer Webb met them on the concrete apron connecting the docks. After a quick round of greetings, Woods ushered them toward three Humvees sitting nearby. Once everyone was loaded, they headed through the flattened area that had once been a thriving Brazilian frontier village. Scores of olive green tents of varying sizes now occupied the land where thatched huts once stood.

Being in Rio Estrada was harder on Sally than she expected. There were a lot of ghosts here for her. This was where her brother had been taken by the harvesters. The last time she'd spent meaningful time with Myra and Keith before the fateful helicopter flight. She remembered the town's people and the quirky shops. The church and the quaint village square with its modest-sized fountain. The small, but neat hotel. Now all gone. Destroyed by a horde of alien monsters and replaced by a large, but sterile military base.

The Humvee bounced up to the Marine headquarters. It sat about a mile west of the old town square, at the edge of the area cleared by the harvesters when they destroyed Rio Estrada. It consisted of a tracked amphibious troop carrier studded with antennae and two trailers. The vehicle was enormous, and if Sally hadn't seen several of them cross the river and then drive out of the water, she wouldn't have believed it could float. There was also a large, open awning with additional equipment set up next to it. In the trees just beyond the edge of the stripped and barren land, several logs were arranged in rows like church pews. A fair number of uniformed men and women already sat

A Harvest of Aliens

there.

Colonel Ames walked out from under the awning with another man to greet the Humvees. She introduced him as her executive officer, Major Mark Sanchez. Sanchez seemed to be a very intense individual of Hispanic background. He had a pronounced accent, though he was easy enough to understand.

After the introductions, Colonel Ames said, "If everyone would excuse us, I would like a word with Colonel Antinasio and Miss Morgan in private. Major Sanchez will get the rest of you settled and set up with translators." It took a moment for the instructions to be relayed in Portuguese and get everyone sorted out. Then Ames led Marcus and Sally into the amphibious vehicle.

The inside was larger than expected. She and Ames could stand upright with ease, and Marcus only had to duck slightly. One side had a padded bench and the other a large map and three computer consoles. Colonel Ames walked to the map, looked at it for a moment, then turned and said, "I have some concerns about our situation that I would like discuss with Colonel Antinasio and you. If you would be so good as to translate for us?"

"Um, well, of course," Sally said in a puzzled tone and then relayed this to Marcus.

"I can see you're wondering about not having Webb translate," Ames said. "Well, this is a delicate matter. Plus, you may have some insight into the situation." She picked up a tablet with headphones attached. "Also, we have these translators, but they sometimes mix things up. Context and all...You know? I prefer the human touch, if that's okay."

"Certainly," Sally said. "What can we do for you?"

"Is General von Jaeger insane? Or merely stupid?" Ames said, her expression dead serious.

Sally was shocked. "Uh, do you want me to say that to Colonel Antinasio? I mean, I hate the man's guts...And I'm sure Marcus does too. But..."

"Yes, ask him...Wait. Tell him I'm not asking out of personal animosity. I admit I disliked the man from the start. But the orders he's giving... Well, they don't make any sense. I've asked for more latitude from the admiral. But communications suck. Before I jump into hot water on my own, I'd like a little more information."

Sally relayed this to Marcus pretty much verbatim. He considered the question very carefully. Sally knew he didn't have any great regard for the general. But he was too honorable to badmouth a superior.

"I believe he is all too sane, Colonel," he said. "I also don't believe he is stupid…Well, maybe militarily, but not when it comes to politics." He frowned at the map. "However, when it comes to battle, he has no experience and a very romantic idea of what it is." He turned to Ames. "I haven't seen a deployment map. I didn't know our forces were so exposed."

Colonel Ames nodded. "He gives orders to move every day. It disrupts any attempts at defense. I've refused to acknowledge his orders the last two days, and he's…well, pissed off." She pointed to a small square on the map. "This is an old rubber plantation house. I have decided to fortify the area around it. Until I receive orders from my own superiors, I cannot accept any more of his…movements."

"I'm sorry. But I don't have any influence on the general. He has ordered my unit back to Manaus in a few days."

"Crap! I'm really sorry to hear that," Colonel Ames said. "I was hoping when your marine regiment arrived, someone could talk some sense into him, maybe you. Any idea who I could discuss this with up your chain of command?"

Marcus shook his head. "Not that would do any good," he said through Sally. "You mentioned before that our command structure is…as you put it, screwed up. We have a lot of political divisions in our government that extend into the military."

"Damn politics," Ames said. "A lot of good people might die if this thing goes south. You see that, don't you?"

"Yes, I do." He frowned at the map." I haven't been privy to the details of his deployments. It looks like he positioned most of our armor too far out to the east. That narrow road would be easy to cut."

Colonel Ames nodded. "I thought so too. When I mentioned it, he got upset and actually moved the units further away. Also, they're now clustered together at the old logging camp. The terrain in that area will make it difficult for them to do much if we get attacked."

Marcus tapped the road between the logging camp and Rio Estrada. "It almost looks like he's moving toy soldiers about in a war of maneuver. I see this area is covered almost solely with infantry. That's not good. Unless there've been a lot of shipments I'm unaware of, most of these troops don't have battle rifles, only the lighter assault rifles." He looked at Sally. "We have firsthand experience how difficult it is to kill demons with smaller caliber weapons."

Sally nodded and relayed this to Colonel Ames, who looked angry. "Jaeger says their weapons are just fine if they are in the hands of…real men. He seems to believe the harvesters are…just a bunch of animals or something."

Sally muttered in English, "I think the little weasel may actually be crazy."

Marcus looked at her patiently until she translated. When she did, he gave a crooked grin. "Maybe, but it doesn't help us here and now."

"Actually, it does," said Colonel Ames. "It helps me anyway. I may get into hot water later, but for now we're going to operate independently of his orders." She turned back to the map. "In addition to fortifying the plantation, I will make plans for a rapid withdrawal."

Marcus's expression became very grave. "There are a lot of good men out there, Colonel. Would you abandon them because our leader is an idiot?"

"No, Colonel," she replied in a terse voice. "However, I cannot help them by being put into a poor tactical position. I'm leaving my armored company in Rio Estrada as part of the reserve. That's the one good idea the general had. And once I have a secure operational area, I will be in a better position to support your men if the need arises."

Marcus peered into Colonel Ames' eyes for several seconds, then gave a curt nod. He turned back to study the map. "I hope this discussion becomes moot. In a few weeks, we'll have much stronger forces. In addition," he tapped the map north of the White Mountains, "there is a decent year-round road into this area. It will support heavy vehicles even in the wet season. General Fernando, commanding officer of the Naval de Brasilia Marines, plans on deploying our forces in this region."

Ames smiled. "That makes good sense. And it wouldn't be logical for them to be under Jaeger's command then, would it?"

"No," replied Marcus with a smile. "In fact, I may be assigned to the marine armored brigade. I served with them before taking command of PBG-31."

Sally glanced at him sharply. This was the first she'd heard of this. *What about showing me around Manaus?* She shook her head, angry with herself. What a stupid, childish thought. *We're at war. My wants definitely come second...But still?*

"Before we go, there's something else," Sally said. "You know about the attack on our camp?" Ames nodded, and Sally continued, "The University of Manaus is getting back into operation. Dr. Allen and the staff think we should move our research there. Except for the physics group."

"It makes sense," Ames said. "No pressure on you to join my staff. I just wanted to give you an option in case Jaeger made things too hot for you." She looked at the monitor displaying the time. "If you'll excuse me, von Jaeger has called a meeting. Interesting, that. He didn't schedule it until he heard I was meeting with you and Colonel Antinasio."

"Figures," Sally said. "When I said he was a weasel, I believe I insulted weasels everywhere."

Ames laughed. "That may well be true." She gestured toward the ramp leading out of the vehicle. "If you'll excuse me, I need to go see what this meeting is about. My executive officer will see to things here."

Lieutenant Woods and Warrant Officer Webb were waiting for the colonel at one of the Humvees. With a final wave, Ames climbed in. The Hummer started up and headed for the Brazilian headquarters. This sat on a slight rise about half a mile away, and a short distance from the old town square. General von Jaeger's large trailer was visible in the center of half a dozen smaller ones. Four tall microwave antennae towered over the cluster of trailers and an even taller flagpole flew the Brazilian flag. Below that was a bright red flag with two stars on it.

"Jaeger wants people to know where he is, doesn't he?" Sally said.

"It's truly stupid," replied Marcus with a frown. "No command staff should make such easy targets of themselves in hostile territory. If you'll excuse me." With a slight shake of his head, he turned and headed toward his men, who were being outfitted with translator tablets.

Evidently the tablets would have to be good enough for this meeting. Sally decided to get one herself to see how accurate they were. The bots behind them had improved a lot over the last few of years, but tone and inflection still confused them and could make a lot of difference in the actual content of what was said—especially for detailed information. Major Sanchez had a woman with him wearing similar insignia to Warrant Officer Webb. Maybe she was a translator too. Sally headed for them.

The woman was Warrant Officer Margert Benson, and she was indeed a translator. However, Portuguese wasn't her specialty, although she did speak it well enough to help hand out the translators. Still, she expressed gratitude for Sally's help in getting things sorted out.

Major Sanchez stepped up to Sally as people were getting settled onto the logs facing a small podium and said, "Webb was supposed to orchestrate the proceeding this morning. Since he's with the colonel, would you mind taking over?"

Sally nodded and said, "I'll do my–"

Gunfire erupted from the direction of the docks, cutting off her reply. As they spun about, the first few shots turned into a torrent, accompanied by distant frantic yells. Everyone was armed, except for Sally. Even Marcus had his pistol. She suddenly felt very naked.

"Form a perimeter," Major Sanchez yelled. He looked at Sally and pointed toward the headquarters vehicle. "Get in the AAV; it should be safe."

"Screw that," she said with a snarl. "Give me a rifle."

He looked exasperated. "I'm not arming a civilian. But do whatever the hell you want. I don't have time for this."

Sanchez ran to join the Marines from the meeting. Two squads who must have been stationed nearby jogged out as well. They formed a loose arc facing Rio Estrada. All of the others either knelt or lay down and sighted down their rifles while sweeping them back and forth, searching for targets. In the distance, people could be seen running in all directions. Some stopped to shoot, but Sally couldn't tell at what.

Sally squatted down also. It seemed the sensible thing to do. Marcus and the other Brazilians joined her. "It must be those damn scout demons," Nelino said.

"But how?" Julio said. "I thought you said they traveled in the trees."

"They travel how they wish," Nelino said. "They probably came from the river. If war demons can swim like porpoises, why not them?"

Waves of ear thumping sound washed over her. BAM, bam-bam, boom. Explosions wracked the area under General von Jaeger's flag. His trailer leaped off the ground by a foot and fell back down with a heavy thud. Smoke began pouring out the door and windows. More explosions went off, and two more trailers turned into raging infernos. One of the microwave antennas toppled over, followed by another an instant later. One of them landed on a burning trailer, crushing it in the middle.

"Dear God," Sally said in a hoarse whisper.

A few organized groups came into view, moving through the camp in a line. Each soldier walked in a half crouch with their rifles on their shoulders. They flicked the barrels back and forth in smooth motions, squeezing off shots as they advanced. The explosions stopped and the shooting died down. But sporadic shots still erupted with occasional wild bursts echoing across the open ground.

"At least someone has it together over there," Marcus said. "Looks like they're getting things under control. But what a mess."

A rumble drew their attention to the right as four Marine LAVs drove out of the forest in front of the loose arc of soldiers. Lieutenant Johnson stood tall in the turret of one, looking very grim, but determined.

"Mount up," yelled Major Sanchez. "Everyone get in or on the LAVs. We need to find the colonel."

Sally hopped up and ran to one of the Hummers. Marcus and the others followed.

Major Sanchez was about to enter one of the Humvees. He stopped and said. "Whoa. Where do you think you're going?"

She swept her arm toward Marcus and his men. "Don't you think you might need some Brazilian leaders over there? And a translator?"

"Uhh. Crap. Yeah, get in."

They loaded into the Humvee. It was a tight fit, so Sally sat on Marcus's lap. Under any other situation, this might have been interesting. Right now, she didn't give it a second thought. The engine roared to life and the vehicle lurched into motion. The LAVs finished loading and started to move as well. The Hummer roared past them and bounced across the plowed earth toward the Brazilian base.

It only took a little over a minute to cover the half mile to the Brazilian headquarters. The two Hummers skidded to a stop, and everyone piled out, weapons at the ready. Except for Sally, who once again felt naked. Less than a minute later, the four LAVs arrived, and the Marines leaped out to form a perimeter around the vehicles.

"There's Colonel Ames's Hummer," Major Sanchez said. "Fletcher, Mahan, go check it out. Second Squad, head into the headquarters area and see if you can render assistance. Shout if you see trouble."

A chorus of, "Aye sir," answered him, and men began fanning out. Smoke swirled thick around the trailers, making the scene a shadowy place. A lot of people were running about in different directions, with no apparent purpose. Sporadic shots still rang out, although no more of the wild bursts could be heard. There weren't any more explosions either. But there had to be a thousand small, dark, deformed-looking, multi-legged shapes scattered over the camp. Scout demons.

A line of men in a loose V formation appeared out of the smoke. They moved like coiled springs, weapons at the ready. A small group of the dark shapes scuttled toward the formation, and two of the men fired several quick shots. The scout demons spasmed and their legs shriveled into their bodies.

The man in front looked familiar. As the group drew near, Sally recognized Sergeant Cyro Araujo. He nodded and smiled at her but walked on over to Nelino and Marcus.

"Sirs," he said in an easy-going tone. "Fancy meeting you gentlemen here."

Nelino gave a wry grin. "I should have known you'd be one of the first people to get their act together." He looked over the still burning wreckage. "Looks like quite a mess."

The sergeant nodded. "That it is, Captain. I'm glad you brought reinforcements. But I think most of the excitement's over." A scream came out of the haze, followed by a short burst of gunfire. "Well, almost anyway," he said, frowning in the direction of the shots. He turned to Colonel Antinasio. "If you'll excuse me, sir, we need to finish our sweep and set up a perimeter."

"Yes, of course, Sergeant. Keep up the good work."

"Yes, sir." He turned and gestured to his men. The soldiers kept formation, swung in a large arc, and headed back into the thick tendrils of drifting smoke. Every few minutes, muzzle flashes lit up the hazy air, accompanied by the sharp retort of gunfire.

"Medic! Medic!" came a voice from ahead. "Major, we found her." This was followed by a cry in Portuguese of, "Médico! Médico!" More frantic instructions in both languages reverberated out of the smoke around the burning trailers.

Sanchez took off at a fast jog. Marcus, Sally, and the rest followed. As they entered the circle defined by the trailers, Sally saw a rifle laying in the dirt. She paused long enough to snatch it up and check it over as she hurried after the others.

The weight told her this was a battle rifle. It was a larger, more powerful weapon than the assault rifle given to her by PBG-31 and felt awkward in her hands. But Julio had shown her the basics and let her fire his a few times. The biggest difference between it and an assault rifle was that it kicked like a mule. She slung it over her shoulder as she neared the smoldering, tattered remains of what had been a large tent near the center of the compound.

Men were poking through the wreckage, and bodies were scattered everywhere. Some had been covered with blankets but most still lay where they'd fallen. To the left, Major Sanchez was with a group of Marines kneeling by three forms on the ground. Before she reached them, the major stood. Still looking down, he shook his head slowly.

*Oh, dear God, did that mean…*Yes, now she could see the uniforms. Colonel Ames and her two companions lay covered in blood. As she watched, the Marines began putting ponchos over their bodies. Tears welled up in Sally's eyes. Linda Ames had been a fantastic leader. A fantastic person. The world would be a little darker with her passing.

Marcus stood with another group nearby, where several more bodies lay. One was very much alive and waved his arms in the air repeatedly. As she drew near, she could hear the petulant voice of General von Jaeger. "This is your fault." It was unclear who he was talking to. "All of you. I see you, Antinasio. You were supposed to patrol the rivers, and that's where these things came from. You're going to fry for this."

Sally noticed none of the men seemed to trying to help the general. They just stood looking down at him. Jaeger spotted her, and his eyes bulged. "You? Morgan. I gave orders! Who?" He looked at Marcus. "Ah. Defying direct orders, Antinasio. I will bury you…and her. Take her to the stockade. Lock her up!"

None of the men moved. She noticed that most of them were Sergeant Araujo's men. Araujo stood beside Marcus. He said, "General, I believe you're in shock. My men will take you to the aid station."

"What? Nonsense! Get me to a vehicle. And why haven't you arrested that woman yet?"

Araujo nodded to a man kneeling beside the general wearing a red cross armband. The man nodded back and gave von Jaeger a shot.

"What the hell's that? What are…What…I…" The general stopped waving his arms about and closed his eyes.

Araujo said, "The general has suffered an extreme shock. Please make sure he gets…proper…medical care."

The man wearing the red cross armband looked up and smiled. "Sure thing, Sergeant." He motioned to two other soldiers, who placed the general on a stretcher and carried him away.

Araujo came to attention and gave Marcus a crisp salute.

"Colonel. My men and I have completed an examination of the area and listed the casualties of this attack. I must inform you that the entire general staff and first tier officer corps have been killed or wounded. At present, you are the senior commanding officer of this region."

"Dear God," Marcus said as the skin around his eyes crinkled in shock.

"What's this all about?" Major Sanchez asked from her shoulder.

She glanced back, surprised to see him there. "It appears Colonel Antinasio has just taken command."

"Hmph. That's the one decent bit of news to come out of this shit pile." He bowed his head. "Colonel Ames is dead."

Sally nodded. "Yes, I saw. I'm very sorry. It looks like Marcus is not the only one getting a promotion in this...shit pile."

"No, I guess not. So–"

An extremely loud roar of thunder echoed out of the east. Only this wasn't a single peal, but an unending roll of explosions. Crackles and pops from thousands of rifles punctuated lulls in the loud blasts. Everyone pivoted in near unison and stared toward the sounds of what had to be the beginning of a major battle in the distance.

"And the shit pile grows," muttered Major Sanchez.

30 David and the Train

The jagged opening that led out of the thunder-chamber turned into a narrow tunnel, barely wide enough for two abreast. It appeared to see little use, and their footsteps kicked up fine dust and left distinct prints in the smooth dirt floor. The passage led upwards at a gentle slope as it snaked back and forth. It was dark too. Darker than they were used to, anyway. There were the familiar blue rods, but these were far apart. Instead of being embedded in the rock, most had been plastered to the walls with webbing, or its close cousin.

There were several places where debris from overhead had fallen and partly blocked the passage. Carrying Paula over these areas was tough, but otherwise they were thankful to be traveling unmolested. Between living in the cave where they'd sheltered and sneaking through this crack in the mountain, David began to feel like a rat hiding under the baseboards of a house. In a way, he supposed that's what they were.

They stopped in a wide spot under a glow rod to rest and examine Paula. The air felt cooler and drier here, though it still smelled strongly of chocolate chip cookies. Thunder continued to echo up the passage behind them, but it was surprisingly muted. The floor vibrated occasionally as it had done back in the cave. At the time, David thought it had been from the blender, but maybe it was the thunder all along. Or maybe both.

Paula's left side was turning bluish-purple from under her armpit almost to her hip. Josh gently probed it, making her squirm and exhale in soft grunts as he did so.

"Well, I still can't find any obvious breaks," he said. "Most likely cracked though." He pulled out the small bottle of ibuprofen and shook out a few more of the precious pills.

Paula looked reluctant to take them and Josh said, "No point saving them. If now isn't the time to use 'em, then there ain't going to be one. Besides, if it will help get you on your feet faster, it'll save on me and David's backs."

She managed a grin that was half grimace and took three of the little brownish-red pills. Then she lay back on the dirt with a sigh. "Give me a few minutes and I'll see if it loosens up."

"Yeah, it would be good to rest for a bit. This is as good a place as any. Then maybe I'll scout ahead a bit."

"Well, at least we're going up," Paula said. "That's a good thing, right?"

Josh shrugged. "I don't know. I think we're already pretty high up."

Alessandra said, "So we should be going down?"

Josh looked at her with a frown. "Look, I said I don't know, so I don't know. All we can do is follow the tunnel and find out. It ain't like we got a lot of options here."

David checked himself over and found four bruises of his own. Two small ones on his left leg. Plus, a scrape and the beginning of a bruise on his shoulder the size of his hand. And a smaller one on his left forearm. Alessandra pulled up her shirt, and he saw an even larger bruise on her right side, just below her bra line. Pedro only had a few scrapes. Being small must have helped. Josh had been hit in the face by something, which made him look like the loser in a prize fight.

That damn conveyor nearly beat us to death. And we may have to go back down it for water? Not a pleasant prospect.

The ground wasn't as soft as the sand floor of their cave, but at least it wasn't hard stone. David found a rock with a pleasing angle and leaned back against it. He really wasn't sleepy since they'd rested in the vat room for a few hours before leaving. But Josh always said, "Never pass up a chance to sleep." So, he leaned his head back and closed his eyes.

A slight scuffing sound and small cough made him blink them open. Pedro was sitting a few feet away with a small smile. "Dots?" he said.

The kid was incorrigible. Here they were, trapped in an alien mountain facing an uphill chance at survival. They had no idea how to get out or even if they could. And less than an hour ago they'd seen…and heard…the most bone-chilling thing in possibly all of human history. And Pedro wanted to play dots.

What the hell. "Sure," he said.

Pedro's smile broadened, and he began pressing his stick down in the dirt.

"Two games," Josh said. "Then try to sleep for at least an hour."

They both nodded and began drawing lines on the board with two small stones Pedro kept for that purpose. The dark gray rocks looked like flint and were long and thin. Perfect for playing dots on almost any surface.

Pedro slaughtered him the first game. Nothing unusual about that. But the next one, David pushed him to the limit and only lost by two squares.

This delighted Pedro. "Game good!" he said, managing to put an even bigger smile on his face. "Again?"

"Sleep," Josh commanded.

Pedro scrunched up his face and shrugged. He crawled over and snuggled up against David and leaned back on the same rock. It felt good and warm to have the boy there. David closed his eyes and managed to drift off.

As always, it was impossible to tell how long they slept. But it couldn't have been too long, probably less than the hour Josh specified. David heard someone talking in low voices, but didn't want to wake up. He felt warm and safe, which was very nice. Pedro was snuggled up on his left and... His right felt warm also. He looked over and found Alessandra snuggled up to him on that side. A very pleasant sensation indeed. Both she and Pedro stirred seconds later.

The three untangled and began to stretch out the kinks. Even Pedro stiffened up a little after sleeping on the ground.

Before they stood, Alessandra clutched David's arm and said, "Do you smell that? It smells like the forest."

David breathed in deeply. A very faint smell of wetness and rotting wood with a tinge of flowery sweetness. A smell he'd loathed back in his tent so long ago when he first arrived. Now it was ambrosia. He nodded. "Yeah, I smell it."

"That is the best smell ever," Paula said. She struggled into a sitting position. "Ouch. I still hurt, but I think I can walk. At least a little."

Alessandra stood and stared longingly up the jagged passageway. "Do you think it is close?"

Josh shrugged. "No telling. Since we haven't smelled anything but that cookie stink and each other, our noses would be sensitive to something new. And who knows what the airflow is like in this place?"

"I want to go look," she said. "At least a little way."

"Me too," said David. "If there's even a chance at seeing out, much less getting out, I want to do it."

Josh frowned and looked at Paula, then around the passage. "If you don't go too far and don't take any chances. This passage looks like a good place to hold up for a while. Paula needs to heal some more anyway. You two go take a look ahead. I'll go back to the conveyor and see if I can snag some food. If I get lucky, maybe we'll get some fruit or something. That would help extend our water."

Pedro looked at Alessandra and said hopefully, "Me come?"

Josh shook his head. "Why don't you come with me, Pedro? I could use some help bringing the water we left stashed anyway."

Pedro looked disappointed for about two seconds, then brightened and said. "Yes, go Josh."

"Go slow," Josh said. He pulled out the Brazilian combat knife and gave it to Alessandra. "Here. It's better than nothing. Go for a count of four or five thousand. I'll do the same. Remember, stop and listen before peeking around corners. Be shadows."

"Just like you showed us, boss," Alessandra said with a smile. David nodded, remembering how stupid he thought Josh's training had been at the time. Now the man seemed a genius, which David had to admit he just might be.

They set out with Alessandra in the lead. She'd always been better at this than David. Her lithe form moved like a ghost. She didn't ever stop to listen at bends and corners, but her movements changed. She'd cock her head, slow, go up on her toes or stoop down in a crouch, take a quick peek, and then flow around the turn looking intently ahead. David did his best, but felt like a lumbering bear treading in her wake. He also let her keep count. She had a knack for it while doing other things. "Multitasking," she called it.

"How long?" David asked.

"Eight hundred. Plenty of time."

The forest scent faded in and out. In fact, it seemed fainter, most likely because his nose was becoming acclimated to it. With a little concentration, he could still pick it out over the cookie smell.

The snaking turns and infrequent glow rods left sections of the passage with little light, but not totally dark. In one part of the passage, he could only see the silhouettes of rocks ahead, backlit by an electric blue halo. It slowed him down as he scooted his feet over the smooth floor with care. Alessandra ended up waiting for him under the next glow rod, looking back patiently as he came up to her.

"Sorry," he said.

"Do not be silly," she said. "We cannot afford an injury. Take your time."

He nodded, remembering the team motto. *Trust your teammates. Do your job. Stay focused.*

"This passage is a lot darker than any of the others," David said.

Alessandra nodded. "Hopefully that is a good sign. Maybe they do not use this one very much."

A short distance later, the rough-hewn passage they were in intersected a large, well-lit, well-maintained tunnel, making a T. No doubt this one saw plenty of use. The dirt floor gave way to hard, smooth stone that almost looked like polished white granite. It was shaped like a half cylinder and curved out of sight to the left and right. The blue light glared off the polished floor and walls with dazzling intensity. Other than being so shiny and the light too blue, it could have been an interstate highway tunnel through the Colorado mountains.

"Fourteen hundred," Alessandra said. "Which way?"

"Which way? Are you crazy? Josh said not to take any chances."

Alessandra looked both ways and stepped out into the tunnel. "Look. Just being in this hell hole is taking a chance. We are going to have to find out where this goes sooner or later. This is the only route we have."

David tried to find a good argument, but couldn't think of one. He shrugged and stepped out into the tunnel and began sniffing at the air. After turning in a slow circle, he shrugged again. "The smell is still there, but I can't tell which direction it might be coming from."

"Me either," Alessandra said. She turned toward the right and nodded. "It seems to slope down a bit in that direction. Down would have to be good, right?"

"I don't know. That big momma thing is down lower, isn't it?"

Alessandra chuckled. "Big Mama? I like that. Makes it seem less frightening."

"I can't take credit; I heard Josh say it."

"That figures," she said. "Leave it to Josh to turn a two-mile long monster, controlling an army of killer fiends, into 'Big Momma'."

David smiled. "Yeah, Big Mama sounds like something we can deal with, even if we can't. But what about the tunnel?"

She made a swoop toward the right with her hand. "This tunnel curves away from that chamber."

"How can you tell that? After all those twists and turns, I've got no idea."

"I don't know," she said. "I can just feel it. Count is twenty-two hundred. What do you say? Go right for about a thousand?"

This felt wrong. But again, he couldn't think of any logical thing to say against it, other than being dangerous as hell. But then, just being in this damn mountain was dangerous, so he nodded. Alessandra went into sneak mode and began moving lightly along the inside of the curve.

David took in several deep breaths and half-whispered to himself, "I don't want to do this." Then he followed, also hugging the wall of the passage.

At first, he peered nervously past Alessandra. Then he realized they had just as much chance of something coming up from behind as from ahead. He trusted her to watch the front and he kept most of his attention to their rear. After a couple of hundred yards, the tunnel leveled out and began to turn in the opposite direction.

Alessandra stopped and frowned. "Well, so much for it being simple. Now it's turning toward Big Momma but going up. I don't think it leads there though, at least not directly."

"Why not?"

She tapped her ear. "Too quiet. If this opened up onto that chamber, these smooth walls would carry the sound right to us."

"Makes sense," David said. "Do you want to keep going?"

"Sure, at least for a little further. The count is three thousand. Let's go to at least four. It will be faster going back."

"Lead on," he sighed.

A short while later, they came upon a long straightaway. Alessandra said, "Let's go as far as the next turn, take a peek, then head back."

"I feel like we're pushing our luck already. Let's head back now."

She wavered. He could tell she desperately wanted to find the source of the smell. To him, it was fainter now, but he couldn't tell for sure. "Oh, come on, just–."

"Shhh!" David held up his hand. "Listen."

They froze, listening intently as a distant clatter-clomp beat tickled the ears. It was accompanied by a warbling squeal that, for some odd reason, made David think of an oversized grocery cart. The clatter-clomp had an odd tempo, not really like a horse galloping, but close enough to make him think of a large animal, very large, judging by the time between beats, and running hard.

He looked frantically in both directions.

"Oh shit," Alessandra said. "Which way is that coming from?"

"I can't tell," he said, his heartbeat climbing quickly. The echoing impacts seemed to come from both directions. They stood with their heads cocked, listening for any clue. In a few moments, as the sounds grew louder and more distinct, he decided they came from behind, going in the same direction they were. He pointed and said, "Run, that way!"

She took off at a dead sprint down the straightaway. David pounded along right behind. During their training, David had become faster than she, but not by much. Not that it mattered. This wasn't a case of, 'I don't need to outrun the bear; I just need to outrun you." They'd become too strong a team to leave anyone behind. *But where are we running to?* David prayed they would find a cross tunnel, a hole to hide in, something.

He swallowed hard when he realized that whatever made the sounds traveled much faster than they did. And despite the conditioning of the last several weeks, at a full sprint quickly began straining his legs and lungs.

They reached the end of the straightaway and paused, panting heavily while leaning against the inside wall of the curve. The noise continued to swell as something big and loud thundered toward them. Alessandra started to run again, but David grabbed her arm. "We can't outrun it. Maybe it will ignore us like the plumbers did. Just pray it passes us by. Up against the wall as flat as you can."

She didn't argue. It was plain that whatever was coming up the tunnel would catch them in mere moments. They went to the far end of the curve and pressed their backs against the wall. The surface quivered behind them. But the pounding of David's heart rivaled the increasing vibrations from whatever charged toward them.

The rapid-fire clatter-clomp continued to get louder and louder.

The squeal became an agonizing screech that sent hot spikes through David's ears as it echoed through the passage. The tunnel wall vibrated against his back, either from the sonic vibrations or heavy impacts on the tunnel floor. Probably both.

A dark shape appeared around the bend. A gatherer! No, something bigger. Much bigger and moving fast. He stood transfixed as the thirty-foot-tall creature sped around the curve. The head was near the ceiling of the tunnel. It had the same praying mantis shape studded with antennas as a gatherer, but twice as large. The head sat perched on a short, armless torso, which in turn connected to a long, wide body. He tried to press harder against the wall, but to no avail. His mouth dropped open in fearful amazement as the thing thundered toward them.

The front pair of legs would dwarf an elephant's but moved faster than a racehorse. The four churning legs behind the front two were even bigger and moving just as fast. He glanced over at Alessandra and saw that her face was as pale as the gray stone they stood against. The whites showed around her brown eyes as she stared up at the fantastic creature.

He looked back just as the alien monster drew abreast. He slipped beyond fear and prepared to die. *It's over. After everything we've been through. This is it.*

The creature's head swiveled and looked down as it thundered past. Large, soulless black eyes of a living locomotive measured him as a possible impediment. It must have decided his existence to be inconsequential because the head swiveled away and resumed staring into the depths of the passageway as it rushed past.

The left front leg breezed by David less than two feet away. He spread his arms out in mock crucifixion to be as flat as possible. The middle leg hurdled toward him and flashed by with only few inches to spare. Then the hind leg went by, coming even closer, causing his shirt to flutter across his chest with its passage. A stream of boxy carts filled his vision. It really was a train. A damn six-legged engine pulling dozens of wagons.

The carts passed, intermittently blocking out the light that sent flickering shadows over them. It reminded him of being on a subway in

New York during a long-ago family vacation. The horrible squealing sound enveloped him. The wail became an intense, shrill pitch that actually hurt his teeth.

At some point, David shut his eyes. He opened them in time to see the dark square of the last cart flash by. As it passed, he stumbled forward slightly, as though an invisible force pinning him to the wall suddenly ceased. His breathing came in a rapid pant, and he leaned forward with his hands on his knees, amazed to be alive.

Alessandra was also bent over with hands on knees. "My God, was that a train? A huge, living train?"

"Yu...Yeah," David panted. "I think so, anyway."

Alessandra stood and stared down the straightaway as the back of the train rounded the far turn and disappeared. The clatter-clomping and squealing noises faded as it did, but the echoes still filled the tunnel. "Come on. I think it is slowing down."

"Come on? If it's slowing down, we need to go that way," he said, pointing back the way they'd come.

"Just to the bend. I am going to take a look. If you do not want to come, stay here." She took off at a jog.

"Shit," David said, breaking into a stumbling run to follow. It was all his legs could manage after their all-out sprint. But after a few dozen yards, he got his second wind and fell into step beside her.

"What do you hope to accomplish?" he said.

"Nothing. I mean... I do not know. I just want to see."

"Why are you so brave all of a sudden?" he said, still panting but beginning to recover. "I thought you were scared of the Devil."

"I am. But seeing Big Mama... Well, now that I have had time to process it, I do not think we are in Hell anymore. These things are something else. From space, I think."

David nodded. "Finally coming around to my way of thinking?"

"I would never sink that low," she said with a small grin. "But I think you may be right about them being aliens."

The sound ahead changed and she cocked her head to listen. The clatter-clomp slowed and the squealing dropped in pinch. A lot of the aliens' equipment seemed to squeal. David wondered if their machinery tended to wear out bearings, or did they just not care?

"See, it is stopping," she said, slowing a little as they neared the end of the straightaway.

"I'm thrilled. Are you sure you want to poke your head around there? I feel pretty damn sure this isn't the way out."

She just gave him an annoyed look and moved close to the wall, slowing to a walk. David did likewise.

"Just pray to God it's not turning around," he said.

She looked at him in surprise, evidently not having considered that. Then she shook her head. "No, it would not just turn around without loading or unloading. It has to be stopping for a reason."

David agreed with the logic, though he didn't like it. With the train stopped, other sounds could be heard coming from ahead—a deep humming with a low rumble, like motors running at low idle. Would a living train idle? It seemed unlikely, but who the hell knew? More likely there was other machinery in operation up ahead. No squealing though.

As they advanced, the sounds became more distinct. There was still the rumbling sound of an engine. It sounded like an old school bus on its last leg. There was also a soft whine and thumping whoosh that made him think of some kind of pump. Each sounded distantly familiar, yet jarringly alien.

"The jungle smell is definitely gone," he said. "But the cookie stink is getting stronger."

"Yeah. Guess you're right about this not being the way out. At least we know for sure now. But I still want to take a peek."

David remembered the old adage about curiosity killing the cat. That was the thing about old sayings. They came to be because they contained an element of truth. He just hoped it didn't apply in this case.

By keeping to the left-hand wall, they tried to remain hidden from whatever might occupy the tunnel ahead. Was it some kind of station or another cavern? David had to admit, after coming this far his own curiosity was aroused too. *The cat be damned.*

As they crept forward, David could see over Alessandra's shoulder that the tunnel opened into another cavern. The floor of the tunnel turned into a ramp that hugged the right-hand wall. It descended in a moderate slope to the chamber floor about a hundred feet below.

The bulk of the chamber and the train were out of sight to their left. As they squeezed against the wall and crept forward, more and more of the space beyond was revealed. In a few moments, the last few carts of the train came into sight and then the engine-gatherer. Finally, they reached the end of the curve and peeked carefully around the few final feet into the heart of the chamber. Alessandra gave a soft gasp. David was too stunned to make a sound.

The cavern dwarfed the train. Though not as expansive as Big Mama's chamber, the space before them was still one of the largest he'd ever seen. The ceiling rose at least four hundred feet from the floor. The space spanned hundreds of yards and thousands deep. It contained a sea of dark, round objects of varying dimensions from the size of a basketball to bigger than a house.

More of these objects were being unloaded from the train by several score of the large gatherers. They took the objects deeper into the chamber and stacked them on or near others of similar size. There had to be hundreds of thousands of them stretching into the distance.

"Eggs!" David muttered. Alessandra nodded, for surely that was what the objects were. A shudder crept up his back as he gazed over the expanse of the chamber and what it implied.

In addition to the eggs, large objects made up of boxes, cylinders, and big pipes were scattered through the area. These seemed to produce the machine sounds. Plumbers that looked slightly different from the ones that repaired the vat attached tubes and wires from these to the objects. Every egg was hooked up to one of the machine arrays, though these differed significantly from one group to the next. Did these support the different kinds of creatures? Or were the eggs being modified somehow? Thousands more of the plumbers could be seen working in the distance, clambering over and around the eggs, diligently performing unknowable tasks.

A very bright whitish-blue flash accompanied by a rumble loud enough to be heard over the chamber's other noises drew his attention to a forty-foot wide hole in the floor. A large mound of rock and dirt that must have fallen from overhead was piled to one side of the hole. There were no eggs on the mound, but repair plumbers crawled all over it.

"I think that queen thing, you know, Big Mama, is down that hole," said Alessandra.

David nodded and pointed at the ceiling where a large, cylindrical structure protruded from the ceiling. "What's that? Do you think it caused that pile beside the hole?"

The structure extended a good hundred feet down from the ceiling and was mostly white. The front was blunted and appeared to have been burned black in many places. It looked only partly constructed, as there were a lot of bone-like struts or girders exposed between sections covered with sheets of a whitish material. More plumbers worked around it, hanging from the ceiling.

Alessandra shook her head. "I do not know. But yes , it looks like the pile is right underneath. Do you think they dumped rocks and dirt down below while they were building it?"

David shrugged. "I've seen enough. Between this and Big Mama, I'll have nightmares for a week."

Alessandra snorted. "I have had plenty of them already. My good friend, we are living in a nightmare."

"Yeah, you're right. Still, let's get the hell out of Dodge."

"Dodge?" she asked as she backed away from the corner. He did likewise and they turned back the way they came.

"Just an old saying from home. Dodge is an old western town. I guess it was a dangerous place to live and people wanted to get away from it."

"Okay," she said, breaking into a jog. "Away from Dodge we shall go."

"And pray that train stays put for a while," he said.

31 Organizing for the Fight

The sudden shock of being put in command froze Marcus for several long beats of his heart. Sergeant Araujo watched him carefully, most likely hoping he hadn't just made a big mistake in helping incapacitate General von Jaeger. Marcus said a silent prayer along much the same lines. *Please give me the strength and wisdom to help my people through this.*

Even as he thought the prayer, a wave of doubt coursed through him, making his shoulders droop. Most of the men around him were army and not even in his chain of command. But in circumstances like this, where the leadership of an entire army had been decapitated in a single blow, he supposed chain of command became a bit fuzzy. Would these men be willing to follow his orders?

Anger flooded through him. *Doubt be damned!* He didn't have time for it; none of them did. The soldiers would listen or they wouldn't. *So, what first?* Resources—he needed to know what he had and where it was. He rolled his neck, took in a deep breath, and set his jaw in determination.

The sounds of explosions and gunfire from the east fueled a smoldering panic around him that was on the verge of turning into an inferno of fear. That could lead to a route. Marcus saw it in the eyes and frantic movements of everyone around him. A lot of soldiers ran around the area, but with no obvious destination or purpose. Except for his own men and Araujo's, all of whom had fought the demons before. The Americans were holding together also, and they'd lost their leader as well. However, their friends and countrymen weren't under attack to the east.

Marcus squared his shoulders and met Araujo's worried eyes. "Very good, sergeant," he said with what he hoped was a firm, calm voice. The other man gave a small nod and relaxed.

"Per your report, we know who the dead commanders are." Marcus gestured to Nelino and said, "Please take Captain Pereira and round up every officer, captain and higher in rank, you can find...senior noncoms as well. I need a list of their ranks, units, and experience. Have them report here as soon as possible."

"Yes, sir," both men responded. They walked off a short distance and pulled out the list Araujo had already made. Nelino had found a note pad in the debris and began writing in it. Within a few moments, the sergeant began sending his men running off in different directions.

"Salina," he said. "Please stay close. I may need your help with the Americans." *But…could she do more?* A crazy idea came to him. *Would she do it? Yes*, he believed she would.

He looked around and saw an overturned table just inside the smoldering confines of the destroyed meeting tent. "Julio, get that table and set it up…" After a quick glanced around for a clear spot, he pointed. "Over there."

"Uh, yes sir," Julio said. He looked about with a confused expression for a moment. Then he spotted the table and hurried to comply.

"Salina, I need your help to rally the men."

"What?" she said. "How? What could I do?"

"The men have come to see you as someone to look up to. Someone who inspires them."

"Um, I don't think–"

"No time for that," he said, somewhat more forcefully than he intended. He pointed at the table as Julio set it up. "Please, get up there and call for the men to rally to the command post. Shout as loud as you can. At least for a few minutes. Just to get them started."

At first, she looked skeptical, but then she nodded and resolve lit her eyes. That was one of the things he admired about her. Once she committed herself, then by God she'd do her best.

With a graceful ease, she hopped up on the table, brandished the rifle over her head, and yelled in Portuguese, "To me, brave soldiers, to me! For Brazil and the sake of your comrades, to me! Rally on the hill."

Gunfire erupted from behind her, and someone yelled. She flinched, as did they all, but only for an instant. Then she resumed yelling. "Rally to the command post. Rally, and we'll show these children of whores they cannot beat us down!"

Damn. That was good, he thought. She was better than he could have hoped.

The effect could be seen at once. Men turned and pointed at her. Cries of *la Demonio Matar*, the Demon Slayer, filled the air. Scores of soldiers stopped their aimless wandering and began heading for the command center. People farther down the hill noticed and began gesturing in her direction.

Marcus turned to Viana and said, "Captain, get them sorted out by unit. Make sure none of them came from the perimeter. If they did, tell them to get back to their positions and hold for orders."

"Yes, sir," he said with a crisp salute.

Marcus saw Nelino and Sergeant Araujo heading toward him. As they hurried up, he said, "Do you have a list for me?"

"Yes, sir," said Nelino. "We should have seven majors who are battalion commanders and maybe a dozen company commanders on the way, including Major Amorim, who commands the reserve force."

Araujo said, "He's a good man, colonel. I'm sure he'll follow your orders. Also, he speaks English and has been establishing a relationship with the American tankers assigned to the reserves by their Colonel Ames."

Something good at last. Marcus already had ideas on how to use the reserves, especially the armor. "Good job, gentlemen. Would you please help Lieutenant Viana get the incoming men sorted out?"

Both men barked, "Yes, sir," and hurried off.

Now for the Americans. For that, he would need Salina, so he headed toward the table. She'd stopped yelling when cries of, "Rally to the headquarters," began to fill the air. Several hundred men now stood in loose ranks in front of her. Fear bordering on panic still marred most of their faces.

"How can we fight demons?" cried out a twenty-year-old corporal. Many around him nodded in agreement.

"They are not demons!" she yelled back. "They're bloodthirsty aliens that are to be hated and killed without mercy, but they are not demons. I killed one, so this I know."

A murmur of questioning voices flowed through the ranks like a wave. Some shook their heads in denial. Others pointed at Salina and responded with hoarse cries of *la Demonio Matar*.

"How?" cried out a voice in the crowd. Others took up the question, which became a chorus. "How?" a score of voices called in near unison.

Salina held the rifle high over her head. Some of her brown hair freed itself from her braid and surrounded her head like a halo. Her feminine form was plain, even in the baggy fatigue pants and loose-fitting top. She looked strong and defiant. To Marcus, she looked like an avenging angel. His heart swelled with pride.

"With this!" she screamed in defiance, brandishing the rifle. "With this and a brave heart fueled by the need to help my friends." She lowered the rifle and continued in a loud, strong voice. "But also, to save myself. To live, you must fight. For to run is death. If not this day, then in the days to follow. These...things. These alien invaders are here to destroy our land. Fight to live!"

The crowd went silent for a moment, then murmurs of assent began to flow through crowd. Still, there was doubt on many of the faces. Another man yelled out, "But how? How do you kill them?"

Salina cradled the rifle in her arms. Her tone went from an emotional cry for action to that of an earnest lecturer. But her voice remained strong and carried over the crowd. Several thousand eyes were now riveted on her. "Team up. Hit them from different sides. Don't shoot for the head. Aim between the front and middle arms if you can. If you must shoot for the head, try for the eyes to blind them. And stick together. That is the most important thing."

Manu of the men began nodding and there were a few whispered conversations as some sought better understanding from those around them. Marcus stepped up in front of the table and winked up at Salina. She nodded back with a grim smile. *Damn, what a woman*, he thought. With a snap, he pivoted and faced the formation in front of the table at parade rest. The crowd quieted down under the eyes of their new commander.

Nelino, Jeronimo, Sergeant Araujo, and the battalion commanders they'd rounded up were walking through the crowd. They were asking people one or two quick questions, then writing on a slip of paper and giving it to each soldier. Then they went to the next person.

The noncoms followed behind, each trailing a growing group of soldiers. They'd give the paper slips a quick glance and either ignore the man and move on, or wave for him to join the noncom's group. The cluster of men quickly began to be sorted and organized into military units.

More and more people began noticing that Marcus was staring out at the formation. The already infrequent whispered conversations began to die down. Despite the rumble of explosions and gunfire in the distance, the voices of the officers asking questions seemed especially loud.

"Gentlemen," Marcus called out. "If I may."

Nelino shouted, "Call your men to order. Call your men to parade rest."

The order echoed across the field and beyond. Each officer or noncom prefaced the command with their unit, saying, "Company," or Platoon," or "Squad," as appropriate. It surprised Marcus when the command echoed from far beyond the immediate area.

Salina jumped down beside him. "Marcus, maybe you should get on the table."

He nodded and looked beyond her at the surrounding soldiers, now standing at parade rest. Their eyes focused on him, with a multitude of different emotions playing across their faces. For the most part, he still saw a lot of fear. But not as much panic. And there was also hope and determination. He needed to tell them something. Give them something to focus on. When he came for Salina, he hadn't planned on giving a speech. But circumstances gave him no choice.

Once on top of the table, he could see over the heads of the immediate crowd and down the slope between the headquarters and the dock area. Black smoke rose in thin tendrils from somewhere down by the river. Hundreds of small, dark scout demon bodies dotted the land on a line from the docks to here.

So, the creatures attacked the docks and headed straight for the command post. As soon as it was destroyed, the aliens launched an attack the right flank. *Right where we're most vulnerable. Very smart.* A bone-chilling realization.

Beyond the men before him, he could see more soldiers forming up on the hillside below the command post. These troops moved with organization and purpose. Apparently, some units remained intact during the chaos. This meant a few organized combat troops should be available. They'd need them to save themselves from this mess. Between them and the men before him, Marcus guessed there to be over four thousand soldiers.

"My fellow countrymen," he called out. *Damn, that sounded corny.* "My fellow soldiers." He turned and looked at the Americans. Lieutenant Johnson sat in his LAV command hatch, watching with interest. The American nodded to him, evidently sensing the importance of the moment, even though he couldn't understand much of what was being said. Marcus nodded in response and turned back to face the soldiers before him.

"I am Colonel Marcus Antinasio. The chain of command has been disrupted by the enemy attack. I have been informed I am the surviving senior officer and hereby assume command of the Brazilian forces operating in this region."

His eyes swept over the assembled soldiers. No defiance, no objections to his statement. *Thank God.* His next few breaths came easier.

"This is a dangerous situation. F or us, our friends, and our country. Our comrades to the east are under attack. We shall be mounting a counterattack to help them. First, we will secure this base and the docks and evacuate the hospital and nonmilitary personal across the river.

"We face a terrible enemy; I shall not lie about that. But they can be killed, and we will defeat them. Work as a team. Combine your fire as Miss Morgan instructed."

He wanted to say more, but time was pressing. Besides, anything he might say would most likely undo the great job Salina had done. He swept his gaze over the officers and noncoms in the formation and said, "For now, please continue organizing the men." His eyes found Nelino and Sergeant Araujo.

"Gentlemen," he said in his best command voice. "Carry on."

"Yes sir," they snapped back in unison.

Nelino yelled out the command for everyone to stand at ease. The other officers and noncoms repeated the command so that it echoed across the field. Then the officers went back to asking the soldiers questions as Marcus jumped off the table.

"Salina, will you please assist me with the Americans? I need to talk to Major Sanchez."

"Of course," she said.

Major Sanchez met them between the table and the parked LAVs. Lieutenant Johnson and Warrant Officer Benson was with him. The latter again looked relieved to see Sally.

Sanchez looked nodded to Marcus and then said something to Salina in English. She replied, "Thank you."

Salina translated his next words. "He says, 'You seem to be getting things organized quickly.' He thought you'd be coming to see him next. He wants to know what you have in mind."

Marcus said. "I need to relieve the men to the east, and I need your help. Then I intend to withdraw back across the river."

Sanchez met his eyes as Salina relayed this. He said, "From what we've seen today, the river doesn't look like that much of a barrier for them."

Marcus shook his head. "The river's not." He turned and waved his arm toward the southern shore. "But that mudflat might be. Especially if we can establish good defensive positions on the high ground."

Sanchez turned and looked across the river. "Makes sense. But it won't be easy getting everyone across. Although our hovercraft should be able to cross that mudflat, which should help some."

Sanchez turned toward the ongoing crackle of gunfire. "What about the fighting to the east? I'd be surprised if the aliens don't come this way for the docks."

"I think so too." Marcus gestured to the northern boundary of the Brazilian camp. "I intend to pull those troops off the line and send them east to help secure the base. I need your forces to take up their positions to protect the north. I will contact the boats and have them get in position to help defend the riverbanks and docks."

Sanchez surveyed the distant positions. Marcus knew he was asking for a very tough maneuver, and it would have to take place fast. Would the Marines do it?

"Mierda!" Sanchez said with a sigh. "Okay. But it will take me a couple of hours to get my people moving and in position. Will that work?"

"It will have to, major. I will begin pulling my men out in a half hour though. I fear we are facing a disaster in the east. I will also need your tanks."

Sanchez nodded. "Colonel Ames already cleared them for reserve duty deployment in an emergency. I guess this fits. But what's your plan for them?"

"I'm still considering that, major. I have an idea but need to talk to my reserve commander first. I'll get back with you, but for now, do I have your tacit approval?"

Sanchez nodded. "Yes, colonel, you do. Now, if you'll excuse me, I have some orders to give. God bless and good luck."

"The same to you, major. And…thank you."

Sanchez and the two other Americans exchanged handshakes he and Salina, then hurried back to the Hummer and LAVs. A few moments later, diesel engines roared to life and they headed back toward their headquarters.

"A good man, there," said Marcus, his voice choked with emotion. "If he hadn't agreed, well…" He shook his head. "Salina, if you would accompany me, I'd appreciate it. The men draw inspiration from you, and we need every advantage we can get."

"Of course, Marcus," she said, her voice sounding unusually husky. Probably from all the shouting.

"Corporal Arente," he yelled as they neared the center of camp. "Front and center."

Julio ran up and snapped off a salute. "Reporting as ordered, sir."

"Corporal. I'm issuing orders and need you to carry them east." He pointed to a camouflaged Land Rover with two stars on a blue field on the bumper. It looked much sleeker than the standard Land Rover Defender used by the army. "Take the general's vehicle up the old logging road and pass orders to every officer and noncom you find. Preferably senior battalion and regimental staff officers." He stopped as Nelino, Sergeant Araujo, and an army officer hurried up to them.

Araujo said, "Colonel, this is the reserve commander, Major Amorim. Major, Colonel Antinasio." The two shook hands.

Marcus said, "Well, Major, we have our work cut out for us."

"Yes sir, we do at that."

Marcus outlined his thoughts to the major. "Will you support the troop movements I am proposing? It would be helpful to have an army officer countersign my orders."

Amorim looked thoughtful and said, "Certainly. I imagine it will help ease the transition a bit."

"Thank you," Marcus said. He turned to Nelino. "Captain Pereira, please write up the following order for me."

"Yes, sir." Nelino flipped a page on his notepad.

"By order of the high command, all units are to advance east until they make contact with the enemy. Using available terrain and resources, establish defensive positions to hinder and stop enemy movements west toward the Rio Estrada docks and surrounding base.

"Reserve force is being assembled to support. This may require two to three hours to complete. Hold the line. Please include a brief tactical overview as well."

Marcus watched as he finished writing. Nelino signed the paper, and Amorim read it and then did likewise. He handed the tablet to Marcus, who signed it and carefully tore the paper free and handed it to Julio.

Marcus said, "You will get bombarded with questions. Answer what you can, but don't let them bog you down. You've got to get this message as far up the line as you can."

"Yes, sir," Julio said enthusiastically.

"Sir, may I suggest one of my men go with him?" Sergeant Araujo said.

Marcus nodded. "Yes. That would be a good idea."

Sergeant Araujo looked over his shoulder and called out, "Sergeant Eduardo! Front and center."

A man in his early twenties left the perimeter and jogged over. He was taller than Julio by about five inches, but probably weighed ten pounds less. He had a very long face and heavy brows over large dark eyes that sat in shadow underneath his Kevlar helmet. A big smile softened the lines of his stretched out, too narrow face.

"Corporal, this is Sergeant Leonel Eduardo," Marcus said to Julio. "Sergeant, Corporal Julio Arente." The two shook hands.

Marcus reached out and grasped Julio's shoulder. "Be quick, but be careful."

Julio smiled grimly, nodded, and ran towards the Land Rover with Eduardo right behind. He got in, started it, and revved the big engine. Marcus felt a light smile cross his mouth. While being one of his best men, Julio still had the spirit of a youth.

The engine's roar softened to a rumble as Julio turned the vehicle around. Then he gave it the gas, and the SUV went racing down the slope. The horn blared occasionally as he encountered groups of people hurrying up the hill.

"Now the fun begins," Marcus said to Salina. Squaring his shoulders, he turned toward Nelino and motioned for the other officers to join them. They had a lot of work in front of them to bring order to a very big mess.

32 David Inside the Tunnels

David smelled burning wood and roasting meat well before reaching the others. The passageway didn't have nearly as good a ventilation system as the cave, and smoke hung heavy in the air. It smelled wonderful compared to the stink of baking too sweet cookies. It smelled of home.

The wide spot in the tunnel came into view. A cheery yellow

light flicked off the walls, pushing back against the blue glow of the tunnel. The small fire burned to one side with a skinned animal cooking over it he didn't recognize. They ate so many different kinds, he didn't even ask anymore. The odor brought water to David's mouth.

Nearby was a respectable pile of camu camu and passion fruit. Pedro sat on the ground, squishing them between two rocks and draining the juice into an empty gourd. David assumed it was intended to help stretch their water supply.

When he noticed them, Pedro leapt up and cried, "Lessandra." He ran over and wrapped his arms around her waist.

She returned the hug with a big smile and said, "My, what a greeting."

Pedro turned to David and said, "Dots?"

David chuckled and shook his head. "Not right now. Let me rest a bit, okay? It was an eventful trip."

Josh looked over the two explorers and said, "We were getting worried. What did you find?"

David and Alessandra took turns telling about the tunnel, the train-gatherer, and the egg chamber.

Josh interrupted them when they described the eggs. "How many?"

Alessandra glanced at David and shrugged. "An awful lot. Hundreds of thousands anyway. They were different sizes from…say, a soccer ball to…big, real big."

"At least the size of a house, and not a small house," David said.

"I thought I saw some really big creatures in the queen's chamber," Paula said. "They were so big, I kinda thought I imagined them. But I guess not."

"We're in big trouble," Alessandra said. "And by we, I mean the whole planet."

Josh said, "Maybe. But for now, we need to focus on our own problems."

"I see your trip to the conveyor went well," David said, sweeping his arm to include the pile of firewood, roasting meat, and the fruit. There were two more white bundles nearby that no doubt contained more food.

Pedro understood this part and nodded enthusiastically. "Easy fishing. Hop, walk, grab."

"That sums it up pretty well," Josh said. "When the belt stops, you just walk around and pick stuff up at your leisure, as long as you keep track of the count."

Alessandra looked thoughtful. "So, water will be the thing." She smiled at Josh and said, "Just like you said."

"It was kind of obvious," Josh said. "But it does put us under a time crunch. The juice will help some, but we need to find water, or go back to the cave."

"Screw that cave," Paula said. "Let's find out where that smell is coming from and get the hell out of here. We need to check out the tunnel going the other way."

"That train scares me," David said. "If it shifts to one side, even a small bit, it could be very bad for anyone in the tunnel."

Alessandra nodded. They'd barely made it back to the opening before the living locomotive thundered past going the other way.

"We'll treat it the same way we did the conveyor," Josh said. "After you eat, go back and start counting. How many trains, how long between them, and anything else you can observe. The data will determine our plan."

"You love data, don't you?" Paula said.

"I know I look pretty dumb, but before I joined the army, I got my degree in engineering from the University of Washington."

"So, how did you wind up a mercenary?" Alessandra said.

"Patriotism," he said, then hesitated. "No, well…that was part of it. Mostly anger, I guess. I was angry a lot in those days. Terror attacks got really bad, and some friends from school got run over by a nut in Barcelona. There was a group called ISIS that promoted bad shit all over the world. I just felt the need to do something."

"You never talk about that," Paula said. "What did you do in the military?"

"If I told you, I'd have to kill you," he said with a humorless smile. Then he shook his head with a snort. "Old joke. Very bad joke. Especially when it's half true."

He swallowed hard. "I did lots of things, actually. Even helped build a bridge. That was one of the best jobs I had. Also went on deep patrols. A lot of stuff I was proud of, especially at first. Then some of it got bad. But the part that sticks with me, that still haunts me was at the end.... when I was part of a black ops team." Then in a near whisper, he said, "That part twisted my soul."

"Black ops?" said Alessandra.

Josh nodded. "'Deep black,' they called it. Basically...we killed people." He drew in a deep breath and let it out in a long sigh. "A lot of people. It was part of some genius idea to strike back at terrorists. It sounded great at first. Some politician said, 'We'll turn the table on their asses.'"

He snorted. "Funny, that became a code word for killing. Orders came out saying, 'Turn the Table on so and so.' That meant kill them and everyone close to them. Once someone had been verified... supposedly... to have committed an act of terror against the United States or an ally...we went after them. Not just the terrorist mind you. Heck, most of the time they died in the act anyway. So our mission was to go after their family... even their friends if we could find a connection. And we did. It was called Operation Retribution."

He hung his head between his knees. "Wives, parents...kids," he finished in a choked whisper. "God help me... We killed kids. We killed them all."

They sat in silence for what felt like a very long time. Josh killed kids. The United States killed kids? David had to struggle to process that. It wasn't what he thought his country stood for. But then, a country is a very big place with a lot of different people in it. Some people were crazier than others.

"I was so damn proud at first," Josh said. "It sounded like a good idea. I mean, at the time, there were a lot of bad guys who were all fired up to die for their cause. They thought they'd go straight to heaven for killing innocent people. The terrorists had a special fund that paid a chunk of cash to their families if they became a martyr. So, they were willing to die, wanted to die. Hell, compared to the shit life most of them had, they were glad to die."

He stopped, his head still hanging down between his knees.

David thought he was finished. But in a moment, he continued.

"But what if their families had to pay the price? You know, then maybe they'd wouldn't see it as all holy glory and shit."

Another long pause. Did David hear a soft sob? The sound was so alien to the iron man Josh had always seemed that, at first, David dismissed it. But then another sob came, followed by a gasp and a sigh.

"I only went on four missions," Josh said, almost mumbling. "It was all I could stand. The last one… Well, it was the last one."

Josh drew in a deep breath, raised up, and ran his hand over his face. "There were three of us. Me, my best bud Sean, and a nut bag named Mark. Sean and I were both getting disillusioned, but Mark… He loved it. The killing, I mean. Maybe countries need folks like that, but he scared the hell out of me."

The sorrow in his eyes turned into something else. Still sad…but anger burned there as well. He seemed to brace himself, then said, "We got a Turn the Table order for a woman's family living in a small town in Saudi Arabia, called Al Majmaah. It was unusual for a woman to be a martyr, but not unheard of. She'd driven a truck through a fence into the Oklahoma state fair. Killed seventeen people. And yeah, I was angry. Anger and hate are great tools for war. Hate helps turn people into objects. Objects are easier to shoot.

"Anyway, we had orders to Turn the Table on everyone in the house. Turned out to be one woman and six kids. It felt wrong. I…I wasn't sure they were even her family. I called off the hit, but Mark… He shot them all. Said he didn't work for me." Josh rubbed his face again. "I didn't shoot any kids, never did. But I was there. I was part of it."

Josh had a brutal face with heavy features. If he was in a room with ten other men picked at random, he'd be the first one picked as being a likely murderer. Now he had tears streaming out of his deep set dark brown eyes and just looked sad and pathetic.

"We had standing orders to put up the slogan after we…did our thing. To make sure the bad guys got the message. We wrote 'The Tables Have Turned' in English and '*tahawalat aljadawulj*' in Arabic all over the walls. We used the blood of the dead. The blood of dead kids. It was all upside down and ass backwards to me. Were we avenging, or just becoming monsters?"

He cleared his throat and said, "After that, I wasn't angry anymore. Mostly just sad and ashamed. We was no better than the shittiest terrorist to ever live. That was my last mission."

Again, they sat in silence for a long while. What could you say to that? Then Josh said, "Anyway, I got out and tried the civilian life. Worked as an engineer. Made good money. But I couldn't cut it. I thought I would be building things or solving problems. But mostly it's just doing paperwork and putting up with bullshit. I decided I had to find something in the middle. I got in touch with some friends who got me hooked up with a civilian contractor doing stuff for the CIA. No killing, just training. That's how I wound up in Brazil."

Josh squeezed his eyes shut and rubbed them with his fingertips. When he looked up, they were very red. "I've never told anyone that stuff before." He shook his head again, as though trying to shake off a fly. "Anyway, about this data stuff. Yeah, I like it. It's clean and honest and mostly non-emotional if you gather it and use it right."

There was silence that lasted for what seemed a long time. Then Alessandra bent down by the fire and poked at the roasting meat. "This should be done in a few minutes. Let's eat, and then we'll go time the trains."

Pedro looked at the adults with confused eyes. He hadn't understood the story, but he understood they were all sad. He went over and gave Alessandra a hug, and she smiled at him. Then he walked over to David and said, "No be sad. Dots?"

The boy's smile lifted David's heart. He chuckled and said, "Sure, why not."

33 Julio on the Logging Road

Julio had never driven a Land Rover before. In fact, cars hadn't been a big part of his life growing up. Manaus had excellent public transportation, and he rarely had problems getting around town. However, the jungle city hadn't become integrated with self-driving vehicles like the rest of the world. So, a fair number of private vehicles could be found around the city. His father had an old Toyota truck and insisted Julio and his five brothers learn how to drive. His father always thought the self-driving car nonsense was just a fad.

The trail down the hill led between various tents and trailers. It was wide in some places and narrow in others. The camouflaged, sleek SUV slipped and slid back and forth across the muddy path as the tires fought for traction, encountering water-filled ruts every few meters.

If people were nearby, Julio slowed and mud only splashed a few feet, but he still soaked numerous soldiers, resulting in a lot of angry yells and gestures. The rest of the time, the Rover's tires sent sheets of brown muck spraying ten feet and more as the vehicle roared and bounced through the slimy puddles. The staff car skidded sideways three times before they reached the bottom of the hill, but Julio managed to get straightened back out before hitting anything.

Sergeant Eduardo looked relaxed except for the white-knuckle grip he had on the small bar over the open window. Between skids, he turned and gazed into the backseat for a moment. "Wow," he said. "I've never been in a Rover like this before."

Julio hadn't paid much attention to the car's interior. Just the controls, which were much more elaborate than his father's Toyota. The SUV's multiple ride and traction adjustments, heated leather seats, padded dash, and automatic temperature controls looked out of place on a military staff car. In fact, other than the camouflage and antennae, this one looked a lot more like a civilian luxury model than a utilitarian service vehicle. Almost a limousine in fact.

Land Rover Defenders were a common vehicle in the Brazilian military. They were reliable and did well over most terrain. Julio had ridden in them numerous times while on maneuvers. They drove much like his father's truck. The general's vehicle handled very differently, but that was a good thing. When he slid the big SUV around a muddy turn, it automatically helped him steer and keep on course. Otherwise, they probably would have driven through a tent by now.

Besides the plush seats and controls, the Rover had a wide center console full of radio gear. That was the least unusual thing about the staff car. He glanced into the rearview mirror and spotted the true difference between this Rover and a standard one.

A partition with a powered window separated the front and back. White and gold filled the space beyond it. Julio had never been in a limo, but he'd seen them in movies. The passenger compartment of the Range Rover would appeal to any Wall Street executive. Like a limo, the only entrance was a double door on the passenger side. A plush white leather couch and two captain's chairs provided seating. Along the side opposite the door was a pull-down desk, a bar, a refrigerator, and a large monitor. All the handles and fixtures were golden.

"Wow," Julio said.

Eduardo snorted and turned around. "Little Fancy Pants really knows how to set an example for the men."

Julio just shrugged and braced himself as the Rover bounced up onto the concrete surface of what had once been Rio Estrada's town square. A three block long, paved road led to another large concrete pad on the ridge above the docks. A short distance from the docks, he turned the Land Rover hard left onto the muddy road that connected the lumber mill to Rio Estrada's modest shipping facility. The forest approached like a green wall as he neared the outer boundary of the land cleared by the harvesters. A moment later, they were in the shadows of the trees.

The SUV came upon a wide rivulet with a submerged concrete pad across it to allow an easy ford. The submerged concrete was twelve feet wide and appeared as a dim gray shadow under the brownish water. Julio slowed and eased across the underwater bridge. In the middle of the crossing, the water came up to the doors of the Rover, but the seals held and didn't leak. They left a curving wake behind them in the sluggish current.

"I've seen them," Eduardo said in a soft voice that almost didn't carry over the motor and gurgling water. "The aliens, I mean. War demons, scouts, the big harvesters. I've seen them all. They scared the shit out of me."

"Yeah, me too," Julio replied, his eyes locked on the watery road ahead. "Not the big ones, but the warriors and the scouts."

"I know," Eduardo said. "I heard your speech. I've fought the war demons, but I don't think I killed any." His long face took on a grim smile. "I killed five of the small ones today, though."

"Good job," Julio said. He thought about Eduardo's statement about fighting the war demons and made the connection. "Ah, were you on Captain Pereira's boat?"

"Yeah. It was a rough one. I got hit in the leg, which won me a free ride in an inflatable boat. I missed the hike out. It sounded...interesting."

Julio nodded. "Yeah, I heard about that. The other boat... Well, I'm sorry about your comrades."

Eduardo bit his lip and nodded. "Yours too. I know you lost a lot of people in the forest. I really liked your speech, by the way."

"Thanks."

They bounced out of the stream and up a slight rise to higher ground. The road was smoother than the abused terrain of the camp, but still little more than a wide space between the trees. The small local logging company built it years ago and kept it reasonably well maintained. However, they constructed it for the use of a couple of oversized pickup trucks to haul lumber trailers to the river. The recent flow of heavy vehicles had churned the lightly graveled surface to muck and left ruts in the surface nearly as bad as the ground around camp.

The road wound a crazy, bouncing route as it followed the path of least resistance between the trees and around large roots, rocks, and gullies. As they switched back and forth, it felt like they were barely crawling through the late morning shadows yet going insanely fast at the same time. Despite the top-notch shock absorbers, the Rover bounced and swayed like an athletic drunkard as it negotiated the torturous course of potholes and ruts. His knuckles turned white from the force of his grip on the wheel. He clutched it as much to keep his seat as to steer.

Mahogany planted by the lumber mill dominated the trees around them. Workers kept the land partially cleared to access the big trees, and numerous small paths branched off the narrow road. This allowed more light than usual to penetrate the forest. Late morning sunbeams slanted down with dazzling energy, painting leaf-shaped shadows across the ground. The sharp contrast of extreme light and dark made it difficult to see along many stretches of the road.

Shadows hid the first outpost so well that Julio almost ran into two camouflaged ATVs blocking the way. He glimpsed the sharp curve of a tire against the chaos of leaves and slammed his foot on the brake pedal. The Land Rover shuddered and skidded to a halt as the antilock system struggled to find a grip on the muddy road. They stopped with three feet to spare. He leaned back in the plush seat, thankful his already pounding heart hadn't exploded during the moment he thought they'd plow into the ATVs.

Two soldiers appeared from the darkness on either side of the road and walked to the SUV. They both wore full combat harness with chest armor and helmets. Julio wasn't sure how much protection any of it would be, but it must be uncomfortable. He was confident if they had to hump it through the jungle, they'd dump most of the hot, cumbersome gear pretty quickly.

The man on the driver's side wore the insignia of a regular army sergeant. His dark eyebrows went up at seeing a Brazilian marine driving the general's vehicle. "Where're you headed, corporal?" asked the sergeant.

"We're on messenger duty." Julio handed him the order signed by Colonel Antinasio and Major Amorim. "Headquarters got attacked; the general and his staff were killed."

"So, this Colonel Antinasio is in command now?" the sergeant said in a shocked, confused tone.

Julio nodded. "Yes. And I'm sure you've heard the fighting to the east. I need to relay this order up the line immediately."

The sergeant's eyes zeroed in on Julio's. "You gave that speech, didn't you? The one with that Morgan woman?"

"Yes, sir. Uh, sergeant."

"Good stuff," the sergeant said with an approving nod. "We developed tactics for killing demons based on it." He handed the orders back to Julio and motioned for the ATVs to clear the road. "Straight for about a kilometer," he said. "There's a wide trail that branches off to the right that leads to battalion HQ. Look for a cross cut into a tree. It's easy to spot."

"Okay, thanks."

As they eased past the ATVs and resumed going up the road, Eduardo asked, "Do you know her very well, Sally Morgan?"

Julio smiled. "Yes, I do. We came out of the jungle together."

Eduardo's long face took on an air of bliss. "I think I'm in love with her."

Julio laughed. "Yeah, you and every other soldier who attended her speech. She's really something special, though."

Eduardo leaned forward and pointed. "I see the cross."

Julio nodded and slowed to make the indicated turn. The ground rose and then dipped, revealing four armored vehicles sitting among the trees. Three of the vehicles were armored personnel carriers called Urutus. These looked a lot like an American LAV except for having six wheels instead of eight. The fourth vehicle consisted of a large, boxy structure perched on top of tank treads. A group of soldiers stood in the middle of the vehicles, dividing their attention between a tablet or gazing off toward the east.

One of the men glanced at the approaching Land Rover and straightened, most likely reacting to the two stars on the bumper. He tapped the shoulders of those around him. As he did so, the soldiers stopped examining the tablet and turned toward them.

Julio stopped the SUV a few dozen paces from the men. He could see their insignia now and identified a captain, three lieutenants, and four senior sergeants. Sergeant Eduardo opened his door and climbed out, and Julio followed.

Eduardo stopped a few paces away from the small group and snapped a salute. Julio did likewise.

"Reporting with a message from headquarters, sir," Eduardo said.

The officers returned the salute, and the captain said, "At ease. Let me see the message."

Julio handed him the paper. The officer appeared to be in his late twenties. He was a little taller and heavier than usual for a Brazilian, but he had the typical light coffee complexion and dark brown eyes, although these appeared strained with worry.

"It's even worse than we thought," he said, lifting his eyes to the group around him. "High command was taken out. We've been ordered to advance east until contact and set up defensive positions."

"Well sir," said the shorter of the two lieutenants. "That's what we're discussing anyway."

The captain nodded and said, "It's good to know a relief force is being organized."

He looked at Julio. "Corporal Julio Arente. I saw your speech. Good job."

Julio began to wonder if his speech was the reason Colonel Antinasio sent him. In hindsight, it made sense. There had been several thousand regular army people there. So, no surprise that people recognized him.

He looked at Eduardo. "Aren't you one of the Sergeant Araujo's men?"

Eduardo nodded.

The captain glanced back and forth between the marine corporal and special forces sergeant. "Wish we had more time. I'd like to hear how you two ended up driving General von Jaeger's personal staff car." He shrugged. "No time now, though. I'm Captain Amaral, Second Battalion of the Forty-Third Infantry Regiment. The telephone lines are out in both directions, so I can't communicate your message forward. But our regimental headquarters is just a few kilometers up the road. They'll make the final decision on our deployment. But we'll mount up and head that way."

Captain Amaral looked eastward, then back at Julio and Eduardo. "Good luck and God's speed to you both. We heard some explosions and gunfire up the road about the same time we heard the attack on the base. That's when we lost communications. All the fighting has been farther east since then. But something happened not far up the road. Keep your eyes open."

"Yes, sir," Julio said. "Thank you, sir. If you'll excuse us?"

The captain nodded, and Julio and Eduardo turned toward the Land Rover. As they hurried toward it, Captain Amaral called after them. "Say, sergeant, you should ride in the back. I hear it's a treat."

Eduardo snorted. "No thanks, sir. Have you seen back there?"

The captain nodded. "Oh yes, I've seen it." He shook his head with a rueful smile. "I saw it being unloaded when we arrived. I found it hard to believe, myself. General von Jaeger likes his luxury. We could have gotten another Urutu here for the space that car took up." With a slight shake of his head, the captain turned and began pointing things out to the men around him on his navigation tablet.

"It's a damn waste," muttered Eduardo as they got in the SUV. "I don't want to ride back there. But if things quiet down, maybe we should check out what's in that small fridge."

Julio smiled. "If things quiet down?... Yeah, if that happens, I could go for that." He started the engine and backed the SUV in a tight turn between two trees. Then he eased the Rover forward to clear another. It was a short, bouncy ride to the logging road. Once there, Julio turned right and resumed picking his way along the tree-lined, rutted trail.

"How long do you think it will be before Colonel Antinasio sends a relief force?"

Julio shrugged. "The base is a mess, so it might take a few hours to get organized."

Eduardo leaned back and said in a low voice, "I'm really nervous about this."

"I am too," Julio said.

After a moment's silence, Eduardo smiled faintly and said, "There should be a checkpoint soon. Don't plow into it."

"I didn't plow into the last one," Julio said defensively.

Eduardo's smile broadened. "No, but you got damn close. Just be careful."

Julio frowned, but then smiled and nodded. It had been close last time. He slowed as they came to the next left-hand turn, palm trees pressing in from both sides. Right past the trees, they came upon the checkpoint. It consisted of one young, scared-looking private standing in the middle of the road, pointing a rifle at them.

"Halt!" he shrieked. The weapon shook in the private's hands. Julio would have guessed him to be sixteen, except the minimum age for military service was eighteen. He appeared to be even smaller than Julio. Compared to the boy's head, his helmet looked comically big. But there wasn't anything comical about the quivering rifle pointed at them. Julio had no doubt the boy's finger was tight on the trigger.

Another private walked out of the shadows on the right. His stance was much more relaxed, almost a slouch. He looked old for a private, at least late-twenties. He was tall and a bit on the heavy side. However, his uniform was tight around his upper arms and thighs from what appeared to be more muscle than fat.

"Soares, you idiot," he growled. "Put down your rifle. The demons aren't going to be attacking us in a general's staff car."

The young private lowered his weapon. His eyes peeked out from under the big helmet, looking sheepish. "I know. But, I, I, well...I–"

"I, I, I," mocked the older private. He snorted and walked over to Eduardo's side of the Rover.

He leaned on the door and said, "Hi, sergeant. Ignore the kid; he's almost a basket case. What can we do for you?"

Eduardo glanced at Julio, his expression puzzled. This wasn't a typical checkpoint challenge. Then he looked back at the private. "We're headed to Regimental HQ. Is there an outpost near here?"

The man barked out a brief laugh and said, "Me and Private Tumandar over there are the outpost." He turned and looked up the road. "About thirty or forty minutes ago, all hell broke loose from the direction of HQ. Our squad leader told us to stay here, loaded up everyone else, and took off."

With the motor slowed to an idle, the stuttered crackles of massed rifle fire in the distance echoed through the open windows. "You're not talking about the fighting we hear now?"

The private turned and shook his head. "No, this was much closer, a couple of kilometers maybe. It stopped about twenty minutes ago. We haven't heard anything but the fighting farther off ever since."

"So, that's how far it is to regimental? About two kilometers?"

"Give or take," the private said. "When you get there, please remind them they left a couple of guys back here guarding an empty stretch of road from who the hell knows what."

"Okay," Eduardo said. "Thanks."

Julio nodded to the young private in the oversized helmet and put the SUV in motion. They bounced along the meandering logging road at a slow, but steady pace. The scent of dead birds in the forest was barely noticeable now. As they drove, the odor of burnt wood and smoldering chemicals overwhelmed it. And before Julio drove much further, the unmistakable acrid odor of gunfire wafted into the vehicle. Tendrils of smoke or fog, he couldn't tell which, hung heavy among the trees. The crackling explosions and rumbling blasts of the fighting didn't sound so distant now. The battle could easily be heard over the revving engine of the Rover.

The right side of the road opened out into a sizeable clearing. An endless variety of light-hungry plants crowded the field's boundaries. A large aluminum building sat near the middle. Not far from the building, an open-sided shed held a modest quantity of mahogany logs. Julio figured this must be a support station for the lumber mill.

The remains of a battle covered the open area around the building and shed. Bright golden sparks glittered across the field from sunlight reflecting off thousands of brass cartridges littering the ground. Blackened circles marked where explosions ripped the earth. The air reeked of burnt chemicals and spilled blood. There was also a faint chocolate chip cookie smell.

The doors to the building stood open, and soldiers lay on the ground inside, covered in dark green sheets. Under the open shed, more covered forms lay between the logs. A handful of soldiers wearing white masks picked their way through the bodies with care while carrying plasma, bandages, or other medical gear.

Near the road was a sizeable pile of small, hideous bodies. Julio estimated there to be several hundred in the mound. Piling them together like this showed how much their coloring varied, more so than Julio would have expected. All of them were dark in color with green, brown, and gray being the most common. But there were also bluish tints and even a few of burnt orange.

Beyond the mound of dead scout demons sat three blackened, shattered trailers. The trailers still smoldered, emitting thin tendrils of dark gray smoke. Beyond them, at the far edge of the clearing and looking very out of place, a bright yellow bulldozer worked at clearing a lane through the jungle. The bulldozer was of an old design, but even at this distance appeared to be in immaculate condition.

Up the road, a couple dozen camouflaged vehicles sat in small groups of four or five. Most of these were small, one- and two-person ATVs. However, several midsize trucks and four standard military Land Rover Defenders sat nearby. A little way apart from them were four steel-sided Urutu armored personnel carriers. A dozen men stood around a table near the road. Other men came and went from this group, walking with quick, determined steps.

A second group of six armed men stood in the road not far ahead. As Julio drove up, a sergeant stepped forward with his hand raised. He eyed the two stars on the front bumper warily and walked toward Julio's window. Obviously, he hadn't expected the arrival of a general's staff car.

With the windows open, it was easy to see inside the SUV. The sergeant's posture relaxed when he realized a couple of noncoms occupied the vehicle, not a general. Then his eyes narrowed with suspicion. He looked back and nodded his head to the men behind him. Two of them stepped away from the others and moved to either side of the road. They didn't raise their weapons, but both soldiers kept their hands on them. The other three stayed where they were and watched.

Julio started to get out, but the sergeant held up his hand, so he remained in the vehicle. The sergeant walked to the window and said, "Would you please explain why a marine corporal and an army special forces sergeant are cruising around in General von Jaeger's staff car?"

"Yes, sergeant," Julio said, pulling out the order and handing it to the sergeant. Then he gave a quick summary of his mission and how they came to be in the Range Rover.

The sergeant skimmed over the written order and nodded. "Park over there," he said, pointing to the left. "I'll take you to Captain Mello." He craned his head and peered into the back seat. "Humph," he said with a shake of his head.

Julio parked and climbed out. The sergeant who stopped them eyed Eduardo for a moment, then nodded and held out his hand. The sergeant emitted another soft grunt and said, "Hi Leon. How'd you get hooked up with a marine?"

Eduardo smiled and shook the man's hand. "Claud, good to see you. Sergeant Araujo wanted me to come along in case some fat ass regular army dude gave the corporal here a hard time."

The sergeant grunted and shook his head. "Damn, you used to be a decent human being. But now I see that special forces crap ruined you."

Eduardo laughed, turned to Julio, and said, "This is Sergeant Claudio Nunes. He and I were in the same company before I volunteered for special forces. Claud, this is Corporal Julio Arente."

They shook hands and Nunes said, "Okay, let's go see the captain."

As they started walking toward the officers, Sergeant Nunes said, "So, a marine colonel's in charge. I've heard a bunch of stories saying he's great and more than a few saying he's incompetent. So, what do you hear? He any good?"

Eduardo glanced over at Julio. Then he shrugged and said in a low voice, "I don't think he can be worse than von Jaeger, do you?"

Nunes grunted but didn't say anything. He seemed to grunt a lot. He said, "I guess you know Captain Mello's the acting commander of the regiment?"

"No, but it makes sense," Eduardo said. "I knew commanders battalion leadership and above went to the general's latest emergency, must-attend meeting. It looks like a lot of folks are getting early promotions today," he finished sadly.

He nodded toward Julio and said, "You don't know who he is, do you?"

Nunes glanced at Julio, then gestured to the orders. "The marine here? I figured him to be one of this Colonel Antinasio's men pulling messenger duty."

"Well, that's true enough. But do you remember that speech I told you about? With the marine private and the American girl who killed the war demons?"

Sergeant Nunes stopped and gazed down at Julio from a good six-inch height advantage. "So, that's you in the newspaper? With Salina Morgan? You killed one of them things by yourself and dragged it out of the forest?"

Julio nodded, then shrugged and said in a low voice, "But not by myself."

"Humph," grunted the sergeant. "It sounded like a rough time." He looked Julio up and down and said, "I thought you'd be taller." Then he turned and resumed walking toward the command group.

The combination of their arrival in a general's staff car and Julio's subtle, but very different uniform caught the attention of the men around the table. As he and Eduardo followed Sergeant Nunes toward the officers, more and more of the men turned to look at them. When they were a dozen paces from the group, a tall captain with light brown hair, visible because he wasn't wearing a helmet, stepped away from the table and walked toward them. Three others followed.

The three noncoms stopped, came to attention, and saluted. Captain Mello returned the salute and said, "As you were." Then they relaxed, and Julio handed the captain the message. The officer read it quickly and looked at Julio.

"All of them...? Dead or wounded?" he asked.

Julio nodded.

"Dear God," said the captain. He stared at the paper for a long moment. Then he squeezed his eyes shut for a second before looking back at Julio. "I don't suppose you have a copy of this order, do you?"

"Uh, no sir."

Mello flipped the paper over and looked at the back, but for what Julio couldn't guess. Probably just a sign of frustration. "I can't believe our communications have been reduced to this," Mello said in a low voice.

He turned and spoke to the three men behind him. "Gentlemen, please review this order and make notes that we received it. Also, that I accept the order and will do my best to implement it. However, as senior commander in the field, I have determined that our current position meets the 'contact with the enemy' stipulation as required by this order. Therefore, we will continue with our current planning."

The three men nodded, pulled out smartphones, and began making notes on them. At least the devices were still good for that.

Once they acknowledged his instructions, he handed the order back to Julio. "I'm already setting up a defensive line here. We're digging in and clearing firing lanes," he said with a wave across the field toward the bulldozer. "The next regiment up the line is taking the brunt of the attack. I've sent several teams to probe and make contact with the forces east of here. Only one's returned...as of yet."

The sounds of battle from the east rose in intensity as machine-guns began firing in sustained, desperate bursts. Then came a rolling cadence of explosions. Julio spun to stare. *Our side or theirs?* There was no way to tell. All activity stopped as everyone paused and stared eastward with worried expressions. The crescendo of battle rose to a climax and then faded. The steady firing of machine-guns, rifles, and cannon remained, but at a lower intensity.

Captain Mello tore his eyes from the east and looked at Julio and Eduardo. "That came from the lumber mill. The one team I've gotten a report from says that's where the bulk of the alien attack hit. The next regiment up the line is in shambles but managed to organize a defensive line about three kilometers from here. But they keep getting flanked by demons swimming upriver."

Julio glanced at Antinasio's order and said, "So this order is out of date."

"Yes and no," the captain replied. "If you're willing to deliver it..." Julio nodded that he was and Mello continued. "Then tell whoever is in charge over there what I'm doing and that I advise them to delay as much as possible. As the retreat, they need to plan on joining my men along this line. That bulldozer has been a godsend, and we're preparing positions to cover the river as well as block the alien advance. I think we can hold at least for a while, hopefully until your colonel's relief force arrives."

"Yes, sir," Julio said.

Mello said, "Good luck, corporal. You too, sergeant." He shook Julio's hand and then Eduardo's.

"Thank you, sir," they replied together. The captain turned, and he and three other officers headed back to the table.

Sergeant Nunes said, "Humph. So, you pampered special forces wimps go to battle in a general's staff cars these days."

Eduardo snorted and then smiled. "Damn straight. Why do you think I volunteered? All special forces noncoms are getting them."

"Humph." Nunes held out his hand. "Maybe we can catch up when this crap is over."

"Sounds good," Eduardo replied, shaking his hand.

Nunes offered his hand to Julio. "You too, corporal. We can grab a beer and swap stories. Sounds like you have a few good ones."

"Be a pleasure," Julio said as he grasped the other man's hand. "Be careful, looks like a storm is headed your way."

Instead of a grunt, the man gave a soft chuckle. "Well, at least I'm not driving straight into it. Good luck."

With a last nod, Julio and Eduardo climbed into the SUV. Julio started it up and got them back on the road. In a few minutes, they left the clearing and the forest closed in around them once more.

The mahogany forest transitioned into the more normal, three-layer canopy typical of the rainforest. Plants closed in around them, making it difficult to see very far to the left and right. The thick foliage would also make turning around on the narrow road more difficult. They crossed another small stream, and the road beyond became muddier and more waterlogged than ever. The Range Rover's four-wheel drive handled it well however. It might be fancy, but the vehicle performed well enough.

The sounds of fighting continued to get louder as they drove. It was no longer a blended sound of destruction. The firing of individual rifles, machine-guns and explosions could plainly be heard over the sound of the rumbling motor. Both men scanned the road and surrounding jungle with nervous eyes. The fighting could only be a few moments away. Brief, intense spats came from the left and right, echoing through the trees and making them flinch.

Eduardo hunched forward with his rifle between his knees. His hands kept fidgeting with the plastic guard around the barrel, sometimes gripping it with white knuckles, then almost caressing it like a lover.

"Should we stop and go on foot?" he said in a low voice. "I don't like being inside this thing."

"Yeah. I know what you mean. A little further, and we'll start walking."

Eduardo nodded but kept his eyes focused ahead. Julio slowed the Rover to a crawl just as the sounds of close fighting suddenly stopped.

Eduardo looked at Julio and said, "Is that good or bad?"

"I don't know," he replied, stopping the SUV.

Distant gunfire still drifted through the trees, but in the immediate area, silence. Had their forces driven off the demons? Or…was everyone up ahead dead?

Eduardo must have had similar thoughts. "There's a whole regiment out here. They can't all be gone, can they?"

"I don't know," Julio replied tersely. Why did Eduardo keep asking him pointless questions?

He took his foot off the break, and they eased forward again. "When we come to a place to turn around, we'll park it and go on foot."

Eduardo nodded. Julio was also eager to get out of the Rover. However, he wanted it close by in case they had to get out of the area in a hurry. While the road conditions made the going slow, it was still a lot faster than walking.

The road curved to the right around a ten-foot-wide jatoba tree surrounded by thick brush. It then widened out a little. Beyond was a rare straightaway. After they passed the tree, the jungle thinned considerably to both the left and right. Most likely, this area had been one the mill harvested recently.

More interesting was the sight of three Urutus and several jeep-like AM2s with machine-guns mounted in back parked on either side of the road. Men were dug in around the vehicles, and more could be glimpsed hiding behind trees and logs further into the forest. A few turned and glanced back at the SUV, but only for an instant. Not even a two-star general's staff car could pull their attention away from whatever they were staring at ahead of them.

Eduardo nudged him and pointed to an opening in a small strand of palm trees to the left across the road from one of the Urutus. Julio nodded, eased the SUV into it, and cut the engine. The silence in the immediate area held. But Julio sensed danger in the silence, telegraphed by the crouched postures of the men around the vehicles and their rapt attention on the road.

As soon as they stopped, Eduardo opened his door and slithered out, staying low to the ground. Julio did the same on his side of the vehicle. They met at the back of the SUV, using the small strand of palms for concealment.

"I guess now we have to find someone in charge," Julio said.

"Over there," Eduardo said, gesturing with his rifle toward the Urutu. Julio nodded and hurried across the road in a low crouch.

Urutu fighting vehicles had been named for a deadly, South American snake. They were old and hadn't received the extensive upgrades of the American vehicles. This meant it didn't have remote-controlled machine-guns and advanced computer systems. But even so, the Urutu was a steel beast carrying a lot of firepower. It'd be the logical place to find whoever was in charge, or at least someone who could direct them to the senior commander.

This Urutu was parked with the front angled partly onto the road. The hatch on top of the turret stood open, and someone's head bobbed up and down from time to time as they cautiously peeked up the road. The two doors on back of the vehicle were open, and Julio headed for them.

He rounded the door with Eduardo right behind to find a middle-aged, slightly overweight sergeant with wide, frightened eyes staring at them. "Has the general come? Are you here to relieve us?"

That this man thought General von Jaeger would be arriving here in any capacity almost made Julio laugh. But the fear and pleading tone in his voice about a relief force made him want to cry.

"No, but one's being organized. We have a message about that for your commanding officer. Where is he?"

Hope fled the man's face, but he visibly steeled himself. He looked like he was on the ragged edge of a breakdown. "Uh, I'm not sure." Then his eyes took on a bit of a wild look, and he emitted a brief maniacal laugh bordering on despair. "He, he, he. Uh, Lieutenant Monteiro. Crap, he's just a kid." He blinked and shook his head. "Uh...Sorry. I...I think he's by the next Urutu."

"Hang in there," Eduardo said. The man barked out another brief, wild laugh, then shrugged as his eyes darted around, scanning the trees behind the Urutu.

Julio started back toward the road, but Eduardo put his hand on his shoulder and shook his head. "These guys are under cover for a reason. Let's go through the trees."

Julio nodded and turned the other way. The Urutu was parked just a few meters beyond the jatoba tree they'd passed. The two men had to push their way through a thin layer of brush, but then the forest opened out. Small, skinny-trunked trees and a variety of low, scruffy plants grew on the other side. Depending on how the randomly spaced trees lined up, he could see a couple of hundred meters into the forest. However, the late morning sun glared as bright here as in the mahogany forest.

The land was a crazy quilt work of light and dark with ground cover that provided lots of hiding places. Every shadow looked like a crouching demon. Staying low, Julio and Eduardo rushed from tree to tree toward the next Urutu up the road.

They found a junior lieutenant kneeling on the forest side of the Urutu. Another junior lieutenant and two sergeants were with him. The lieutenant was young, only a couple of years older than Julio. But his face had deep lines and was streaked with dirt and sweat. Most of the men's uniforms had blood on them, but as none of them seemed hurt, it probably wasn't theirs.

As they approached, the young officer looked them over with old eyes. Julio knew those eyes. The survivors of the first battle with the demons had looked much the same. But then, better old eyes than panicked ones.

Julio squatted down beside him. "Orders from high command sir," he said, handing him the message.

The lieutenant maintained a neutral expression as he took the paper, most likely a mask of self-control and calmness he wore for his men. If so, he was doing a pretty good job. Much better than the middle-aged sergeant at the last Urutu.

The lieutenant handed the message to a gray-haired master sergeant kneeling beside him. He also had old eyes, but at least on him they looked at home. He scanned the message and said, "Ha. Advance to contact. Well, we've got that covered."

Eduardo looked back and forth between the young officer and senior noncom. Then he said to the lieutenant, "Sir, Captain Mello is now in command of the 43rd Regiment. He's setting up a defensive line about three kilometers west of here. He asked that you delay as much as possible, but for you to withdraw to his positions at your discretion."

The master sergeant shrugged. "At least we have a place to pull back to. Not sure how much more we can delay, though. We're barely holding it together."

The lieutenant nodded, then motioned for three men taking cover behind some low brush nearby to join them. Once they arrived, he said, "Go to your battalion commanders and tell them to maintain current operations and tactics. But as they fall back, keep an eye out for the 43rd to their rear. Once we reach them, be prepared to dig in."

Julio wondered what kind of tactics they were talking about. But now wasn't the time to ask.

All three soldiers said, "Yes, sir." Then hurried away in different directions. They ran in half-crouches as they darted from tree to tree.

"Not wild about digging in," the master sergeant said. "That didn't work so well at the tree line."

The lieutenant shrugged. "Yeah, but how much more can the men take?"

"I don't know, but—"

"Here they come!" someone screamed. Other soldiers took up the yell. Several machine-guns opened fire, and seconds later Julio was surrounded by the roar of weapons. The men beside the Urutu ducked instinctively, although they couldn't see what started the shooting from behind the combat vehicle.

Julio met Eduardo's eyes and saw his own alarm mirrored there. Eduardo broke the gaze and jumped into motion with Julio right behind. Staying low, they moved to the front of the Urutu and dove behind a fallen log along with three other soldiers. Julio poked his head up to search for targets. They were easy to find.

"Oh, my God," he muttered as his gut constricted.

Hundreds of war demons were swarming down the road. Behind them, the Urutu opened fire with its big fifty-caliber machine-gun. Julio's chest thrummed and his ears went numb as the weapon roared over his head. By now, he had so much adrenaline coursing through his veins that he didn't even flinch. He rested his battle rifle on the log and began firing along with the others.

The demons looked like a dark wave rolling down the road. There were so many, it was difficult to pick out individual targets. On the other hand, he couldn't miss hitting them. Hitting the vulnerable spot between the front two appendages was another matter.

The aliens got hit plenty. Some had limbs blown completely off by the heavy weapons, but still they leaped forward—or, in some cases, dragged themselves along. However, they still kept coming.

A thunk sound came from the soldier to his left. Julio turned toward him as he collapsed like a towel dropped to the bathroom floor. Blood flowed down from his helmet, and Julio saw a sizeable hole in it. He ducked down and reached over to check the boy's pulse, only to find his neck cold and lifeless. Looking up, he saw at least a score of men lying motionless around him. More soldiers, most painted with the red roses from various wounds. Some crawled slowly away from the battle.

When he looked back at the demons, he was surprised to see that the advancing wave had been reduced to a few dozen. Hundreds of the odd-shaped aliens carpeted the road. The sight filled him with savage pride. *We did that!* Then doubt filled him. *What was the point of this charge? Just to kill a few soldiers?*

The heavy machine-guns on the combat vehicles did the most damage. As he watched, more demons fell. The few dozen dwindled to a handful. Two more fell as they neared the first Urutu, and then there were only three of the leaping, twisting forms left. But now they were only a score of yards from the combat vehicle. Julio watched in sick fascination as they closed the gap. *What the hell were they doing?* Two of the remaining demons suddenly convulsed and fell, tumbling across the ground. But the last made an incredibly long leap and landed on the front of the lead Urutu.

Lightning filled Julio's vision as thunder shook him to the bone. A gust of hot air plucked the bush-hat from his head. The strings tied around his chin made the hat flip back onto his left shoulder. Half blinded by the blast, he could still see far more than he wanted to.

The front of the Urutu disappeared, engulfed in a sudden cloud of smoke and dust. The Urutu's turret leaped out of the smoke, flipping end over end before smashing into a tree with a loud clang. Julio felt sick and stunned as he watched the turret bounce off the tree and fall to the ground with a muffled thump. Silence fell across the jungle ever so briefly as everyone stopped firing, shocked by the loss of the precious armored vehicle as much as the intensity of the explosion.

"Oh, my God," Eduardo said from beside him. To Julio's abused eardrums, it sounded as if he spoke with a pillow over his mouth. "If a few more made it through…" He didn't need to finish the thought. The Urutu behind them was only a dozen meters from the one just destroyed. Now the point of the charge was clear.

The silence lingered over the road for several long slow seconds. At least it was silent for Julio, other than a constant ringing sound. It felt like he had a wet towel wrapped around his ears. But it didn't last long. After a few seconds, a machine-gun began chattering in the distance to their right. Dozens of rifles soon joined in. Julio guessed the new battle to be about a kilometer away.

A soldier to his right, his face streaked with dirt and tension carving deep lines around his eyes said, "They're trying to flank us again."

The horn on the Urutu behind him sounded three times. The unexpected noise made Julio jerk in surprise. More horns and several whistles began blowing, each giving three successive blasts. Men began running about in every direction. It looked confusing, but he saw there was an order to the chaos.

Several soldiers hurried to help those dragging themselves down the road or lying prone on the ground. Others mounted up on the AM2 trucks or the Urutus. In a few minutes, several ATVs began retreating down the road. The two remaining Urutus and three Land Rover Defenders stayed behind while soldiers loaded wounded onto them. Off to their right, the firefight continued. The crackle of gunfire rose and fell as the battle surged and ebbed.

Julio saw a prone figure on the far side of the road. *Had he moved?* He nudged Eduardo and said, "I'm going to check on the guy; he may need help."

Eduardo nodded, and they hurried across the road, stooped over like old men. The soldier stirred feebly just as they reached him. A large red stain marred his upper right thigh. While Julio put pressure on it, Eduardo took out his medical kit and began preparing a pressure bandage. They managed to stop the worst of bleeding, but by then the soldier had passed out.

While they worked, the two Urutus pulled out and headed up the road with a roar of big motors and the crash of smashed brush and tree limbs. A few moments later, the AM2 light trucks began to move out as well. All were packed with wounded. In the surrounding trees, men could be seen moving west along with an occasional ATV or motorcycle. Motorcycles were common in Brazilian infantry units, especially in rough terrain like this.

One of the trucks, a Toyota with a machine gun in the bed, stopped next to them. Bleeding and bandaged men crowded the bed around the gun. In some cases, they lay on top of one another.

"If that guy looks like he'll live, we might squeeze him in back," said the driver.

Eduardo frowned and said, "I don't think he'd make it back there."

"We've got a vehicle," Julio said. "We'll take him."

The driver shrugged, and the motor of the Toyota revved as he began moving away. Before it reached the bend, the shooting from the right stopped. It was far from silent however, as motors and men crashing through the brush came from the sides and behind. But compared to the shooting, if felt as though an ominous quiet gripped the land. Eduardo nudged Julio and nodded up the road. Dark shapes moved at the far end of the straightaway.

"Time to go," he said.

The two stood with the wounded man cradled between them. Julio took the legs and Eduardo locked his arms around the man's chest. They moved to where the SUV was parked at an awkward, though rapid shuffle.

The vehicle was where they left it, but not in the same condition. The back-left corner had been smashed and the Fender driven into the wheel well. From the tracks, apparently the Urutu with the hysterical sergeant had plowed into it while turning around. Anger boiled up in Julio, but it faded quickly. Living through hell made him stoic beyond his years. What was the point of being angry?

After the two stared at the wrecked Rover for several moments in semi-shock, Julio glanced behind them. Demons moved down the road, though not as fast as when they charged the Urutu. He glanced at Eduardo, who shrugged and nodded toward the road. They resumed the half-shuffle jog with the wounded man between them, moving as fast as they could.

They rounded the jatoba tree, and Julio felt some measure of relief at being out of sight of the demons. Already the two men's breath came in quick pants from carrying the soldier and moving at such an awkward gait.

Eduardo shook his head and said, "Man, now we're really in trouble."

"We'll make it," Julio puffed.

"Oh, sure we will. But the general's going to be really pissed when he sees what you did to his fancy ride."

Despite everything…the tension, their defeat, and their desperate run, Julio burst out laughing.

34 Marcus Makes Preparations

The sounds of combat echoing through the jungle hammered at Marcus's heart. His countrymen faced a desperate situation out there. And despite the distorting effects of the trees, he could tell the battle was getting closer. Reports came in that the demons were destroying Urutus by leaping on them and exploding. So much for the general's belief that armored vehicles assured victory. The man had a true talent for underestimating the aliens.

Captain Viana hurried up to him, looking grim. "All communications are out, but you already knew that, but maybe not the extent. We still have one microwave tower, but all the transmitters were destroyed. The telephone lines, every one of them, have been cut. The scout demons must have had them located before the attack."

Salina was translating for Major Sanchez, who shook his head at the report. "This is a very well planned and executed attack then."

"Obviously. The creatures can read maps and plan very well,"

Major Augusto Amorim said, his face grim. As commander of the reserve force, he was the most senior army officer remaining after the disaster at the general's headquarters. He was not a typical Brazilian in that he spoke English and had blond hair and hazel eyes. The major shook his head in frustration and said, "Another cornerstone of von Jaeger's planning has been shattered. He was confident that they were basically too stupid to do that."

Marcus snorted. "You should never plan on your enemy being stupid. But it doesn't matter now. We must determine what to do going forward. What've we got left?"

Viana said, "Well, the reserve, of course. And we've pulled everything from the northern defensive line, including three battalions of mechanized infantry with twenty Urutus. There is another battalion of pure infantry with no vehicles to support them." A series of explosions echoed out for forest from the east. He glanced that way and said, "But from the sound of it, they shouldn't have a very long march to get into position."

"We need to move as much as we can to the east. How are they armed?" Marcus said.

"Mostly with assault rifles. The bulk of the units with battle rifles are at the lumber mill. We can beef up their firepower by pulling machine-guns from the patrol boats."

"No, we'll need them elsewhere, I'm afraid. I fear the demons might try attacking from the river again. They'll have to make do with what they have."

Viana frowned and shook his head. "You know how tough it is to kill one of those damn things with an assault rifle? You'll be putting them in a really bad spot."

"You don't think I know that, captain?" Marcus snapped. "We're in a bad spot everywhere." He drew in a deep breath. "I will also need ten of the Urutus from the mechanized companies to be reassigned to the reserves." Jeronimo started to say something, but Marcus held up his hand to cut him off.

He looked away and gave his head a small shake, then backed up as he squared his shoulders. "Jeronimo, I'm going to have to put you in a bad spot as well. The reserve will stay where it is for the moment. I want you to take everything else east and take over command of the defense there. I plan on withdrawing the hospital and non-combat personnel back across the river. But we'll need time to do that."

Jeronimo looked grim, but he nodded. "If that's what you need, sir. I'll do my best."

"I know you will. And believe me, the reserve force isn't in for a picnic either."

Jeronimo smiled at Major Amorim. "I'm sure he isn't."

"Actually," Marcus said, with a humorless smile, "I'll be taking command of the reserve force." He turned to Major Amorim. "As most of these people are army, and you're the senior army commander, I want you to take command of the evacuation and base defense."

"What?" Amorim exclaimed. "That's my unit. I...I mean–"

"No, major. This entire base is your unit." Marcus turned to Nelino and said, "Captain Pereira will take charge of the river crossing itself. Commandeer any boats, civilian and military, as you see fit."

"Major Sanchez, can we count on your hovercraft for the effort?" Marcus said through Salina.

He hesitated, obviously concerned for his own men, but then nodded. "Yes, of course. And my forces should be moving into the northern defensive positions within the hour. I have gotten reports of demon activity in our sector, but no attacks. However, I will have to leave screening forces in place until we finish moving here."

"Very good. Thank you," Marcus said. He turned to Major Amorim. "Okay, let's go check over the reserve force. There are a few preparations we need to undertake for what I have in mind."

35 Daniel and the Attack on the Marines

A steady wind stirred the leaves with a rustling murmur. The noise was surprisingly loud, but the coolness of the breeze was a nice change from the usual airless humidity on the ground far below. Daniel lowered his binoculars and shook his head. "You're right, Tom. It doesn't look good at all."

The man beside him, Private First-Class Tom Black, looked up from the scope on his sniper rifle and nodded. "Yes, sir. I think we're about to get seriously rained on."

Daniel grasped a branch for support and looked over the edge of the narrow platform at the ground a hundred feet below. He yelled down at a group of upturned faces, "Hey, Gunny, get 'em ready. It doesn't look like we have much time."

The darkest face in the group below saluted and began addressing the others. Daniel turned to the slender, blond private. "Good job on this platform," Daniel said. "You can see for miles from up here."

Private Black smiled. "Thank you, sir. But the whole squad helped."

Daniel nodded. "I'll have to buy them a beer when this is over." He raised the binoculars and looked once more at the war demons pouring out of a large, sinister opening at the base of the Dark Mountain. It looked different from here, but he was sure it was the same one they'd come from before attacking his platoon last time.

Heat shimmered in the moist air and slightly distorted the distant image. But it was clear enough to make out individual demons as they piled on top of one another in clumps, making it difficult to determine exactly how many there were. Daniel estimated at least five thousand, probably more.

He sighed. "Damn, if only we could get a message to artillery. A few shells with them bunched up like that, and we wouldn't have any problems."

Black looked at him with concern. "Do you think that's why they cut our communications? Have they figured that much out about us?"

Daniel nodded. "Yeah, I do. I think somebody badly underestimated their ability to plan and adapt. I only hope the demons underestimate us as well."

He lowered his binoculars and looked over the torn and ravaged orange land between the bright green of the rainforest and the mountain's bone-white spires. His chest felt tight as he took in the stark contrast at the forest's boundary—life versus death.

From this vantage point, gazing at the barren terrain

surrounding the mountain, it seemed as if a terminal disease was attacking the jungle. In a sense, he supposed it was. And to think some parts of the world still denied this was even happening. Daniel knew that anyone who saw the mountain and the growing desert around it would have no doubt about the dangers it implied.

He said, "Well, I guess I better get back to my LAV. Are you sure you want to stay up here alone?"

Black's smile was a thin, tight line. "Yes, sir. You need some eyes up high, and I guess I can do it as well as anyone." He tapped the large rifle sitting on a bipod at the edge of the platform. "And maybe I can pick off a few of the buggers on their way in." He nodded to a rope hanging off a nearby branch. "If it starts to get too hot, I'll just take the express elevator down. Be better with just one."

"Okay," Daniel said. "Don't' forget, though, I owe your team a beer when this is over."

Black raised an eyebrow. "Hell, sir, I ain't forgetting. Just make sure you remember!"

Daniel turned, grasped the rope, and then looked back with a smile. "Why, Private Black, I believe you're coming dangerously close to insulting the integrity of an officer." Black just snorted. Daniel chuckled as he wrapped his legs around the rope and slid down to the ground.

Gunny came up as Daniel kicked the rope off his leg and rumbled loudly in his gruff, drill sergeant voice, "Welcome back to planet earth, sir!"

Daniel could hear more than a hint of disapproval in the older man's tone. Gunny did not like an officer wasting valuable time doing things like climbing trees to see with their own eyes what a perfectly good private could easily report on.

Daniel gave a half smile. "Okay, Gunny, I know you don't approve of me doing any real work. But I really wanted to see what we're up against firsthand."

Gunny's eyes widened with mock innocence. "Why sir, I have no idea what you mean. Why would I disapprove of you removing yourself from command and communication to climb a tree? That's the lieutenant's prerogative, sir!"

Daniel sighed. "Okay, Gunny, okay. I'll try to be a good little officer, at least for the rest of the day." He took off his helmet and wiped sweat from his brow. "What about the other snipers?"

Gunny shrugged. "They're in place, but I'm not sure how much good they'll be. Those Barretts are great at a distance, but not so good against fast-moving targets."

Daniel nodded, replacing his helmet. "I know." He glanced back up the tree. "But it's one of the few rifles we've got with enough punch to do those things some major damage at range. They know to pull out as soon as things get dicey?"

Gunny nodded and then looked at the mountain. "I sure hate seeing them things massing like that. If they come, how long are we supposed to hold this tree line, Lieutenant?"

"Until Company A passes behind us. Then we've got the backdoor all the way to Rio Estrada."

"We got the weapons platoon setting up east of us," Gunny said, with a nod in that direction. "Are they going to try dumping some ordnance on them?"

"I think so. The major told 'em to take some shots if they got a chance. And that big bunch out there looks like a good target to me."

"Roger that," said Gunny.

A series of loud chuffing sounds came from the adjoining unit as they opened fire. The weapons platoon contained the unit's big mortars and antitank missile squads. "Speak of the devil," Gunny said. They both scrambled up behind the turret of Daniel's LAV and raised their binoculars.

"Son of a bitch!" exclaimed Gunny as the first salvo of 81mm and 120mm mortar rounds burst ineffectively about two-thirds of the way to the demons. "The dumb asses must be using prox fuses. That shit ain't going to work with all that electronic mumbo jumbo in the air."

Daniel nodded. Proximity fuses were supposed to detonate the shells just above the ground, spraying the target with deadly steel shrapnel. They worked by sensing radio pulses reflected from the ground. It had been discussed in briefings that interference from the White Mountain might make them misfire.

But the next salvo met the same fate, and the next. Daniel shook his head. "I don't think that's from prox-fuses. Surely, they'd have gone to time delay by now," he said, propping his elbows on the turret to steady his binoculars.

Details were blurred by the thick, humid air, but numerous war demons, perhaps one in ten, seemed raptly focused on the air above, the arms containing their weapons pointing skyward.

"Crap," said Gunny. "Please tell me they ain't shooting those shells out of the air."

Another salvo of explosions bloomed black clouds high over the demons, and Daniel nodded. "I think that's exactly what they're doing. Remember in that briefing with the scientists? They said these things can see radio waves. Like natural radar. They must be able to track the shells."

Gunny lowered his binoculars and leaned forward against the turret, shaking his head. "That shit just ain't right."

Daniel looked to the east, where the crackle of machine-guns and rifles, punctuated with the heavier thumps of explosions, could be heard in the distance. Daniel looked at his watch; it had been over an hour since the scout demons devastated the Brazilian headquarters.

"I wonder how the Brazilians are doing. I know the lack of battle rifles is a really bad deal for them."

Gunny cocked his head for a moment, listening to the distant battle. "I ain't no expert in the capabilities of the indigenous military, but offhand, it sounds like they're getting the shit kicked out of 'em."

Daniel smiled grimly. "Gunny, you have such an eloquent way of putting things."

He shrugged. "It is what it is."

The platoon of four LAVs were set up right at the edge of the forest. They had a clear field of fire if the demons came at them. In addition to the snipers, beside each LAV were log-covered firing pits with machine-guns at the ready. Everybody looked as prepared they could be. "Okay, Gunny, let's…"

A muffled explosion followed by an agonized scream interrupted him. The blast made him duck. He looked up just as Gunny pulled him to one side, nearly spilling both of them off the LAV. A second later, a thirty-pound Barrett .50 caliber sniper-rifle careened off the steel where he'd been standing. Sadly, this was followed a second later by the twisted body of Private Tom Black.

They froze, staring down at the body. More muffled explosions erupted from the left and right, causing them to duck down again. Someone else screamed, sending a forlorn wail echoing through the jungle. Daniel and Gunny looked around frantically, trying to locate the source of the explosions and screams. The anguished wail faded away, leaving an unnatural silence along the tree line.

Gunny said in a low voice, "What the hell?"

Corporal Sharon Bennett, standing in the gunner's hatch on top of the turret, pointed and screamed, "Here they come!"

A fifty-cal on one of the mortar platoon's Assault Amphibious Vehicles opened fire on their left. A second AAV joined it and less than five seconds later, the Recon Platoon's chain guns also began shooting.

Gunny jumped off the LAV and dove into the log-covered pit with the gun crew on the right. Daniel climbed up on the LAV's turret and wiggled into the command hatch. As he snatched up his helmet, put it on, and adjusted his microphone, he glanced up and saw a mass of leaping dark shapes in the distance. *Oh shit, here they come, is right.*

Sliding into his command seat, he powered up the three monitors. He tabbed the left hand one onto the rear camera. Through the foliage, he could see the road. It was empty. *Damnit, where was A Company?* They should be moving by now. His platoon couldn't hold this line for long. They'd be outflanked once the supporting units moved east.

"Fletch, be ready to kick the pig."

"Foot's cocked, LT."

Sharon was focused on her screen. The turret lurched back and forth as she tracked targets with both the main gun and the coaxial machine-gun mounted beside it. Her fire was devastating to the charging demons. But it didn't slow them and for sure wasn't stopping them. Dying didn't seem to be a problem for these assholes. *Well, by God, we'll just have to kill them all.*

Daniel triggered the overhead gun from his center screen.

Bursts of fire began arcing out. Bright streaks that left smoke trails in their wake were the tracers. Impacting rounds from the LAVs kicked up small orange explosions of mud around the demons. It seemed to Daniel that far too few found their mark, however. It took a long time for someone to strike home and send an alien tumbling across the ground.

Damn, how'd they gotten so close so fast? The surprise from the explosions allowed them to get a big jump at crossing the open ground. Daniel wondered what happened to the observers who were supposed to have sounded the alarm. *Did the explosions kill all of them? How could every observer and sniper be targeted and killed at the same time? Scout demons? Maybe.*

He looked around his position, suddenly fearful of more mysterious explosions. *Is this the same type of weapon they used at the Brazilian headquarters?* The Marines left before anyone knew how the aliens pulled that off.

He pushed the worry aside, no time for it now. Regardless of the cause of the explosions, the blasts had been comparatively small. Though deadly to his soldiers, once everyone was mounted up, they'd be okay.

Placing the top gun on automatic to find and engage the closest target, he focused his attention on the center screen. The demons were a little over a quarter mile away and closing fast. There were fewer than he expected. Thank God for that, maybe five hundred or so. The bulk of the horde still sat at the base of the mountain. He frowned, wondering once again why they didn't commit more of their forces. *They must have their reasons, but why?*

The weapons platoon to their left were packing it in. Why wouldn't they? Their mission had been to drop mortar rounds onto the creatures and thin their ranks. That'd been an obvious bust. Now they'd take their AAVs and go take up assigned positions in the new defensive line north of Rio Estrada.

Movement on the left-hand monitor focused on the road caught his eye. Company A's AAVs and support vehicles were on the move at last. *Thank God.*

"Fletch, sound the horn. We'll be boogying out in a minute."

The LAV's horn sounded three short blasts, signaling the gun crews in the bunkers that it was time to mount up. Meantime, he watched with anxious eyes as Company A filed past. *Damn, couldn't they go any faster!*

The LAV's massed fire continued to whittle down the demons, but at a disturbingly slow rate. The creatures had spread out and were leaping in complicated patterns that made targeting them difficult. And they were fast! They were much further apart than when they attacked his platoon last time. But being spread out like that meant their attack should have had little effect. Daniel again wondered what they hoped to accomplish. He thought about how they'd disrupted communications. If they were smart enough to figure that out, this crazy charge must have a reason, but what? And what about those explosions. His already uneasy feeling ratcheted upward.

At last, the final vehicle from Company A passed, marked with a red pendent on its antennae. That meant Recon was clear to withdraw. He cycled his monitors through the various cameras mounted outside the LAV. The gun pits were clear. Time to get going.

"Kick the pig, Fletch," he said.

"Putting the boot to her," came the reply. With a roar that sent vibrations through the vehicle, they lurched into motion.

The other vehicle commanders were keeping one monitor on his LAV and when they began to move, the rest followed within seconds. They fanned out in a staggered formation to keep their guns' fields of fire clear.

The route was already planned: follow the tree line for one mile, then swing through a cut in the trees that led to the road. Two miles after that, and they could get covering firing from the units already in Rio Estrada.

Again, the speed of the demons surprised him. They were nearly on top of the platoon. But this at least concentrated them, and as he watched, a dozen fell in the span of a few seconds. There were maybe twenty still coming, then twelve, and then five. Sharon yelled triumphantly, "We got 'em, LT. Sons of bitches. That'll show 'em."

At thirty yards, the two leading demons launched themselves toward Gunny's LAV, which was on the outside rear of the formation next to Daniel's. He watched the demons sail through the air, seemingly in slow motion. The LAV's chain gun and top machine-gun blazed away, trying to claw the alien shapes out of the air, but to no avail. The LAV made a sharp turn, and one of the demons missed while the other bounced off the fender and fell in front of it. A second later, two powerful explosions erupted that lifted the front of the LAV and flipped it over on its side. Daniel was thrown violently sideways, slamming his head painfully into the steel side of the turret. His helmet saved him from a fractured skull.

"Gunny!" Daniel yelled. He frantically played his cameras over the stricken vehicle, trying to see if there was any hope. Smoke and dust billowed around the LAV, blocking most of his vision.

"Oh God," Fletch muttered. And then yelled, "Shit! There's another one."

"Where?" Daniel and Sharon yelled in unison. He gave up on the monitors and looked through the periscopes ringing the command hatch.

"Ten o'clock! Ten o'clock!" screamed Fletch.

The turret jerked around and Daniel spotted it, already in the air. Only one, but he feared that would be enough. Now he understood the purpose behind the attack. He cringed, but there was nowhere to go. Sharon desperately tried to elevate the LAV's guns, but they were swinging up too slowly, too damn slow by far.

"Oh, my God," muttered Daniel helplessly as the war demon sailed toward him.

The engine revved to a shriek, and the LAV lurched in an abrupt left turn, throwing Daniel's face into the padded rim of the periscope with a thud. An instant later, a burst of fire from the LAV's co-axle machine-gun lanced out and caught the demon on its left side. The stream of bullets did not stop it, although they did spin the creature sideways. The LAV's wheels churned frantically as Fletch forced the armored vehicle into a tighter turn.

Daniel tried to keep the demon in sight, instinctively switching to another periscope as it sailed by the side of the vehicle but lost it as it fell. He flinched in fearful anticipation as it disappeared from view. His heart beat one, two, three times. Then with a flash and a roar, a wave of pain swept him into blackness.

36 Julio in the Forest

Julio and Eduardo carried the wounded man along the winding, muddy road for about a kilometer. Julio's arms quivered with the strain of supporting the wounded man. His legs threatened to cramp from the awkward gait, and sweat ran off him in glistening rivulets, soaking his shirt and pants. At last, they rounded a strand of bamboo and saw the next Brazilian defensive line.

Two Urutus sat at the end of another straightaway in the logging road. They'd been backed into the forest and faced west, ready to run in the event of another mass charge. After the last attack, it made sense to be ready for a quick getaway.

About halfway to the Urutus, three camouflaged trucks blocked the road, their backs faced toward Julio, also positioned to head west in a hurry if needed. All three had heavy duty machine-guns mounted to their beds, with metal shields on them. On either side, men peeked around trees and from hastily dug foxholes. As Julio and Eduardo staggered up the road with the wounded man, four soldiers came out from around a large mahogany tree and ran to meet them.

"Thank...God," Eduardo panted. "Let's put him down."

Julio nodded gratefully. He almost dropped the man as they eased him to the ground. Then he and Eduardo collapsed onto their knees beside him, both breathing fast and hard.

"Looks like you could use some help," said the corporal leading the soldiers as they approached. Two of the privates went to check on the wounded soldier.

"Yeah... Thanks," Julio gasped, trying to slow his breathing.

"He's in bad shape," said one of the privates. "We need to get him to the aid station right away."

The corporal nodded, and the two soldiers picked up the wounded man and hurried off. As he watched them go, Julio whispered a silent prayer that the man would be all right.

The corporal reached down and helped Julio to his feet. "We

need to get under cover. The demons must b–"

A thok sound interrupted the corporal, turning his last word into "ulk." The man's light brown eyes showed surprise. He looked down and put his hand over a half-inch hole that had appeared on the left side of his chest. Blood gushed through his fingers as he toppled backwards.

Julio dove back down and rolled into a small ditch on the side of the road. Eduardo and the remaining private did the same on either side of him. As he reached to grab the corporal's boot and pull him to cover, someone screamed, "Demons!" A second later, the familiar crackling roar of massed machine-guns and rifles erupted from up ahead. At the same time, though at a far slower rate, thok sounds echoed through the forest from behind them. Thok, thok-thok...thok.

A quick check of the corporal's pulse revealed he was dead. *Damn, damn, damn.* Julio fumbled to get his rifle off his back, where he'd slung it to free his hands. Even as he got the sling over his head, Eduardo and the private began shooting.

Shadows moved on either side of the road. At least the demons weren't charging...yet. Julio brought up his rifle, but Eduardo glanced at him and shouted over the din, "No! Head toward the line. I'll cover you."

Julio started to protest but realized that would be a waste of time. Instead he said, "Leapfrog it." Julio tugged the private's shoulder and they began low crawling along the muddy ditch toward the Brazilian lines.

"Roger that," said Eduardo. He continued to fire short, three round bursts at the approaching aliens.

Julio and the private slithered along, moving like eels through the mud. Halfway to the Brazilian lines, they stopped and pivoted around, then began searching for targets in the gloom under the trees along the road.

An alien form with an oversized arm held high caught Julio's attention. He zeroed in on it with the enhanced sight of his battle rifle and fired a three-round burst. The rifle's retort was noticeably louder than the assault rifle he normally carried. He aimed at the intersection between the arms and front set of legs as Sally had taught him. But the creature turned as he pulled the trigger.

The demon's head jerked as two holes appeared in one of the oversized eyes. This didn't seem to bother it much, and it swung its spike weapon toward Julio. The junction between the front two limbs wasn't in view, so Julio sighted in on the torso to the side of its head. He fired and hit his mark. The battle rifle's more powerful bullet must have punched through the shoulder to its heart. The demon sagged, and its weapon arm thumped down to the ground.

"Yes!" Julio barked out in triumph. He spotted another one behind a tree. The demon only had its head and the oversized weapon hand poked out around the trunk, making it difficult to hit the vital kill zone. He popped off a few shots and then ducked back down.

Eduardo stopped firing and began crawling along the ditch toward them. Bullets and spikes crisscrossed overhead with faint buzzing sounds. Being in the middle of a battle meant you had to avoid getting hit from every direction, especially since a lot of soldiers fired blindly from behind cover. This wasn't a healthy place to be.

Eduardo passed them, pressing lower into the mud as he did so. Getting closer to their own lines meant the fire from that direction now passed only a few feet over their heads. He gave Julio a crooked smile as he passed.

"This has turned into a lovely day. Don't you think?" he said.

"We'll have to do it again sometime," Julio said, smiling back as his new friend slinked past.

"They're attacking different," said the private. He lifted his head, fired off a few shots, and then buried his face against the side of the ditch.

"Yeah, they're not charging," Julio said. "And they're using cover."

The demon's new attack style was probably the only reason Julio and the private were still alive. They must be adapting to the human's tactics. If they'd charged, their position would be quickly overrun otherwise. But he wasn't sure what it meant going forward.

Eduardo reached the mahogany tree where the poor corporal lying in the road came from. He leaped up and around it out of sight.

Julio nudged the private. "Start crawling."

The man nodded and put his rifle in the crook of his arms. He began crawling by using his knees and elbows to slide along in the mud. Julio did the same a few meters behind. The ground felt cold and wet against his body. Cold, wet, and safe. Though the safety was comparative and no doubt more illusion than reality.

The thok sounds ceased a few moments before Julio reached the mahogany tree where Eduardo had taken refuge. The gunfire tapered off more slowly and then stopped as he and the private reached it. Both men leaped out of the ditch and sprinted around the tree to get under cover. Even as they found shelter in a shallow foxhole dug behind the tree, a series of explosions sounded from the east.

"Well, that was fun," Eduardo said with a faint smile. He raised his head and peered out over the roots of the tree. "Looks like they wanted to pin us down before they launched an attack on the lumber mill."

The sounds of battle grew. The noise of thousands of rifles and machine-guns being fired in unison was momentarily drowned out by a long string of explosions. Julio could feel the ground vibrate under him. The first wave of concussions stopped, as did the gunfire. But only for a moment. The gunfire resumed and more explosions erupted, though at a less fervent pace.

"Shit," Julio said. "That was intense. Were those explosions from the aliens?"

"I don't know," replied Eduardo. "At least our side's still shooting back. They're still in the fight."

"Yeah. Good point. So, what do you think we should do next? Head back to base?"

"I guess–"

His response was cut off by a burst from a truck-mounted machine-gun behind them. The Brazilian green and black vehicle shook from the recoil of the heavy weapon, and Julio's already abused ears sent sharp needles through his head. A muffled scream jerked his attention back to the road, and he saw demon shapes moving toward them in the shadows. Distant thok sounds filled the air. Then, through the din, came the cry, "Spies! Spy demons!"

Grotesque, multi-legged shapes the size of dinner plates fell out of the surrounding trees by the dozens. Three landed in the bed of the

Toyota behind them, and the gunner drew back with a scream of terror.

BANG! The explosion was nowhere near as big as the one that destroyed the Urutu, but it was more than sufficient to kill the gunner. A spy demon must have gotten inside the truck too, because the rear window blew out with another loud bang and the cab became engulfed in flames.

The private who'd been on the road with Julio jumped to his feet and fired at the spy demons using full auto. His face lit up in savage satisfaction as he swept bullets around the burning Toyota. Then it twisted in pain and fear as he dropped his rifle and fell to the ground with a large red stain spreading across his back.

The spies scuttled across the ground around Julio's shallow foxhole. Staying low made them hard to see; raising up to shoot gave the larger aliens up the road a good target. These things truly were demons. Plus, the battle rifle wasn't nearly as effective on the close, small, fast-moving creatures. The recoil made it hard to keep on target shooting full auto, which would be the way he'd normally shoot at the spies.

At least not all of them were exploding. So far, anyway. That was small consolation when four of them hopped into the foxhole. Julio didn't even try to fire his weapon. Instead, he raised it up as high as he dared and slammed the rifle butt down on the closest spy. There was a distinct crunch, and purplish fluid erupted from its back. The legs twitched, and went still.

Eduardo's rifle blasted from close by, and a neat purple hole appeared in the creature next to the one Julio crushed. It, too, went still. The special forces sergeant was apparently a better quick shot than Julio.

A blaze of pain lanced up Julio's left calf. He jerked his leg back and flipped around to spot the spy demon that slashed his leg with its menacing, three-inch, razor-sharp claw. He used the roll to help propel his right leg around in a vicious kick that knocked the demon out of the foxhole. It landed in a rolling tumble, but as soon as it stopped, the creature darted back toward the foxhole.

Despite the incoming fire from the large demons, Julio rose to his knees and brought his rifle up. Instinct took over as he sighted, shot, and killed the foul thing with a bullet that shattered the creature's head and drove all the way through its body. Then he ducked back down in time to hear the whispers of several spikes slice through the air overhead.

Where was the last one? Four spies entered the foxhole, and he looked about with frantic eyes. A surge of relief raced through him as he spotted it squirming on the ground to his left with Eduardo's knife sticking through its back. He relaxed long enough to take in two deep breaths to settle his nerves, then poked his head up high enough to look for more threats. There weren't any more living spy demons in sight, and the thok sounds from up the road stopped. The air was full of black smoke from the Toyota and smelled of burning plastic, hot metal, and other odors he didn't want to think about.

"The gun," Eduardo said, leaping up and running to the burning truck. "We need to save the gun."

Ignoring the pain in his leg, Julio jumped up and followed. Machine-guns were the best weapons they had against the demons. They couldn't afford to lose any if they could help it.

The front of the truck was engulfed in flames. He tried not to think about it getting hot enough to set off the tins of fifty-caliber ammunition stacked behind the cab. Eduardo leaped into the bed, then hesitated as a wave of flame rushed out at him. He crouched down and began tossing ammunition off the back of the truck. He must have had the same fear as Julio.

Julio leaped up and swiveled the weapon around to put the gun's shield between himself and the fire. As with most mounted armaments of this type, it was secured to the pedestal with a large, heavy-duty retaining pin so that it could be taken off the truck for maintenance. He pulled out the locking cotter key and tried to pull out the pin. But it resisted him with mechanical stubbornness. The weight of the heavy gun resting on it held it frozen in place. Despite the shield, heat sizzled against his exposed arms. He struggled to lift up on it but couldn't get any leverage. The metal beneath his fumbling fingers began to grow hot.

Eduardo gave up on the remaining ammunition and turned to help him. With both men lifting, Julio managed to free the pin. They jerked the gun free and tumbled off the back of the truck in a heap. The heavy machine-gun landed across their stomachs with a painful thud and they both went, "Oomph."

Before they could recover, a series of loud bangs erupted over their heads as the fifty-caliber bullets still behind the cab started exploding. They curled up below the truck's tailgate with their arms over their heads as bullet fragments, casings, and other bits of flying metal whizzed around them. Thankfully, Eduardo had gotten most of the ammunition off the truck and the fusillade only lasted a dozen seconds or so.

Silence settled around them after the last pop from overhead. Eduardo uncurled, rolled over on his back, and stared up at the clear blue sky for a moment.

"You know, my friend," he said in a low voice. "I'm beginning to think this line of work might be a bit hazardous."

Julio flopped over on his back beside him. Then snorted, smiled, and nodded.

37 Marcus at the Tanks

Marcus straightened his shoulders and concentrated on projecting an air of calm as he walked through the Urutus preparing for the assault. No easy task with the frenzied activity underway around him. The vehicles of the reserve force were always kept loaded and fueled, so at least that task didn't add to the general confusion. The main activity involved filling canvas bags with the heavy, orange soil common to the Amazon and affixing them to the six-wheeled combat vehicles.

A sergeant in the reserve platoon came up with the idea of reinforcing their light armor with sandbags. No one knew if it would help, but as the old saying goes, "It couldn't hurt." And the added weight might help with traction on the churned soil between the White Mountains and the tree line. At least the extra padding gave the crews some hope they might survive the battle.

The ten additional Urutus he'd pulled from the line were getting a similar treatment on the other side of the base. They'd join them when they headed out and bring the reserve force to a total of thirty Urutus and five Leopard 1 main battle tanks. In addition, the four American Marine Abrams M1A3 tanks would join them as well. That was a lot of firepower. Was he using it wisely? Would his plan work? *Dear God, please help us make it work.*

He paused to watch a crew as they strapped a heavy bag to their vehicle. He nodded with satisfaction as they made sure the Urutu's turret would turn all the way around and the weapon ports weren't blocked. The bags might be helpful, but functional weapons would be essential. The best chance they had, at least for the Urutus, would be to carve their way through any demon attack with sheer firepower.

He took a deep breath and held it, then let it out slowly to help push down the fear and doubt coursing through his mind. Then he felt a light touch on his shoulder, turned, and looked down into the worried face of Salina Morgan.

"Why you?" she said.

He hesitated a moment, confused by the question. "Why me?"

"Why do you have to be the one? The one to lead this?"

He looked over her head toward the sounds of explosions and machine-guns from Captain Viana's embattled troops. He said, "I…I can't say, really. It just seems like something I have to do."

She shook her head angrily. "Why do you have to be the hero? You've already done more than anyone here."

He smiled down at her, shaking his head. He pulled her away to a more sheltered area. "Salina, I hate what General von Jaeger said about me and my men. But there was an element of truth to it. I'm a river guard, a police officer really, not a general. But I served in the Urutus before and know them well. It's the job I'm most qualified for.

Not being a theater commander."

She opened her mouth, but he held up his hand. "Besides, I couldn't let these men go without me. I'll be honest; this will be very dangerous. They need to know the man who came up with this crazy plan is willing to see it through."

Salina looked away and slowly nodded with a small, resigned sigh. "That's what I thought you'd say." She met his eyes with an intense and somehow proud look. "Hit them hard, Marcus, but remember to let go. Please stay alive."

The corners of her mouth twitched upward in a smile, but it looked forced. "Remember, you promised to show me around Manaus." She stood on tiptoes and kissed his cheek. Then after a moment's hesitation, she brushed her lips softly across his. "Come back safe!" Tears began flowing down her face as she turned and hurried away.

Marcus stood in stunned surprise. Before he could recover, she was gone. He gingerly touched his cheek where she'd kissed him, then his lips. A smile came to his face, and for a moment concerns about the battle, the fear, and the doubt vanished, pushed aside by a wonderful surge of joy. He noticed some of the men looking at him. Many had silly grins on their face as if they, too, found a brief respite from reality by living vicariously through him.

He was unaware of it, but none of the men were surprised by the exchange. The inevitable rumor mill of the camp had marked them as a couple right after her speech. As the men looked at each other, a small warm current flowed through them as they thought of their own loved ones. Out of place perhaps on the cusp of a life and death battle, but appreciated nonetheless. Or maybe not out of place after all. For love of family is one of the bedrocks of all soldiers.

The moment ended when a sergeant barked, "All right, that's enough wasting time! Back to work!"

But for Marcus the glow continued a little longer as he pondered her words and the brief, sweet kiss.

Sally

Sally paused not far from where the reserve force was preparing for battle and tried to get her emotional firestorm under control. She'd gone to tell Marcus to be careful and say goodbye… just in case. Tears welled up at even the thought of his possible death. *Damn him for being so noble!* First Myra and then David, and now Marcus was going into the middle of what seemed a hopeless battle. She didn't know how much more loss and pain she could stand.

Not only Marcus, although there was no denying he held a special place in her heart now. Julio was out there, along the Jeronimo. Her new brothers and comrades in arms. It amazed her how fast she'd grown so close to them. Going through hell together probably accounted for most of that. Plus, they were truly decent people.

The sounds of battle came nearer by the hour. *Does that mean we're losing?* She prayed they were okay, but something told her she might lose more friends this day.

Now, from the west, came the sharp crack of multiple explosions. The Americans were being attacked as well. She'd seen several of their big amphibious vehicles moving to the north side of the camp. How many were still out there? Could they hold the demons back while the hospital staff and the growing number of wounded were evacuated? If not, she could well lose more than just friends. She touched the butt of the rifle slung over her shoulder. *But not without a fight*, she thought grimly.

She shook her head. *Enough of this drama. I don't have time for this crap.* She'd promised to get back to the headquarters after seeing Marcus. If she'd had her head on straight, she wouldn't have left at all. Her skill with English and Portuguese was more important than ever. Major Sanchez had made that plain enough, as had Nelino and Major Amorim. The evacuation would require close coordination between the Brazilians and Americans. It was time to get back to work and do whatever she could to help save some lives.

38 Julio and the Gun

Silence descended across the line of desperate soldiers, at least locally. Ripples of gunfire and explosions still echoed through the forest from farther east as the Brazilians at the lumber mill continued to fight for their lives. The noon sun fought to penetrate the interlocking branches overhead, casting odd shadows all around them. The men squinted as they cast anxious stares into the surrounding shadows.

Julio peered with apprehension through the maze of trees, searching for movement while his fingers tickled the firing lever of the fifty-caliber machine-gun. He'd lost count of the number of men they'd lost lumbering the gun through the forest during the fight. How he managed to still be alive was a mystery. Just lucky, he guessed.

The weapon was an awkward affair at best. In almost any other situation, no one would have even dared fire it. It was designed to be mounted on a fixed swivel. Instead, he and Eduardo had lashed it to a slender mahogany log with utility belts. A man knelt on either side of Julio and supported the makeshift gun mount with their arms and belts looped over their shoulders. The gun had dents along the barrel and receiver. The handles were partly melted and the metal scorched. However, despite its obvious shortcomings, the men clung to it like a raft in a furious storm. It was a true case of having something that was better than nothing, but not by very much.

Ghostly white tendrils of mist crept through the trees, floating on air that was hot, heavy, and laden with the sharp tang of gun smoke. The acrid chemical odor overlaid the moist smell of decaying wood that permeated the rainforest. The combination made Julio's eyes water, and he had to constantly fight the urge to sneeze. The smoke, mist, and shadows often tricked the eye with false movements. Of even more concern, it covered up movements the men desperately needed to see, at the worst possible time.

He and Eduardo ran out of ammunition for their rifles not long after rescuing the gun from the burning truck. As men fell, they'd gone from guarding it to manning it. Eduardo stood behind him with his pistol drawn, ready to help fend off scout demons, as they liked dropping down on the unwary. In his left hand, he carried a long stick for a pointer to help the gun crew pick out targets.

"There! There!" Eduardo screamed, pointing the stick over Julio's head. It was long enough for the men on either side of Julio to see it too. They began scooting around on their knees, trying to stay low as Julio traced the line of the stick to the base of large trees thirty meters away. A shadow within the deeper shadows caught his eye. The men with him strained to get the heavy, ungainly machine-gun around. It seemed to take forever. Julio strained against the belts to help turn it while his heart thumped wildly in his chest. Sweat coursed down his face as the snout of the weapon came slowly around.

The shadowy shape took form as a war demon scuttled forward, weapon claw up and ready to fire. At last, the gun lined up with the menacing silhouette, and he squeezed the trigger. The gun bucked as a short burst lashed out. Bullets stitched a line across the alien, sending up a spray of dark blood. The creature lurched and went still. The fifty-caliber slugs were death to a demon, no matter where he hit it. Once more, the group cheated death.

The aliens had gotten good at using cover. Also, the smoke and strange shadows didn't seem to hinder them much. Thankfully, they only had a limited number of spikes stored in their weapon arms, just as Sally Morgan had predicted. But they were deadly shots, and their spikes often found flesh.

The crew did not relax with the small victory. Demons large and small were everywhere. The soldiers continued to peer into the forest and overhead, sweating profusely from the heat, the humidity, and the strain. Tension and fear hung like a cloud over the Brazilians, seemingly more tangible than the smoke and mist. In between the thunderous bursts from their weapon, the labored breathing was nearly a collective pant, giving voice to both their exhaustion and stress.

Shots erupted from the right, quickly swelling to a roar as another demon assault pressed home. The soldiers listened intently, knowing their fate to be intimately linked to whoever fought beside them. *Would they hold? Or would they break and run?* That had happened twice already. The entire line would be threatened if the demons succeeded in breaking through, forcing the Brazilians into yet another desperate retreat.

The roar of combat from the right continued without pause, indicating a major push by the aliens. The echoes permeated the forest, seeming both close and yet, somehow unreal and far away. Occasional screams of rage or pain or terror could be heard, even over the clamor of heavy weapons—the sounds of desperate men fighting for their lives.

Several sharp explosions overshadowed the roar of gunfire, followed by a sudden silence. The quietness hung in the air for a few heartbeats; then came a scream and the sounds of bodies crashing through the foliage. Frantic whistles began blowing up and down the line. That was the signal to retreat. The Brazilians' line broke yet again.

Julio and the other men shuffled backward awkwardly. It was hard to keep the gun trained in the right direction while moving. The panting of the men turned to grunts as they worked both with and against each. Fallen branches snagged at their feet and thorny vines plucked at flesh. Julio stumbled several times and barely kept his feet.

Eduardo started yelling at the men around them. "Stay focused! Get the ammunition! Stick together."

Three of the men broke and ran by the gun crew with terrified eyes and empty arms, carrying neither ammunition nor weapons. The men on either side of Julio looked fearfully at one another. For a moment, he thought they would run as well. But their expressions firmed with resolve, and the three continued their grunting progress through the forest.

The few remaining soldiers around Eduardo responded reluctantly to his frantic shouts and began gathering up ammunition. Raw fear tinged with panic was plain on every face. The incredible stress carved deep lines into their features, furrowing their brows and transforming youthful faces into old men.

A yell of alarm that transitioned horribly into a scream of agony came from the shadows nearby. Julio peered into the forest where the sound came from. But before he could spot anything, the machine-gun grips were jerked out of his hands as the branch dropped on his left. The man who'd held it was on the ground, gurgling and clutching at his bloody throat. Multiple thuds from impacting spikes came from all around. One of the men gathering ammunition collapsed in a heap while the others dove for cover. Julio searched the shadows frantically and spotted the dim outlines of several war demons scuttling towards them.

He leaped over the wounded man and lifted the branch while

yelling, "Man the gun! Man, the gun!"

Eduardo and the last remaining soldier helping him gather ammo froze for a split second when they saw the demons. Eduardo dropped the two tins he carried and dove for the gun. The soldier with him dropped his tins also but ran into the forest behind them. Eduardo reached the machine-gun and grabbed the handles while Julio and the other soldier swung the weapon toward the demons. He fired just as one of the creatures launched itself right at them. The bullets missed, kicking bark off the trunk of a large tree.

The demon was in the air, but Eduardo strained the gun upward and fired another burst. The heavy bullets went a little wide, but still raked along the demon's side, ripping off two of its legs and sending it spinning sideways. The demon hit hard and tumbled across the ground to their right. Mangled but not dead, it immediately began dragging itself toward them. The stumps that been its legs trailed purple gore behind it.

The soldier holding the right side of the makeshift gun mount tried to pull the gun around toward the crippled demon crawling toward him. At the same time, Julio and Eduardo tried to aim it at the remaining war demons to their front. This resulted in a brief, crazy tug-of-war that lasted several critical seconds.

"The front!" screamed Eduardo. "To the front!"

Julio glanced over at the private. His face was pale and his eyes showed white all the way around his dilated pupils. His gaze darted back and forth between the demons in front and the one slowly but surely approaching him on the right. A look of resignation swept over his face, and tears began to flow down his cheeks as he nodded. The gun came around, and Eduardo fired a burst at the three aliens in front of them.

Fire and steel lashed outward from the gun. A line of small eruptions kicked up along the ground from impacting bullets before Eduardo adjusted his aim. The stream of death from the gun stitched across two of the demons, and purple gore flew up from their backs. Both went instantly still. He missed the third, however, and it fired its weapon. Thok!

"Unh," Eduardo gasped as a fountain of blood burst from his

chest. "Momma," he said softly as he fell backwards.

At nearly the same time, the private screamed as the crippled demon reached him and drove its sword-claw through his neck. The scream turned into a gurgling sob as he collapsed and his end of the gun mount fell to the ground.

The remaining demon launched itself toward them. Julio dropped the log and threw himself to the side. He spotted an assault rifle dropped by one of the soldiers and rolled toward it. It wouldn't be as effective as a battle rifle. But it was close, and there was no way he could operate the fifty-caliber by himself.

The demon thudded down where he'd just been. Still in motion, Julio snatched up the rifle in midroll and came to his knees with it in his hands. With practiced fingers, he found the safety and found it already off.

"Please be loaded," he prayed under his breath as he swung the weapon toward the demon.

But he didn't get the chance to find out. The demon's sword-like claw flashed toward him before he could pull the trigger. Instinct took over, and he brought the rifle up to block it. The claw smashed into the weapon's stock with ferocious force. The move saved him from being impaled, but the powerful blow knocked the rifle from his hands, and it flew half a dozen meters away.

The three-fingered hand at the end of the weapon arm slammed down on Julio's shoulder, pinning him to the moist ground. Each finger ended in a stubby, sharp claw. For some odd reason, Sally's voice about how these connected to the war demon's nervous system and probably controlled the spikes drifted through his mind. One of the claws cut into him, drawing blood.

The alien drew back the sword-claw, and Julio saw his approaching death. Thoughts of his family filled his mind. *Would mother and father be proud of me?* He prayed they would. Funny how slow things became when you were facing death. Why was the demon waiting?

"Get it over with, you spawn of a whore!" he screamed up at it. The creature's big eyes were each the size of Julio's palm and had a slight sheen to them, but no hint of emotion. However, they had an evil-looking shape. They made him think of a shark's eyes. Still, the demon didn't strike.

It seemed frozen. The sword-claw twitched downward, then back up in small, jerky movements. Like a machine with a locked bearing. The sounds of combat from the lumber mill stopped, as did those from the left and right. Silence settled on the forest. All that could be heard was what sounded like the rumble of dozens of distant engines accompanied by clanks that might be tank treads.

The pressure pinning him to the ground ceased as the demon spun and leaped away. It almost hit a tree and then began scuttling through the forest. In seconds, it disappeared from sight. The aliens, for all their speed and leaping ability, didn't seem to like the trees. They almost looked awkward at times moving between them.

Movement caught his eye, and he saw the crippled demon dragging itself along in the same direction as the other one. Rage filled his heart, and he got up and retrieved the assault rifle. The alien ignored him and continued moving slowly across the ground. The burning rage tempered down to a seething simmer, and he took time to pull out the magazine to make sure the rifle was loaded. Shiny brass met his eyes, and the mag felt heavy enough to be over half full. He slammed it back into the weapon, cocked it, and took careful aim. The weapon roared and shuddered in his hands as he fired a long burst into the demon's exposed side. Purple holes and purplish mist covered its back, and the demon went still.

The satisfaction of killing the thing was short-lived, however. It vanished when he remembered Eduardo. He hurried over to his new friend, but Eduardo's vacant and staring eyes told him nothing could be done well before he reached him. With a sigh that turned into a sob, Julio sank down on his knees beside the bloody body. Gently, he reached down and closed the empty, brown, staring eyes.

With a start, he remembered the private on the other side of the gun. His mind just wasn't working right. No surprise, really, considering the last few minutes. But a quick glance showed he was just as dead as Eduardo. The man had been incredibly brave. He'd held his position while Eduardo fired at the demons in front, knowing the whole time a living nightmare was crawling closer and closer. Right up to the end. He reached over and removed one of the private's dog tags. He left the other with the body.

"Private First-Class Jesus Simoans," he read out loud in a low voice. "You were a good man. A brave soldier." Fresh tears formed in Julio's eyes. *If I survive this mess, I will see that you are remembered.*

His legs felt weak, and he had to use the rifle to stand. A dozen men lay dead around him. As much as he wanted to bury Eduardo and Private Simoans, to do so and leave the rest seemed disrespectful. Besides, he had no idea why the demons ran off or how long they might be gone. With a heavy heart, he turned and began staggering west, back toward Rio Estrada and whatever dubious safety it might provide. Maybe he could get some people to come back and help bury them. Maybe

39 Armored Assault

The rumble of powerful motors surrounded Marcus. Thirty-nine armored vehicles tended to make a din. Except for the four American tanks, which moved along with a soft whine that seemed eerie for such large vehicles. The noon sun shone in a brilliant blue sky, but the temperature felt remarkably cool for the Amazon. It was one of those rare dry-season days that would've been ideal for cruising on a patrol boat.

The cool air was deceptive though. The sun heated the dark-painted steel to an uncomfortable swelter, but it could have been worse. For now, the hatches were open and most of the crews sat outside their vehicles, as did he. The breeze flowing over the outside of the Urutu felt good on his skin. Soon enough, they'd have to button up. Then the sweating would begin, and from more than just the heat.

They followed the same cut the harvesters made through the trees that the American LAVs led by Lieutenant Johnson used on their mission. That seemed like a long time ago. Marcus received word just before leaving that the lieutenant's LAV had been destroyed covering the Marine's movement to Rio Estrada. Marcus hadn't known him well, but the young officer had impressed him nonetheless. A sad loss indeed.

They reached the end of the cut after an hour of waddling up the wide track of torn and broken orange ground. The same kind of terrain could be seen expanding out into the desolated land surrounding the mountains. The comparatively dry weather of the last few weeks provided better traction out here than he'd expected. However, sun dried big clumps of soil made for rough traveling nonetheless. As if on cue, the Urutu gave a sudden lurch, forcing him to grab onto the side of the hatch to keep from being tossed off the turret. They were lucky no one in the assault force had fallen overboard during the trip. He's considered ordering them inside earlier as a safety precaution. But considering what they were headed for, that seemed kind of silly.

Sitting next to him was Sergeant Alexander Pachulia, the Urutu's gunner. He had his head tilted way back, looking up at the massive granite mountains. "It's kind of beautiful, isn't it sir?" he said over the com system. "It looks really white and glittery."

"I guess it does," Marcus replied. The mountains usually had a bit of a yellowish tint, like old dead bone. But in the noon sun, it did indeed look very white. Quartz deposits sparkled like diamonds across the surface.

"Yeah. And really, really big," the sergeant said with a thoughtful nod. "Too bad it's so damn terrifying."

Marcus chuckled. "I know what you mean."

He could understand why many people still claimed the creatures were demons… or in some cases angels. It was hard to believe that what amounted to an entire mountain landscape twice the size of Aruba could come down from space. Marcus had seen the data and read the reports, but still struggled to comprehend it. The struggle intensified the closer they got.

And they were driving straight toward it. That was the plan. No great military maneuvers. No wonderful strategy to turn the tables. Basically, the entire force was bait to lure the attacking demons away from the men trapped at the logging camp and the assault on Rio Estrada. Of course, they may well entice even more demons out of the mountains. But he couldn't see any other way to relieve pressure on his trapped and struggling army. His plan, his responsibility for whatever happened. His mouth went dry at the thought.

But if they were bait, they were bait with teeth. Every vehicle had at least one machine-gun that could be fired from inside without exposing the gunner. The Leopards had two and the American tanks had three. In addition, Marcus had loaded four machine-guns into the troop compartments of every Urutu. These could be fired through gun slits situated along the sides and rear doors.

Also, the tanks had powerful cannons, though how much use they'd be against the comparatively small, fast-moving demons remained to be seen. Finally, two of the American tanks had makeshift add-ons dreamed up by the machine shop on the USS *Bataan*. Since none of the ship's aircraft could fly near the mountains, they'd taken two attack helicopter Gatling guns, attached them to the tanks' cannons, and beefed up the turrets' traverse system to handle the extra weight. No one knew how effective these would be, but they looked very intimidating.

Yes, they definitely had teeth. But would it be enough to keep the war demons at bay with sheer firepower? Out in the open land between the mountain and forest? That was the million-dollar question, wasn't it?

"Please be enough," he said under his breath. "For my people's sake, please be enough."

"Did you say something, sir?" Sergeant Pachulia said.

"Uh, no. Sorry. Just saying a prayer."

"I been doing a lot of that today," Pachulia said. "I've got a feeling all of us are."

Marcus looked over and gave him what he hoped was a reassuring smile. The sergeant smiled back and resumed staring at the mountain. Pachulia had a laid-back accent from one of the big coastal cities. *Rio de Janeiro* probably. He had the trim body of a surfer and brown hair tinted with red highlights. But despite being easygoing, he seemed quite competent. That was the problem with assuming command at the last minute. Marcus hadn't the time to really get to know his crew. The sergeant had a good attitude, and as long as he could shoot, that was all that really mattered. They weren't going to be doing any complicated maneuvers. If he survived this, he promised himself to get to know them all really well.

They passed the boundary line of trees that marked the end of the cut and entered the four-kilometer-wide open area. The region was bordered on one side by the forest and the other by the thousand-meter-tall jagged wall surrounding the mountains. The space between was an orange desert with dark gray boulders scattered around, from the size of a skull to some bigger than a house. Most of the experts assumed these fell from the cliff face when the aliens landed.

Once in the open, the formation angled eastward toward the large opening reported by Lieutenant Johnson during his recon. That was where the war demons had emerged before attacking his platoon. The lair of the beast. There had to be at least five thousand war demons, and God alone knew how many scouts attacking the Brazilians right now. If this didn't pull them off…well, Marcus didn't want to think about it.

Were there more war demons in the mountain? It seemed likely. If so, how many? It was a frequently asked question with no good answers. Some guesses put them in the hundreds of thousands and few even higher. The thought made Marcus shudder and his gut tighten.

Per the plan, the crews started to crawl inside their vehicles after they made the turn. Commanders and gunners moved inside as well, but stood in their hatches and kept watch over predetermined sectors around the formation. Marcus doubted they'd have long to wait for the aliens to react. The formation was undoubtedly heading into what Captain Viana would call, "a target-rich environment."

Marcus didn't have an assigned sector to watch. But for now, he kept his binoculars trained on a large, dark shadow at the base of the mountain. *Was that the reported opening?* It looked like one, but it was hard to tell due to the shadows cast by the noon sun. Stalagmites hung down that caught the light and glistened, making the shadowy area look like a huge gaping mouth with jagged fangs. So far, he hadn't seen any activity there.

"Movement! Movement!" Sergeant Pachulia cried. "Four o'clock at the tree line. Sound the horn, Menderes."

Bwamp! Bwamp! The horn blared out two quick blasts. That was the spotting alert for the three to six o'clock sector. Each quarter of the clock had been given a number one through four to communicate the direction of possible threats. With radio communications blocked this close to the White Mountain, it was the best way they'd come up with to focus attention where needed. The other vehicles also sounded their horns in double blasts to ensure the whole formation was alerted.

Marcus spun around and trained his binoculars on the tree line. There! Boiling out of the forest like a kicked anthill. Thousands of them. The sight thrilled and sent chills through him at the same time. The thrill came from knowing his plan had pulled at least some of the demons away from the lumber mill and Rio Estrada. From the numbers he could see, it had to be a pretty large proportion, if not all of them. The chill came from the idea that in a few minutes, the creatures would undoubtedly head his way. The price of success. How many would die for it?

All the tanks and half the Urutus had remote controlled machine-guns mounted on top of their turrets like the Marine LAVs. However, fifteen of the Urutus' top guns had to be operated by the vehicle commander. These commanders had been instructed not to take any chances, but Marcus feared they would. There was a sense of power shooting such weapons that sometimes led to overconfidence in the gunner—especially those with no combat experience, which was the case with every soldier in the formation except himself. He supposed they'd get plenty in the near future, although gaining such experience tended to be bad for your health.

From the right and left loud booms sounded, startling Marcus and sending faint vibrations through the Urutu. He spun around, fearing the demons had managed to sneak close enough to attack the formation. Instead, he saw smoke billowing over the formation and realized the concussions had come from the lead tanks firing their cannons. They'd been given free rein to shoot if they saw the demons grouped together as they now were at the tree line.

Each high explosive round included a tracer, and five streaks flew toward the alien lines. The American tankers followed suit, sending four more high explosive rounds at the aliens. Five blew up at a hundred meters short. As incredible as it seemed, the demons must have intercepted them. Four continued on and impacted with large blossoms of smoke and fire. Dust and debris filled the air, making it impossible to tell if the shells caused any damage.

But they did do one thing—they told the aliens it was time to charge. A fast-moving black wave flowed away from the trees right toward the humans.

"Range?" Marcus called out. It surprised him how high-pitched his voice sounded. He cleared his throat.

"Twenty-one hundred meters and closing," replied Sergeant Pachulia.

"Call every hundred meters."

"Yes sir." A second later he said, "Two thousand meters."

Damn, that was fast. The tanks fired again. The shells impacted in the middle of the charging demons, and at least one of the creatures went cartwheeling sideways. Hopefully it was dead. But the effect of the cannons was minimal, as had been feared.

"Nineteen hundred."

That had only been a few seconds. How fast were these things? At least forty to fifty kilometers per hour, he estimated. That was nearly double what the Urutus could manage across this torn and battered landscape. So, there wouldn't be any running away from this battle. Not for him and the Urutus, anyway. The tanks might be able to outrun them, maybe. *Pray God they didn't need to.*

"Eighteen hundred."

Marcus turned and focused his binoculars on the base of the mountain. Still nothing. So, he pulled out a flare gun, loaded it with a red shell, and fired it into the air. Then he loaded a green shell and fired again. This was the signal to assume a line formation. Since the demons were only coming at them from one direction, this would allow the vehicles to have unobstructed fields of fire along the entire right flank.

Pachulia's laid-back accent was missing as he said in an excited tone, "Seventeen hundred meters."

"Open fire at fifteen hundred," Marcus said.

"Fifteen hundred. Yes, sir."

Once his Urutu fired, the others would fire as well. The max range of the heavy machine guns was about two thousand meters. But they didn't have an unlimited amount of ammunition. During planning, it'd been decided to let them close to twelve hundred, but that was before he'd seen how fast they truly were. *Was he losing his nerve? Maybe.* But at the speed the war demons were closing, he felt it better to start whittling them down as soon as possible.

The aliens spread out like a dark flood as they came. He noticed only about half of them left the tree line. He focused his binoculars at the edge of the forest and saw thousands still waited there. Their bodies quivered as if wound up tight and ready to spring, but held back by an invisible hand. He didn't know whether to be relieved or concerned about that. No time to worry now.

The demons charging across the open ground brought back memories of the first time he'd encountered them. It'd been in the forest, just after Julio rescued Salina from the helicopter. The damn things killed over half his men. "Hello, my old friends," he mumbled as a wave of hate swept into his heart. "This time I have much better guns than just a stupid pistol."

"Sixteen hundred meters. Did you say something, sir?"

"No, nothing important. Sorry. Get ready."

"Oh, I'm ready, sir. Believe me."

The snout of the fifty-caliber rose slightly as Pachulia adjusted his aim. Marcus ducked down and slid into his command chair. He checked the monitor and set it on the camera to give him the same view as Pachulia. For a second, he felt a stab of envy thinking about the triple monitors in the American LAVs that Lieutenant Johnson showed him a couple of weeks ago. It faded fast as he watched the numbers on the laser range finder at the bottom of the screen click down the range.

"Target fifteen hundred," said Pachulia.

Despite the bumpy ride across the rough ground, the Urutu vibrated noticeably as the heavy machine-gun opened fire. In an instant, the odor of burnt cordite filled the turret, along with snake-like wisps of smoke. Marcus's helmet earphones made the gun sound oddly distant. But even with the hearing protection, the sounds of the revving motor, and the roar of the fifty-caliber, there was no mistaking when the strange contraptions on the American tanks opened fire.

RRRRUUUURRP. The noise was so strange that once again Marcus feared a new alien attack. It brought to mind the mating call of a house-sized bullfrog. Two bright lines of white lanced out from the American tanks and played across the charging demons. The Gatling guns fired long, sweeping bursts that sent out over a thousand 20mm explosive shells in less than fifteen seconds. This tsunami of steel, coupled with the less impressive but still substantial fire of the other heavy machine-guns, slammed into the charging war demons with incredible and satisfying results. The heavy caliber shells ripped through the creatures like the scythe of an avenging angel. Hundreds were sent tumbling in the span of a few heartbeats to lie unmoving on the orange soil.

As the Gatling guns swept back and forth and the heavy machine-guns fired burst after burst, the alien warriors continued to fall by the score. But the demons did not hesitate in their headlong rush. They merely spread out and kept coming. Even so, over a third of them died before reaching the next critical range for the assault force—the eleven-hundred-meter mark of the medium machine-guns.

Marcus switched his camera view to the remote gun on top of the turret. Below, he could hear the gun crews getting their own weapons ready to fire through the two gun-ports on the right side. This was taking place in all thirty Urutus. Counting the top mounted guns on the armored vehicles, over one hundred more machine-guns were now aimed at the charging demons. The crews were poised and ready, waiting on his vehicle to fire first.

The demons crossed the line on his screen marking the range. Again, they needed to be careful of ammunition, so he counted to five before barking, "Fire!" At the same time, he hit the trigger button on his console. A split second later, the men below opened fire, followed immediately by the rest of the formation.

A fresh sheet of steel and fire lashed out from the human vehicles. Over a thousand rounds per second were added to the guns already firing. This produced a storm of metal that swept through the demon formation with incredible fury. During that brief time, it did not matter how crazily they leaped and dodged; the demons were literally torn to pieces. Their scaly hides erupted with purple blossoms, and limbs were shorn from their bodies before they could even hit the ground. One minute after the concentrated fire began, the demon attack ended.

As the last alien tumbled to the ground, cheers erupted from the crew and the men in the troop compartment below.

"That ought to give them something to think about," came the awed voice of Sergeant Pachulia over the headset.

"Indeed," Marcus replied quietly, keeping to himself the thought that this was only the opening round.

He rotated the gun camera and saw with dismay that a much larger horde was now massing at the foot of the mountain. As awe-inspiring as their display of firepower had been, the victory had been too easy and couldn't last. Marcus doubted the demons would be so obliging as to attack from only one direction the next time.

40 Sally at the Camp

The fighting to the east slackened noticeably not long after Marcus and the reserve force headed out. This had been a godsend as it allowed the hospital a chance to get caught up triaging and stabilizing the wounded. Trying to decide what to move and what had to stay was a nightmare, requiring Sally and Nelino to literally make life and death decisions. There was no telling what medical apparatus would be the most helpful, as every doctor and expert had a different opinion. More wounded flowed into Rio Estrada every hour. And while equipment was being packed up and shipped out, it couldn't be used to save lives.

With the sounds of battle getting closer by the minute, her biggest fear was not moving fast enough. The idea that any of the four surgical wards might still be on this side of the river when the demons arrived terrified her. The alternative was to pack up and move just as the influx of wounded was at its peak. Bleeding men lay on stretchers everywhere. It reminded her of the scene in *Gone with the Wind* where Scarlett O'Hara visited the Atlanta train station.

She really would have preferred to stay with Majors Sanchez and Amorim to get quicker reports on how Marcus's attack was going. But Nelino had requested her help since the hospital compound was a cooperative set-up between the Americans and Brazilians. The language barrier hadn't been a big problem during normal operations. But the current situation wasn't the least bit normal. The efforts to get ready to move across the river resulted in chaos. It didn't help that almost none of the staff wanted to go with so much to do on this side.

The hospital compound was a collection of tents set up in front of a pile of rock that had once been the Catholic church. Before its destruction, it'd been the social and spiritual center of Rio Estrada. One of the strangest things about the harvesters' demolition of the building was that they apparently took the cross from the top of the spire and the bells from the belfry. Sally couldn't begin to imagine why.

However, it'd added fuel to people's fears and led in no small part to the term demon being applied to them. Not that it took much. *Why would they bother? Just to study us?* Or… Well, she was too much of a scientist to believe the creatures were actual demons. But that didn't mean they couldn't have demonic intentions. Besides, the point was moot as far as she was concerned. By all definitions she held dear, the damn things were evil.

About three-fourths of the hospital was Brazilian. The American section was set up on what would have been the center of the old town square. Three large diesel generators provided power to the compound. In addition to four operating tents, there was a large tent for triage and two others for recovery and intensive care. There were also multiple trailers for administration, tents for individual and group housing, and even a large laundry—a lot to evacuate in a short amount of time.

Add two thousand wounded in various stages of care with more arriving by the minute, and it was easy to see why Nelino needed her help. After several intense arguments, things had finally been worked out with the staff. Now he wanted her to go across the river to help reestablish the hospital on that side.

"I really feel I'm needed here," she said. "I told Major Sanchez I'd come back once we got things smoothed out."

"But... Please, Miss Morgan?" The pleading tone in his voice was tinged with a whine that didn't fit him at all. He began chewing his scarred bottom lip with vigor. "I know they could use you at HQ. But things are a total mess on the other side. The translator apps are causing as much confusion as helping, and the few bilingual speakers we have just don't have your skill. And...well, your level of respect. People listen to you."

She noticed that also, which surprised her. It had happened with the military and now with the medical staff as well. Whenever she expressed her opinion on what the doctors and nurses should do, they usually shut up and went along.

Her masters in biology certainly wasn't the reason. It must have had something to do with her reputation. That took getting used to. She'd frequently felt overlooked during many discussions in the past. It was especially bad in Brazil, where everyone, both men and women, tended to defer to the oldest or tallest or...any male, present. It really pissed her off sometimes.

But something had definitely changed in this regard. As soon as people learned her name, they tended to look at her with awe. It seemed stupid, but also kind of nice. Overall, it just reaffirmed her opinion that people were generally crazy.

"Let me check in with Major Sanchez. If it looks like he doesn't need me, I'll go," she said, hoping the major needed her to stay. She just wasn't ready to go back across the river. Funny, in a way. Just a few hours ago, she'd dreaded coming over and facing the bad memories of Rio Estrada. Now, she dreaded leaving it.

After Nelino reluctantly agreed, she turned and saw a very sweaty Dr. Allen coming out of a nearby tent. He flipped the canvas flap out of the way, then turned and reached back inside. He tugged out a large cart full of folded sheets and towels. A moment later, an equally sweaty Paul appeared, pushing it from behind.

"Dr. Allen? Paul?"

Both men looked over at her, and their faces lit up with smiles. "Sally, thank God," said Paul, jogging over to her. "We were worrying about you."

She thought they'd already gone back across the river. "I've...Well, I've been busy. What are you doing? Laundry?"

Dr. Allen laughed and said, "Sweating, mostly. But yeah, we volunteered. They got swamped with more casualties than they were really ready for."

Sally nodded. That was an understatement.

"Do you have any idea how many sheets, both normal and sterilized, this place uses? A lot, we can testify to that."

Paul said, "You've been busy? I'll say you have. The men in the wards swear you pretty much single-handedly rallied the entire Brazilian army. The Marines also, to hear some people tell it. What did you do?"

"Me? Nothing really. I just stood on a table and yelled."

Dr. Allen chuckled. "Some of the wounded said you spoke personally to every person there. Gave them words of encouragement and blessed them, or something like that."

"I talked to some. But come on, to all of them?" She shook her head. "Rumors."

"Now you're not only the Demon Slayer. They're calling you the Angel by the River," Paul said.

"The legend of Sally Morgan grows," Dr. Allen said. "Or as most of the Brazilians say, Salina Morgan."

"I've never heard you called Salina before," Paul said. "Is that your actual name?" She nodded, and he said, "I've known you for four years and didn't even know that. It kind of fits you. You know?"

Sally shrugged. It sounded weird to her ears—except when Marcus called her that. "It's my grandmother's name," she said. "But no one ever–"

A roar of heavy weapons erupted from the north, and the three spun around to face it. She'd been told what to expect when the aircraft multi-barreled cannon strapped onto the American tanks opened fire. Sure enough, the weapons sounded like massive croaking bullfrogs. A short time later, the sound swelled as more guns began shooting, making an incredible din that drowned out all the other fighting. It lasted for one, two, three minutes. Then stopped. It took a moment to realize that with the cessation of the shooting, the entire area went silent.

Did he win? Is it over? She knew it wasn't likely, not yet. But the hopeful thought still rose in her heart. The one that came from her fears was... *Is he dead?* It was agony not knowing something you dreadfully wanted to know. Needed to know. And it wasn't just her concern for Marcus, but for the soldiers, the wounded, herself. *Whoever said, "Ignorance is bliss," was the stupidest son of a bitch ever born.*

"I've got to get back to Major Sanchez," Sally said. It was hard to tear her eyes away from the north, but she managed it and looked at her two friends. She shook her head. "Laundry volunteers. I need to get you two the proper credentials."

Their eyes kept flicking northwards, but they managed nervous chuckles.

"Believe it or not, the laundry has a pretty high priority for crossing," she said. "So, I guess I'll see you on the other side."

"That statement can be taken a lot of ways," Paul said dryly. "Why don't we just say, see you soon?"

"Fair enough," she said with a nod. "See you soon."

41 Armored Assault Interlude

The triumphant feeling of being in an invincible armored force didn't last for long among the crew. After the first round of excited cries, the Urutu cruised onward in comparative silence. He imagined it was the same in all the vehicles. And storm clouds gathered in the form of the demons at the base of the mountain. *Best take advantage of the calm to reload and do a weapons check.*

Marcus activated his comm and said, "Corporal Menderes. Signal to halt."

"Yes, sir," came the reply.

Two long horn blasts sounded. The signal was taken up by the other drivers and echoed through the formation. It felt strange commanding a modern fighting unit with horns and signal flares. Almost like cavalry buglers and flag wavers of old. But one did what one must in battle.

The Urutu gave a final lurch as it stopped, and Marcus opened his hatch. All over the formation, the others did likewise to help air out the gun smoke from cramped confines. In the troop compartment, the gunners began checking over their weapons and doing a quick clean to prevent them from jamming. Some would change out barrels that had gotten too hot if required.

Marcus detached the ammo box on the remote gun and swapped it out. The other commanders did so as well. Meanwhile, the Americans fed belts full of dull silver and black shells into the large green boxes attached to the Gatling guns. In a longer engagement, these would most likely run dry.

Only the sound of idling motors and the clink and clunk of mechanical parts being worked on carried over the light wind. The shadowy area in the side of the cliff Marcus thought to be an opening proved to be just that. Thousands and thousands of war demons now massed outside it. The crews gave them a lot of apprehensive looks, along with glances at the looming monolith towering over them like an evil sentinel.

It took him longer to reload the gun than it should have. His fingers felt thick and slow and didn't want to work properly for some reason. Frequent glances at the base of the mountain didn't help. With an act of will, he shut the aliens out of his mind and focused on placing the belt in the proper position. It clicked into place, and he closed the receiver and pulled back the bolt. *There, loaded and ready.*

The momentary relief this gave him was dispelled by a single short horn blast. The alert signal for the twelve o'clock to three o'clock sector. Other horns repeated the alert as he fumbled for his binoculars and focused them on the tree line.

More demons flooded out of the forest to the east of the ones that launched the initial assault. Thousands of them. Far more than he'd estimated. These must have been the ones that had been attacking the lumber mill. He hoped so, anyway. Surely it would take pressure off the soldiers in the forest and at the mill. He'd given Captain Viana instructions to be on the lookout for such movements and try to break the trapped men free if possible. He scanned westward and saw the demons that hadn't taken part in the first attack were still at the tree line. Add a couple more thousand on that side, at least. His hands began to feel slick on the field glasses.

Three deeper horn blasts made him flinch. These came from the American tanks at the rear and indicated the six to nine o'clock sector. He spun about and looked past the tanks, noting that the crews were closing up the big ammo boxes and preparing to move out. Beyond them, a dark line about four kilometers away moved across the open land. These must have been the demons that had attacked the Americans. A further success he supposed, but not one he wanted.

He thought about holding where they were, then shook his head as he reconsidered. The plan was to advance along the cut toward the mill once the demons began attacking. No point in changing it now. There was no way to know which would be more effective at this point. Besides, this was a mobile force, so they might as well fight on the move.

"Give the signal to advance corporal," he said over the vehicle's com system.

"Yes, sir," came the reply, and the corporal sounded three short horn blasts followed by one long.

Marcus was thrown back against the padded edge of his command hatch as the Urutu lurched into motion. He bounced off it with practiced ease and continued to scan the war demons surrounding them on three sides. He supposed when the time came, they'd close in the front to completely encircle them.

Marcus looked over at Sergeant Pachulia, who was standing in the gunner's hatch. He smiled as reassuring a smile as he could muster and said, "Well, it looks like we managed to pull them off our people."

Pachulia nodded, though his expression made it clear that attracting thousands of demons was a dubious victory at best. Marcus had to agree. It was easy to make plans from the safety of a tent and start them in motion. Seeing the result of that plan was another matter altogether. Of course, he couldn't let that show. He sucked in a lungful of air and gripped his binoculars lest his true feelings be betrayed by the shaking of his hands.

He surveyed the wave of war demons coming up from behind and estimated they were traveling twice as fast as his command. That would put them in range of the Gatling guns in about fifteen minutes. He considered ordering the formation to speed up, but rejected the idea. While the tanks glided effortlessly across the torn land on their steel tracks, the six-wheeled Urutus were already struggling, slipping and sliding over the barren ground and having to steer around small arroyos and holes the tanks skimmed over. They really couldn't go any faster without taking serious risks. It wouldn't do to lose one of his precious vehicles to a stupid accident. Also, it would most likely disrupt their formation and weaken the effect of their combined fire.

God, please help us in this, our time of need. The tanks might or might not be able to withstand a demon blast. But the Urutus certainly could not, unless the sandbags proved to be more effective than he expected. In all likelihood, they'd soon find out. Things certainly looked bad as he studied the enemy around the slowly moving vehicles. Thousands upon thousands of quivering war demons surrounded them preparing to attack. Very bad indeed.

42 Exploring the Train Tunnel

David and Alessandra learned a lot watching the train-gatherers roar up and down the tunnel. First, there were two trains, one big and one little. Not that the little one was really that little, but it didn't fill the tunnel from side to side like the larger of the two. Alessandra pointed this out the fourth time it roared by.

"Yeah, that's great," David said in response to her observation.

"As long as it stays more or less in the middle."

"It has every time so far. Why would it not? I think we could go up the tunnel after the large one goes by, and then stay near the wall when the small one passes. We should be fine. Right?"

David couldn't think of an answer she didn't already know, so he just shrugged. She was probably right. But, 'probably,' could get them killed. It didn't matter how big the train was. Sharing a tunnel with one wasn't a good time. They'd been there, done that.

"There is an average count of fifteen hundred between trains, but three thousand between the big one going and coming. I say we go take a look after the next train, at least as far as a twelve hundred count. If we do no t find a side passage, then we turn around and come back."

David really didn't want to go back into the train tunnel. What Alessandra skipped over was that they'd be in the tunnel during at least one trip of the small train. The thought made his gut quiver. But he wasn't going to admit it. Then he remembered the promise he made to himself…and his dead sister, to be a better person and felt ashamed. Besides, what the heck else could they do? He was part of a team now, and they all had to do their part, wants be damned. And now was as good a time as any.

He squared his shoulders, nodded, and said, "Okay, let's go for it."

The big train passed a few moments later. David bowed and waved his hand toward the tunnel. "After you, my lady."

"Thank you, kind sir," Alessandra said with a smile.

She took off at a quick jog and David fell in right behind. No skulking about this time; they wanted to cover some ground. They both ran as quietly as they could by using their toes as Josh had taught them. But Alessandra now wore the soldier's boots David pulled from the vat. They fit her reasonably well, but made a distinct clomp, clomp sound when she ran. Like a miniature Josh. David's leather walking shoes did a bit better. It was the only time he could move quieter than she.

"You sound like one of the trains," David teased.

She looked back at him and stuck out her tongue. A fine sheen of sweat made her forehead shine. Her long hair was pulled back in a ponytail and bounced against her back as if dancing in time to her clomping feet. She looked beautiful. Then she smiled and turned back to focus on the tunnel.

The small train had a different sound than the big one. The clatter-clomp rhythm was just a bit faster, and it wasn't accompanied by the godawful squealing noise. They heard it a few heartbeats after Alessandra called out, "Nine hundred."

"Now I guess we find out how well it stays in the middle," David said, trying to keep his voice level and calm.

Alessandra nodded, but kept up the pace. They'd already decided to plaster to the wall when it got close, rather than search out a curve. But it turned out they didn't have to. An opening appeared in the tunnel wall a dozen yards further on.

"Look," cried Alessandra. "Come on."

They pounded along the tunnel at full speed. David was panting like a train engine himself by the time they reached the large tunnel mouth. It could have been a major intersection to the one they were traveling based on the wide, arched opening. Their mad dash paid off and they reached it with plenty of seconds to spare.

The clompity-clomp of the smaller train grew ever louder until the strange six-legged beast-engine reached the tunnel and rushed past. It didn't even glance in their direction as it went by with a soft whoosh of moving air and the hiss of dozens of turning wheels.

David said, "Well, that wasn't so bad."

Alessandra was examining a mound of debris blocking the tunnel about fifty feet in. "No, but this is not so good though," she replied in her always formal English. "A dead end."

The short tunnel had a smooth floor and arched ceiling. The floor had a worn look, as if it had seen a lot of use at one time. David wondered what had happened to block off so many passages. Had the gatherers done it on purpose? Or maybe it happened when they landed. There was no telling, and he decided they might never know.

David went to the debris and sniffed around it. "I don't think the forest smell is coming through here, at least. There must be another way for the outside air to get in."

"This makes a good rest point, anyway. Wait for the big train to pass, and then maybe go a little further?"

"Sure, why not?" he said. But he had to wonder how long their luck could hold. Not with the trains, but if there were thousands, even hundreds of thousands, of creatures living in the mountains. How long before they encountered something that noticed them and didn't like them being here? The trains saw them, but other than making sure they weren't an obstacle, they didn't seem to care. Neither had the plumbers. Why was that?

He shuddered at the thought of what would happen if they ran into one of the big gatherers. Or one of those dark lumpy shapes he'd seen attacking people before he was captured. He muttered under his breath, "God, please keep protecting us. I pray for your guidance. Amen."

"What was that?" Alessandra said. "Did you say something."

"Just a quick prayer."

She cocked her head at him. "I did not think you believed in God."

He shrugged. "I believe there's something beyond us. God is a good word for it. I just don't like all the mumbo jumbo people mix up with him...or her. Or when they try to tell you what God wants. Even worse is when folks use God as an excuse to judge other people, even hurt them. But I feel better when I think there is a God. So yes, I believe. And I pray sometimes."

"I can respect that." She crossed herself. "As for me, I pray all the time."

They waited at the opening until the big train squealed past a short time later. "Let us go," Alessandra said, and began her soft clomp-clomping up the tunnel again.

She only called out the hundreds in her count. A few dozen paces beyond "eighteen hundred," they came upon another opening and ran inside it. Or tried to. It was so narrow, running wasn't an option. And to David's relief, there was no sign of any gatherers or any other creature. In fact, it would be difficult for even one of the plumbers to navigate it.

The opening was a tight squeeze for David. "This can't go far; it's just a crack," he said.

Alessandra took in a deep breath and smiled, her eyes bright.

"Can you not smell it? The forest. This is the strongest it has been so far." She began working her way along the passage.

David swallowed hard watching her lithe form wiggle forward through the rocks. If she had a tough time, then this would be really fun for him. With visions of getting stuck, David followed. He had to turn sideways in several places to get through. Thank God, he'd lost a lot of weight. In other places, there wasn't even a floor, just a narrow fracture that disappeared from sight below them. They had to place their feet on ledges and boulders on both sides of it and scoot carefully along.

The only sign of the gatherers was an occasional glow rod plastered to the wall. There were several sections where they had to feel their way through in the dark. But the crack kept snaking back and forth through the granite. And the forest smell was indeed stronger. After what felt like a very long time, but was most likely only a few minutes, it began to widen out.

David squeezed through a section and heard Alessandra gasp in the dim light ahead. "What? What's the matter?" he said.

"Not a thing. Daylight. I see real, honest to God daylight." She gave a soft sob. "It is…it is the most wonderful thing I have ever seen."

David pushed past the last rock blocking his way and rounded a slight turn. A fair-sized cave lay before him—not as big as the one they'd lived in for so long, but not much smaller. The opening to the outside was maybe a hundred yards further on and glowed bright and beautiful. The sunlight cast long shadow fingers toward them from a variety of boulders, columns, stalagmites, and stalactites that festooned the cave. The bright sunbeams were indeed glorious. David's eyes started to ache and his throat constricted at the beauty of it.

Alessandra began picking her way over the rugged floor of the cave toward the opening. It was covered in loose shale and very uneven, with lots of boulders large and small. David set off behind her with his heart soaring. *Was this a way out?* Then fear hit him like a blow.

"Alessandra, stop. Be careful. What if it's guarded?"

She paused and looked back doubtfully. If this was a way out…or in, it would make sense that someone, or something, would keep an eye on it. After a moment, she nodded and went into sneak mode, going from shadow to shadow and easing around corners. David lost sight of her in the jumble of rocks. Damn her for taking chances. He began scrambling forward, taking too many chances of his own. If something were up there, it would have to be deaf not to hear the shale clicking under his shoes and the frequent small rockslides he left in his wake.

After climbing down a boulder taller than he was, he landed on a smoother floor. It was still rocky, but more like pea gravel than shards of shale. Then he saw Alessandra at the opening, silhouetted by the sunlight. Apparently, it wasn't guarded. Or if it was, it was by the universe's worst sentry.

A far-off crackling thunder could be heard as he walked up to her. It reminded him of Big Mama's chamber, but distant and muted. There was also a faint rump sound, like a frog. But the sky beyond was a clear, beautiful blue. *Is this actually a view of the outside? Or is it an illusion?* But the smell told him otherwise. The smell of wet wood, and flowers, and life filled the cave. So, yes, this was a view on the outside.

Then where did the thunder come from?

He stepped up beside Alessandra and gasped. The whole Amazon forest seemed to stretch out before them. They stood at the edge of a precipice that had to be several thousand feet high. Below them was a wide swath of orangish brown soil and beyond that a vast sea of green. Thunder still boomed and crackled out of a clear sky.

Alessandra took his hand and pointed. In the distance, a mass of specks flowed across the orange. Other specks, slightly larger but fewer in number, could be seen moving in some kind of formation. Flashes and puffs of white erupted everywhere. Though due to the distance the sounds didn't match with the action, there was no doubt this must be the source of the thunder.

"It is a battle, is it not?" she said.

"I think so. I hope whoever it is kicks their ass."

She lifted his hand, looking almost surprised to find she was holding it. With a shy smile, she let go and stepped forward to lean cautiously over the edge of the cliff. "That is a lot of rope to braid," she said.

David eased forward and gave a quick glance down, then

stepped back. It made his chest and stomach feel funny being this close to the drop—a weird, tingling sensation like he was already falling or something. It was a long, long way straight down. *Could they climb it?* He didn't look long enough to tell for certain, but it looked doubtful. It was nearly a sheer rock face the entire distance and with what appeared to be a negative incline part of the way. Of course, let them spend another few weeks trapped here and his opinion might change. He hadn't been able to imagine getting out of the vat room not long ago.

"Do...do you think you could make a rope that long?"

Alessandra shrugged and stepped away from the edge, much to David's relief. "I do not know. Probably not. The sheer weight of the material might be too much. Maybe if we can figure out how to do it in stages."

David said, "Well, Josh is pretty good at this stuff; maybe he can figure something out. We also have to keep an eye out for gatherers. They might not appreciate us dangling off the side of their mountain."

"It would be better if we can find another way down," she agreed. "For now, I guess we should go tell the others. Just to get to see the sky is worth a lot."

"So, I guess we aren't in Hell after all?"

She wrinkled her nose at him. "Maybe not. But it is close enough for my tastes. I think I will consider it Hell for now."

David laughed. "Fair enough. Let's go dodge some trains, shall we?"

She smiled and said, "Yes. Let us do so."

43 Armored Assault Round Two

They were surrounded by a dark sea of alien monsters bent on their destruction. The second attack by the demons would be hell on earth—a cliché Marcus had heard applied to many past battles. And no doubt, it would be said of future battles as well. But this was Marcus's battle, and he could think of no term more apt.

They came in from three sides—the rear and from the front left and front right. This was smart because it limited the ability of the machine-guns inside the Urutus to engage them. The fields of fire from the side gun ports would be partly blocked by the sandbags reinforcing the armor. If anyone called the creatures from the White Mountains a bunch of dumb animals again, Marcus swore he'd punch them in the face.

"Oh my God, my God," mumbled one of the gun crewmembers over the intercom.

"Belay that," Marcus said in a soft voice. "Keep your head. Pick your targets."

"Yuh, yes sir," came the voice.

"Corporal, please begin weaving when I give the signal. That might give our side gunners a better chance to engage. Feel free to swerve as you see fit to give them targets."

"Yes, sir," said the corporal firmly, though with a slight tremble in his voice.

Marcus reviewed the paper with the agreed-upon signals listed on it. He knew them by heart, but didn't trust himself. With all the stress hormones flowing through him, it was best to verify. The short list covered twelve commands or alerts, seven for horns and five flare signals. Tracing his finger down to the desired command, he double-checked it, and then pulled out the flare gun and a green flare. Although he felt calm inside, his fumbling fingers indicated otherwise. At last, he got the flare gun loaded, held it over his head, and fired.

The gun went pop when he pulled the trigger. A loud bang came when the flare ignited overhead and a green ember floated down, trailing a line of smoke. Marcus looked around at the commanders and saw them wave in acknowledgement. The vehicles began to spread out in a loose oval formation.

The machine-guns and Gatling guns had delivered savage retribution to the enemy during the first fight. It would be more difficult this time. At least a third of the formation's guns wouldn't be able to engage, or at least not very well. In addition, with the enemy coming in from all sides, their firepower would be diluted significantly. They wouldn't be able to send out one massive wave of deadly metal like last time.

Marcus's Urutu was on the mountain side of the formation. Over five thousand war demons charged toward them from that direction alone. Nearly as many came from the tree line, and another three thousand or more approached from the rear. He ducked inside, closed the hatch, and checked the range indicator on the monitor. Two thousand meters. It seemed pointless to conserve ammunition at this point. Either they'd stop them or not. Best to start hitting them as soon as possible.

It surprised him how calmly his voice came out as he issued orders. "Corporal Menderes, please begin to swerve as you see fit."

"Yes, sir."

The range dropped to eighteen hundred meters. He took a deep breath and said, "Sergeant…open fire."

The command was met with the now familiar muffled roar of the fifty-caliber. The turret vibrated in time to the pulsing chatter as heavy slugs left the barrel. Acrid smelling smoke began to drift through the cabin. All as before. The difference this time was the effect. Half as many guns were firing at more than twice as many demons.

The aliens fell by the score. Purple gore splattered, and mangled bodies tumbled. However, instead of launching a hurricane of steel, it was more akin to a stiff wind. The demons had no concerns about losses and pressed forward in a relentless wave.

The bullfrog roar of the American Gatling guns reverberated over the battlefield. He glanced out the periscope facing in their direction and saw twin white lines of death dance along the charging war demons. The effect was dramatic as exploding shells ripped the aliens apart. But even with the added firepower of the five American fifty-calibers covering the rear of the formation, it wasn't enough to slow the aliens, nor appreciably dent their numbers.

He glanced back at his monitor and saw the front of the charge was down to eleven hundred meters. *Already in range of the medium guns?* Time was distorted, going fast and slow at the same time. Excitement overrode discipline, and gun crews up and down the formation began shooting. Despite everything, a flash of irritation washed through him. But the feeling seemed silly a second later.

One thousand meters.

"Fire," he barked, hitting his trigger button.

The additional guns provided better results. The front rank of demons seemed to melt away. At least the crews were following the standard orders for the green flare. Fire toward the center of your side of the formation to try to drive the demons to the front and back. The demons hadn't faced tanks before. With their much thicker armor, they'd have a better chance of surviving if…when the demons started reaching the formation. Plus, Marcus and his crews had one more trick to play.

Well before this battle, one of the Brazilian tankers noted that the main guns might not be effective due to the demons' speed and mobility. During discussions on how to deal with this, the Americans mentioned an obsolete cannon round that might help. They'd taken the idea up with the armors aboard the USS Bataan. The technicians had been delighted with the idea and modified dozens of shells into canister shot. They built shells containing fifteen hundred half-inch stainless steel squares, which were much easier to make than the rounded balls used originally. These were close relatives of canister grape shot that killed so many during the Civil War.

Both the American and Brazilian tank crews could fire a shell every two to three seconds. In effect, the main gun of each tank was transformed into a huge shotgun. Or as one tanker put it, "A pump action with a five-inch-wide barrel."

The demons' attempt to avoid the Urutu's side guns by attacking the formation's front and rear, pushed them right into the path of these industrial killing machines. At five hundred meters, the tanks opened fire, and the results were everything Marcus could have hoped for. The nine tanks smoothly traversed their turrets as they fired, sweeping the battlefield with over thirteen thousand half-inch chunks of steel every three seconds. The blasts cut thirty-foot-wide swaths through the charging demons, shredding them by the hundreds. But it still wasn't enough.

The first demon to break through headed straight for a Leopard tank in front of Marcus. He saw it sail through the air, legs and claws spread wide just before it hit. It landed right on top of the turret and clung there for a long heartbeat. Then it exploded with a dazzling flash that made the monitor dim, sending out a shock wave that rocked the Urutu.

But a main battle tank was a different breed from an Urutu. The Leopards used by Brazil weighed forty-five tons, the Marine Abrams sixty-five—a very far cry from an Urutu fighting weight of fourteen tons. In addition, both countries had added armor to enhance survivability. It paid for itself now as the Leopard emerged from a cloud of orange-brown smoke. After a brief pause, no doubt to allow the crew's heads to clear, it continued firing its main gun every three seconds, sweeping the turret back and forth in a slow arc as it did so. The only major damage was the loss of the remote-operated heavy machine-gun mounted on top, although it couldn't have been a picnic for the men inside.

"Damn, did you see that!" Sergeant Pachulia yelled. "Go, you son of a bitch, go!"

Regretfully, the first hit wasn't the last. Far from it. But here the demons made a major mistake. They went after the tanks with a vengeance. Blast after blast rocked the lead Brazilian tanks, and within minutes the same began happening to the Americans behind them. Even steel behemoths such as these couldn't take such punishment for long. First one then another of the Leopards ground to a halt as smoke started to pour out of every seam.

The death of the Leopards forced the formation to split, and the battle became a melee with each human vehicle blazing away in every direction while surrounded by demons. However, there did seem to be noticeably fewer of the aliens now. Marcus began to have some hope they could pull this off.

The demons must have realized their mistake at leaving so many chattering machine-guns untargeted, because the Urutus began to take hits as well. The first sent a spray of orange dirt flying as the sandbags protecting the hull burst violently. But they did their job and the Urutu kept moving, spewing fire from every gun. It didn't fare so well at the next blow, however. A demon landed just behind the turret and exploded, shearing it off and leaving the vehicle a mass of flames.

"Sweet Jesus, sweet Jesus, sweet Jesus," Sergeant Pachulia

muttered over the intercom. But he stayed on his gun, sending out streams of smoking tracers. Killing one demon after another.

"On the right!" screamed one of the men below.

Marcus spun his gun camera around to see a dark shadow in the air headed right for them. The Urutu swerved hard left but the demon landed on the right deck. Bright light filled the cabin with an explosion that seemed soundless. The Urutu lurched violently, and Marcus's ears lost the ability to hear. His teeth, head…whole body convulsed in pain as dust and smoke filled the cabin.

"We're still alive," came an unbelieving voice from the troop compartment. It sounded muffled, very far away, and barely understandable through the cacophony of bells now clanging inside Marcus's head.

His vison rocked back and forth, making his stomach spin. Then he realized it was his head bobbing around. With a painful shake of his head, he forced it hold still. It was hard to focus. *Is it over? No, it couldn't be.* His brain didn't want to think. An explosion from nearby rocked the Urutu rocked and he looked through one of the periscopes while trying to blink tears from his eyes.

Heavy dust still fell onto an over turned Urutu a dozen meters away. Fire licked up from the engine compartment and black smoke billowed upward. *No, it isn't over.*

"The turret hydraulics are out!" screamed Pachulia, his voice at the edge of hysteria. "I need someone to crank."

Marcus shook his head again, which hurt like hell, but it seemed to help. Gritting his teeth against the pain, he shook it once more and looked at his monitor. The screen was blank. No doubt the outside cameras had been knocked out. Pachulia was working the hand crank for the turret while trying to line up a shot with his periscope. His monitor must be out as well.

"I've got it," Marcus said, turning his seat around and reaching for the hand crank.

Pachulia nodded and leaned into the padded frame of the gun scope. "Keep coming left." Marcus cranked as fast as could and felt the turret slowly turn. The heavy thump of the big machine-gun vibrated the turret, and Pachulia yelled, "I got you, you–" Then, "Keep cranking, keep cranking. Left! Left, left!"

Since he couldn't command without radios or shoot since his gun was out, he focused on cranking and let the crew run the fight. For the time being, turning the crank became Marcus's world. That and listening to the heavy machine-gun fire accompanied by explosions going off around the Urutu. Also, he prayed.

Time lost meaning as Pachulia screamed in excitement, fear and frustration. "Right, crank right. No damnit, the other way." The gun roared the turret shook. "Die, die you bastards." Over and over. Crank left, crank right. Marcus's chest and back burned. His arms felt much too heavy and he feared he couldn't keep going. But he did. Crank right, crank left, crank right.

Smoke filled the cabin, burning his eyes and throat. The ventilation system must have been knocked out along with the hydraulic system. It was amazing the battered Urutu was still in the fight. As he cranked, his head started to spin from the fumes. He worried that if the demons didn't kill them, asphyxiation would.

The vehicle lurched back and forth as Corporal Menderes weaved around in tight turns across the battlefield, dodging God knew what. There was little chance they'd survive another hit, so he forced such thoughts out of his mind and only focused on Pachulia's voice as he called out which way to spin it. From below came the frequent chatter of the medium machine-guns. It made him proud that they had taken a hit and yet remained in the fight. He just wished he knew who was winning.

"My God, I think they're running. Thank you, sweet Jesus," Pachulia said. The sound of explosions dropped off noticeably.

Marcus abandoned the crank and threw himself back into his chair. The monitor was still dead, so he raised the seat to look through the ring of periscopes around the commander's hatch. What he saw sickened him and filled his heart with joy at the same time. Only eight Urutus still moved; the rest lay shattered and burning around them.

Why were we spared? Thank God, thank God. I'm not worthy but thank God.

One Urutu was further away than any of the others and sat immobile, its wheels shredded on one side. Yet still it fired burst after burst into the demons streaming past until one leapt upon it and silenced it with a shattering blast. Seven Urutus left. Two Brazilian Leopards and three American Abrams still moved as well, although they looked like losers from demolition derby. Charred and twisted metal covered their outsides. Not a one of them had a functioning top gun, but still their cannons fired blast after blast at the retreating demons.

But the sons of bitches were running. Never had he seen a more beautiful sight. Less than a few dozen bounded away toward their damned mountain. Piles of twisted and mangled corpses of their dead littered the ground around the remaining armored vehicles.

Victory? He supposed it was if they quit attacking the lumber mill and Rio Estrada. But it was an ugly victory. Seeing the number of burning vehicles brought tears to his eyes. Such bravery in the face of such long odds.

"Corporal," he said into his mic. It was obviously dead, and he snatched it away from his face. He yelled, "Corporal Menderes, get us to the nearest Urutu. We need to see if anyone's still alive."

"Yes, sir," came a shouted reply. The vehicle made a hard-right turn, bounced along for a short distance, and lurched to a stop.

Marcus threw open his hatch and climbed out. He vaulted to the ground and ran toward the still burning Urutu, but stopped short. It was easy to see there would be no survivors. When the Urutu's armor failed, it did so catastrophically. He looked around through watery eyes and saw this to be the case over and over. Other crews were leaping from their vehicles to search, but it was obvious they'd find few if anyone alive. Even the dead tanks were little more than smoldering funeral pyres.

He turned and with a heavy heart said, "Mount up. We need to get to the mill in case they come back."

The half dozen men who followed him to the Urutu returned with heavy shoulders but raised heads. Surviving a battle such as this carried a savage mix of emotions. Pride, joy at being alive...and a lot of guilt. *Why me? Thank God it was me.*

A handful of survivors were pulled from the wrecks. Marcus delayed climbing back into his vehicle to check on them. Every one of them were in bad shape. The crews made them as comfortable as possible in the remaining Urutus, and they set out for the lumber mill. Marcus intended to reach it as quickly as possible and then move everything back to Rio Estrada.

To him, it seemed vital to maintain a foothold on this side of the river, especially with the wet season approaching. He intended to make the vanquished village a formidable fortress until relieved, which should be soon. The docks and ramps built by the engineers would prove invaluable when reinforcements arrived.

If what he had been told was true, two hundred Leopards and a hundred more Abrams would be here in a few weeks, along with many more Urutus and other armored vehicles. Then they'd show these damn bastards something. With God's blessing and men such as those around him, they'd make the demons curse the day they came to his planet. To his country.

Viva o Brasilia, he thought proudly.

44 A New Home

Josh pulled himself up and over the ledge at the cave mouth opening and David breathed a sigh of relief. Now hopefully his heart would stop sending unpleasant sensations across his chest. It was unnerving to watch the big man climbing across the face of the cliff, often dangling by only one hand over a two-thousand-foot drop. David could barely tolerate kneeling close to the edge.

"I don't see how you do that," David said, his voice a bit unsteady. "That's a long, long way down."

"Don't really matter after the first forty or fifty feet," Josh said with a shrug. "You just have more time to enjoy the view if you fall."

David looked down, cocked his head, and gave it a small shake. He couldn't argue with the logic, but looking over a fifty-foot drop didn't make his insides twist the same way. Just the idea of trying to climb the face of the cliff made his arms quiver.

"So, what do you think?" he asked, not sure what answer he wanted to hear.

"It's not too bad for the first hundred feet or so, but after that there's an undercut in the cliff and the climb becomes real technical. I don't think we could do it without special gear, at least a hammer and a few dozen pitons to set some rope." He leaned out and pointed up and to the right. "There's a ledge up that way and maybe an opening. We might want to check that out, but not right now. You said you guys found two more tunnels?"

Alessandra nodded. She'd stopped watching several minutes ago. David wasn't the only one uncomfortable with Josh's acrobatic climbing. She gestured with her head toward the back of the cave on the left side. "They are both down there, about twenty feet apart. One is not much bigger than the passageway we came in by. But the tunnel on the far left looks pretty big. We did not push down either of them very far, though."

Josh glanced toward the back of the cavern and said, "We'll get to them. This cave looks like a good place to hole up for a while. There are signs of moisture around the opening. Probably drips down pretty good from above when it rains. We can use that poncho David got from the soldier to catch water. We'll have to go easy on the firewood, though. But with a little luck, and by God we're due some, we won't have to go back to our old camp."

That would be very good luck indeed. The idea of going back to the blending chamber to fetch water had caused the small group more than a little concern. They'd still have to go to Big Mama's cavern for food and wood. But now that they had the trains figured out, it wasn't too bad of a trip—provided nothing else used the tunnel. There was always the worry of running into something that would take an unpleasant interest in them. But that was true to some extent, no matter where they were in this godforsaken mountain.

Paula must have been thinking along the same lines. She sat nearby, propped up against a boulder beside the opening, soaking in the sun. It'd been tricky getting her through the cramped tunnel. She wouldn't be going to the conveyor anytime soon, but she seemed to be making progress.

She said, "At least this cave does not have anything that might interest the gatherers. I feel safer here than anywhere we have been so far."

Alessandra nodded, but looked a little doubtful. She pointed to the blue rods that started in the middle of the cave and ran back. "Someone, or rather something, came through here at one time. There are not so many of those light rods in this section, but still… they are here. Why would they even bother putting them there? And how long do they keep glowing?"

David said, "No telling. But I hope they're not radioactive."

Josh chuckled. "Lordy, I hope we live long enough for radiation to be a problem. There's no point in wasting energy thinking about that. We have other concerns, like where will we do PT?"

The others groaned, but in a good-natured way. There was no doubt the training Josh put them through had paid off many times over. Without it, they never would have gotten out of the blending chamber and made it this far. In fact, David kind of missed it, especially the team exercises. He'd never felt so much a part of any group before. Not since his mother and father died, anyway.

While Josh explored the cliff face, Pedro had with the fascination of a child at the circus. But now he looked uncharacteristically unhappy. He kicked at the rocky ground with his scuffed-up, blue-canvas tennis shoes, muttering to himself. For the first time, David noticed what large feet the boy had. It fit with his puppy dog demeanor.

"What's the matter, Pedro?" David said.

Pedro looked up with a sad smile and said, "Dots? Floor bad. No Dots."

Alessandra laughed and said, "Do not worry so. I think I saw some dirt by those other tunnels. I will help you bring some to where we set up camp, and we will make a nice playing area. Then you can start kicking David's butt again."

Pedro looked hopeful and his smile returned. He looked over at David and said, "Dots? Dots fun."

David smiled back and nodded. "Sure, Pedro. Checkers too, if you want. And I bet we can use some of these rocks to make chess pieces. I've got a feeling you'll love chess."

Josh grunted. "Now there's a game I can get into. I'll help you.

Some of this rock is limestone, and we should be able to chip out some decent-looking pieces."

David looked around the cave and let out a sigh. There were occasional, faint vibrations from time to time, no doubt offshoots of Big Mama's electric freak show somewhere below them. But they were barely noticeable. The air was cool and fairly dry, most likely due to their being several thousand feet up. The sun felt wonderful and the air sweet. It didn't feel exactly safe, but this cave didn't provoke the constant dread and feeling of oppressiveness their old one had.

Yes, this would be a good place to, "Hole up," as Josh put it. Odd as it seemed, here in an alien nest of impossible monsters, David felt happy. And in this small group of survivors, he'd found a family.

The End of Book 2

70852424R00216

Made in the USA
Middletown, DE
21 April 2018